THE LIGHT SHINES THROUGH

Janet Joanou Weiner

Also by
Janet Joanou Weiner

Though Darkness Descend, The Huguenot Resistance Series Book 1

Good Tidings, A Christmas Anthology by the Lady Lits
Short story - The Greatest Gifts

Dedication

To my children and grandchildren.
Beloved! Fear not.

I will turn the darkness into light before them
and make the rough places smooth.

Isaiah 42:16 (NIV)

A Note from the Author

The context of this novel is the conflict between the Catholic King Louis XIV and the Huguenot Protestants in early 18th century France. It was a different era, one full of fear and misunderstanding, as well as differences in faith practices. At that time, each side believed the other to be heretical.

The author wishes to make it very clear that she does not hold this opinion.

Table of Contents

PREFACE

From the resurrection of Jesus until the early sixteenth century, only one form of Christianity existed in western Europe, the Roman Catholic Church. With no separation of church and state, kings considered themselves God's earthly representatives and the guardians of the "one true faith."

When German monk Martin Luther created a list of abuses occurring within the Roman Catholic Church of the sixteenth century, he aimed to bring reform within that church. Instead, the resulting Reformation gave birth to Protestantism, which spread throughout much of Europe.

About two million Protestants existed in France by 1562. Called Huguenots, possibly after Swiss political and religious leader Besançon Hugues, the Protestants believed in each person's ability to read the Bible and pray without a Catholic priest as intermediary. Their high valuation of individual responsibility, literacy, and hard work led many of them to prosperity. Despite Huguenot loyalty to the king, rulers perceived these influential people as a threat.

Following almost fifty years of conflicts known as wars of religion, King Henri IV established the Edict of Nantes at the end of the sixteenth century, giving Protestants the right to exist legally. Huguenots could worship freely in their manner and could marry, baptize, and register their children outside the Catholic Church.

During the almost one hundred years under the Edict of Nantes, Huguenots flourished. That changed in the late seventeenth century, when King Louis XIV, believing himself appointed by God, styled himself *le Roi Soleil,* the Sun King, with everything revolving around him. He refused to tolerate people outside his Catholic faith. His motto "One king, one law, one faith" rhymes fluently in French—*Un roi, une loi, une foi.*

After Louis XIV revoked the Edict of Nantes in 1675, Huguenots faced four hard options: convert to Catholicism, execution, endure life in prisons or convents, or leave the country. Despite the king's closure of the French borders, at least 250,000 Huguenots fled from France to Switzerland, England, the Netherlands, the Cape Colony of South Africa, and the American territory that would later become the United States.

Most Huguenots who converted in France did so in name only. In the Cévennes region especially, they went underground, meeting and worshipping in caves at night. Their children attended Catholic schools but were reeducated at home, using hidden family Bibles. Prison and death awaited Huguenots caught in such clandestine activity.

Around 1701, an outpouring of the Holy Spirit occurred in the Cévennes, mainly affecting young Huguenots who came to be called *inspirés*. In their sleep or during worship services, *inspirés* as young as five or six years old cited long biblical passages and exhorted listeners to repent and to actively live out their faith. Even people observing the phenomenon with the intention of discounting it wrote incredible accounts of what they witnessed.

By 1702, an uprising against the King's persecution of the Huguenots stirred in the Cévennes. Leading the movement were brave *inspirés* called prophets, young adults who chose to act as they heard God lead.

CHAPTER 1
INVADED

17 July 1702
Grotte de la Roquette
Near St. Hippolyte du Fort
Southern Cévennes

With eyes closed, Suzanne joined the Huguenots in song, lifting her voice in worship. Even as the lyrics flowed from her mouth, she sensed a shift. Something charged filled the atmosphere. Her eyes flew open.

Nothing had visibly changed. Why, then, did her heart pound so? Tingles rippled up her arms, every survival instinct in her rising to high alert. She stepped forward in the flickering torchlight, a warning on her lips at the same moment shouts sounded near the mouth of the cave. Footfalls thundered.

"They're here!" Her mouth dry, the warning was but a croak and came too late.

The silhouettes of dozens of King Louis XIV's soldiers flooded the entrance as they filed down the steep incline into the cave. Hard-heeled boots churned the damp earth between the boulders, replacing the fresh mineral-laden atmosphere with the scent of fear. Gathered illegally in an underground service, the trapped Huguenots scattered. Shots echoed, and the faithful bowed not in reverence but to protect themselves.

Everywhere Suzanne looked, mothers shielded their young with widespread arms and stood firm against the onslaught. Fathers rushed forward, attempting to defend and protect. Those who bore arms fired. From her position in the middle of the cave, she glanced up toward the single opening, now devoid of soldiers, as solitary Huguenots slipped out and away.

Choking on smoke from the gunfire, she turned, searching wildly through the tumult and the tears blurring her vision. Where was he? *Oh Lord, where?*

She pushed through the chaos, shouting above the din. "Gabriel-Isaac! Gabriel-Isaac!"

Not far from her, a soldier leaped onto a boulder. "Round up the leaders! They must not escape!"

Suzanne pressed flat against a side wall, hiding in the dark, barely registering the piercing cold. Though of medium height, she stood on tiptoe, straining to see through the mayhem. Torchlight burned, flickering ominous shadows onto the surrounding limestone walls. She peered through the blur of the troop's red coats tangled with the earth-toned garb of the stunned Huguenots.

Soldiers seized Pastor Etienne and hauled him toward the exit. Suzanne knotted her fist over her mouth, stifling a gasp as she watched armed men drag off her family's longtime friend. Another shot rang out. Another Huguenot hit the ground, blood seeping into the mud.

Despite everything within her wanting to flee, Suzanne forced herself to focus. She had to stay and find Gabriel-Isaac. It was her job to keep an eye on him. She'd been charged with keeping him out of trouble while Maman and Papa led people to the assembly. Where were *they* now?

Suzanne searched through the haze and turmoil as she inched away from the wall. Why hadn't she insisted Gabriel-Isaac sit with her? Because he was thirteen years old. *Not a baby,* as he made loud and clear. She didn't see him among the Huguenots near the cave entrance.

Although the cave had seemed the perfect place for a nocturnal service, its low opening slowed the Huguenots' escape. Her stomach clenched as screams and groans permeated the atmosphere. Soldiers fired off more shots. Bloodstained bodies fell. Neighbors, friends, and fellow believers created horrific obstacles as the beleaguered Protestants scrambled, attempting to get away.

"Suzanne!" Her father's voice reached through the fog of fear and revulsion. "*Suzanne!*"

She blinked, then saw him across the havoc. Two officers shoved Pierre Lacombe toward the opening, his hands bound behind his back. Suzanne stifled a scream. *Non!* This couldn't be happening.

Not far behind Papa, soldiers held Maman by each arm, hauling her along. A flash of terror, unlike anything Suzanne had ever known, jagged through her entire body, rooting her to the spot.

Papa turned and called to his wife. "Jeanne! Stand firm! Until eternity! We'll meet again, beloved."

Maman lifted her head and nodded. Suzanne read the words on her mother's lips. "Pierre! Beloved, I'll see you there." Her parents' great love for one another and for God shone bright, palpable through the swirling darkness.

Soldiers forced Papa's head down at the cave's mouth, then pushed him out into the night. Others hauled Maman up and over boulders as she resisted, searching right and left. Her gaze landed on Suzanne. Peace radiated from Maman's face. "Be strong!" she mouthed. "I love you."

Within seconds, Suzanne's parents disappeared into the darkness. Would she ever see them again? She shrank back against the wall.

Find your brother now. The Voice sounded like Papa's but came from somewhere deep within her yet far beyond the human realm. This Voice jolted her back to her task. She must find Gabriel-Isaac and get them both safely out of here. But how?

She stepped out of the shadows. *Help me find him. Show me the way.* A hand grabbed her wrist from behind. She jumped and whirled, letting out a small shriek. It took a second to grasp that her brother held on to her. She pulled him back to the wall, her finger to her lips.

Hands clasped tight, the pair made their way toward the opening, stepping around bodies, ducking behind boulders when soldiers strayed near. *Keep us unseen, hidden.* Lights flashed and dimmed as torches swayed and extinguished in the fray. Shouts from Huguenots and soldiers charged the atmosphere.

Suzanne and Gabriel-Isaac crouched behind an enormous slab of stone not far from the cave door. Chilly night air flowed over them like a whisper of freedom. But how could they slip unnoticed by the steady stream of royal soldiers dragging their prisoners to the exit?

Gabriel-Isaac motioned they make a run for it. She shook her head. "Wait," she mouthed, eyes stern. He hesitated, then pulled back. Every aspect of his posture conveyed his desire for action. This was nothing new. He'd long talked of joining his uncles in Mialet, who believed it was God's will to fight the authorities. Despite the rigid determination etched

5

across his face, she read trust in his eyes. He needed her, and she'd do everything possible to ensure his safety, even if she died trying.

Time expanded and contracted until she no longer knew if they'd remained hidden for minutes or hours. Her stiff limbs testified to the latter, but that didn't seem possible. Huddled next to her, Gabriel-Isaac had dozed off as the noise and turmoil lessened. Asleep, he looked younger than his thirteen years. And she felt bereft, orphaned, despite her seventeen.

She fought against the pull of sleep. A part of her wanted to shut down, shut out all she'd seen that night. More than once, she drifted, her head tipping against the limestone boulder, then jerking up at the cold contact. Finally, she resorted to pinching her arms. Alone, she might have given in to the blankness of sleep, anything to blot out the horror of the attack on her Huguenot community and her parents' arrests. But she wasn't alone.

It was one thing to be charged with Gabriel-Isaac's safety when her parents were nearby. Now they were gone. *Gone!* Governor Bâville rarely released prisoners unless they truly converted to the "one true faith" of the King. Neither of her parents would do such a thing, even if it led to their deaths.

Outwardly converting to the King's religion when he revoked the Edict of Nantes had allowed the population of St. Hippolyte to survive. She'd watched Maman and Papa inwardly hold on to their faith and take active part in the underground church, Papa spreading word of the secret nighttime assemblies as he delivered wine, Maman leading pastors and others to their meeting places. The decisions of her parents shaped the course of her life and led to this moment in time.

Suzanne bit her lip. Her attention needed to be here and now. It was her turn to show extraordinary faith. She didn't feel ready. Would she measure up? Could she get herself and Gabriel-Isaac out of here and then safely home?

Go now! Suzanne stiffened, looked around, but knew it was the Voice. She welcomed the guidance, but could she trust the Voice to keep her focused? The last thing she needed at this moment was for her attention to succumb to a vision.

Now, Suzanne! She grabbed Gabriel-Isaac's hand and pulled him swiftly to his feet. Their eyes met. Already her height, he'd soon pass her up—if they made it out of here alive.

"We're going *now*," she whispered. "Keep your head down. Follow me."

She glanced toward soldiers down deep in the cave. What if they looked up toward the opening? What if there were more of them outside, beyond where she could see?

Go! At the divine command, Suzanne bolted with Gabriel-Isaac close behind. They scurried along the wall like the pair of badgers they'd seen skimming the riverbank earlier in the summer. Suzanne didn't dare look back and couldn't see any farther ahead than the opening. They must be quick. Escape was now or never.

She ducked beneath the low opening and took one step into the night. Thud!

"Ow!" Gabriel-Isaac cried, rubbing his head with his free hand.

"Shhhhhh!" Suzanne yanked him down and through the mouth of the cave.

To your right. An enormous outcropping of spiky rocks surrounded by thick bushes was just within reach. Sister and brother scooted behind the rocks and huddled close.

A rough voice pierced the night, the accent northern. "Hey! Did you hear something?"

Footsteps approached their hiding place. Suzanne peeked between boulders. Two soldiers stood directly on the other side, the buttons on their red coats glowing faintly in the moonlight.

"Maybe," his companion said, scanning the area.

Both men stayed in place, surveying the surrounding terrain, their bayoneted muskets at the ready. Silence. The soldiers lowered their guns.

The stockier one spat on the ground. "I didn't expect them to fire on us."

"Many escaped. Governor Bâville will be mighty angry."

"We'll get 'em, though. The Governor's not giving up till we've put every last one in prison or the galleys. Or best of all, dead."

"They know every nook and cranny of the land, scurrying and hiding like rodents. It's possible some of the rats are still out there."

Suzanne held her breath as the soldiers began stomping around, slashing through the nearby brush with their bayonets. Gabriel-Isaac's whitened face practically blended in with the boulder concealing them, but she read strength in the set of his jaw. *Help, God! Make us invisible.*

One of the soldiers moved close. Suzanne kept her eyes open despite a strong desire to squeeze them tight. The soldier's knee-high stockings and buckled leather shoes were within touching distance. She fought a crazy impulse to laugh out loud at the frippery contradicting his wretched mission.

A branch snapped somewhere in the forest. Both soldiers froze, heads lifted, listening, then took off toward the sound. Shouts echoed through the woods, then silence. The soldiers must've captured some Huguenots. Relief wove through her, followed by a wave of guilt. Why were others taken and not them? How was any of this just?

No time for pondering; she must get her brother to safety. They needed to go, but where she did not know. Maybe the Voice would continue to guide and protect them. It had led them out of the cave and kept them hidden from the soldiers' eyes. Thankfully, it hadn't come with any outward manifestations, though her hands shook for obvious reasons. *God, please guide us to safety. I'll try to welcome your voice. Even if the trembling comes upon me, even if I'm thrown in prison. Don't let me fail to bring Gabriel-Isaac safely home.*

A wisp of breeze swept past her cheek, swirled, and lingered. It was time to move.

CHAPTER 2
NOT ALONE

17 July 1702
Near St. Hippolyte du Fort
Southern Cévennes

The first pale rays of dawn filtered through the leafy canopy above as the sun rose over the eastern mountain range. To the west, the cliffs of Le Cengle mountain, the constant backdrop to Suzanne's life and town, jutted into the morning sky. St. Hippolyte du Fort was in sight for her and Gabriel-Isaac.

Grotte de la Roquette was only an hour's walk from home if they walked straight there in broad daylight, twice that when hundreds of Huguenots streamed to secret night services in the cave, traveling in pairs and taking circuitous routes to avoid drawing attention. As then, she and Gabriel-Isaac had stayed in the thickest parts of the forest, off the main paths.

Suzanne tucked a chestnut-colored curl back under her linen cap, then glanced at her brother. His steps slowed, his shoulders drooping despite his efforts to appear strong. They'd been up all night. First at the service, then walking for several hours, stopping to hide at any hint of soldiers still combing the woods, looking for the dispersed Huguenots. Grateful to have made it this far without detection, she breathed a prayer of thanks. But she and Gabriel-Isaac were literally not yet out of the woods. *Please lead us all the way home.*

She tipped her head toward a cluster of beech trees. "We can rest for a moment," she whispered. Gabriel-Isaac shook his head. Both understood the need for haste, to make it back to their Planque neighborhood and home before day was fully upon them. She turned and continued pushing through tangled vines and prickly berry bushes.

Sister and brother trudged along in silence, Suzanne's thoughts drifting like the occasional green leaf that fell in the soft dawn breeze. She drew a long breath of cool morning air full of fresh herbal scents released by their footsteps, almost able to imagine this an ordinary walk for the sheer pleasure of being in nature. Not that she'd been much able to enjoy such a thing. The presence of Governor Bâville's mounted dragoons and foot soldiers had overshadowed her entire existence. From what she'd witnessed in the cave, they were more determined than ever to wipe out the Huguenots. Still, it was nice to dream of freedom, of moving about without fear.

The sun peeked over the southern mountains behind them. Le Cengle, its silhouette resembling a reclining woman, glowed in peach hues against the cerulean sky. Suzanne picked up the pace, eager to be in the relative safety of her family home. The lighter the sky became, the more dangerous their journey grew.

Suddenly, Gabriel-Isaac grabbed the edge of her cloak and pulled her behind thick brush. He held a finger over his lips, his eyes full of alarm. She listened hard. Sure enough, the crackle of branches underfoot sounded nearby. *Lord, you've brought us this far. Don't stop now, please.*

Silence. Had they imagined the sounds? Gabriel-Isaac nudged her side, almost knocking her off balance.

"Hey!" she muttered, then clamped her mouth shut. Now was not the time to tell him off. He pointed toward a clump of scrubby undergrowth farther along. She shrugged in return. Most likely they'd heard a beaver or a fox searching for breakfast.

Gabriel-Isaac stabbed at the air with his finger. Sure enough, the bushes moved again, rustling in a manner that could only be caused by something much larger than a ground animal. Holding up a hand, Suzanne signaled they'd stay put and wait.

A young man emerged from behind the shrubs, brushing off bits of twig and leaf. Medium tall, he looked like a Huguenot in his brown wool breeches, beige stockings, and leather walking shoes. Who was he? She knew every single Huguenot in St. Hippolyte, even those of nearby villages. They were a tight-knit community. Being forced underground had only strengthened their bonds.

Suzanne looked at Gabriel-Isaac, her eyebrows raised in question. He shook his head. He didn't know the man either. The stranger removed his cap, revealing auburn hair, and fanned himself with it while scanning his surroundings. After a moment, he replaced his cap, then leaned toward the bushes and said something she couldn't hear.

Leafy brush jostled and shook. A pair of hands reached through, pushing aside branches, and one by one, seven young people emerged. Disheveled, they darted their eyes left and right like hunted animals.

One spoke in a low voice to the first man. "Massip, you're sure you heard something?"

"Are you sure there's no one out here now?" asked another.

"I've been a guide for many journeys," said the one called Massip. "I know when I hear humans."

Without warning, Gabriel-Isaac stepped out from their hiding place. Suzanne tried to pull him back, but he'd moved out of her reach. Lips pressed tight, she rose and joined him. He couldn't be out there alone. Whatever this was, they'd face it together.

Eight slightly dirty faces turned and stared. Suzanne took several steps toward them, hands spread wide.

The guide moved forward, his emerald eyes curious, assessing. Suzanne raised the gold cross on her necklace, showing the specially designed symbol Huguenots used to recognize one another. She stood her ground, praying this wasn't a mistake. Despite their bedraggled appearance, could these people be spies for Governor Bâville?

She met Massip's gaze, only slightly higher than her own. Gabriel-Isaac moved to her side.

Finally, the guide spoke. "You're Huguenots?"

"Yes. And you?"

Massip waited a moment, continuing to study her face. "We are as well." The others in his party inched closer. "I'm Jean Massip."

"And I'm Suzanne Lacombe. What are you doing out here? I've never seen you before. Were you at the assembly last night?"

"Lots of questions!" Jean smiled. "We're just passing through."

Gabriel-Isaac piped up. "Did you know Bâville's men raided the gathering?"

Suzanne threw him a warning look. She wanted to take it slow.

"Oh!" exclaimed one dirty face. "That explains why soldiers swarmed the area like ants all night."

11

Suzanne stared at the stranger. "You're a woman! I thought . . . I mean, you're all dressed as men."

Jean shot a look at the girl, who clamped both hands over her mouth. "Madeleine can't resist speaking out, no matter how many times I warn her." He rubbed his neck. "Three of our group are girls, sisters. May I present the Mademoiselles Celestin? The other four and myself . . . Well, obviously, we're men."

Nothing seemed obvious at this point, but Suzanne didn't think it wise to point that out. "So, if you weren't at the gathering, *why* are you out here?"

"I'm a guide, helping them travel to Geneva."

"Why are they going?" She already knew the answer. There was only one reason for traveling as they were: fleeing the unending persecution from authorities and priests who knew many Huguenots secretly practiced the Protestant faith. Harassment, hefty fines, arrests, imprisonments—that none of it stamped out their beliefs raised the ire and frustration of their tormentors.

Madeleine, who appeared to be the eldest of the sisters, stepped closer. A few strands of pale blonde hair peeked out from under her cap. Her blue-gray eyes reminded Suzanne of her own. The women studied each other for a moment. Finally, Madeleine spoke. "We're all *inspirés*. The Holy Spirit falls on us and we shake, preach, and prophesy."

"It's happened to me, too," Suzanne said, her voice soft. "I've tried to hold it back so my family won't be in danger." Could they see her underlying terror of imprisonment and torture? Or her greater fear of not being strong enough to be faithful to the end?

"You could've been arrested if you hadn't held back," said Gabriel-Isaac. "So, I'm glad for it."

Madeleine touched Suzanne's arm. "I understand. It took me some time, but I learned that we're able to control it, to make it stop." She gestured at her sisters. "Although she's the youngest, Claire knew this from the beginning. Rachel, well, she's still figuring it out."

"It's frightening, isn't it?" asked Rachel. "Yet, it's plainly God speaking through us. Sometimes we don't even remember what we've said. When the others tell us later, it's way beyond what we've learned or could say."

"Yes!" Suzanne gathered her thoughts. "It's shocking when the community affirms the words coming through me. Whole biblical passages, followed by a related teaching. I certainly don't know how to do all that."

"And why did God choose us for this?" asked Claire. "I'm only twelve."

"The fruit is good," one of the young men said. "People repent and turn fully to our Savior."

"I'm honored to receive and impart whatever the Holy Spirit brings," said another. "Though it's come at a cost."

A torrent of emotion unleashed within Suzanne, as if constricting cords wound tight around her heart were suddenly cut loose. Tears stung her eyes, and she fought the urge to cry out in relief. They understood! There'd been other youth overcome by the Holy Spirit in their assemblies, but in her family, she was the only one. Even her parents were unsure what to do with it, with her.

Suzanne swallowed hard. "So, you're fleeing?"

"We'll join relatives in Geneva. Bâville's authorities have targeted us; they know who we are."

"We became *réfugiés* rather than face prison or worse," said the shortest man. His entire manner exuded fearlessness. Their flight was not for lack of bravery. In fact, they were possibly now at a greater risk of arrest, with more dire consequences.

"A new life of freedom awaits us in Switzerland," said another, his face shining at the thought of it.

"All our parents are in prison or gone on to their reward," said Madeleine. She shut her eyes for a moment, as if to block out the grief.

Suzanne couldn't speak. Their reality was now hers as well.

Jean lifted his cap and tipped his head toward the rising sun. "We need to get going. There's a safe house farther north; we're headed there."

"And we must get home to St. Hippolyte du Fort," said Suzanne.

"You could come with us," said Madeleine. Her sisters surrounded Suzanne and Gabriel-Isaac, hope filling their faces. "Right, Jean?"

The guide scanned the forest. "All right. But we need to go *now*. We've been standing here far too long as it is."

Gabriel-Isaac bounced on his toes, energy emanating from him like heat waves from sunbaked earth. Given the chance, he'd go with them. Maybe not to Switzerland, but at least to their uncles in Mialet.

"Thank you for the offer, but we need to go home." Suzanne held her voice firm. "Our grandmother and siblings must be sick with worry by now."

Gabriel-Isaac's shoulders sagged. "Yes, we must return to St. Hippolyte."

They all exchanged the three *bisous*, cheek kisses for Father, Son, and Holy Spirit.

"Go with God!"

"Go with God! May we meet again, in better circumstances, whether on earth or in heaven."

As they parted, an enormous pull rose within Suzanne, an almost overwhelming desire to join the sisters and follow the guide to a different life. How strange! Usually, she longed only for home, for her family gathered, safe. She shook off the unusual thoughts. Grand-mère and her younger brother and sister needed her now more than ever.

Suzanne and Gabriel-Isaac turned west while Jean led his little troop toward the north. Both groups disappeared into the forest once again. Suzanne carried a lightness she hadn't experienced since receiving the outpouring. The young people's courage and shared experiences bolstered her heart and strengthened her step.

Yet, as she and Gabriel-Isaac darted through the trees and bushes, unease slowly built back up and slithered around her soul. She'd been determined to let the Voice come, even at the risk of drawing attention. However, talking with the refugee *inspirés*, while comforting, had reminded her of the dangers of her "gift."

St. Hippolyte's prison-fort was one of many packed with *inspirés*, some as young as five and six years old. Bile rose and stung the back of her throat at her thoughts of the torture meted out to expose their supposed playacting.

With her parents gone and only Grand-mère Isabeau at home, she couldn't afford to be imprisoned. Who would take care of the children while Grand-mère attended a birth? Now that she thought of it, would she be able to accompany her grandmother and continue her training as a midwife?

A branch snapped under her foot.

"Pay attention!" Gabriel-Isaac muttered.

Suzanne watched her step and came to a firm conclusion. She could not leave the family or put them in danger. Her "gift" must stay hidden away.

CHAPTER 3
ABBÉ DU CHAILA

17 July 1702
Pont-de-Montvert
Northern Cévennes

Not bothering to wipe his greasy fingers, the Abbé du Chaila broke the wax seal and scowled at La Violette, as if the valet were responsible for timing the report's arrival. The servant knew better than to interrupt *déjeuner* or any meal. The priest bit back the correction on the tip of his tongue.

As Governor Bâville's right-hand man, Du Chaila had been waiting for this letter to reach him. Both the Governor and the Abbé had a vested interest in last night's raid near St. Hippolyte du Fort. The priest grimaced and rubbed his round belly as he perused the contents.

Governor Bâville's message was definitely not good news. The officer in charge had ordered his men to open fire on the worshippers, killing twenty. Only twenty! Some of the Huguenots dared to fire back, hitting several soldiers. Outrageous. How dare they bring arms to their illegal gatherings, even if most were antiquated weapons once belonging to their grandfathers. Three of the Governor's men had succumbed to their wounds.

Several hundred Huguenots attended the illegal service, but the soldiers only arrested a few dozen. Which meant that the majority got away. How could that be?

The Abbé finished reading, then pushed away from the table, soup sloshing across his bowl and onto the white linen tablecloth. His appetite disappeared. Why had the cook made such a hot meal on a blazing summer day? With his brown linen sleeve, he mopped the sweat off his face before it dripped into the folds of his neck.

You'll never amount to anything. You're an utter failure. Du Chaila flinched at his father's voice running through his head. He glared at La Violette, standing by with his gaze straight ahead. Had he discerned the moment of weakness?

With a growl, Du Chaila dismissed the valet, watched him leave the room with rapid steps, then poured another glass of his preferred Bordeaux. He sniffed the wine, gave it a sharp swirl, drained the crystal goblet, and threw it against the cold marble fireplace, still relishing the sound of shattering glass as he exited the back of the house.

Shuffling down a small set of stone stairs and the length of his garden, he barely noticed as he moved from sweltering shade to burning sunshine. At the garden's far end, he stopped and stared at the *potager*, noting its struggle to produce vegetables in the unusual heat. Tomatoes had cracked and split under incessant high temperatures. He kicked over one of the wooden stakes, uprooting the vine attached. An overripe tomato rolled to the side, and the Abbé stomped it flat.

His gut wrenched, the searing pain returning in force. The physician had warned him to abandon rich meals, avoid wine, and opt for simpler fare. Where was the pleasure in that? Besides, those infuriating Huguenots were the cause.

In nine long years of attempting to remove any trace of the heretics from France, hadn't he, under Governor Bâville's authority, applied every form of coercion possible? Still, the Protestants carried on with their illicit meetings. Unbelievable. They read the Bible without a priest and called praying to the saints idol worship. He wrenched a dead branch off a black alder and tossed it toward the river beyond the garden wall.

Even worse, attendance was down in the King's church. Many people simply stopped going. It must be those troublesome *inspirés*. Ever since they'd started their phony trembling and prophesying, the underground Huguenots had grown bolder. Many who'd converted to the true church had returned to their Protestant roots.

Bâville had hundreds of *inspirés* in jail. What to do with them now? They endured separation from their parents, deprivation and punishment, and *still* held fast to their faith. Often, they carried more courage than their elders.

You failed in Siam! You actually thought you could be a missionary! Ha! Weakling! You don't deserve to be called Abbé despite your ordination. And Inspector of the Cévennes? Bâville's title for you is laughable.

Du Chaila pressed both hands to the sides of his head. If only he could squeeze away the thoughts besieging him in his father's voice. *Our family does not tolerate failure. You are a failure.*

His family had fought in all wars of religion since the first wave of Protestantism arrived in France nearly two centuries ago. Now, he carried on the tradition of suppressing Huguenots. This was his time, his mandate.

How was it that the Huguenots continued to exist despite actions that should've exterminated the vermin long ago? They found inspiration in the biblical accounts of God's deliverance of his people from their enemies. The gall! Apparently, they called their nocturnal gatherings "desert assemblies," drawing inspiration from the Almighty's provision for his original children. Persecution seemed only to reinforce their faith and firm up their nonsensical resolve.

Hadn't he ensured that many had died for their treason? Requisitioning this house from a Huguenot noble, turning the cellar—all but the wine room—into a veritable prison, complete with torture chambers and cells. Servants had replaced piles of papers and old furniture with stocks, chains, and instruments of coercion.

A thrum, a thrill, sparked at the memory of his prisoners pleading for mercy, especially the women. Nothing gave him more satisfaction than watching them cry and beg for life as he stretched their limbs to the breaking point on his specially designed rack. That they almost never renounced their beliefs only added to the challenge. He'd order executions whether or not they recanted, but they certainly gave him every excuse to do so.

He sent quite a few of the young women to convents for life, though. Maybe he'd been too lenient after all.

Then there was the escape last month, after soldiers incarcerated Jacques Couderc in the dungeon for prophesying. In a rare moment that might be mistaken for mercy, the Abbé allowed the prisoner's mother to visit. *And then you left them alone, didn't you?* Du Chaila clapped his hands over his ears. It was because the evening meal had been growing cold on his table. While he dined upstairs, Couderc and his mother sawed through his ankle stocks and fled.

18

It's you. The problem is you. You're weak and a failure at everything you attempt. Du Chaila pressed his lips together to keep from screaming. Sparks of light appeared before his eyes and his vision grew dim. He grabbed a nearby beech branch that promptly snapped under his weight, sending him to his knees. As quickly as his bulk would allow, he lumbered back to his feet and glanced up at the house. It wouldn't do for the servants to observe his malaise.

On top of everything else, the Governor's letter had reported the escape of a young man from Mialet, Rolland Laporte. Rumors circulating through the Cévennes said Laporte was gathering men in his hamlet to fight. Du Chaila scoffed out loud at the very thought. It would never work. The Governor's trained soldiers would crush them without delay.

Du Chaila turned his back to the house and gazed across the river Tarn to the bridge that gave the village its name, Pont-de-Montvert. An image returned of the execution of another upstart Huguenot, Françoise Brès, a young woman they'd called a prophetess. *Fanatique* was more like it. She'd traveled through the Cévennes, exhorting fellow Huguenots to stand firm. Her capture several months ago was a big prize, and he'd made sure that many attended her hanging on this very bridge.

Pain shot through his gut. He leaned against the garden's low limestone wall and stared at the river's meandering waters.

Only twenty-five years old, Brès prophesied all the way to the end. On the scaffolding, the noose already around her neck, she proclaimed the demise of the Abbé du Chaila. "He who exposes me to this torture will end his days here, this very year!"

Ha! There was proof the prophets were fakes. The execution of Brès had been at the end of January almost seven months ago. Was he not standing here, alive? Why then did her words cut deep as if etched into his memory with shards of glass, the sound of her voice reverberating through his dreams?

Hot summer sun continued to beat down on Du Chaila. He stroked his hands across his bloated belly, straightened, and plodded toward the shade. Seated on a stone bench beneath a wide chestnut tree, he mopped the sweat off his face with his handkerchief, then patted back his long mouse-gray hair. He pulled the parchment from the folds of his habit, fanned himself, then read the report once again.

The cave raid had yielded a few successes. They'd finally captured the well-known preacher Etienne Gamond. Excellent. Also arrested, two pillars of the underground church, Jeanne and Pierre Lacombe. All three had never been caught in the act. Until now. A whiff of breeze touched the Abbé for the briefest of moments, gone as quickly as it came.

Usually, the Governor gave swift and clear sentences. Pastors publicly broken on the torturous Wheel, male prisoners sent to row in the galleys of Marseille until death, women imprisoned for life, and children sent to convents for reeducation at the family's expense. But sentencing those captured wasn't enough. Hundreds of Huguenots had simply disappeared during the raid. One could almost believe that God was on their side.

The Abbé scanned the letter again. The Governor called for greater measures to be taken to extinguish the Huguenots, with proof no longer needed of their hidden faith. Even better, Bâville was sending two more detachments to aid in the rounding up. The soldiers should arrive on the morrow. The thought lifted Du Chaila's spirits, as did the sight of spiky green-brown chestnut pods dangling from the branches overhead. He reached up and touched one, enjoying the pricking pain of its spines. Squeezing tight, he crushed the needles into his palm until tiny rivulets of blood dripped across his wrist and down his arm. He released his grip and studied the sight.

The Abbé's appetite returned. He'd give some thought to new and creative ways to shatter the heretics. Licking his lips, he stood, straightened his habit, and returned to the house to finish his meal.

CHAPTER 4
ST. HIPPOLYTE DU FORT

17 July 1702
St. Hippolyte du Fort
Southern Cévennes

The sun continued its slow trajectory in the bright blue sky as Suzanne and Gabriel-Isaac arrived at the edge of St. Hippolyte du Fort. She shielded her eyes and tried to come up with a plan. How would they get inside the fortified walls with soldiers guarding every entry point?

She'd planned to arrive in the dark and slip through the gates unnoticed by the sentries who often dozed during the night shift. Now the day was full, the guards wide awake and on the alert. After last night's raid, they'd be on the lookout for Huguenots returning with no valid reason for being outside the walls.

Sweat trickled down her back as she surveyed the rampart walls around the town, including five gated and guarded entry points. Two years before her birth, the King had ordered them installed along with a fort, now on the western edge of St. Hippolyte. Such features were usually meant to protect the population inside. The opposite was true in St. Hippolyte du Fort, where walls enclosed and restricted movement. The villagers were essentially prisoners in their own town.

Suzanne and Gabriel-Isaac stopped to rest in the fragrant shade of a wild fig. The spicy-sweet aroma of ripening fruit permeated the air. She almost laughed as he stuffed another fig in his already full mouth, a dribble of red-purple juice running down his chin. Good thing they both loved the fruit. It would strengthen them for this last leg of their journey.

"We'll have to avoid the gates all together," Gabriel-Isaac said.

She stared at him. Why hadn't she thought of that? Of course, that was the best plan. Her brother had a good head on his shoulders and was thirteen going on thirty. Hadn't Maman said that?

Maman! Gone! Papa too, most likely forever. With the pressure of getting home, Suzanne had forced grief down deep, and now was not the time to deal with it. If she peered too long into her churning pool of emotions, it would suck her in and under.

"You're right, which means we must climb the mountain behind the Planque neighborhood outside the town walls. It'll take us another hour."

Gabriel-Isaac shrugged, his hazel eyes so like Maman's. "We'll go along the back wall of the Château de Planque, then down to the road. Crossing the Route de Lasalle to home will be the trickiest part. But I think it's far enough from the guard station at the other end of the bridge. Unless a soldier patrols the street, we can make it across unseen."

He'd figured out their path. She admired his ability to find a way around the gates, but wasn't their safety her job?

The pair trudged along the rocky hill, pausing occasionally in the shade of green oaks and wild olives. The sun arched across the sky, and the heat bearing down on Suzanne threatened to burn her fair skin and add more freckles to those sprinkled across her nose and cheeks. She stopped for a moment, lifted her linen cap and wrestled her chestnut curls back into a chignon, then put the bonnet back in place. At least it protected part of her face and light eyes from the constant glare.

Below them, the backs of homes at the far end of their neighborhood came into view. If they could walk down the narrow road in front of the houses, they'd be home in less than ten minutes. She longed for this journey to be over. But with soldiers patrolling the streets day and night, sticking to the mountain path was the wisest course. They needed to avoid any form of questioning after last night's raid.

Her mother loved this type of adventure, secretly crisscrossing the countryside, avoiding troops while guiding preachers and others to the hidden meetings. Besides assisting Grand-mère at a birth, Suzanne preferred helping at home. Safe, as opposed to this journey with Gabriel-Isaac. Yet something deep inside her yearned for more. Of what, she didn't know. In school, she'd loved studying history and reading anything she could get her hands on. Through stories she could travel far and experience much from the security of home. But what was she supposed to do with that?

She pushed a branch out of her way, forgetting to hold it back for Gabriel-Isaac. Wham!

"Ow! Hey! Be careful!" He rubbed the red mark on his cheek.

"Oh! Sorry! My mind's elsewhere."

From the shade of a scrubby green oak clinging to the mountainside, Suzanne glimpsed the water-powered *moulin*'s rooftop. She leaned against the tree and rested her eyes for a moment, imagining the cool interior of the mill containing the enormous stone olive press. The spacious limestone structure, with eight tall windows, looked out on the river Vidourle. Her parched throat craved a few handfuls of its icy water.

Her eyes flew open. Marguerite! The daughter of the mill managers, the Marolles. Her best friend. They'd waved to each other across the cave before the raid. Had she been among those taken? If so, that would've been something to see. Born days after the first dragoons came to St. Hippolyte, Marguerite was a fighter by nature. She wouldn't have gone without a great struggle.

Gabriel-Isaac nudged her. "Time to go."

Without a word, she started hiking across the rocky mountainside. Far too many feelings piled one upon another, tangling and twisting.

Maybe he didn't need her help to stay safe. Hadn't their father always said Gabriel-Isaac was aptly named after Papa's younger brother? Uncle Gabriel was a born warrior, as was Maman's brother, Uncle Paul, who'd joined Uncle Gabriel in Mialet years ago.

"Suzanne, over here, behind the back wall of the Château grounds." Gabriel-Isaac led the way.

What was she thinking? While she had always struggled with a sense of direction in more ways than one, her brother had inherited Maman's innate ability to find the best path, at least in the physical sense. Of course, he could manage just fine without her. But what of the other siblings? Marc-André was only a year younger than his brother, yet had an entirely distinct personality. A dreamer, he loved his books and his drawings. And Marie, so bright and inquisitive and only eight years old. Suzanne hated to think what could have happened if Grand-mère hadn't kept the younger ones home with her last night? At least they'd avoided the trauma of the soldiers' raid and seeing their parents' arrests.

Marc-André and Marie still needed guidance and care. Grand-mère Isabeau would fill in for their parents as best she could. Already in her sixties, she was slowing down a bit, although Suzanne would never say so in Grand-mère's presence. A giggle bubbled through the weight in Suzanne's chest at the thought.

Her step quickened. She was needed at home and couldn't wait to bring comfort and care to her family. Finally, she and Gabriel-Isaac reached the back of the Château de Planque property and trudged along the path outside the tall limestone wall. They would need to hide should the current owners or their workers appear. But for now, it was a relief to no longer crouch and dart from bush to bush. She inhaled the green scents of summer, thankful for the shade provided by the trees in full bloom.

The pair scrambled over an enormous granite outcropping where sunshine released mineral scents, adding them to the midsummer fragrance. On the other side, they brushed dirt off their hands and continued their trek. High on the hill, they approached the back corner of the property.

Gabriel-Isaac stopped and crouched behind dense foliage. "Suzanne, wait. There's the small watchtower. Lord Valmalle allows the authorities to use it for surveillance."

She joined him behind the bush. "Looks empty to me. How do you know this?"

"Never mind. Let's wait a little more to be sure no soldiers roam the area."

After a few minutes, they crept forward until they confirmed the tower was empty. Suzanne stepped inside. She'd grown up with tales of the medieval structure, with its terra-cotta roof and rounded walls, complete with slits for archers' arrows. Before the dragoons came to St. Hippolyte, her parents had enjoyed its sweeping perspective up the valley to the north, across to Le Cengle mountain, and on down to St. Hippolyte.

"These views are incredible," she said. "Just like Maman and Papa described."

Gabriel-Isaac gazed at the scenery, his face solemn. She rested her hand on his arm, not sure if he would welcome the physical comfort at age thirteen. He pressed his lips together and turned his head away. After a moment, he spoke. "Yes, I always love it up here."

"You've been here before? Papa and Maman told us to never . . ." She didn't know why it surprised her. Of course, he came here on his own. Independent, sure of what he wanted from a young age. "Have you come here often?"

"Yes. I know it was risky, coming onto the Château property. But I always waited to see if Lord Valmalle was out hunting or if any of his workers or soldiers were around."

She could barely hold back the scolding ready to flow forth. He'd trespassed on land belonging to a loyal subject of the King. Lord Valmalle relished reporting any errant activity by the Huguenots to the authorities.

"You know," she said, "when the Valmalle family bought the Château, they changed their name to Valmalle de Planque, as if they were actual nobility. They're all staunchly on the side of the King and love to take any opportunity to prove it."

Normally, her brother would've rolled his eyes, then ignored her. Today, he nodded slowly, distracted. He finally spoke, his voice as distant as the interloping blue-green hills to the north. "It turns out Papa knew I came here. I don't know how he found out. He just seemed to know things."

Suzanne remained silent, grief lodging like a stone in her throat.

"But Papa never stopped me. After I returned from a visit up here, I'd find him waiting for me. Probably praying. He'd meet my eyes, nod once, and then return to his business."

Tears welled and flowed, and neither sibling could hold them back. Gabriel-Isaac reached and took Suzanne's hand, astonishing if on any other day. Today, she received the gesture of shared pain.

The beauty of the wide vista before them brought a measure of solace to their souls. Brother and sister drank it in. Below, the curved terra-cotta tiled roof of their home, the Lacombe manor, peeked through the trees.

"We'd best be going," said Suzanne after a while. "Grand-mère will be very concerned about us by now. Knowing her, she's invented some story for Marc-André and Marie, so they won't worry."

Gabriel-Isaac drew himself up. Without another word, he led the way down a steep, overgrown trail. Suzanne followed, still stunned at his admission of trespassing. And with Papa's knowledge! At least Gabriel-Isaac knew the way. But what if soldiers had caught him?

Her feet skidded on the rocky slope. She grabbed the edge of a large boulder, steadied herself, then continued on, relieved to be off Lord Valmalle's land. She'd grown up in the shadow of the Château de Planque but had never been inside. From Maman and Papa's descriptions of the interior, she'd created a mental picture of each room.

With the arrests of Suzanne's grandfathers, everything had changed for Maman. Her mother, Grand-mère Suzanne, died soon after. Then dragoon soldiers forced out Maman and Papa, who'd lived in the Château since their marriage. Their move into the Lacombe house across the street, along with Maman's siblings, was a comfort to Grand-mère Isabeau. Suzanne loved that she was born the following year into a big and noisy extended family.

She looked down the hill. Almost there!

A shout pierced the air. Farther down the path, Gabriel-Isaac dropped to the ground. She ducked behind a berry bush.

Another loud call rang out, closer this time. They waited as the soldiers changed the guard like any other morning. Troops marched the length of the Planque bridge, fulfilling the ritual for the end of one shift and the beginning of another. The replacements settled in the entry gate at the far end of the bridge.

Silence reigned. Brother and sister rose to their feet, brushed themselves off, and continued with caution. At the foot of the hill, they hid behind boulders, waiting for the right moment to cross the road. Heat rose from the land and beat down from above, yet a cold weight lay in her belly. It was one thing to deal with her own loss, but to share it with Grand-mère and the rest of the family brought their new reality to the forefront.

Beloved, I am with you. Suzanne stilled. The Voice. It came, even though she'd determined to shut it out. *You are never alone. I am with you always.*

Her home was within reach, but suddenly she wished for more time to reflect, to take in the words. *Beloved. Never alone. I am with you.* The edges of her battered, fear-frozen heart thawed the tiniest bit.

Could it be true? Was she worthy of such love? Of such attention?

Gabriel-Isaac craned his neck, scanning the road up and down. He turned back and nodded. Time to go. Her foot bobbled and slipped on the loose gravel, releasing a small cloud of limestone dust. She grabbed a pine branch, ignoring the prickly sting of its needles and the sap smearing across her hands. There were challenges ahead, and she must focus on getting through them, starting with crossing the road to home.

CHAPTER 5
CHEZ LACOMBE

17 July 1702
St. Hippolyte du Fort
Southern Cévennes

Gabriel-Isaac heaved a noisy sigh, releasing a small portion of pent-up emotion. The terrible news Suzanne and he brought home overshadowed the family's relief at their safe return.

Needing a break from the grief-filled atmosphere, Gabriel-Isaac stepped out into the small front garden. Beyond it stretched one of the vast vineyards belonging to the Château de Planque. Gabriel-Isaac could only think of the vines as his father's. Lord Valmalle reminded the Lacombes often that they inhabited their home on his property solely due to Papa's role as vineyard manager. Would Valmalle force them out now?

Papa had been training Gabriel-Isaac to take his place someday. Gabriel-Isaac would miss the time spent with his father patiently explaining the timing and techniques of vine pruning. That aspect had interested Gabriel-Isaac, more so than weeding and watering. Yet passion for the terroir, for tending and cultivating the land with all its particularities, simply did not run in Gabriel-Isaac's veins. Papa truly enjoyed nurturing the vines, and his experimental vintages carried a favorable reputation. Gabriel-Isaac's heart longed for greater adventure, something more significant. Like fighting injustice.

The journey back home after the raid had given him time to reflect. His innate indignation at the abuse the Huguenots suffered from the King's authorities had flamed into outrage. Until last night, he hadn't witnessed soldiers raiding a worship gathering. Images of his parents bound and dragged away burned in his brain and stoked the fire in his soul. He'd locked eyes with Papa through the chaos and read the words on Papa's lips. "Son, be courageous." Gabriel-Isaac's throat tightened. He hadn't even been able to say goodbye. Hands clenched; he replayed the chaotic scene. Hundreds of Huguenots struggling to flee, to make it to the mouth of the cave against a steady stream of armed soldiers. Some worshippers at the gathering had fired at the invading troop. He may have seen a soldier or two fall, but Bâville's men had shot first. Gabriel-Isaac had watched Rolland, the leader in Mialet, disappear into the crowd. Through the smoke and screams, the thought came to follow him. That maybe the opportunity had come for Gabriel-Isaac to join his uncles in their plans to fight.

But just as the idea sparked, Suzanne had appeared in his line of sight, scanning the crowd, looking for someone. Him. Grave concern, almost a wild panic had been etched across her face. He hadn't had the heart to slip away. Instead, he'd reached for her hand and they'd escaped together.

By now, he could be in Mialet. But he'd have to wait for another moment. The sooner the better.

He squared his shoulders and readied himself to go back inside and face the family. Maman always said he was thirteen going on thirty. He'd have to live up to that estimation now.

———————

In the salon, Grand-mère Isabeau sat tall on a straight-backed chair, and Suzanne knelt on the parquet floor beside their youngest sister, Marie. The eight-year-old had crumpled with the news of their parents' arrests, shattering like a broken vase. Her tiny frame bent and heaved as she wept into her hands. Suzanne stroked her back. "Marie, *chérie*, Suzanne whispered, her own cheeks wet with tears. "I'm here. We'll get through this together."

On the opposite side of the salon, his younger brother by a year stood silent, taking it all in. Marc-André's golden-brown eyes, so like Papa's, surveyed the room in his quiet, observing manner.

The front door's iron knocker rapped loud. Suzanne's head shot up. Gabriel-Isaac looked from his sister to Grand-mère. No one moved. The knocker thundered a second time. Grand-mère stood and started toward the door. Gabriel-Isaac shook his head. He'd deal with it. After all, he needed to be the man of the house.

He left the salon with swift, firm steps and moved through the small entryway. What if the soldiers were searching for those who escaped? Spine straight, chin lifted, he opened the front door. Sun-warmed air met his face.

Aunt Anne! Relief trickled through all the ragged places inside him at the sight of Maman's youngest sister.

"I came as soon as I heard," she said, stepping inside the cool entryway. He ducked his head and stepped back, avoiding her outreached arms. Afraid to speak, he turned and led the way to the salon.

She followed him into the room, stopping to take in the scene. With three *bisous*, she greeted Grand-mère, lingering, murmuring softly. The two women embraced for so long they appeared to hold each other up. Gabriel-Isaac had to look away.

Finally, the women pulled apart, both wiping away tears. Aunt Anne drew a long breath, then moved to Marc-André, where he continued his solitary stand. He greeted his aunt politely but kept his distance. Was he also afraid of losing control, of crying like their sisters? Maybe Marc-André wasn't so different from Gabriel-Isaac after all.

"Marc-André, our heavenly Father will never fail or forsake us," said Aunt Anne, resting her hand on his arm. His lower lip quivered, and he dropped his head on her shoulder with a shuddering sigh. Gabriel-Isaac spun toward the window, tears stinging his eyes and threatening to spill.

He had to get out of here, to *do* something. The weight pulling at his soul threatened to envelop and drag him under. The only way to end such a loss was to fight back.

Could he leave now, go straight to Mialet and finally respond to all the wrong with action? Join his uncles even if he should be the man of this house? Maybe Marc-André could tend the vineyards that stretched out in front of and behind the Château, although he'd barely begun training with Papa.

It wouldn't be too difficult to go unnoticed while the family's loss preoccupied them. Almost without realizing it, Gabriel-Isaac started toward the door.

"Gabriel-Isaac, come sit," called Aunt Anne. "We need to hear about everything that happened. You've been through a terrifying experience.

Talking about it will help those of us who weren't there." She held his gaze, then turned to Suzanne. "And both of you as well. It'll be difficult. But I know from experience that speaking about trauma, bringing it to the light, is a step toward healing."

Gabriel-Isaac huffed and dragged a chair into the family circle. He sat silent as Suzanne answered her aunt's questions about the raid and escape.

"And Pastor Etienne? Gabriel-Isaac, do you know what happened with him?"

"Yes. They arrested him right away."

Aunt Anne nodded, her eyes shining through unshed tears. "Ever since he returned from seminary in Lausanne, he knew this day would come. He often said that his diploma equaled a death sentence."

Gabriel-Isaac stared at his knees, blinking hard. He had long admired the pastor's courage and commitment. Now, unless a miracle happened, Gabriel-Isaac would never see Pastor Etienne alive again. Or his own parents.

"God protected you," said Grand-mère. "For that, I am eternally grateful." She fingered the golden Huguenot cross on the chain around her neck. "Still, I'd like to know where the soldiers took Jeanne and Pierre, which prison or . . ." She breathed in as if the air held strength. "Or if they sent Pierre to the galleys."

Aunt Anne agreed. "Yes, we must find out. If they're imprisoned in St. Hippolyte's fort, it might be possible to visit and bring them food and supplies. I'll ask my father-in-law. As the former town *notaire*, he'll know how to get the information."

"I can also make discreet inquiries during my visits to expectant mothers," Grand-mère said.

"But why?" asked Gabriel-Isaac, his voice harsh. "Why did God let the soldiers arrest them?"

Aunt Anne pulled a linen handkerchief from her sleeve and dabbed her eyes. "Your parents are extraordinarily faithful and brave. We've all depended on their work with the underground church, and they'll be greatly missed by all. They understood the risks and that this could be the result. They were ready. I know their biggest regret is leaving you all behind."

"God has chosen we live in a time such as this," said Grand-mère. "We each have a part to play. Mine has been to trust him through Grand-père André's death in the galleys and Uncle Gabriel's absence all these years. And now, once again, through the loss of my firstborn, Pierre, and my beloved daughter-in-law, Jeanne."

Grand-mère lowered her gray head, then lifted it again, her face shining through the sadness. Deep silence filled the room.

After a moment, Gabriel-Isaac spoke. "Anyway, how did the soldiers know where we were? We've gathered many times without being discovered."

Aunt Anne and Grand-mère exchanged glances, lingering longer than normal. Gabriel-Isaac looked from one to the other, then to Suzanne. Their eyes met and held for a moment.

"You think . . ." Crimson filled his cheeks. "You think someone betrayed us? Who would do such a thing? Only Huguenots know the time and place of our meetings. Sometimes even then we've had to follow the Holy Spirit's leading as we go."

Heat boiled through Gabriel-Isaac. There was no other way the soldiers could have known the location of the hidden service. The authorities offered rewards for such information, but the Huguenots of St. Hippolyte and villages nearby had remained loyal to one another. Until now.

Gabriel-Isaac looked down at Marie, seated on the floor, quaking in confusion and grief. Marc-André sat rigid in his chair, while Suzanne jumped to her feet and paced circles nearby, shooting him worried looks. Gabriel-Isaac had to get out of there.

"There's something else I'd like to do," said Aunt Anne. "I've desired this for so long."

Gabriel-Isaac stared at her. He couldn't imagine what she meant. What now?

Aunt Anne's focus landed on him alone. "We need to retrieve a precious item, something special I hid with your mother's help years ago, in the Château de Planque."

CHAPTER 6
ROLLAND LAPORTE

17 July 1702
Mialet
Eastern Cévennes

Rolland Laporte pushed aside a prickly stem and stepped through a berry bush, glad for the thick serge sleeves protecting his arms. Out the other side, he fanned his face with his round brimmed hat. The midday sun blazed down in full strength.

He ran his fingers through his nearly black hair and replaced his hat. The going was slow, taking much longer than the usual six-hour walk from the worship gathering outside of St. Hippolyte du Fort to his tiny hamlet of Mialet nestled in the hills. Once again, he thanked the Lord for his escape during the raid and for his safe journey so far.

Sorrow weighed heavy across his broad shoulders at the thought of Pastor Etienne's arrest. Even as Rolland fled, he'd witnessed the soldiers' rough treatment of his friend. The penalty for a minister caught tending to a Protestant flock was a painful, drawn-out torture and execution. There'd be no leniency.

Nor would there be for Rolland, if caught. He bent his tall frame under a low pine branch. Everything changed after he became an *inspiré* earlier in the year. Now, almost every time he attended a Huguenot gathering, including the one he'd just fled, the anointing fell on him to speak biblical truth and to prophesy. An honor, yet one that carried significant risk.

Though spared this time, he knew his life could be forfeited at a moment's notice. He didn't relish dying. But who was he to question if

God saw fit to give the task of preparing an army to an uneducated twenty-two-year-old, who normally spent his days combing raw wool, straightening the fibers for spinning into yarns?

Under the Holy Spirit's direction, Rolland had trained those willing to fight the authorities at the right time. Last night, about a dozen of them had accompanied him to the service. In the event of a raid, the plan was to flee and regroup later. Had they all escaped the soldiers? Avoided arrest? He'd soon find out; home was just around the next mountain bend.

He kept his guard up. The Lord hid him from the eyes of his enemies, but that didn't mean he shouldn't also use his own senses.

Pushing through the brush at a brisk pace, he became increasingly impatient to arrive at Mas Soubeyran, his family home, and reunite with his men. There was much to report.

Two men in particular would welcome what he had to share. For many years, Gabriel Lacombe and Paul Tessier had lived next door to him in Mialet. It had been a challenge to keep those two in check, especially Gabriel. Although he was only thirty-four and Paul twenty-eight, they were the elders of Rolland's troop.

He lifted his hat again and fanned himself, moving the heavy air across his face. His father had done a good job of spiritually leading and guiding them all until his arrest. Now, it fell on Rolland. Maybe that's why God had gifted him with the anointing of the Holy Spirit. Like all the *inspirés*, he was young and not theologically trained, yet he could preach the Word of God at Huguenot gatherings. He chuckled. It *had* to be God speaking through him. He certainly didn't have what it took to do anything like that.

Rolland continued up the mountain until the uneven skyline of Mialet's red-tiled rooftops came into view, quickening his steps. Within a half hour, he ducked through the low threshold and stepped into the ground floor of his home, barely noticing the pervading chill as he hurried through the entryway and up the narrow stone stairs, two at a time. Like cool spring water, relief washed over him as he entered the living and dining area on the second floor. His men all sat around the table, including those who'd attended the St. Hippolyte gathering. Until this moment, Rolland hadn't realized the full extent of the burden he carried for their safety.

The men jumped to their feet and surrounded him.

"You made it!" Gabriel pounded Rolland's back. "We kept the faith, praying." He glanced at Rolland's mother, standing next to the oak sideboard laden with food for the men. "We've all been back for hours," Gabriel continued in a low voice. "If they'd arrested you and figured out you are an *inspiré* . . . Well, we're very glad you're here."

"Yes, the Lord has seen fit to save me, to save us all for his purposes." Resting his hand on Gabriel's shoulder, Rolland smiled across the room to his mother. He went to greet her with three *bisous*.

She grinned. "They think to protect me by not stating the obvious. Of course, we all wondered . . . And now you're home. Safe." Peace glowed from her face, so like his own, with angular cheekbones under dark, intense eyes. "The Lord has plans for you that aren't yet fulfilled. I never truly doubted your return today. Now, sit and eat. You must be hungry."

He hugged her tight, grateful for her unshakeable faith. And her cooking. His belly rumbled, and they both laughed as he pulled up an oak bench and sat with his hands on the table, palms up. One of his sisters brought him a plate piled high. The men returned to their places around the table and peppered him with questions between bites of pork sausage, sheep's cheese, and chestnut bread.

"Did you have any trouble with the soldiers?" Paul asked.

Rolland drew a long drink of ale from his pewter tankard, then wiped his mouth with the back of his hand. "The Lord concealed me multiple times. As the prophet Isaiah wrote, 'Your ears shall hear a word behind you, saying, 'This is the way, walk in it,' whenever you turn to the right hand or whenever you turn to the left.'"[1]

He caught a look between Gabriel and Paul. Like most Huguenots, Rolland could read. But he hadn't the level of education of those two and seemed to surprise them often. His lips lifted in a slight smile.

Rolland chewed a bite of sausage, then continued. "At one point, I hid in a clump of berry bushes, and several soldiers stopped close by. I overheard their conversation. Apparently, Governor Bâville knows of us and of our intention to one day take on his soldiers. From what they said, the Governor will be extremely upset that I escaped. They expect he'll raise the stakes and strike back hard."

---

[1] Isaiah 30:21 (NKJV)

"I don't see how they can actually do us *more* harm," said Gabriel. "This has gone on for years, decades, and only gets worse. What else can they inflict on us?"

Paul spoke up. "They could abandon the tiny semblance of justice they still maintain."

"Go on," said Rolland. He valued the man's logical thinking that often brought clarity.

"Until now, they apprehend us only if we're caught in an assembly, praying, or reading our Bibles. They could abandon those stipulations and arrest us with no proof of illegal activity."

Across the table, Rolland's mother remained serene. He regarded each of the men, assessing what they were ready to receive. "What you say is true, Paul. I think the Governor will direct his men to take greater aggression against us. Some of you know of Abraham Mazel, the prophet from St. Jean du Gard. He's a wool comber like me. His home is a little over an hour's walk west from here, and our families have always been friendly, helping one another if needed."

"At the end of last year, the Holy Spirit visited Abraham in a dream in which enormous black cows devoured all the vegetables in a garden. A loud voice ordered him to chase them out. Mazel refused. The command came once again, and in the dream, he obeyed."

Rolland ran his finger around the rim of his tankard. "Over time, Abraham has understood the garden represents God's church, his true followers. The cows are the corrupt priests who ravage and destroy the people's sustenance."

All eating and drinking ceased, every eye on Rolland. "Abraham resisted taking up arms and fighting against our persecutors. But in the following months, God continued to speak, telling him to rise and carry iron and fire against the priests. Several of the most respected prophets have received similar directions."

Silence filled the room, broken only by the persistent chirping of cicadas outside. Of course, the dream and its confirmation by revered spiritual leaders was welcome news for these men.

Rolland focused his eyes far away. "Last night, the older prophet Esprit Séguier told me now is the time."

"Now?" asked Gabriel, jumping to his feet.

"What's the plan?" asked Paul, leaning forward.

"When do we leave?"

"The sooner, the better!"

Questions came fast, voices overlapping one another. More than one man stood, ready to go. Rolland held up his hand for silence. "We'll wait for God's timing. I believe it's soon, but I must receive clear direction from the Almighty before we move."

As quickly as it arose, excitement evaporated from the room.

"At least let some of us go," said Gabriel, his body shaking energy. "We can scout out what strategies the prophets are now hearing, as well as information on Bâville's plans."

The thought crossed Rolland's mind that he'd be dead if Gabriel's eyes shot bullets. The man was over a decade older and had known Rolland since he was a boy. If Rolland weren't an *inspiré* held in esteem among the larger Huguenot community, his authority wouldn't go very far with this one.

"Let me pray on it," Rolland said, his voice firm. "I believe it won't be long."

All the men drifted away, returning to the tasks of the day. Rolland lingered at the table while his mother stood and stacked empty plates. After the two youngest sisters carried the dishes to the kitchen, his mother circled the table and settled on the bench next to him.

She smiled. "You already know, don't you?"

"I think so, yes. I'll pray about it some more to be very sure. The questions are who goes where and when. But I believe we'll be in an open war against Governor Bâville and the King within the next few weeks."

Rolland and his mother sat side by side, a moment filled with eternity. Their lives were always tenuous, both physically and spiritually. But now, change was coming. Maybe it already had. The Laportes, mother and son, remained rock solid in their faith and experienced no fear.

CHAPTER 7

HIDDEN TREASURE

17 July 1702
St. Hippolyte du Fort
Southern Cévennes

Suzanne shivered despite the summer heat. Everyone gave Aunt Anne their full attention, even Gabriel-Isaac. No one knew where her call to action was headed.

Aunt Anne composed her hands on her lap. "You all know of the dragoons' arrival in St. Hippolyte many years ago. Well, the officers and several of their men moved into our home, the Château de Planque. Originally, a Colonel Arnault seemed somewhat favorable toward us. I suppose he was a man of faith in his own way. He respected my father, and they seemed to have an understanding. However, his orders soon sent him elsewhere. The next batch of dragoons who moved in with us were far worse."

She paused, a line etched between her brows. "Although it's been almost twenty years, I can well remember our shock as we understood this was our new reality. I guess we'd expected the soldiers to move on and life to return to normal. But that didn't happen. One of the hardest aspects of the dragoons living with us was concealing the Bible and our evening readings."

Grand-mère bowed her gray head. Dragoons had invaded her home as well.

Aunt Anne looked at each of the Lacombe children. "When the dragoons first moved in, we slept, ate, and spent all our time in one bedroom. It was safer that way. During the day, we stored the Bible in your mother's wooden trunk, which also served as our dining table. At night, once the soldiers were busy eating and drinking, my papa, your Grand-père Isaac, brought it out and read to us. The rest of us took turns standing guard at the door, listening for approaching dragoons."

Suzanne glanced at Gabriel-Isaac, her eyebrows slightly raised. Why was Aunt Anne telling them what they already knew? With a tiny tilt of his head, he shrugged. He didn't know either.

"You must wonder why I'm bringing this up now," Aunt Anne said. "Well, as pressure increased, your grand-père created a better *cachette* to conceal the Tessier Bible from the dragoons. Of course, if they'd ever found our family treasure, they'd have confiscated and destroyed it, plus handed out fines and punishments."

Everyone looked across the room at the oak-framed mirror hanging from a thick velvet ribbon over the sideboard. The Lacombe family Bible nestled safely in the space between the mirror and the backing, which Grand-père André made for this purpose long ago. From Suzanne's earliest memories, her papa also brought the Bible out each night after dinner and read passages to the family. Then he and Maman took great care to explain the meaning.

A new cord of sadness twisted around her heart. How she'd miss those evenings. Like all the children and youth throughout the region, she'd been required to attend school run by priests and learn the catechism. Governor Bâville was determined to eradicate Protestantism through education. But each night, parents in every true Huguenot home carefully reeducated their children in biblical precepts and the tenets of their faith.

Aunt Anne's voice brought Suzanne back to the present. "To better conceal the Bible, Grand-père Isaac added a wood plank shelf in the armoire where your mother, Aunt Catherine, and I kept our clothes. He constructed it so that under the top of the armoire, there was a hiding place. It was ingenious really, as no one ever thought to lift that upper portion unless moving the entire piece of furniture."

"What are you saying?" asked Gabriel-Isaac.

"After Grand-père Isaac's arrest, the dragoons forced us to move out of the Château de Planque. We couldn't get the Bible without discovery."

"So now you want to get it?" asked Gabriel-Isaac.

Aunt Anne shook her head. "That would be too dangerous. The bedroom is on the second floor, and you know Lord Valmalle is a loyal ally of Governor Bâville. If we asked for the Bible, Valmalle would have every excuse to arrest us. Even asking for the armoire would raise suspicion."

Her gaze rested on Gabriel-Isaac. "We owned a small psalter as well. How I loved that book, with its beautiful illustrations."

"I remember you telling us about it, but I thought it had been lost," Suzanne said.

"I believe I told you we didn't have it anymore. Before we moved out, your mother and I hid it from the dragoons to keep it safe."

Gabriel-Isaac studied his aunt. "Where?"

"On the ground floor, in the pantry off the main kitchen. One stone was loose in the wall behind the storage sacks of grains and flour. When Marion, our housekeeper, wasn't around, your mother and I used large soup spoons to carve into the mortar behind the rock. We created enough space to hide the tiny psalter. I doubt anyone would ever find it."

Grand-mère's mouth dropped open. Apparently, this was news to her as well.

Tears brimmed in Aunt Anne's bright blue eyes. "Now more than ever, I'd like to have the psalter back. It's a significant piece of our family heritage."

Suzanne could understand her aunt's desire to have the Tessier psalter. Its words of truth and the special family memories connected with it would bring comfort with Maman gone. But why invite more trouble?

"I'll go," said Gabriel-Isaac. "I'll get it. How hard could it be?"

Aunt Anne smiled through her tears. Had she expected him to volunteer?

Suzanne stood, hands fisted. "*Non*. Don't we have enough to deal with already? Couldn't we just keep out of harm's way and try to go on with our lives?"

Beloved! Fear not. This is my will. All will be well. Suzanne buried her face in her hands. Despite the turbulent thoughts shaking her, a quiet reassurance washed over her. There was no trembling, only a profound and unexpected peace.

She lifted her head and found Aunt Anne observing her. Somehow, it seemed her aunt understood. But why would she send Gabriel-Isaac into danger? Did she hear the Voice? Had God led her to do this?

The Voice assured Suzanne all would be well. Could she trust it? It had led them out of the cave, through the forest, and safely home. Would it continue to come in such a quiet, still manner? Could she truly live without fear?

How could that be so when many of her loved ones, including Papa, had suffered? Had been thrown in jail or worse? She stood abruptly, escaped to the kitchen, and began stacking dirty dishes, clanking them hard. A huge part of her wanted to throw the lot of them on the floor. Instead, she gave them a ferocious washing up.

A quarter hour later, she placed both hands against the granite sink under the window and strained forward to look out. Directly across the road, Gabriel-Isaac jumped through the Château de Planque's kitchen window and disappeared. Fear froze any kernels of faith in her, and she found it impossible to formulate thoughts. She tried to pray for his safety. Maybe God would take the hammerings of her heart as a plea for help.

Beloved! Fear not.

Those words again! They kept coming unbidden. Each time, resistance rose within her. *Non!* Freedom from fear wasn't possible. Yet, the words brought stillness amid the ongoing storm.

The Voice whispered *Beloved* as if that were her name, as if that should overshadow every fear in her life. Could that be so? She'd never *not* believed in Jesus. The Bible said he loved her, so that must be why she was called Beloved. But their relationship felt rather distant.

Suzanne reached up and unlatched the window. Summer heat flowed into the chilly room. Built on the slope of the Route de Lasalle, the lower half of the Lacombe kitchen was partially under the ground. Normally, she welcomed the coolness during the hot months, but now she couldn't get warm. She rubbed her arms and opened the window wider. It didn't help. Her body trembled from a cold that originated in her interior, as if she was shut down until Gabriel-Isaac returned safely.

She determined to keep her vigil at the window until Gabriel-Isaac reappeared. Across the street, the Château's ground-floor kitchen compound should be empty at this hour. It made sense that Aunt Anne and Grand-mère had chosen this moment.

But Suzanne didn't like it. Why had Aunt Anne put Gabriel-Isaac at risk? Lord Valmalle would have no qualms hauling him before the Governor's authorities. Valmalle would be delighted to bring punishment to the Lacombe family. Although they faithfully cared for his vineyards, he resented that they'd inhabited the land long before he arrived. It was no secret he suspected their conversion was in name only, that he desired to catch them in some Protestant activity and turn them in.

Suzanne leaned out the window, scanning the road. Her breath caught. Charles Fesquet emerged from the Planque bridge and walked toward the Château. Why was he, of all people, here now?

She couldn't let him knock on the Château's front door and draw someone from inside to the ground floor. Not while her brother was trespassing in that same area.

Her heart thumped above the butterflies dancing through her stomach. Why did seeing Charles always provoke this reaction in her? Yes, he had those eyes, rich brown, and that wavy hair. And incredibly full red lips. With a frown, she banished those thoughts. She and Charles had become friends during their school days, but that's all they could ever be. His family were true Catholics, and she, of course, must marry a Protestant.

Suzanne untied her long linen apron and threw it over the back of a straw-bottomed chair. She grabbed her bonnet off its peg, pulled it on, and stepped out of the kitchen door. Heat rose and flamed across her face. Hopefully, he wouldn't notice or would blame the weather if he did.

She strode across the street, calling out before he entered the Château courtyard. "Charles! Bonjour!"

He stopped and tipped his cap, then leaned in to give her three *bisous.* "Bonjour Suzanne! How nice to see you! *Ça va?*"

Suzanne tried not to think about his lips brushing her burning cheeks. And had those eyes lingered on her face? Surely, that was just her imagination.

"Uh, I'm very well, thank you. And you?" Aware she sounded overly formal, she rushed on. "I haven't seen you in a long time. How's your family? And how's the Fesquet wine business coming along? What brings you to this side of town?"

Charles smiled wide and leaned a little closer, none of which helped quiet her racing heart. "So many questions! Yes, it has been a while. And we're all very well, *merci*."

He looked around at the Planque vineyards. "But the vines on our side of town are suffering. Distance from the river and lack of rain have caught up with us. This year's harvest looks to be sparse. In fact, that's why I'm here." He shaded his eyes with his hand and glanced at the Château.

"Since the Château de Planque has that immense cistern behind the outer courtyard wall, we figured your vines have the water they need. And, unlike our domaine, yours is close to the river." He turned his gaze back to her. She tried to concentrate on his words and not his vibrant eyes or the timber of his voice.

"So, my father wishes to set up a meeting with Lord Valmalle to discuss combining our harvests, forming a cooperative venture. If he agrees, I suppose your papa will also take part."

The dancing butterflies in Suzanne's belly crashed to a halt. What would happen when word got out of her father's arrest? Would Charles ever speak to her again?

CHAPTER 8
CHÂTEAU ADVENTURES

17 July 1702
St. Hippolyte du Fort
Southern Cévennes

" Suzanne! Charles! Bonjour, friends!"
Suzanne swiveled to her best friend's voice. Marguerite strode toward them from her home down the street, her long legs covering the distance quickly. The Marolles had long managed and lived above the Château's *moulin à huile*. Suzanne turned her face from Charles, hiding her relief that Marguerite had escaped the soldiers' invasion. Marguerite's timing was perfect, a more than welcome distraction.

"Bonjour, Marguerite!" As the young women leaned in for three *bisous*, Suzanne held her friend's gaze for a brief moment of shared gratitude. They'd both made it through the cave raid and returned home safely. Marguerite squeezed Suzanne's arm, then turned to greet Charles.

"What brings you to our side of town?" she asked after the customary *bisous*. "Checking out the wine competition?"

Suzanne grinned. Marguerite's voice almost always carried a slight sarcastic edge. That, plus her sharp wit, brought levity and humor into most situations.

Charles laughed. "Actually, I'm here to see if Lord Valmalle would welcome a collaboration. Our grape production is down this year. Also, my father and I think we can increase profits, not to mention create some interesting vintages."

Suzanne wracked her brain for a way to veer the topic away from *her* father, known for his successful wines. No words came; grief clogged her throat.

Marguerite grabbed Charles's arm and started dragging him away from the front of the Château. "You know, I've been wondering about this white powdery stuff on the grapes. Could you tell me what it is and why it's here?"

What was Marguerite doing? Her friend couldn't care less about the agricultural aspects of the fruit of the vine.

"Suzanne, come look at this!" Marguerite ordered, a slight urgency laced through her voice.

Too surprised to do anything else, Suzanne followed. The trio crossed the small street in front of the Château and stepped through the tall wrought-iron gates in the stone wall that surrounded the Planque domaine. Marguerite peppered Charles with one question after another.

Suzanne listened and swatted away mosquitos as Charles patiently explained that the problem was powdery mildew and that only a few vines were affected. Would this change the Fesquets' proposition of collaborating with Lord Valmalle? Not that she really cared about that, but why was Marguerite drawing Charles's attention to the issue?

And how was it going for Gabriel-Isaac? Everything in Suzanne wanted to look back toward the Château, but she didn't dare. Was he still inside?

Marguerite's voice broke into Suzanne's thoughts. "Thanks, Charles, for filling me in. I pass by here every day. Now I'll know it's nothing to worry about."

Finding it highly improbable that Marguerite came anywhere close to worrying about Lord Valmalle's vines, Suzanne stared hard at her friend. Marguerite gave her head a tiny shake.

"You're welcome." Charles smiled at them both. Did his eyes rest on Suzanne a little longer? Casting her eyes down, she pressed her lips together. She really had to stop reading more into his every gesture.

"Well, I best go see Lord Valmalle with our proposal," he said.

"*Bien sûr!* Of course! Don't let us keep you."

In the street dividing the Château and the vineyards out front, they said their goodbyes. Suzanne and Marguerite watched Charles pass through the wrought-iron gate into the Château's front courtyard and then walk across to the massive double front doors. He lifted the heavy iron ring serving as a knocker, rapped it several times, then turned and waved. Marguerite and Suzanne returned the wave as a servant opened the door and gestured for Charles to enter.

"What was that all about?" Suzanne whispered to Marguerite. She glanced back at the Château as they walked toward her home across the street.

Marguerite laughed and tossed her long, ebony hair over her shoulder. "Surprised by my sudden interest in grapes and mildew? It was that or risk Charles seeing your brother climbing out the Château's kitchen window."

Suzanne froze. "Oh my goodness! You saw him! What if Charles had . . ."

A wave of dizziness threatened that she might pass out on the hot road. She clung tight to Marguerite's arm.

"Don't worry! Charles didn't see Gabriel-Isaac. And since your brother's not out here, he must be inside your house. I can't wait to hear what on earth Gabriel-Isaac was doing sneaking in and out of the Château." Her sage-green eyes danced. "Trespassing in the biggest home in town, owned by the vengeful Lord Valmalle. This story should be entertaining!"

Suzanne couldn't decide if she wanted to laugh or weep. Once she saw Gabriel-Isaac was safe, she might just do both.

The friends took their time walking to Suzanne's home. One never knew if unfriendly eyes gazed down on them from the Château de Planque windows. No need to draw attention. They stepped into the entryway of the Lacombe home, the brisk air welcome after the intense heat outside.

Suzanne raced into the salon. Gabriel-Isaac stood beaming by the unlit fireplace, a small linen-wrapped item in hand. "Good. You're here, Suzanne. Bonjour, Marguerite!"

The dam of tension gave way. Suzanne's tears overflowed.

Marguerite, hands on her hips, turned to Gabriel-Isaac. "So, young man, what have you been up to? I saw you climbing out the Château's kitchen window. I can't wait to hear this story!" She crossed the room and greeted Grand-mère and Aunt Anne with three *bisous*, then flopped down in a chair. "Gabriel-Isaac, tell us all!"

Suzanne smiled through her tears. Marguerite always got right to the point, like family. They did share Aunt Catherine, Maman's prickly sister married to Marguerite's uncle. Since words flew hot and fast between her and Marguerite, it was just as well that Aunt Catherine lived down the road, in the village of Sauve.

Facing Gabriel-Isaac, Suzanne narrowed her eyes. "It's a good thing Marguerite saw you. I'd gone out to distract Charles Fesquet." Why did her cheeks flame every time she said his name out loud? "He was on his way to speak with Lord Valmalle about a new wine venture. Then Marguerite came along and dragged Charles off to check the vines as you emerged from the window."

"You're welcome for the distraction," Marguerite said, sardonic grin in place.

"*Merci!*" said Gabriel-Isaac. "I didn't see any of that! I'm glad you were there to keep Charles and any Château people away from the ground floor."

Gabriel-Isaac quickly updated Marguerite on the existence of the Tessier psalter, then launched into his adventure story. "Thankfully, the Château's cook hadn't latched the window after the midday meal. One push and it opened. As in our kitchen, there's a granite sink right inside. I stepped onto it and then jumped down to the floor."

"No one else around, then?" asked Aunt Anne.

"No, just as we expected. The servants weren't there, probably busy elsewhere or resting."

"What would you have done if someone had seen you?" Suzanne demanded. Images of imprisonment and worse rose in her mind. If he'd been caught, authorities would've thrown him into the St. Hippolyte prison-fort, to languish with the other youth there. If he'd been accused of thievery, they would've put him on display in public stocks.

"I'd have made up some story." Gabriel-Isaac lifted his chin. "Anyway, no one was in the kitchen, at first. But I'll get to that." He ignored Suzanne's sharp inhale. "Then I went through a few small rooms next to the main kitchen before I found the pantry. There are huge woven sacks full of grains and ground flour. I've never seen such a quantity! Behind them are wooden shelves lining the walls, filled with crocks of preserved vegetables." He looked at his aunt. "I hadn't expected that, and it took me some time to move them while looking for your hiding place. Finally, I found a loose stone. I'd been close to giving up, but there it was. With some jostling, it finally came free. And voilà!"

He held up the small package in triumph. "Still there, after all these years."

Gabriel-Isaac handed it to Aunt Anne. With great care, she unwrapped it, turning the psalter over in her hands. Then she pressed it to her chest, tears sliding down her cheeks, her lips moving in silent prayer.

"Gabriel-Isaac, you said no one was around *at first*," Suzanne said. "Did anyone see you?"

"Just as I put the crocks back in place, I heard someone in the next room."

Suzanne sat down hard on the nearest chair.

"I crouched as low as possible behind the flour sacks. Good thing they're huge!" He chuckled, obviously impressed with the volume of the storage bags compared to his own height.

"None of this is funny, brother."

He rolled his eyes. "I heard footsteps coming closer to the pantry, but stop. Maybe they'd heard something when I replaced the vegetable crocks. Anyway, whoever it was left after a minute. Clearly didn't see me."

"God be praised!" said Aunt Anne. "For Gabriel-Isaac's protection and for the return of the Tessier psalter. I've always believed that the Almighty would keep it hidden. And now, to have it in my hands once again! Have I told you I took it with me when the Huguenots of St. Hippolyte moved to Le Cengle mountain right before the dragoons arrived?"

The entire family nodded.

"Aunt Anne, you've told us *many* times!" Marc-André said, his voice serious.

Laughter burst forth, releasing the last bits of pent-up anxiety over Gabriel-Isaac's escapade. They all gathered around Aunt Anne as she turned the beautifully illustrated pages of the psalter. The tiny tome even contained pages with intricate lace-like cutouts. Marie seemed especially enthralled and snuggled in close to her aunt to take it all in.

Judging from Aunt Anne's joy, the Tessier treasure was almost worth the risk taken. Not only was she a young widow, but she'd now lost her dearly loved older sister and her brother-in-law. Though nothing could change all that, the psalter clearly brought her great comfort.

Suzanne stood and moved away from the family. Jangly after the tension of the afternoon's activities, she wrapped her arms tight around her middle. How could she take care of Gabriel-Isaac and keep him safe if he took such risks? Even though the retrieval of the psalter hadn't been her decision, she'd never have forgiven herself if the outcome was bad. She must keep the family secure, for all their sakes and for Maman's and Papa's.

With the continuous pressure surrounding their family, was security too much to ask? All she'd ever wanted was for them to be all together, for some form of stability. Why was that always just out of reach?

CHAPTER 9
EVIL PREPARATIONS

22 July 1702
Pont-de-Montvert
Northern Cévennes

The Abbé du Chaila rarely stepped outside in late afternoon, by far the hottest part of the day. But he couldn't contain himself. He needed to move about.

Even under the shade of the trees, the sunbaked air hung thick and still. With a summer rainstorm well overdue, the parched land crackled underfoot like tinder waiting to ignite. Down the slope, at the bottom of his garden, the river Tarn barely trickled. Large and small boulders that were usually submerged protruded along its borders.

Success against the heretics was finally within reach now that Governor Bâville had raised the stakes, sending a hundred additional soldiers to Pont-de-Montvert a few days ago. Du Chaila had barely allowed the soldiers to rest and refresh themselves before sending them out again. They were sweeping through villages, forests, mountains, and valleys—anywhere and everywhere—looking for Huguenots. The priest rubbed his fleshy hands together and flicked his tongue across his lips. This effort was almost too easy.

Yet another mosquito lazed around his face, whining by his ear. He stopped and waited. Finally, it landed on his neck and he slapped it dead, leaving a red splotch of bright blood on his palm. He bared his teeth. This campaign must suck the lifeblood out of the Huguenot movement. The King exerted great pressure to get the job done, and the Governor had run out of patience. Bâville could not fail. Nor could Du Chaila.

The Abbé licked his dry lips again and ran a hand across his thinning gray hair. What would happen to him if his authority were removed by the Governor? Unthinkable.

Du Chaila stepped into the ground floor of his house. He relished the permanent cool aided by the dirt floors and wide walls. Once his eyes adjusted to the relative dimness, he walked down the hallway, stopping at each door, checking each cell. Stocks and chains lay ready to secure his prisoners, alongside tables and various instruments prepared to provoke confession. Soon they'd be more useful than ever.

The farthest room was his personal favorite. On the other side of the unbreakable iron door was the rack. Here, he did his best work. A side table held his pliers and other tools, cleaned, polished, and lined up in neat rows. Whatever met his particular fancy or promised to produce the best results was at his fingertips, ready to go. La Violette did his job well. He'd even remembered to spread fresh straw over the packed-earth floor, covering the bloodstains from his last batch of prisoners.

Soon, there'd be a new group. Fresh meat, so to speak. Pinpricks of excitement shot through his chest at thoughts of those first moments: palpable fear in the prisoners' eyes, waves of terror radiating off their bodies. The thrill faded at memory of past prisoners' courage. Something on their faces, some inner strength, baffled him every time. They were afraid of him and what he'd do to punish them and force conversions, but at their very center, they seemed unshaken, immovable. How was it that a strange peace lingered in and on them, one that surpassed everything around them?

Irritation flamed into fury. He slammed the cell door and strode down the hallway, his pulse racing. He'd crush and toss aside this new set of Huguenots, exterminate them and their false religion. This time, his efforts *would* make a difference.

Back upstairs, he entered his grand salon. La Violette rushed in, face flushed.

"They're here! The soldiers have returned with prisoners."

"Already? That's good. That's very good indeed."

The priest waddled to the tall window. In the street below, soldiers rustled the prisoners along. Du Chaila's heart leapt. Eight heretics! And they were young, as he liked them.

"Don't stand there, man!" he bellowed. "Show them the way to the dungeons."

La Violette scurried away. Du Chaila paced and contemplated creative new ways to inflict pain. Anticipation bubbled through his soul. He laughed out loud.

Down in the street, he questioned the capitaine in charge of the day's arrests. The hunt had yielded a group of young people fleeing to Geneva, led by a guide called Jean Massip. The Abbé pasted a decorous expression onto his face to cover his exhilaration. He barked directions, and the soldiers led the prisoners around back to the dungeons.

Du Chaila followed and watched the soldiers lock away his prey. He couldn't wait to get his hands on them. By the time he was done with Jean Massip and his little band of Protestants, terror would reverberate throughout the Cévennes. The priest ordered the capitaine and his men to ride out again. Surely, this would mark the beginning of the end for the Huguenots.

How stupid the young people had been. Stopping at an auberge for refreshment, probably expecting a safe Huguenot abode. Ha! Plenty of people throughout the region were more than willing to bring him information about Protestants fleeing or in hiding. With the enticement of a few coins, the fools willingly betrayed their neighbors.

Only Jean Massip and three others had sheltered in the auberge. The soldiers found the rest later. Apparently, they'd split up for greater safety. Du Chaila sneered. As if they could outsmart royal soldiers.

However, the capture presented a slight problem. Three of the prisoners were women, albeit dressed in men's clothing. He didn't have enough cells for lodging them apart from the male prisoners.

Stories circulated of immorality among the *inspirés*. Lodging males and females together would give opportunity for spreading false rumors, one of the many tools in his arsenal. In the past, though, he'd found that separating them produced better results. That they appeared to remain stronger together was probably just bravado, but he'd take every step necessary to weaken them, including isolating the leader, Jean Massip, in the most secure cell.

Du Chaila swatted a mosquito away from his sweat-drenched face and paced the length of his garden. He'd need to expedite the women's treatment and then send them north to the convent in Mende. The nuns would see to the prisoners' reeducation and ensure they never again saw the light of day. Too bad he couldn't keep them longer for himself, but he must deal with the men.

Ducking his head, he stepped through a low arch and into the cold corridor leading to the dungeons. At the first door, he lifted the wood panel covering a tiny window and checked on the men inside. Chained by hand and foot to wooden blocks, they weren't going anywhere. He'd made extra sure this time. Hot anger boiled at the memory of that prisoner who escaped with the help of his mother. His tiny mother! Du Chaila ground his teeth and pushed all discouragement down deep, especially his father's condemning voice ringing through his head. Since that event, he'd reinforced the cells. No one would ever elude him again.

He studied the four male prisoners through the portal. Despite their pale faces, their eyes held no terror. Each of them returned his penetrating gaze, not one backing down. He didn't like that. Not at all. He'd soon teach them what it meant to fear. First, though, he had to deal with the women. He slammed the wooden panel shut.

When he entered the next cell, his spirit lifted at the sight of the three girls, apparently sisters, huddled on the dirt floor. He closed the door firmly, and as he approached, they sat straight, chins held high. The eldest even dared to meet his eyes. Courage and that same certain strength filled her face, striking him like a punch to the gut. Why were they not cowering, afraid? He brushed his unease away. Clearly, they didn't know what was coming to them.

The Abbé stepped to the table and ran his hand over his tools. Which one to use first? He picked up a pair of pliers, then turned to study the girls. One crumpled, dropping her head, low sobs escaping her lips. Perfect. He'd start with her. The other two would lose their strange fortitude once they saw him at work on their sister.

An otherworldly sound rose from down the hall. Prickles spread through his scalp, and the hair on his arms stood on end. A strange melody, the swell of a song, scraped across his nerves like nothing he'd ever experienced. The pliers clattered to the ground.

"Don't think this is over." His snarled words tangled in his constricting throat. He strode from the room, slamming the door behind him.

The priest stalked back to the first chamber. He pulled the long iron key from his pocket, unlocked the door, and thrust it open hard. Inside, the chained Huguenot men sang with a force that struck him like a physical assault. Vaguely familiar lyrics wove through an unknown tune, producing excruciating pain in every part of his being. Gritting his teeth, he balled his fists and restrained himself from clapping his hands over his ears. No sign of weakness in front of the heretics! What would his father say?

The song continued.

Let God arise, let his enemies be scattered.[2]

How dare they sing the words of this psalm against the Abbé du Chaila? He picked up a wooden plank he kept in the corner and approached his soon-to-be victims. He would squash them, starting with their heads, and snuff out the wretched noise.

The prisoners continued worshiping.

As smoke is driven away,
So drive them away;
As wax melts before the fire,
So let the wicked perish at the presence of God.[3]

He swung the board wildly. Darkness rose and engulfed him, pinpricked with sparks of white. His fury receded, leaving an icy chill in its wake. The singing was pure torture. He shook himself. He needed to stay present and put an end to the infernal sound before he lost all control, including bodily functions, like his victims did.

His eyelids fluttered. Why was he on the ground, gravel and dirt grinding into his face? *Non!* What had happened?

He pushed himself up on all fours, his belly grazing the floor. Lifting one foot, then another, he stood, feeling slow and heavy, his head swimming. He placed one hand on the stone wall to steady himself and brushed his face off with the other. His vision cleared, and the four Huguenots came into view. Each watched him, eyes wide. Nearby, the wooden plank lay on the ground, the men unharmed.

A fresh wave of dizziness caused his vision to dim yet again. He had to get out of there before a disaster occurred. With leaden feet, he shuffled from the room, one hand groping along the stone wall.

---

[2] Psalm 68:1 (NKJV)
[3] Psalm 68:2 (NKJV)

In the frigid hallway, his gut twisted. He doubled over until the spasm passed.

You're a coward and a weakling. A failure. His father's oft-repeated words cycled through his clouded brain. The Abbé opened his eyes, lifted his head, half expecting to find his papa towering over him with a raised hand, ready to beat out weakness.

Sweat soaked through the Abbé's robe. He drew his sleeve across his brow. An episode like that must not happen again. Ever.

He could wait out this spell, whatever it was, whatever its cause. Then he'd return and finish the job. And this time, he'd make sure the results were exactly what he desired.

CHAPTER 10
PROPHETS ON THE MOVE

22–23 July 1702
Rabiès
Northern Cévennes

Abraham Mazel lifted his iron lantern and made a slow arc around the stone sheepfold, filled with the flock of God in human form. Although he'd been an *inspiré* for some time, the incredible leading of the Holy Spirit amazed him. With no human communication, a small group of Huguenots gathered in the dark of night to worship. In this limestone *bergerie* above the tiny village of Rabiès in the northern Cévennes, they sought specific direction for their next move.

Abraham set the lantern on the rock wall and lifted his sandy hair up off his neck, attempting to cool off. Even at night, the heat was unrelenting, as was the bad news. Word of the Abbé du Chaila's arrests of the guide Massip and seven others had spread like wildfire throughout the parched lands of the Cévennes. The priest's violent reputation was no secret.

Within days, relatives of the arrested youths had dared to confront the Abbé at a regional fair, begging him for mercy. They'd offered a substantial sum for their release, met only by a haughty refusal. Du Chaila's plans to send the Mademoiselles Celestin to the convent in Mende horrified all who heard of it. No one ever left that place of innumerable tales of torturous abuse.

As devastating was Du Chaila's proclamation that he'd send for the executioner on returning to Pont-de-Montvert. He'd make an example of Jean Massip with a public hanging, ignoring the legality of a trial.

Abraham ran his hand across his face, remembering his extraordinary dream. He understood that the dark beasts in it were the priests, such as Du Chaila, who destroyed the Huguenots and what they needed to survive, their practical and spiritual nourishment.

It made sense. Over the past two decades, the Huguenots lived under the persecution of the King's authorities, including the clergy. Still, it was hard to accept the words in the dream. Someone telling him— Abraham!—to chase them out. In the dream, he'd refused to do so at first. Since deciding to obey, he'd struggled with the reality of actually doing such a thing. He didn't own a gun and had never taken part in any kind of battle. The priests' evil actions were widely known, but it had never occurred to Abraham to do something about them. Why would God talk to him about all this?

He'd received more instructions several times after the dream. The Huguenots were to carry iron and fire against the priests. The most unusual direction had been to burn their homes and overthrow them. Could God truly want the faithful to engage in violence?

Abraham had spent hours searching the scriptures for confirmation of it all. In the Old Testament, the Almighty had led his people to take up arms and fight. David started with Goliath but went on to defeat numerous enemies. And wasn't David a shepherd to begin with? Not that different from a wool comber like Abraham, only twenty-five years old and with no experience other than the family business.

While at work straightening raw fibers of lambs' wool for spinning, he'd demanded of God, *Why me?* Immediately, the reminder came. The Almighty chooses the weak and foolish of this world to confuse the wise and the strong. Abraham had shaken his head. *Are you sure God?* To his astonishment, respected prophets he'd shared his dream with confirmed the message. Many had received similar divine direction.

He looked around the *bergerie.* Several of those prophets gathered here now, including the well-known Pierre Séguier. Called "Esprit" for his fervent prophetic proclamations, he was the oldest *inspiré.* Mazel suppressed a smile, imagining that the fifty-two-year-old, with his fiery intensity and wild gray hair, resembled Elijah on Mt. Carmel. That Séguier left everything he knew a few years prior to follow God's call to preach throughout the Cévennes served as a great inspiration to them all.

Sparks of light flashed through Abraham's body, the stirrings rising from deep within. Then came the tremors. He recognized the beginning of a prophetic flow. Greater shakings would follow. As usual, it started slow and small, then increased. He stood and waited.

Like the others, he believed in the biblical truth that the spirits of prophets are subject to the control of prophets. If desired, he could shut down the violent agitations, but he'd learned that it lessened the flow of the Holy Spirit. The Abbé du Chaila's latest, intensified actions had provoked a shift in the inspirations, and their instructions now headed in a new direction. He didn't want to miss out on any of God's guidance. Maybe that was why the tremblings were coursing through him with more power than ever.

Esprit Séguier moved toward him. "Speak, Mazel. The Spirit is upon you."

As usual, Abraham didn't fully know what he was going to say until his mouth opened. Words from heaven streamed through him like a torrent of living water from an abundant rain. Loud and clear, the instructions came. "Brothers and sisters! The time has come. We must *now* take up arms, without delay, and go deliver our brothers from the persecutor holding them in Pont-de-Montvert."

Abraham waited a moment, then stepped back. There was no more direction for now, at least through him. He shut his eyes, letting the reality of the prophecy sink in. The very thing he wrestled with, had resisted and even dreaded, was upon them. Now was the time.

Another prophet, Salomon Couderc, stepped forward. "The Spirit confirms it. *Now is the time.*"

"Yes!"

"Amen!"

Séguier spoke loud. "We'll obey God. *Now is the time!*"

"No matter the outcome!"

Séguier knelt and the others followed. "Almighty God, we commit all this into your hands. Guide us to walk only in your ways."

"Amen," the men spoke as one.

Séguier stood and looked at the gathered. "We go, now."

Mazel nodded. "Remain on high alert! Soldiers roam the region."

"We go with God."

After two hours marching through the dark, the men stopped by a stream as the sky pinked with the first rays of dawn. Abraham knelt and lapped water from his hand. Thirst quenched, he splashed his face, then stood and used his white linen shirtsleeve to dry off. His fellow prophets leaned against boulders along the water's edge. He couldn't believe it was finally happening. They were on their way to Pont-de-Montvert. He still didn't know how they'd liberate the prisoners from the Abbé du Chaila. Only a few of them carried weapons, ancient guns, and most knew nothing about using them. Could he shoot another human being? Would it come to that?

His gaze landed on their guide. Rampon had served Séguier on his travels of preaching and prophesying through the Cévennes. Best of all, Rampon was from the mountain village of Pont-de-Montvert, the very place where Du Chaila lived and conducted his operations. A gift from God. As was the privilege of working with Esprit Séguier and Salomon Couderc. *Thank you, Lord, for your clear directions and this blessed unity.*

The Voice spoke low. *You're never alone.*

Peace descended. He wasn't alone. God would remain with him to the end, whenever that came.

The four travelers continued across the river. Within a quarter of an hour, they arrived at the edge of village of Bougès, still not sure why the Holy Spirit led them to that place.

The sun peeked over the tiled rooftops as the men stood at the edge of town, considering their next move.

"Food would be nice," said Salomon.

"Man lives not by bread alone," said Séguier.

With a half smile, Rampon shot the older man a look. "So often we do just that."

Abraham spoke up. "If we're to engage in a physical confrontation, we should fortify ourselves. Let's continue on to the village center. Women fetching water there might give strangers a morsel."

Rampon patted his empty belly.

Without a word, Séguier started walking into the village, and the others followed. They wound their way through small cobblestone alleys and, within minutes, stepped into an open area with a raised stone fountain in the center. Several women there busied themselves filling ceramic jugs and catching up on gossip before the tasks of the day.

The men approached with caution. Abraham pondered what reason to give for their arrival in town so early in the morning. One never knew who sided with Governor Bâville and the Abbé du Chaila.

He stepped forward. "Bonjour, mesdames."

"Bonjour, messieurs," the women replied more or less in unison. A few eyed the strangers, wary expressions on their faces.

The men moved around to the opposite side of the fountain. Clean water poured through an iron pipe into the limestone basin. Rampon reached his hands under the stream, drinking some and declaring it icy, then dabbing his face.

Abraham opened his mouth to speak, then stopped at Rampon's swift nudge in the ribs. The guide tipped his head toward two men emerging from a small side street.

One of the pair called out. "Bonjour, messieurs and *dames*."

The women mumbled their responses and then scurried away. Evidently, they'd had their fill of outsiders for the day. Rampon's shoulders sagged, clearly disappointed they'd have to find sustenance elsewhere.

Salomon stepped forward, shielding his eyes from the sun. "Jacques?" he said to the taller man. "Cousin? Is that you?"

"*Oui!* It's me, Cousin Salomon. What are you doing here?"

"I could ask you the same, Jacques. We know the story of your escape from Du Chaila's prison last month, with the help of your brave petite Maman."

"*Oui!* Somehow, she convinced the priest to let her visit me. Once he left us alone—I think he went upstairs for his meal—she pulled a small saw out of her stocking. We cut through the wood stocks around my ankles, then slipped out into the forest."

"A miracle from the Almighty!" said Séguier.

"Indeed," said Jacques. "Certainly, the angel armies were at work conducting us to safety."

"So, why are you here now?" asked Salomon.

"After hearing of the Abbé's plan to execute the guide Jean Massip without a trial, we spent time in prayer." Jacques glanced at his traveling companions. "God led us to come here. We didn't know what or who we'd find. But we believe now is the time to take action."

Abraham bowed his head for a moment, grateful for this confirmation.

Séguier spoke up. "We believe the time is now as well. We're moving toward Pont-de-Montvert."

"What will you do there?" asked Jacques.

"God is our guide."

"Let's go!"

The men walked on together. At the edge of the next tiny hamlet, a covered stone *lavoir* appeared, a cool oasis in the sweltering heat. They had the place to themselves. No villagers lingered laundering clothing and sheets.

Inside, the travelers settled on the ground, leaning weary backs against the low stone wall surrounding the rectangular washbasin. Jacques pulled dried berries and roasted chestnuts from his knapsack and passed them around. When he also produced a few cured sausages and two rounds of sheep cheese, Rampon could barely contain his glee.

"The Lord does provide! If we only had some fresh bread." He cast a longing glance toward the closest home.

"Let us be grateful for the bounty before us," said Abraham. He thanked God for the provision.

Séguier didn't partake. He stood apart, his head tipped upward.

"Esprit, come eat!" said Mazel.

Rampon shook his head. "Leave him. He's listening to God. Anyway, he eats little. Sleeps little too. Mostly prays through the night."

"He's a tough one," said Salomon.

"Yes. He has one foot already in eternity. Any more of that sausage?"

Without a word, Salomon jumped to his feet and strode to the edge of the *lavoir*. He peered out, then pulled back.

"Several men approach. Quick! We need an explanation for why we're here."

The strangers entered, pulling up short at seeing the laundry occupied by men.

Abraham rose and took a step forward. He narrowed his eyes, then smiled. Fellow Huguenots! He'd met them recently at a midnight gathering. The newcomers explained God had led them to stop by this spot on their way to Pont-de-Montvert. Mazel shook his head. Again, the Lord had sent men to join the cause. It was no small matter to take on the powerful Abbé du Chaila, yet God continued to send support.

Excitement at the Lord's latest confirmation gave way to questions. Men spoke out, over one another.

"I know God led us here, but . . ."

"I've heard Du Chaila has dozens of King's soldiers guarding his home and throughout the village."

"We lack training."

"We lack numbers and arms."

"Can we really do this?"

"I'd consider it an honor to die fighting for my God."

Séguier held up a hand. "We face an enormous challenge. But we're not alone. We go with God."

"Above all, the battle is the Lord's," said Mazel. He paused as the Voice whispered the next step. "If my fellow prophets agree, we go out from here in pairs to recruit more men and seek arms and supplies."

Séguier nodded. "Exactly what the Almighty spoke to me. We'll meet in one day's time on Bougès mountain."

The men murmured their agreement, then set to organizing into pairs. In one day's time, they'd rendezvous on the mountain. From there, they'd follow God's orders and set out to deliver the prisoners at Pont-de-Montvert. Whatever the consequences.

CHAPTER 11
ARRESTS

23 July 1702
St. Hippolyte du Fort
Southern Cévennes

Curled up in the salon, Suzanne yawned and tried to concentrate on her book. She cherished Sundays, when family and friends gathered for the entire day. All had been calm since the raid and Gabriel-Isaac's escapade in the Château de Planque earlier in the week. Maybe everything would settle down now. Maybe they could live with some semblance of stability, despite the loss of their parents.

She was always sleepy after their big midday meal and from the ordeal of attending morning mass, but even more so today. She'd have much preferred staying home, in her cocoon, relatively safe. Everything about being in church grated on her nerves.

Her double religious life wore on her now more than ever. Pretending to follow beliefs that were not her own was nothing new. But since the cave raid, she'd grown uneasy attending Mass. Surely their Catholic neighbors noticed her parents' absence, even if no one said anything. At least Charles hadn't acted any differently. He'd turned around in his pew and beamed a smile in her direction. Thinking of it sent flutters through her chest and made idly reading impossible.

Across the room, Gabriel-Isaac stared out the tall front windows at the front vineyard's rows of burgeoning grapevines. His thrill at the successful outcome of his Château adventure four days ago had disappeared. More pensive than ever, he seemed far, far away. She stood and stretched, then joined him.

"Our vines—I mean the Château de Planque's—are thriving as always. Charles said his father expects a lesser grape yield in the Fesquet vineyards this year. It's interesting that they wish to merge their harvest with Lord Valmalle's."

"Uh, yes, I guess so." Gabriel-Isaac's eyes still fixed on something invisible, to her at least.

It pained her to see him so withdrawn again. Why couldn't he be content with life here?

"Gabriel-Isaac, what's going on? You were so happy with the victory of retrieving the psalter. Why are you now so . . . ?" Suzanne searched for the correct word. "Why are you so downcast? Like David in the Psalms?"

She followed his glance across to the wooden mirror, where they'd hidden the Tessier psalter along with the Lacombe family Bible. Gabriel-Isaac turned and looked her full in the face. Soon he'd have to lean his head down to meet her gaze. Thick brown hair hung over his forehead, framing his misery-filled hazel eyes.

The main substance of his grief was related to their parents, of course. But she sensed there was more. The hungry, desperate look that had long been growing in him was now ripe. Keeping him safe and helping the family carry on with their lives seemed more impossible by the minute.

"Hey, you two," Marguerite called from her seat next to Marc-André. Free from work at the mill on Sunday, she often came for a visit in the afternoon. "Have you heard the news? I almost forgot to tell you."

Suzanne and Gabriel-Isaac turned back to the family. Marguerite's commanding voice was not to be ignored by anyone in hearing distance. Aunt Anne and Grand-mère shared a look under raised eyebrows.

"Governor Bâville considers the raid on our people in the cave last week unsuccessful. Not enough arrests." Marguerite's nostrils flared. "Bâville's furious. So, he sent that foul Abbé du Chaila even more soldiers and lifted restrictions, as if that spineless vulture had any to begin with."

Grand-mère shot a pointed look. "Marguerite! Please refrain from critique and stick to the facts. How did you come by this information? I know you Marolles hear all manner of tales in the mill when people drop off their wheat or olives. Can you trust the source?"

"Yes, ma'am," Marguerite said, dipping her head slightly. Beneath her tough exterior, she was intensely loyal to those she loved, and that included the Lacombe family. She'd reign in her caustic tongue out of respect for Grand-mère. "This I heard directly, in the mill. The source is not from around here but has traveled frequently through St. Hippolyte. My parents trust him. So do I."

Marguerite's eyes flickered with the constantly simmering outrage she carried deep in her soul. Dragoons had slashed her mother's face while she was pregnant with Marguerite, hoping to force conversion. When that hadn't worked, the soldiers used pliers on Marguerite's father, crushing his fingers and leaving him incapable of doing his job unassisted. Marguerite ran the mill now, with her father's oversight. She didn't mind the hard work, but her bitterness resided just below the surface. Suzanne prayed it never got her into trouble with the King's authorities.

"And now," Marguerite continued, "with the help of these additional soldiers, the Abbé arrested eight young people fleeing for Geneva. Apparently, there's a guide called Jean Massip, plus four other young men. Also captured were three sisters dressed in men's clothing."

Suzanne dropped into a chair, her hand fisted against her mouth.

Gabriel-Isaac gestured wildly. "We met them in the woods on the way back from the gathering." He looked at Suzanne, then addressed Marguerite. "When were they captured?"

"Yesterday. Word traveled fast."

Suzanne shut her eyes, trying to block out the images of Jean Massip and the others, especially Madeleine and her sisters. The youngest was only twelve years old! Everything inside Suzanne blazed, then extinguished, like a fire doused with a bucket of frigid water.

How much more could they take of ongoing persecution and repression, no end ever in sight? Although it had been this way her entire life, she longed for the freedom to live without constant fear.

Beloved! Fear not.

Non! She jumped up and hurried from the room, slamming its door shut behind her. Love meant security and that those she loved would be well. And now that seemed less possible than ever.

Gabriel-Isaac watched his sister rush out of the salon. After their quick conversation with Jean Massip and the young people he led, they'd all continued their journeys. Suzanne had said nothing about them since. It was terrible that the Abbé du Chaila had their forest friends in custody, but Suzanne seemed unusually upset.

Now that he thought about it, something had come over her when talking to them in the woods. What was it? Not joy. Surprise, maybe. Relief. Her eyes had brightened while talking to the young people. Especially as they explained the reason for their flight—that they were *inspirés*.

Gabriel-Isaac chewed his lip. Suzanne had experienced the flooding of the Holy Spirit and all that came with it. That hadn't happened in a while, though. Maybe meeting others like herself had helped his sister.

Also, she'd acted a bit differently while talking to Jean. That he couldn't figure out, but she'd seemed . . . a bit more awake. He shook his head at the odd thought. A walk outside would do him some good, even if the temperatures were still soaring.

He stepped out into the front vineyard. Taking his time, he wandered down the first row of vines and up the next. The heat released scents of vines, grapes, leaves, and dirt. As the terroir filled his senses, tears rose. These odors and sights were linked inextricably with his father. Papa. Gone, probably forever.

Gabriel-Isaac brushed the moisture off his face and walked faster. He stopped and lifted large green leaves to check the clusters of purple-black grapes clinging to the vine. Although he didn't share his father's passion for the vineyards and all that went with them, he couldn't let Papa's efforts go to waste. Lord Valmalle's anger would ignite, and it would dishonor the years Pierre Lacombe had invested in these very plants and his unique wines.

Did that mean Gabriel-Isaac could never leave this place? He kicked a stone out of his way and darted in among a group of large trees on the edge of the field, needing a break from the beating sun. The river Vidourle trickled along just beyond, barely moving at all. Like him.

He found a boulder in the shade of a black alder and sat staring at the slow-moving water. How much more waiting could he take? From his earliest memories, the tales of the men in Mialet who prepared to fight their royal oppressors had ignited something in his soul.

For the hundredth time, he considered running away to join them. He was meant to be part of that battle. Getting to Mialet on his own didn't concern him. In fact, he welcomed the challenge of a secret journey. But his departure would surely distress Grand-mère and Suzanne.

How else could he get on with his call in life? A light breeze stirred the ridged leaves overhead. Light flecked through. A spider scurried over his boot and vanished under a pile of twigs and leaves. Maybe he should do the same. Dash away to Mialet in the night, hiding in the abundance of forest and caves along the way.

"Gabriel-Isaac! Woohoo! Where are you?" Suzanne's voice wafted through the heat from somewhere in the vineyard. He wished to be small, to follow the spider and disappear.

"There you are!" She pushed aside branches and stood at his side, hands on her hips, looking around at his sanctuary. "It's so pretty here! We need rain, though, the river is terribly low. But we'll manage with the well until the next storm."

When he didn't respond, she focused in on him. "Aunt Anne's gone home to care for her ailing father-in-law. Marguerite left at the same time. Anyway, Grand-mère needs help moving her old armoire to a new spot in her room."

"Why now?" Gabriel-Isaac asked, still staring at the nearly dry riverbed.

"I don't know. Maybe she's trying to keep us occupied as a way to cope."

Gabriel-Isaac met Suzanne's eyes, then watched as she pushed back her linen bonnet and fanned her face with her hand.

Of course he'd go help. He needed to be the man of the house. But for how long could he stay and fill that role?

CHAPTER 12
LETTING GO

24 July 1702
St. Hippolyte du Fort
Southern Cévennes

S uzanne dropped her head into her hands. *Non!* This couldn't be happening. Every fiber of her being screamed against it. Grand-mère wanted to give Gabriel-Isaac permission to join their uncles in Mialet! He was only thirteen. How could this be a good idea? Her grandmother's opinion shook Suzanne like a ferocious wind uprooting everything she tried to protect.

Grand-mère drew a chair close and sat. "Suzanne, I know you're upset."

She couldn't answer.

"I understand it frightens you to let Gabriel-Isaac go. Would you like to know my reasons?"

She lifted her head and gave a curt nod. There were no words, at least not any appropriate ones, to express how appalled she was at this turn of events.

"You know the story of my younger son, your uncle Gabriel, how the dragoons shot and wounded him. And that we let Josué Noguier take him to Mialet to recover. It was our only choice."

Suzanne stared straight ahead, hands clasped tightly in her lap, her knuckles white.

Grand-mère brushed back a strand of her silver hair. "Gabriel wanted to fight the dragoons from the minute he heard they were coming. Grand-père André and your father had to keep the family gun hidden away from him while we were on Le Cengle mountain."

A hint of a smile lit Grand-mère's face. "Gabriel liked to remind us that since we Huguenots call ourselves the Lord's army, we should use arms and fight."

Suzanne glanced at her grandmother. This part was new.

"Of course, we explained the guns brought to Le Cengle mountain were to be used in self-defense only and that we were taking a stand of *passive* resistance. That never sat well with your uncle. In the end, he ran away to join the faction who prepared to battle the dragoons here in town. Twice. The first time, he twisted his ankle, and your papa brought him back home. But within hours, he left again, injury and all. He joined Capitaine Noguier and took part in their first and only skirmish with the soldiers."

Suzanne sighed. What was Grand-mère's point?

"Your brother is much like his namesake. Gabriel-Isaac is also a born fighter, and I believe he'll eventually leave on his own, run away just like his uncle. I'd rather we release him and plan for his departure. Danger and risk are slightly reduced this way. Also, I trust your uncles Gabriel and Paul to keep good watch over him. Can you see?"

"But—" Suzanne swallowed hard. "How will he get there? And isn't everything here already hard enough, especially now, with Maman and Papa gone?"

Grand-mère reached out and covered Suzanne's folded hands with her own. "Yes, life is challenging. God never promised it would be easy. But he remains with us in every single situation. His presence provides what we need: love, strength, wisdom, security, and so much more."

Suzanne looked away. She wanted to gather the family around, like a mother hen protecting chicks under her wings. Yet she'd seen her brother's growing restlessness. Despite everything within Suzanne screaming *non*, maybe Grand-mère was right.

"Will we ever see Maman and Papa again?" The words caught in her throat.

Grand-mère gave her hand a gentle squeeze. "I don't know the answer to that. My inquiries as to their whereabouts have not yet yielded information. When I know something, I'll tell you without delay."

"Do you think they sent Papa to the Marseille galleys?" Suzanne didn't need to be told what that would mean. For the men chained to boats day and night in all forms of weather, death usually came within the first two years.

Grand-mère's shoulders sagged for a moment. "It's likely. We've learned that Governor Bâville sent a dozen of the men captured that night to the boats. At some point, the authorities will notify us if your father was among them."

"Why is it taking so long for us to receive the information?"

"I cannot answer that with certainty. My guess is that they consider delay to add to our suffering, that it's just one more way to pressure us to give up and truly convert."

There was no question of that happening. Especially now. How could anyone in the family let her parents' sacrifice mean nothing?

"And Maman?"

"I suspect she's imprisoned in one of Governor Bâville's towers or forts. I promise you, I will not give up searching until we know. Aunt Anne is working on it as well. We must pray for revelation soon and that your mother is somewhere close enough for us to bring her supplies."

"Would they let us see her?"

"It's hard to say. It depends on the individual guard at each location. Some can be bribed."

Hearing her grandmother speak all this out loud made certain possibilities more real: Papa's exile, essentially a death sentence, and Maman's imprisonment. It was hard to breathe.

"Suzanne, child, look up! We must keep our eyes on Jesus, not the wind and the waves of the surrounding storm."

Suzanne tried to picture Jesus. An image came of him walking on water through the tempest, strong and unafraid. His face was full of love, his eyes fixed on her.

"When we focus on Jesus, when we remember who is ultimately in charge of the world, it changes everything," said Grand-mère. "We find more than enough strength and courage to carry on."

Beloved! Fear not. The tender whisper curled around Suzanne like a wisp of sweet air, and the tightness in her chest lessened ever so slightly.

Grand-mère patted her hand. "So, I know a way to get Gabriel-Isaac to Mialet."

"You do?"

"I believe you are friends with Charles Fesquet, correct?"

"Uh, yes, I am. Why?" Suzanne ignored the random butterflies now zinging through her stomach.

"His father sent him to the Château to discuss combining grape harvests with Lord Valmalle, right?"

"Yes, Charles said the Fesquets' harvest this year looks to yield less fruit than usual."

"So, I wonder if he'd be open to a trip to the area below Mialet. As you know, my sister Florence and her husband, Philippe, have a vineyard in Tornac, which is only an hour's wagon ride from here."

"And then?"

"Charles could meet Uncle Philippe, check his vineyard and wines, and discuss the possibilities of a joint venture with him."

"But what will happen with Lord Valmalle and the Château de Planque vines? Especially now with Papa gone?"

"We don't know how Valmalle responded to the Fesquets' request, do we? He's not an easy man to work with. Your father knew this from experience."

"True, Papa found him very inconsistent and difficult. Who knows what he'll do without Papa here to oversee the vineyard workers and wine production? But I don't see how Gabriel-Isaac fits into all this."

"Since your papa was preparing him to work the vines, it makes sense. Even more so now. We'll say Gabriel-Isaac needs to finish his training at Uncle Philippe's vineyard. Charles could take him there. After he leaves, Philippe can take Gabriel-Isaac on to the uncles in Mialet. It's only an hour by horse up the mountain from Tornac."

Everything in Suzanne still struggled with the whole idea. Gabriel-Isaac leaving the relative safety of their home was monumental. That he'd be joining his fight-focused uncles made it worse. But maybe they wouldn't actually battle the royal soldiers. The men gathered in Mialet had prepared to take on the authorities for years with nothing concrete ever happening. She could only hope.

It was quite evident from Gabriel-Isaac's demeanor that something had to change. Even if physically fighting for their rights never occurred, being around others who were of like mind would be beneficial for Gabriel-Isaac.

"I'll go too," Suzanne announced, then clapped a hand over her mouth. The words had flown out unplanned. Yet, deep down, she knew it was the right thing. Her soul filled with peace for the first time in a long while.

"I thought you'd say that," said Grand-mère.

"You did?" Suzanne didn't think her surprise could be greater.

"Yes. It'll bring you comfort to accompany your brother and see him safely settled, first in Tornac, then all the way to Mialet. Knowing he's secure and what his surroundings are like will ease the pain of this change."

Dazed, Suzanne nodded. It was all happening so quickly. Yet the conviction remained that it was the correct choice, for Gabriel-Isaac and for herself. Otherwise, he'd surely run away to Mialet. This was the safer option.

"I'll come back. My place is here. What will you do for help with Marc-André and Marie while I'm gone? Who will attend births with you?"

"Don't you worry about that, *chérie*. God provides all I need and more. Aunt Anne will help with your siblings as she's able. As for births, we'll see. Your assistance is invaluable, but I delivered babies by myself for years." The spark in Grand-mère's eye spoke volumes of her passion for midwifery and of her capacity to manage on her own.

"Have you shared this with Gabriel-Isaac?" Suzanne asked.

"He knows that I have given him permission to go. But I wanted to speak with you first as to logistics."

"What about Charles Fesquet?"

The twinkle in Grand-mère's eye blossomed. "Would you like to go to his father's domaine and present our idea? Marguerite would surely be willing to accompany you."

Suzanne's face flamed. Both hands flew to her cheeks.

"I thought so," Grand-mère said, her laughter filling the room.

CHAPTER 13

HEADING OUT

24 July 1702
St. Hippolyte du Fort
Southern Cévennes

In the early morning hour, the cicadas chirped in the warming of a new day. Blended with birdsong, this was the musical background of Suzanne's best memories. In summers past, she'd accompanied Papa on wine deliveries. Fierce pain squeezed through her chest. She missed him terribly.

"You ready, Suzanne?"

Reminding herself to smile, she looked up at Charles Fesquet, seated in his wagon. The sun rising over Le Cengle mountain shone bright in her eyes, framing Charles in a golden glow. Beside him sat Gabriel-Isaac, ready for the past half hour.

She counted the blessing of Marguerite accompanying her to the Fesquets' Domaine la Grand'Terre and finding the right words quickly for asking if Lord Valmalle had been open to combining harvests. When Charles and his father shook their heads, concern etched across their faces, Marguerite had easily proposed the plan involving Suzanne's winemaking uncle in Tornac.

Suzanne hadn't cared for the high-pitched way her voice came out when she joined in the conversation. "Would you be willing to take a day trip to visit my uncle and see his domaine? The Delapierre vineyard will have more grapes than needed this year. The weather in their valley has been optimal for the vines. And Uncle Philippe is looking for a buyer or partner to experiment with blends for new vintages."

Charles's busy father had insisted his son make the trip and drive their two-horse wagon. The point of departure had come around so fast.

She nodded at Charles. "We're almost ready. Grand-mère is putting together a basket of food and Château de Planque wine for Uncle Philippe and Aunt Florence." Did her voice betray her excitement for the day ahead in his company?

"You sure she doesn't want to send some of our wine too? Domaine La Grand'Terre vintages are the best!" He grinned. Their back and forth banter, honed over the years, often centered around the rivalry of their father's wineries.

Hands on her hips, Suzanne said, "I think you'd get a debate on that from my papa!"

Her breath hitched at the mention of Papa. She looked away.

"Oh, Suzanne! I'm sorry, I didn't mean to . . ." He lowered his voice, leaning toward her. "I heard about your father and mother."

He knew! She had wondered if the news of her parents' arrests had reached the true Catholics in town such as the Fesquets. Apparently it had, which also meant he knew the Lacombes were secretly Protestant. Yet he seemed unfazed by the information.

Throughout their school years, she'd assumed Charles believed in the authenticity of her family's conversion to the King's church. He'd said nothing to the contrary. Along with Marguerite and others, they'd sat through the priests or nuns teaching the catechism and recited the prayers. Plus, the Lacombe and Marolle families attended Mass as regularly as the Fesquets.

"How long have you known?" she asked, her hand shielding her eyes against the sun's glare. Sweat beaded across her forehead under the narrow rim of her bonnet.

"I overheard one of our field workers talking about it."

"No, I mean, how long have you *known*? That my family's not . . . I mean, that we are . . ." Suzanne couldn't bring herself to say the labels out loud.

"Oh! Well, always actually." His earth-brown eyes carried compassion. "My papa said your family, both the Tessier and the Lacombe sides, would never renounce their Protestant faith. He admires your integrity."

"But my parents converted the year I was born!" Suzanne tried to make sense of it all. "My siblings and I went to priest-taught schools and attended Mass."

"Yes, but my father understood your parents did so to protect their family. The risks of being involved in the underground services must've been hard for them."

Suzanne couldn't believe it. "You know about those as well?"

Charles shrugged. "I think most of us are aware of who believes what, along with your, uh, nighttime activities."

"And you don't mind? Think we're heretics?"

"Some do. But not me or my family. Someone who did wouldn't consider engaging in a business venture with your relatives."

Suzanne stared up at Charles. She'd no idea the Fesquets and others knew the Lacombes remained Protestant. Even more shocking, people had more or less accepted it. She didn't know what to think of it all.

"Hey, Gabriel-Isaac! Could you please stop that?" Charles placed a hand on her brother's knee. Gabriel-Isaac jiggled one leg in a rapid staccato beat, practically bouncing himself and Charles off the wagon seat. "I didn't know you were so excited to join your uncle Philippe!"

Suzanne wished time would slow down, delaying her brother's departure. Still, it was the right thing. God made him to fight injustice in an active, concrete way. He'd join the cause with or without her support.

A question niggled at the back of her mind. What exactly was *she* made to do and be? Everything in her centered on helping others. But Grand-mère insisted she'd manage fine without Suzanne at home and at births. Soon, Gabriel-Isaac would live in a new place and wouldn't need her any longer.

She'd return home after this trip, and then what? Carry on with midwifery, yes. Continue to help raise her younger siblings and run their home, yes. Those were good things, but was that all there was for her? It was possible she was made for something different. But what service to the cause of freedom could there be for a girl who'd rather have her nose in a book?

Charles hopped down from the wagon to adjust a harness. He patted the chestnut gelding's nose. Traveling to Tornac with him was a welcome distraction from the changes ahead.

Grand-mère emerged from the house, carrying a basket laden with gifts for her brother and her sister-in-law. She placed it in the wagon bed, then embraced Suzanne. Gabriel-Isaac's goodbyes with Grand-mère had been earlier, in private.

Suzanne accepted Charles's extended hand as he helped her up to the passenger seat beside her brother, who remained firmly in the middle. Her brother had always looked up to Charles and was not about to trade places. She ducked her head at the thought of even asking, grateful her bonnet partially shielded her blushing cheeks.

Charles settled into the driver's seat. With a light tap of the reins, the horses set out across the bridge. Gabriel-Isaac leaned forward, as if to hurry the journey along. Suzanne elbowed her brother, and they both turned and waved goodbye to Grand-mère.

As they exited town, a welcome breeze stirred through the sun-dappled forest, fragrant with scents of green oak and pine. Beyond the clip-clop of horses' hooves and the rumble of wooden wagon wheels, Suzanne listened to the cicadas' rhythmic serenade. If only the journey to the Delapierre vineyard was much longer.

Charles focused on the road ahead. What was he thinking? How could she engage him in conversation with Gabriel-Isaac between them?

They emerged from the woods into bright sunshine and began the short but steep descent into a vineyard-filled valley. Suzanne loved how the road's sharp curve to the left at this spot provided a sweeping view of grapevines nestled between sloping mountains. The cerulean sky filled out the picturesque vista.

"This is my favorite part of the route!" said Charles, glancing over Gabriel-Isaac's head. "I don't travel through here much, but when I do, I always enjoy this view."

"Yes! Me too!" said Suzanne. It was as if he'd read her thoughts.

Soon they'd arrive at Uncle Philippe's vineyard. Charles wouldn't stay long, just enough time for lunch and to discuss the potential collaboration. She had only a little more time with him in this journey. What should she say?

Be honest with him. Suzanne shut her eyes. Not now! She'd not heard the Voice much recently. The last thing she needed now was to come under an inspiration and make a scene.

Beloved! Fear not. Be honest with him.

Her eyes flew open. Oh! Was it possible her heavenly Father understood such concerns as what to talk about? Did he care for her like that?

What did the Voice mean? Be honest with Charles about what? God couldn't possibly mean for her to tell Charles how she felt about him! Not in Gabriel-Isaac's hearing!

Her thoughts returned to the conversation with Charles before they left. She still reeled from his admission. Her family's practice of their forbidden faith wasn't such a well-kept secret after all.

She turned a bit in her seat. She'd just have to talk around Gabriel-Isaac. He scanned the horizon anyway, lost in his own world, probably imagining his adventures ahead.

"Charles, I'm surprised you and your family have always known where my family's true faith lies." Her cheeks flared hot again. Maybe having her brother sitting between them was helpful after all.

Charles threw her a glance, a small smile on his lips. "I didn't know that you didn't know!"

They both laughed a little, a pleasant release.

"So, you really don't mind that we're on opposite sides of the wars of religion?"

"We believe in your right to follow your conscience. Despite some differences, we share much as Catholics and Protestants."

Suzanne observed his profile. His words and the openness of his demeanor conveyed sincerity. It would take time to get used to the idea of him and others knowing the truth and not turning her family over to the authorities. Of course, some *had* betrayed them, as was surely the case for the recent cave raid. But his family had never shown hers anything but kindness and respect. That they'd done so while knowing the truth touched something deep in her soul.

She shut her eyes and tipped her head back to bask in the sunlight. There were Catholic neighbors who didn't see them as enemies! Maybe there was less to fear than she'd imagined. And the Voice's encouragement to be honest with Charles had led to this greater openness. Maybe God actually did see and love her. Like sunflowers whose bright faces turn toward the sunshine, she warmed to the idea.

"I'm truly sorry about your parents," said Charles. "They are loved and respected."

Gabriel-Isaac tensed, then dropped his head. Suzanne dared to put her arm around his shoulders, grateful he didn't shrug her off. His body relaxed slightly, and he leaned into her side. She treasured the moment. Soon, he'd literally be out of her reach.

Charles steered the horses around the last sloping curve and into the valley. "You know, Gabriel-Isaac, my papa truly appreciated working with your father. He always said that Pierre Lacombe's wines were remarkable. His vintages reflected our terroir so well."

Gabriel-Isaac looked up and nodded through shining eyes. "I helped him store wines in oak barrels in our cave, plus many more for Lord Valmalle in the Château de Planque."

"We'll continue to enjoy the fruits of his labors, as will others," said Suzanne.

They rode along in silence for a few moments, then entered a portion of the road lined with plane trees. Lush and full of summer foliage, they created a leafy tunnel. Beams of light broke through, creating enchanting patterns.

"This is also my favorite part," Suzanne and Charles said at the same moment. Their eyes connected and they laughed out loud.

The rest of the journey passed in peaceful camaraderie. Between stolen glances at Charles, Suzanne pondered all they'd talked about. She released a huge breath, blowing away a layer of anxiety.

When the Tornac town hall came into sight, Suzanne motioned to turn right. Traveling the long lane leading to the home of Uncle Philippe and Aunt Florence, they passed through rows of healthy vines laden with fruit. She watched Charles take in the abundance, his eyes wide.

Suzanne reveled in the winey scent of sun-warmed grapes. For a moment, all seemed well in the world. The loss of her parents and the pain of letting go of Gabriel-Isaac receded to the background, at least for now.

Sparks of a new hope arose within her. Grand-mère had suggested this trip and a collaboration between their families. She didn't seem to have a problem with Suzanne's friendship with Charles. If the Fesquets weren't against the Huguenots, was it possible for them to be together after all? She didn't know how it would all work. But daring to dream of a life with him filled her heart with joy. For now, that was enough.

CHAPTER 14

THE SUMMIT

24 July 1702
Bougès mountain
Northern Cévennes

Abraham watched as Huguenot men streamed to the summit, their designated meeting place. As the blazing sun dipped into the lower half of the sky above Bougès mountain, his spirit soared at the number of those arriving to engage in battle.

The results of yesterday's efforts by several pairs of prophets to recruit men and arms were impressive. When he and Salomon Couderc traveled to a nearby town, they'd again found Huguenots gathered to worship and pray. All had perceived a spiritual shift, a heightened sense that change was in the air.

Abraham lifted his head in gratitude for these multiple confirmations of the Almighty's guidance. He craned his neck as an eagle floated past, then returned to hover directly above him. The majestic bird stayed in place for several moments, its eyes focused on his face.

Finally, the eagle flapped its enormous wings and drifted away on a current of warm wind. Abraham shaded his eyes with his hand and watched until it was out of sight. Another sign! Throughout the Cévennes, eagles were a symbol of the prophetic, of God speaking to man. Here was one more affirmation.

Around forty more men had joined their band. He shouldn't be surprised. Above all, this was God's mission. That the three sisters arrested by the Abbé were from this region helped their cause. After Du

Chaila's blunt refusal to grant leniency, the girls' family and friends jumped at the chance to take action.

Séguier called the assembly to attention, then led a fervent prayer, joined by all. Although many were exhausted from two nights without sleep while traversing great swaths of the Cévennes, there was no time to waste. This was the hour! By God's direction, they would deliver the prisoners from the Abbé's dungeons.

Abraham glanced at Rampon, again grateful for his knowledge of Pont-de-Montvert, his hometown. That and Jacques Couderc's firsthand experience of the inside of Du Chaila's dungeons would serve the band well.

"Everyone with a weapon, place it here," Séguier ordered, pointing at the ground before him.

One by one, the men brought forth ancient muskets, half-working pistols, a couple of swords, a few axes, and a scythe, laying them before their leaders. Some held back, holding large sticks, their only defense. Abraham wiped the sweat from his brow with his forearm and looked at Salomon Couderc. Both men turned to Séguier. The older prophet gave one curt nod, his eyes lit with holy fire. It would have to do.

Abraham stepped up on a boulder and observed the pale faces of the newly gathered band of brothers. Murmurs and fear-filled mumblings grew, especially among the newest volunteers. The reality of the venture they were about to embark on became more evident by the minute, especially after the assessment of their paltry lot of arms. Discussions, questions, and challenges erupted.

He raised both hands until all fell silent. "Men, we're here by the call of God! It is *he* who has given us the orders to free the prisoners from the clutches of the devil's henchman the Abbé du Chaila."

Nicolas Jouany, a new recruit with past military experience, called out. "You're Abraham Mazel, correct?"

"Yes."

"The very one whose dream we've talked about for months."

"That's true," Mazel said, taken aback that his message from God was so widely known.

Jouany stepped forward. A roof tiler by trade and older than most of the men, he carried a certain authority. "In this dream, you were told to rid the garden of ravaging beasts, were you not?"

"Yes, that is so."

"Then, we shall do so!" shouted Jouany. Several others nodded in agreement.

Séguier spoke up. "Many of us have received the same guidance over the months. We're certain our mission comes from God. Now is the time!"

"Fear not!" said Salomon Couderc. "We follow God's orders, whatever the outcome." He paused, scanning the crowd. "It's highly likely the Governor's soldiers will kill or imprison many of us. But take heart! He who loses his life in this world gains eternity in the next. We know where we're going! We know who we'll be with!"

"Would any of you turn back from obedience to the Almighty?" said Séguier, his bushy gray eyebrows a straight line over flashing eyes.

"The God of heaven's army is our strength!" shouted Mazel, arms spread and lifted high.

"He *will* assure our success!" Séguier proclaimed. Again he led as the Huguenots bowed their heads and prayed, vowing to remain united in their mission.

As the sun sank behind the mountaintop, the temperature dropped, a welcome relief from the sweltering day. Séguier set about organizing the men into rows of four. From time to time, he paused, tilted his head, and looked up, clearly listening to God's instructions. Then he moved to the front and called out in a loud voice. "Only the most determined, fierce, and formidable belong at the head of their troop."

Along with himself, Séguier placed Jouany in the front ranks, then added another former soldier, Gédéon Laporte. The older prophet turned to Abraham. "I believe the Almighty has already told you where to stand."

Mazel stepped into place in the front row. He'd never get over God sending him into a battle against evil. *May your will be done on earth as it is in heaven.*

A few hours before midnight, the Huguenot warriors descended the mountain and began marching north through the Vallée Française. They followed the river as it wound toward their destination, the men singing Psalms along the way. Fervor reached a crescendo as they turned the last bend in the road and entered Pont-de-Montvert. At the top of their lungs, they sang a paraphrase of Psalm 51.

Have mercy upon us, O God,
According to Your lovingkindness;
According to the multitude of Your tender mercies,
Blot out my transgressions.[4]

Several of the men waved their muskets in the air, others brandished wooden torches, setting the night ablaze. Abraham's blood pounded through his veins. The time had come.

To avoid unwelcome surprises, Jouany sent men to act as sentinels at each of the four entry points to the village. Villagers cracked open wooden shutters, peered out the windows, then slammed them shut. Governor Bâville's soldiers were nowhere in sight. No matter. They were not the target.

Rampon gave directions to the home and prison of the Abbé du Chaila. Mazel, Jouany, Séguier, and Laporte led the way through the town. At their approach, a parish priest rushed onto the stone bridge in front of the Abbé's house and ran straight into Mazel.

Abraham stepped back. "Your name, sir!"

"Father Roux. Get out of my way!" He waved a trembling hand, his fear clear despite the show of indignation.

In one accord, Mazel and Jouany grabbed him by the arms and dragged him across the bridge and up to Du Chaila's door on the other side. Faced with more than fifty determined men, the few soldiers standing guard beat a swift retreat.

Father Roux struggled against his captors while shouting up toward the second floor. "Abbé! Du Chaila! Armed Huguenots are at your door and throughout the village."

After a moment, the Abbé stuck his head out the window. "What do you want?" he demanded, his face a snarl of disdain.

Time stood still for Abraham as he stared up at this face of evil, this man who tortured and killed men, women, and children. It chilled him to the core. Then, like a flood, a strength and courage far beyond what he normally possessed rose up and poured out.

"We ask for the prisoners' release, by the will of God!" he cried.

After a long silence, Du Chaila gave an abrupt nod. "Give me a minute."

---

[4] Psalm 51:1 (NKJV)

Was that a hint of a smile on the Abbé's face? This man was certainly not to be trusted.

Minutes passed with no further contact. Holy fire raging through his entire being, Abraham grabbed an axe from a fellow fighter and smashed it into the Abbé's front door. A few swift strokes, then he crossed the threshold and entered the house.

Séguier and a handful of men remained in the street to stand watch. Jouany, the Courderc cousins, and a few dozen others followed Mazel inside.

"Infiltrate the house!" he ordered. "Half come with me to the prisoners."

Jacques Couderc found the stairway leading down to the dungeons. Mazel and the men followed him below. He stopped in front of a closed door.

"This was my cell," he said, his voice tight. "Usually, soldiers guard this corridor. Appears they've all gone."

Couderc stepped aside, and Abraham positioned himself in front of the heavy wooden door. With several strikes of the axe, he broke off the lock, then stepped inside. Torchlight revealed four captive men, watching with wide eyes.

"Don't fear!" said Mazel. "We're here to liberate you!"

Jouany grabbed the axe and smashed their ankle chains, setting them free. The young men stood on shaky legs, relief spreading across their faces. Abraham ordered several men to lead the freed prisoners outside to safety.

Mazel, Jouany, and Couderc continued down the hall. The door to the next cell swung open without resistance. Vacant. A woman's linen cap, ripped and dirty, lay on the ground.

"The Abbé must've sent the sisters to the convent already," said Abraham. "We still need to find the guide."

A few steps farther, they turned a corner, then stopped at a formidable iron door.

"Anyone there?" Jouany shouted, pounding hard against the metal.

"Yes! Me! Jean Massip!" The guide's voice was barely audible.

"We're friends sent by God! Here to set you free!"

Jouany and Couderc took turns heaving the axe against the lock and the door, but the metal wouldn't yield.

"Jean!" Abraham shouted. "Where's the key to this door? Quick! Do you know?"

"No, but I've seen the Abbé put it in his pocket."

Mazel ordered a quick search of the hallway. No key. He directed Jouany and several others back upstairs. "Search everywhere. Get into the Abbé's salon. Search *him* if you have to."

Jouany nodded, then raced down the hallway with his men and disappeared around the corner.

"Hang on!" Abraham yelled into the cell door. "We'll get to you soon."

Somewhere in the house above, a shot rang out, followed by furious roars.

"Stay here with Jean," Mazel commanded Couderc, then he dashed upstairs faster than he'd have thought possible.

Arriving at the scene, reality hit him like a dousing of icy water. Crumpled on the ground, one of the Huguenots screamed in pain, shot in the face. Several men worked hard to staunch the fast-flowing wound.

But that was not all. Father Roux lay dead, blood pouring from three scythe wounds.

Mazel's vision blurred, then righted itself. The divine orders had been to free the prisoners, not kill priests. Yet, deep down, he'd known it might come to this. And now it had.

CHAPTER 15

REALITY

24 July 1702
Tornac
Southern Cévennes

Although they'd been *à table* for several hours, Suzanne wished it could go on forever. Charles chatted with her aunt and uncle, flashing his grin over at her from time to time. Maybe one day, enjoying the midday meal with him would be the norm. Her heart danced.

Uncle Philippe stood, looking at Charles. "Time to show you the vineyard."

Charles rose. "*Merci*, Madame Delapierre. The meal was delicious."

"You're most welcome, Charles." Aunt Florence cleared her throat and threw her husband a pointed look. "And Gabriel-Isaac will join you of course."

Suzanne frowned. Was it still necessary to cover her brother's actual mission? If Charles and his family were not against their faith, why not tell him the truth? Hadn't the Voice said to be honest? It would be a welcome relief to stop pretending.

Charles and Uncle Philippe crossed the threshold, followed by Gabriel-Isaac, who quickly shut the door against the blast of hot air from outside. The fair amount of coolness limestone walls held in gave welcome relief from the sometimes oppressive summer heat.

Suzanne stacked the empty plates, then carried them to the large kitchen. The Delapierres had some help, but mainly outside with the vines.

Aunt Florence washed the ceramic plates with a bar of olive oil soap she said she'd made in a vat in the wide fireplace. Suzanne rinsed each dish in a bucket of clean water, then set each to dry in a wooden rack on the wall. She enjoyed the time of washing up after a meal, a time to think as she brought cleanliness and order.

Suzanne placed another plate in the rack. "What chance do you think there is of Charles and his father collaborating with the Delapierres?"

With a wet hand, Aunt Florence batted away a mosquito. "Hard to say. We'll know more once he's seen the vines up close. Of course, Monsieur Fesquet will give the final approval based on Charles's report."

"Charles and I had an interesting conversation on the way here."

Aunt Florence passed her the porcelain serving platter. "Go on."

Suzanne plunged the vessel into the rinse water. "He told me his family knows we're Huguenots!" She looked at her aunt. "Even more surprising, they don't seem to care. Charles said his father actually admires our conviction and courage."

"That bodes well for a potential partnership. Here in Tornac, I know of at least a few villagers who feel the same way. They let us know in subtle ways, by a kind look or gesture at the open market or with offers to help when we most need it."

"This is all new to me. I don't remember hearing Maman, Papa, or Grand-mère mention such acceptance."

Aunt Florence set a freshly washed pewter cup on the edge of the stone sink. Her focus appeared to reach far into the past. "The suppression of our faith has forced divisions unwanted by many people, maybe even most." She turned her gaze to Suzanne. "Of course, some strongly believe we're heretics. They fully support the drastic measures of Governor Bâville and the Abbé du Chaila. But I'm certain those people are in the minority. Far more of our neighbors desire to live in peace with us, despite our differences."

Buoyant hope filled Suzanne's spirit. "Then why not let Charles know the *real* reason Gabriel-Isaac's here? I'm so tired of pretending, covering up who we are."

Aunt Florence grabbed Suzanne's arm. The clean cup she'd sat on the sink's edge clattered to the floor.

"Don't even *think* of such a thing!" Alarm filled Aunt Florence's face. "It's one thing for true Catholics to tolerate our beliefs. It's quite another for them to know of preparations to fight the King's troops."

"But Grand-mère encouraged me to invite Charles on this trip. She understands, um, our friendship." Suzanne took a step back as her aunt retrieved the dropped cup. Aunt Florence stood and looked her full in the face.

"You must understand how serious this is! There's no harm in a friendship or even a joint work venture with a Catholic. But if true Catholics learn of plans to resist the authorities and don't report it, they're liable to treason, which carries a death sentence. While the Fesquets are supportive of us in general, support for our men engaging in battle is an entirely different matter. That's what your brother is heading toward. Make no mistake."

Suzanne swallowed hard, still resisting the idea of Gabriel-Isaac in combat, even if that was the purpose of this trip. She hated hearing it said out loud. Maybe, in the end, it wouldn't actually come to that. The Huguenots had already endured for almost two decades without entering into overt war.

"If you shared more with Charles," Aunt Florence continued, "we'd never be sure who else would hear of it. News of Huguenot men in Mialet planning to fight against Governor Bâville and his soldiers would be used against us. This particular knowledge would be highly valued and earn a substantial sum for the bearer."

Suzanne's earlier joy drained away like dirty dishwater, the glimmer of freedom to be completely open with Charles extinguished. If she couldn't be honest with him, what chance did they have for a future together? Her stomach churned. Would her life ever stop being turned upside down? No matter how hard she tried to do the right thing—helping, serving, caring for others, even letting go of Gabriel-Isaac—it seemed never enough to secure her longed-for peace. A blanket of exhaustion covered her.

After the vineyard tour and much discussion with Uncle Philippe, Charles walked to his wagon. Suzanne couldn't bring herself to look at him as he gave her three parting *bisous*. She managed a quick glance from under her bonnet as he settled on the wagon seat. He tried to hold her gaze, his face filled with questions. She flicked her eyes away and stared at the ground.

Charles tapped the horses lightly with the reins, then waved as the wagon lurched forward and on its way. She watched until he disappeared from sight. What was left for her in a world where she continually found herself left behind?

———————

Gabriel-Isaac bounced up and down on the balls of his feet. Watching Charles Fesquet drive away made Gabriel-Isaac's new reality all the clearer. He was one step closer to joining his uncles.

"Can we leave now?" he asked Uncle Philippe.

"No, you and your sister will spend two days with us. We haven't visited in a long time, and you might as well learn a few more things about the vineyard. Never know when it will prove useful."

That was not at all what Gabriel-Isaac wanted to hear. It didn't help that Aunt Florence chuckled under her breath, muttering something about the impatience of youth. He sighed and gazed across the vines as twilight descended.

Earlier, when he toured with Uncle Philippe and Charles, he'd played along with the ruse. It actually wasn't that hard to do. He simply followed along while they inspected the grapes and discussed business possibilities. If they addressed him, he answered. He knew more about vineyards than he'd thought. Papa had taught him well.

With Charles on his way back to St. Hippolyte, he could drop all pretense. Day after tomorrow, Gabriel-Isaac would join Rolland's men. Men! Would they accept him as one? When Grand-mère sent Uncle Gabriel the request for the group in Mialet to accept his nephew, the answer had been immediate and positive.

The last time Uncle Gabriel had returned to St. Hippolyte for one of his brief visits, Gabriel-Isaac had only been ten. At thirteen, he'd grown considerably taller and had a few more muscles. He was ready to train and then take part in battle. Surely, they wouldn't hold him back from the action once he was there. And surely the time for battle was drawing closer. The men in Mialet must have heard of Abraham Mazel's dream. Wouldn't Rolland and his uncles in the east wish to join Mazel in the north when the time came?

He turned and followed Suzanne into the house. For the next few days, he'd attempt to engage with the family, especially his sister. A slight tinge of sadness mixed into his anticipation. He didn't know when he'd see Suzanne or any of his family again. But he had a call to fulfill, and nothing or no one would stop him. He'd just have to make the most of the time together before he stepped into the life for which God made him.

CHAPTER 16
IRON AND FIRE

24 July 1702
Pont-de-Montvert
Northern Cévennes

Abraham scanned the bloody scene. "What happened here?" Esprit Séguier and his troop stood on the opposite side of the room. Séguier glared at the scene before him as he shook his head.

"When we came up the stairs from the dungeons, we encountered Father Roux," said Jouany.

"Wily priest slipped away from us out front," growled Séguier. "As did a man claiming to be Du Chaila's secretary. I don't know which way he went."

Jouany's eyes blazed. "Father Roux pulled a pistol from his robe and fired, hitting our man in the face. He then proclaimed it was our just due as heretics."

Another Huguenot fighter raised the bloody scythe in his hand. "This is his just due. Father Roux assisted the Abbé in torturing and raping my sister before sending her to the convent. Relatives who live nearby told us."

Abraham held up his hand. "While this is not why we came here, we are waging war. Violence, bloodshed, and even death are bound to come when fighting for righteousness."

"King David understood that well," said Séguier.

Mazel turned to Jouany. "Any sign of the key to Massip's dungeon?"

"We didn't get far with our search. If it's with the Abbé, he's barricaded in his room upstairs. With servants, it appears."

"They have guns," said Séguier. "Someone up there fired shots at us down in the street. We could hear Du Chaila screaming orders."

"Find that key," said Mazel. "We must liberate Massip and the other prisoners."

Jouany ran upstairs with several men. Abraham and the other prophets huddled together, consulting God for their next step. Waves of the Holy Spirit tumbled through Mazel. He shut his eyes and bowed his head, listening.

His eyes flashed open. The direction could not have been clearer. "Brothers, the Almighty directs us to set fire at the foot of these stairs! The inhabitants of this house must be exiled!"

The men jumped into action. Gédéon Laporte, followed by several other men, ran outside to the woodpile and grabbed armfuls of pine logs. Back inside, they stacked them at the bottom of the staircase. Three men carried out the wounded Huguenot as Laporte set the wood on fire.

"Go up and warn those searching for the key," ordered Mazel. "They must evacuate. Now!"

Within a minute, they came back down, along with Jouany and the other fighters, holding out empty hands.

"Du Chaila must have the key on his person," Jouany reported. "We couldn't get into his room. Through the door, he begged us to have mercy and let him go."

Abraham offered up a quick, silent prayer for help.

He watched as fire filled the pine-framed house. Well dried from the summer sun, the wood burned hot and fast. Flames licked up the stairs and across walls. Abraham followed the last fighter out of the building.

"The prisoners. Have they been liberated?" asked Séguier.

"All but one. We couldn't penetrate the guide Massip's door."

"With this blaze, he won't last long."

"I left Jacques Couderc outside his cell," said Abraham.

"Jacques is over there." Séguier pointed across the crowd of fighters.

Abraham understood that the violence of the fire and quantity of smoke left Couderc no choice but to exit. But where was Massip?

"We must get the guide out now!" Couderc yelled.

Gédéon Laporte stepped up. "There are thick tree trunks lying out by the woodpile. We can use one to ram through the exterior wall to his cell."

"Do it now!" Séguier and Mazel shouted in unison.

Laporte gestured for several strong men to follow him, and they raced off as flames shot through the house's windows.

Séguier and a dozen men remained stationed at the front, guarding the door and street. The rest surrounded the building. Abraham ran to the footbridge arching over the river Tarn directly behind the house. From there, he'd have an overall view of what was happening.

At the highest point on the limestone bridge, he turned and watched the blaze devour Du Chaila's house. Scarlet and yellow-gold flames reflected and amplified off the river below until the entire world seemed alight. Abraham surveyed the surrounding area, then shook his head. Not one of the surrounding structures had caught fire. Only the Abbé's prison burned.

Gunshots pierced the smoky atmosphere. Abraham took a few steps forward, his eyes narrowed. Down the side of the house's outer wall, a rotund figure in priests' garb lowered himself using a rope made of bedsheets. The Abbé du Chaila! Huguenot fighters close by fired at him and at two of his servants, who followed him down the wall and into the garden below.

At that instant, the roof of the Abbé's home succumbed to the fire and collapsed. Light flared and illuminated the garden. From his post, Mazel watched one domestic take flight, then hit the ground, felled by a gunshot. The other servant flung himself through the flames, straight into the hands of Huguenots.

A figure huddled behind the garden hedges. Abraham blinked several times, straining to see through the smoke and shadows. Yes! The fearsome Abbé du Chaila, in a white nightshirt, hid in the bushes.

Pointing at the cowering priest, Mazel shouted to his men below the bridge. "Bring him to me."

Within seconds, they found and dragged Abbé du Chaila from his hiding place. The men surrounded the Abbé and rustled him up to the footbridge.

Arms crossed, Abraham watched them approach. Du Chaila presented quite the spectacle, his nightshirt soiled with dirt and blood, one leg twisted, obviously broken from his descent into the garden. Heat roiled through Mazel as the priest whimpered and pleaded with the Huguenots gripping his arms, hauling him along.

Even propped between two men, the Abbé could barely stand. The injured leg dragged behind the priest, reduced to a groveling mess before men he had long persecuted, men whose families he had tortured and abused. He mumbled and seemed to speak to his father.

In a flash, he gained strength and yelled out. "I'm not a failure! These heretics commit evil here today!"

Séguier and Jouany ran to the bridge and stood beside Mazel. The men holding the Abbé thrust the priest before the leaders. Du Chaila immediately sank to his knees, his injured leg at an awkward angle.

The Abbé lifted his chin. "You know, messieurs, that God prohibits murder."

Jacques Couderc couldn't hold back. "Then you are indeed unfortunate. How many have you condemned to die by hanging? How many have you stretched to the breaking point and then had beaten to death on the Wheel? How many have you exiled to galley ships and convents to perish in misery? We're here to judge you according to what *you* have done."

"Oh, messieurs! I will follow you anywhere! Or, if you let me go, I swear I will no longer persecute your people. I will retire, stay in my home, and no longer involve myself in religious affairs."

Abraham towered over the priest. "Abbé du Chaila, you waste your time negotiating with us. It would be better for you to pray and ask God's forgiveness for your heinous sins and for the cruelties you've exercised on children, women, and men. Beg *him* for mercy on your soul."

Séguier's fierce eyes scrutinized the priest. "God wants not this sinner's death but his redemption! Let us grant him life if he renounces his deeds and joins in the ministry of the merciful Eternal One."

Du Chaila's mouth dropped open, his face dark with fury. "Absolutely not!" He spat, his spittle landing at Abraham's feet.

"Then you must die. Your sin rests on you!" Without hesitation, Esprit Séguier lifted his saber high and brought it down hard upon the Abbé's head.

Jouany did the same, administering the second blow.

Emboldened, several men followed suit, one after another.

"Voilà! This is for my parents, whose death came at your hands."

"Voilà! This is for my wife, for the torture you administered unto her death."

"Voilà! This is for my father, whom you had burned alive."

"Voilà! And this is for mine, who died in the galleys by your order."

"Voilà! This is for my daughters, who you abused and then sent away."

"Voilà! This is for my sister, whose nails you pulled off one by one and whose hair you ripped out."

"Voilà! And this is for burning our fields and destroying our livelihood."

Each Huguenot fighter present voiced a long-endured grievance. Trauma flowed out of their bodies and on to the Abbé.

Finally, Séguier held up his hands, acknowledging the deed was finished.

Rampon's sword raised, ready to strike another blow. "It's said he's a sorcerer, a magician. How can we be certain the man is truly dead?"

Mazel raised his voice. "Enough! Brothers, it's clear. He's gone. The Abbé du Chaila now stands before the judgment seat of God." He paused a moment as men, chests still heaving, stepped back. Bloody swords, knives, and batons lowered slowly to their sides.

Abraham stepped to the edge of the bridge and gazed into the trickling river below. After a moment, he swiveled and scanned the crowd. Had Laporte freed Massip?

He sent a few men to find out, then looked at the remaining fighters. An unexpected memory rose. "Do you remember the prophecy of the young woman Françoise Brès?"

The fighters exchanged glances, some shrugging, others nodding.

"In the first month of this year," Abraham continued, "Du Chaila executed her on this bridge. I'd not remembered it until now." He shut his eyes as the scene arose in his mind. "With the rope around her neck, she prophesied that the Abbé himself would die within the year, here on the bridge, on this very spot."

Comprehension dawned on the men's faces. Some looked upward, while other heads bowed, as in prayer. Esprit Séguier lifted his arms high to heaven. Then, one by one, men fell to their knees. Fervent gratitude poured forth to their heavenly Father as the village's clock tower rang out the midnight hour.

Through the praise, Mazel listened for guidance. What would the Almighty have them do now? There was no going back. A major line had been crossed. The long awaited holy war had begun.

CHAPTER 17

UNCLES

26 July 1702
Mialet
Southeastern Cévennes

Suzanne sniffed the dry air as Uncle Philippe's wagon bounced toward Mialet. She found it hard to draw a deep breath; anxiety rose and squeezed it short. How she wished the time with Aunt Florence had been longer. On the wagon seat next to Uncle Philippe, Gabriel-Isaac strained forward, again hastening toward his destination. For him, their departure hadn't come soon enough.

Suzanne massaged her temples. She had come to terms with her brother's need to join their uncles and take some sort of action, understanding that Grand-mère's plan was best, that it was better to take him there rather than wait for him to run away. But logic didn't help her hurting heart. Why couldn't everyone just stay home together and live as peacefully as possible?

"You alright back there?" Uncle Philippe called over his shoulder. Not up to conversation, she'd chosen to ride in the wagon bed.

"I'm fine." Not really, but what was the point of saying so? With this trip, her brother moved toward danger. But Uncle Gabriel and Uncle Paul had been in Mialet for years, preparing for an eventual war. Maybe Gabriel-Isaac, too, would train for a battle that never came to fruition. The weight on her chest lifted a little. Maybe he'd even get bored and wish to return home. She could hope, couldn't she?

The cicadas sang and chirped at full volume as the wagon rounded a tight turn up the mountain.

"Almost there!" said Uncle Philippe.

Gabriel-Isaac sat up even taller, if that was possible. Had he grown in the few days since they left home?

"Can we see it yet?"

"Patience, nephew."

Suzanne rolled to her knees and pushed her bonnet back a bit. She'd never been to Mialet and had only met Uncle Gabriel a few times. Uncle Paul had left when she was very young; she barely remembered anything about him.

Shy at the thought of seeing them, she felt tiny butterflies jitter through her chest. They reminded her of the more exciting ones that came whenever she was around Charles Fesquet.

She shook her head to dispel that line of thinking. Her talk with Aunt Florence had made it quite clear that any relationship with Charles besides polite friendship was out of the question. Suzanne wished her heart would catch up to her understanding that their world was complicated.

Uncle Philippe tapped his horses firmly with the reins, calling out encouragement as they struggled up the steep path. Suzanne gripped one of the wagon's slatted sides and couldn't decide if she wanted to curl up in the wagon bed or keep her eyes wide open as they approached the tiny hamlet. She opted for the latter.

"Whoa," cried Uncle Philippe as they came to the first of several stone houses in Mialet. "This is the Laporte home."

Before the wagon came to a full stop, Gabriel-Isaac jumped down and started toward the house. Suzanne shielded her eyes from the sun and watched as the door flung open. Several men poured out, exchanging *bisous* and handshakes with Gabriel-Isaac.

Uncle Philippe came to the back of the wagon and offered his hand to help her down. She accepted, attempting to smile.

A tall, sturdy man approached them. "Bonjour! I'm Rolland Laporte. Welcome!"

So this was their leader. At first glance, apart from angular cheekbones, broad shoulders, and stocky legs, nothing about him was remarkable. Yet he exuded a sort of confidence she found intriguing.

Two other men gathered around.

"You must be Suzanne! You might not remember me. I'm your uncle Paul."

With his kind blue eyes, narrow face, and slender frame, Maman's youngest sibling resembled Aunt Anne. Suzanne warmed to him instantly.

"We've met a few times," said the older of the pair. "But in case you don't remember, I'm your uncle Gabriel." Although more muscled than Papa, this man was clearly his younger brother. The focus of his gaze and the way he raised his left eyebrow, reminded her of Papa. She pushed down a well of rising emotion. He even had Papa's wiry brown hair, though in a darker version than she'd inherited.

She returned their three *bisous*, grateful for the distraction of the others who came to greet them. Gabriel-Isaac stood wide-eyed and speechless in the presence of his heroes.

A middle-aged woman approached, introducing herself as Madame Laporte, Rolland's mother. "We women need to band together," she said, reaching her arm around Suzanne's shoulders. She led the way up the steps into the Laporte home.

Once inside, everyone gathered in the dining room. Suzanne offered to assist Madame Laporte with meal preparations. With a chuckle, Rolland's mother insisted she had plenty of help from her four daughters. She motioned for the new arrivals to take a seat at the long oak table with the rest of the men.

"Well, there's some big news to share, isn't there?" Madame Laporte said, looking at her son.

"*Oui*, Maman," Rolland said with a tight smile. "As usual, you get right to the point."

Madame Laporte sat down and folded her hands on the rough table.

"Incredible information came to us yesterday," Rolland said.

At the change in his tone to grave, Suzanne looked to her uncles, all three of them. Uncle Philippe tugged his chin, waiting. Uncle Gabriel and Uncle Paul stood off to the side, stone-faced, their arms crossed. Gabriel-Isaac shifted in his seat.

"A troop of Huguenot prophets, led by Abraham Mazel, Esprit Séguier, and several others, recently formed as they followed God's instructions to travel through the northern Cévennes." Rolland gazed out the window as if he could see to their location.

"You know of Mazel's dream," he continued after a moment. "Big black cows devouring and destroying a garden—all the people's sustenance."

Everyone nodded. Was there a Huguenot in the Cévennes who hadn't heard of this dream by now?

"Three days ago, Abraham Mazel received more instructions: go even farther north to Pont-de-Montvert and liberate the current prisoners from the Abbé du Chaila's dungeons."

Suzanne and Gabriel-Isaac exchanged hopeful looks. Their forest friends! Were they now free?

"After gathering more men and arms from the northern villages, this band of Huguenots did just that."

This was wonderful news! But why did Rolland still look so somber?

"There's more. They received divine instructions to set the house on fire. The Abbé du Chaila escaped, but our men caught him. He refused to repent." Rolland squared his broad shoulders, his dark brows knit tight. A thick silence filled the room, the only sound the slow ticking of the mantel clock. "So they killed him. The Abbé du Chaila is dead."

The evil Inspector of the Cévennes was dead? Killed by Huguenots? Suzanne couldn't contain her questions. "They killed a priest? Under God's orders?"

Rolland looked her in the eye. "Our men didn't go there with that intention. Violence escalated when one of the Abbé's men fired on them, killing one of our brothers."

She didn't know what to think. *God, is this what you intended?*

"Are you sure this information is reliable?" asked Uncle Philippe. "How did it come to you?"

"Through me," said a young man. "I was there."

Moments earlier, Suzanne had noticed a flicker of movement as someone entered the dining room. The person had stayed in the corner, in the shadows, until now. As he stepped forward, she gasped and jumped to her feet.

"You're the guide! Jean Massip!"

"Guilty as charged," he answered with a lopsided grin, moving closer with a limp she hadn't observed in the forest.

"How are you here?" Suzanne looked around the room, then through the open door into the entry area. "Where are the sisters and the others?"

Jean's smile faded. "I'm sorry to say that the Abbé sent the Celestin sisters to the convent before our rescuers arrived. The rest of our group are with relatives."

Suzanne sat on the wood bench, the spark of joy at possibly seeing Madeleine and her sisters extinguished. Madame Laporte put a hand on her arm, and Jean turned the cap in his hand around in circles.

"Tell the rest of the story, Jean," said Rolland. "They need to hear it."

Suzanne caught the concerned look Massip directed her way. Why did he care? They barely knew each other.

The guide drew a breath. "Mazel's men broke through the door to the other prisoners with an axe and set them free. But the Abbé had locked me in a separate cell."

He paused and rubbed his neck. Something about the gesture reminded Suzanne of her father. She batted that thought away.

"My door was unbreakable, made of iron, so they couldn't get me out. Some men went to find the key, but they didn't return for ages. Then it suddenly seemed everything around me was on fire. Smoke filled my cell." Jean's voice trailed away, as if even the memory robbed his ability to breathe.

One of the Laporte sisters offered him a chair. Wincing, he lowered himself into it slowly.

While the guide gathered himself, Rolland filled in some details. "My uncle, Gédéon Laporte, brought Jean here yesterday and recounted the full story of what happened. He left early this morning to rejoin Mazel, Séguier, and the others. They have unfinished business."

Suzanne leaned forward. They'd already set the prisoners free and killed the Abbé. What else was there to do?

"Besides bringing me here to recuperate," Jean said, "Gédéon Laporte was also the one who finally got me out. With the aid of a thick tree trunk, he and a few others broke through the outer stone wall of my cell."

Rolland filled in the rest. "Uncle Gédéon and his men found Jean passed out from the heavy smoke. Using an axe, they broke the irons around his ankles, then pulled him into the garden just as the home's roof collapsed."

Suzanne shuddered and struggled to breathe. Could there be anything more terrifying than being chained inside a building engulfed in flames?

Jean lifted his chin, his bright green eyes serious. "For that rescue, I'm eternally grateful."

"As are we all," said Madame Laporte. She stood and motioned for her daughters to accompany her to the kitchen, shaking her head at Suzanne when she rose to help. "You stay and hear the rest. It's important."

Suzanne turned her attention back to Jean and found him watching her. She looked away, her lips compressed.

Rolland stood. "Uncle Gédéon reported that the Abbé's valet, La Violette, lowered himself into the garden from an upper window, following the priest. He flung himself through the flames in surrender. Brought before my uncle and Esprit Séguier, the man begged for mercy. Séguier listened for God's instructions. While he waited, a village woman came forward declaring that La Violette had sometimes helped the prisoners, brought them extra food and such. Séguier then offered the valet his freedom if he renounced the evil course prescribed by Du Chaila. He agreed immediately and they released him. He disappeared into the night."

Rolland looked through the window to the terrace of the summer kitchen where his mother and sisters prepared food. Suzanne sensed he was processing the events he'd shared and more. He turned his attention back to the room and took a seat next to Jean. "The Huguenot fighters worshipped the rest of the night. In the morning, the inspiration came to go to a nearby village and rid the earth of another evil priest. About half the men declined, saying they'd return to their homes and take part in no further violence. Abraham and the rest left right away, singing hymns as they went. Then my uncle borrowed a horse and cart from a local Huguenot to bring Jean here to recover from his ordeal. Uncle Gédéon left early the following morning to return to the northern Cévennes and join in the purge."

Suzanne's forehead pinched. More fighting? The Huguenots planned to kill another priest? A purge? How far would it go? Could this be God's will?

Rolland looked directly at her, as if he read the questions in her mind. "I believe they are following God's leading in all this. These prophets hear and then obey the directions given. Wasn't this the case in the Old Testament events? With King David and his mighty men?"

She sat back but kept her focus on Rolland. Why did he keep addressing her? Did he know she was an *inspirée*? For once, she wished the Voice would come, so she could understand what all this meant.

Rolland stood, his dark eyes fierce. "I leave shortly for Nîmes, to recruit more men to our cause. I believe the Almighty has finally released us to go forth and fight. The Governor and his men have long abused their power. We must fight for our lives and our liberty."

The men began talking among themselves. At the far end of the table, Gabriel-Isaac sat listening to his uncles. She caught snatches of their conversation, their voices full of exhilaration.

War was finally upon them. Cold dread crept through her belly. How had it come to this?

Gabriel-Isaac leaned toward his uncles, eager to keep up. She shut her eyes against the boy he was and the man he wanted to be, wishing she could make all danger go away. *Oh Lord, please protect him. Please keep him out of it.*

Someone sat next to her. She lifted her lids a bit and threw a sideways glance. Jean Massip. Why was he there? Why did he keep watching her with those emerald eyes? She turned her head away, then leaped to her feet and went to help with the meal.

CHAPTER 18
DIVIDED

28 July 1702
Le Plan de Fontmort
Central Cévennes

Inside the dim cave, Abraham Mazel stood assessing the remnant of fighters. Despite the noon hour, most of the men curled up on the ground in exhausted slumber.

Through the last days' raids of nearby villages, they'd evaded the royal troops' relentless pursuit. Abraham thanked God for this hiding place nestled high on a mountain ridge, for the respite it provided from the blistering summer sun and from Governor Bâville's soldiers.

Over half the men who accompanied him after Pont-de-Montvert had returned home. How could they abandon the directions from God, given through Abraham himself and Esprit Séguier?

He understood the mission had changed. The band had marched to Pont-de-Montvert only intending to free prisoners, and the violence had escalated. Abraham ran a hand over his face, still shocked that the Spirit had led them to end Du Chaila's life. But if they hadn't, how would the Huguenots have found justice? The King gave them no right to defend themselves, no reason to expect fair trials.

When the Lord's direction came to burn churches and more homes of clergy, only places connected to the King's "one true faith" had gone up in flames. Just as in Pont-de-Montvert, adjacent homes remained untouched by fire. Surely the recurrence of such miracles was a sign, an affirmation of the justice they were carrying out. When God so guided,

Huguenot fighters had granted mercy as he did yesterday, sparing the life of a priest called Father Martin in the eastern Cévennes.

In all cases, were the fighters not simply being obedient? When the Almighty spoke, shouldn't one obey? Abraham didn't understand how a person of faith could act any other way.

"Mazel? May I ask you a question?" One of the younger fighters stood before him.

"What is it?"

The man shifted from foot to foot. "Please don't take offense, but I'm wondering if killing the entire family at the Château de la Devèze was necessary."

It had been three days since Esprit Séguier had received instructions for the band to go to yet another town high in the Cévennes mountains and target the Château de la Devèze, inhabited by a family of former Protestants detested by local Huguenots for their cruel complicity with Bâville's authorities. If only the family hadn't responded to the demand to surrender their arms by firing on Huguenot fighters.

Abraham looked up, as if seeing beyond the ceiling of the damp cave. The relative calm of their hiding place allowed sorrow to surface. A boulder of grief weighed heavy on his chest. He'd miss his friend and comrade Jacques Couderc, who'd been the first to fall in that skirmish, dying almost immediately. Their shared experiences had forged a bond between them.

Mazel had pondered the same question now asked by the sensitive fighter. He studied the young man. "What's your name?"

"Simon Bourguet, from St. Hippolyte du Fort."

"Well, Simon. As I'm sure you remember, we let the servants go. We even let them take whatever they wished from the Château first."

"Then we burned it with the family inside."

"Simon, is there any other way for us to stop the evil?"

"Isn't that God's affair to carry out?"

"Ah, I see. Yes, I believe it is. I also believe that he's using us to do so."

"That family *was* very cruel, especially toward our kind."

"And beyond that, we acted on God's clear direction through Esprit Séguier."

Both men looked across the crowded cave to the old prophet, pacing back and forth, his hands clasped behind his back, his lips moving in silent prayer.

"Our scouts report hundreds more soldiers now roam the land, looking for us," said Simon.

Abraham put his hand on the young man's shoulder. "We'll wait for the Holy Spirit's guidance. The Almighty won't stop guiding us now. This is indeed a holy war."

Simon nodded, then returned to his spot on the ground.

The men were not complaining, but pale faces and constant discussion about food made it clear they were hungry. After two days in the cave, supplies were low. Not wanting their own people to suffer, the fighters had only taken food from people who'd harmed them through the years.

Abraham sat on the ground, his back to the cave wall. *Show us the way, Lord.* His eyelids grew heavy. He dozed off, his head bobbing forward, until he jerked and woke with a start. His body trembled hard as Holy Spirit waves crashed through him. A message came to him, loud and clear now that his eyes and ears were wide open.

He stood, then wove his way through the sleeping Huguenots to Séguier.

"Esprit! The Lord has spoken!"

The older man didn't respond. Mazel blocked his path and took hold of both of Séguier's arms. "Listen! I've received guidance! God spoke!"

His intensity roused those around him. Several men gathered around the two prophets, interested to hear their next marching orders.

Séguier said nothing.

Abraham squeezed his arms. "Esprit! We're in danger of being discovered! The Lord has made it clear. We must leave, *now.*"

Séguier turned his gaze upward, his focus elsewhere.

Again Mazel shook the older man's arms and repeated the warning. As the information spread through the cave, the men quickly gathered their meager affairs.

Finally, Séguier lowered his eyes and looked at Mazel. "My son, no. We are to stay."

Abraham dropped his hands. Never had the prophets received conflicting instructions. What did that mean?

Maybe Séguier hadn't heard him. Maybe he remained in his own private world with the Lord. In a loud voice, Abraham repeated the warning.

Séguier looked deep into his eyes. "We're not to move."

Murmurs rippled through the fighters.

"Mazel says God's guidance is to leave," said one.

"And Séguier says we're to stay," said another.

"This has never happened before."

"They've always agreed. Until now."

Conviction and clarity filled Abraham. Not having the agreement of another prophet was new, but he didn't have time to figure that out now. Confident he'd received an urgent warning from God, he'd follow the instructions.

"Men, danger approaches. We must not allow them to trap us in this cave. Follow me!"

Without waiting to see Séguier's reaction, Mazel grabbed his gun and small knapsack and led the way out and into the surrounding brush. Running fast, darting around individual trees and rocks, they finally disappeared into a copse of trees dense enough to conceal them despite the midday sun.

Abraham took stock. Séguier was with them! They'd have to discuss their conflicting revelations later. At least the old man hadn't stayed behind.

On high alert, Mazel tuned in for further instructions from God. Shaking came, but not through him. The earth beneath their feet vibrated, and the surrounding trees trembled and quaked. As best he could tell, at least a dozen horses pounded through the forest.

Like hunted animals, the crouched Huguenot fighters lifted their heads and listened. Suddenly, Séguier stood, his chin held high. Without a word, he walked away from the group, disappearing into the forest.

Abraham opened his mouth to call him back but decided against it. They couldn't afford to draw attention. What was the old prophet doing?

Confusion broke out, and several men fled. Others followed Séguier into the woods. A remnant remained with Mazel.

He couldn't think what to do next. Until today, the prophets had always operated in effortless unity. What was happening?

A mounted officer burst through the forest. At least eighteen dragoons on horseback followed, weaving through the trees, curved sabers raised and ready.

On instinct, the men lifted their ancient muskets. Mazel pulled himself together and gave the order to fire. Not one Huguenot bullet met its target. The officer charged through the shots, waving his sword.

One soldier closed in on several Huguenots. "Over here, Capitaine Poul!" he shouted, pressing toward his prey.

The capitaine closed the distance to the Huguenots within seconds. Before Mazel could respond, Poul killed four, wounding another he then took prisoner.

"Go!" shouted Mazel, gesturing for the remaining fighters to disperse through the woods they knew so well, their best chance of eluding these skilled dragoons. He waited, ensuring they obeyed, then ran like the wind. Darting through the trees, he arrived at a cluster of huge boulders and slipped into a narrow crevice.

Moments later, the soldiers thundered past, their hoofbeats reverberating off the surrounding stones. Then the forest fell silent, except for a few birds chirping, timidly testing if all was well. Abraham drew a deep breath.

He sank to the ground in the tiny space. Listening for any returning soldiers, he prayed the hand of God would continue to cover his men, wherever they were. Being on foot had its advantages. Also, the Almighty's particular brand of protection seemed to render them invisible before.

In the quiet, questions without answers churned through his head. Why had Séguier walked away? Where did he go? What about the others who'd abandoned their divine task and fled? What now, God? Was this righteous war, long awaited and barely begun, over already?

CHAPTER 19

BELOVED! FEAR NOT

28 July 1702
Mialet
Southeastern Cévennes

Suzanne treasured her time with Madame Laporte, helping with the last of the dinner dishes. Full of wisdom, Rolland's mother seemed to possess no fear, like her son. While comfort enveloped Suzanne in this mother's presence, she missed her own mother terribly.

Madame Laporte washed the last drinking cups in the granite sink. "Your uncle Philippe informed me you'll both leave early tomorrow morning."

Suzanne placed a stack of clean pewter plates in the cupboard carved into the stone wall. "Yes, he needs to get back to his vines. But first, he'll take me home to St. Hippolyte."

"Which means you'll be saying goodbye to your brother."

"Yes. Our two days here have passed so quickly. I wish everything would slow down."

The older woman put her arm around Suzanne. "I'm sure you know that you have to let him go."

"I know I do. Still, I wish he'd stay home." Suzanne gulped air. "With Maman and Papa gone and war breaking out, it's all just too much." She covered her face with both hands.

Madame Laporte led Suzanne to a large ladder-back armchair by the kitchen fireplace. Nestled in a nook to the left of the wide chimney, it would be the best seat in the house when a fire roared during the winter months. Today the hearth remained pleasantly cool, as the women had cooked outside in the summer kitchen.

Madame pulled another wooden chair alongside Suzanne's and settled her stalwart self on the straw seat. She shut her eyes. Was she taking a little nap? Praying?

Suzanne stared at the cold hearth, inhaling the smoky odor that permeated the room. She wasn't ready to say goodbye to Gabriel-Isaac, but the time was upon them. He needed to join the fight wherever that led. The past few days only confirmed this; she'd never seen him so alive.

Hands clasped tight in her lap, she rubbed one thumb with the other. Would she ever feel secure? How could she, with her family torn apart? Would she ever see her mother or father again? Or Gabriel-Isaac?

Rolland had left yesterday to gather more men to fight, while her uncles continued training the ones here in basic combat skills. Gabriel-Isaac threw himself into every exercise with his entire being. She wished with *her* entire being that he'd never actually fight.

If she was honest with herself, that didn't appear likely. As soon as God gave the word, Rolland and her uncles expected to join the revolt. Suzanne shivered, as cold on the inside as the fireless hearth at her feet.

Madame Laporte placed her hand firmly on Suzanne's arm. She startled and stared at the older woman. Madame spoke with her eyes still shut. "My child, you are beloved. Your heavenly Father says, 'Fear not.'"

Suzanne stilled. Time seemed to stop. Those words again!

Madame opened her eyes and gazed into Suzanne's. "God's perfect love drives away all fear."

Suzanne dropped her head, unable to express her myriad of emotions. She wanted to tell Madame Laporte that she wasn't afraid, just sad. That all she desired was for her family to be together and to live in safety.

Beloved! Fear not. Why did these words about love and fear come to her together so often?

"I know you're grieving the loss of your parents and now Gabriel-Isaac," said Madame Laporte. "You wish your family would remain intact, then all would be well. Of course you are sad."

Suzanne studied Madame Laporte. The woman seemed to know exactly what she was thinking.

"But fear can lurk beneath sadness and even make an idol of the desire for all to be well. Our Good Shepherd promises to be with us in the darkest valley. He sets a table for us in the presence of our enemies."

"Why do we even need to have enemies?"

"We certainly can't understand all God's ways, but they are higher and better than ours. All he does streams from his great love for us."

Suzanne rose and began pacing. "I just . . ." She stopped in front of Madame's seat. "I really don't understand all this."

A gentle smile played on Madame's lips. "That's alright. Walk with him, link your arm through his. He's always with you. Draw close and listen. Understanding will grow." She sat back and shut her eyes once again.

How odd that Madame's words echoed those of the Voice. Maybe it was time Suzanne gave more thought to what it meant to be Beloved and how that could affect her feelings about the constantly changing circumstances. Could it be that her desire for some kind of normalcy stemmed from fear? What exactly did she fear? She had a lot to think about.

Madame's breathing slowed into a gentle whiffle. Suzanne tiptoed across the red clay tiles and out of the kitchen. She shut the door carefully behind her, turned, and bumped straight into Jean Massip.

He took a step back, holding up both hands. His crooked grin stretched wide. "Suzanne! I was just looking for you."

She peered at him, not fully focused. Embarrassment at colliding with him mixed with the thoughts and emotions still circling through her head and heart. Was fear the root beneath her longing for nothing more to change? Of course, there was nothing wrong with desiring a quiet life, with those she loved kept safe and nearby. But that life continually moved beyond her grasp. Maybe it didn't work to wait for people and circumstances in her life to line up as she wished. Could more fully receiving God's love remove her fear? Could she have peace and well-being *despite* the difficulties?

"Would you care to go for a walk?" Jean asked. "The sun's just gone down, but it'll stay light for a little while."

She blinked while he waited for an answer. "Alright."

His face lit up, his already brilliant eyes shining brighter. "Let's go!" He crossed the tiny entryway and pulled open the heavy wooden door. "After you, mademoiselle."

The pair descended the stone stairs and walked through narrow passageways between homes in the tiny hamlet. They stepped out onto the main road, and fresh air swirled around them. The sun, recently sunk behind a mountain ridge, tinged the sky with soft pastels—pink, coral, and gold. One and then two stars appeared in a bluing corner of the sky. A waft of thyme mixed with wild mint crushed underfoot filled the air with the perfume of summer.

Out of the corner of her eye, she observed Jean. He still walked with a slight limp, which she'd learned came from torture on the Abbé Du Chaila's infamous rack. Further injury had come from the leg irons and their rapid removal, plus a great deal of smoke inhalation, leaving Jean in need of time to heal. It seemed a good sign that he felt up for a stroll.

For the past two days, they'd spoken little, despite their eyes meeting several times across a crowded room. At first, she found him irritating and a bit confusing. His enthusiasm and optimism grated for reasons she didn't understand. Despite his near-death ordeal in Pont-de-Montvert, he didn't seem depressed or angry. She couldn't quite figure him out. He was unlike anyone she'd ever met.

She decided it might help to get to know him some. "So, Jean, how did you become a guide?"

He laughed, breaking off and holding a stalk of something like wheat, then a spiky, sepia-tinted pod on a long stem. "Ever since I was little, I loved adventures. My parents would find me up on the ridge behind our home, exploring on my own. They called me their little mountain goat. Soon enough, I learned how to pay attention to my surroundings and find my way back."

"Where are your parents now?"

"In heaven."

Suzanne stopped and faced him. "They're both gone?"

"Yes. They refused to convert and paid the price about five years ago. I was fifteen."

"I'm so sorry. You must miss them." Her own sorrow surfaced. "I mean, how do you go on?"

"I still miss them, but the pain lessens over the years. I treasure wonderful memories of our life together; they bring me comfort." He looked her full in the face. "Suzanne, I know of your parents' arrests in the recent raid. Your grief is new and sharp."

She dipped her head, not wanting him to see her brimming eyes. There was nothing she could do about the red splotches that were surely breaking out on her neck, a telltale sign of her upset. She hadn't expected the conversation to go in this direction.

Jean continued. "Also, I've learned to keep busy. Guiding our fleeing brothers and sisters to safety has helped me a lot. I believe I'm doing something significant for our cause."

"You are!" She hadn't even known the strength of her opinion until the words formed. "You are truly helping people. The Celestin sisters and the others you led when we first met, they needed your knowledge and skills. I certainly would. I get lost in the mountains near my own home."

His crooked smile appeared, and a shock of auburn hair fell across his eyes. "I also love the adventure of it, despite the danger."

"That is not something I understand. All I want is for everyone to avoid taking risks and stay safe, unlike my brother, who has longed to be here in Mialet with Rolland and our uncles. And my best friend, Marguerite, is always ready to fight for what she believes is right." Suzanne chuckled. "Grand-mère calls her fiery but my Aunt Anne says she's just feisty." Suzanne's smile faded. "But with my parents' involvement in the underground church, I've always had a sense that something bad could happen. And now it has." She drew a long breath, and as she exhaled, something pent up in her released. Until now, she'd never verbalized those thoughts so clearly.

"God made each of us differently, didn't he? It seems to me, Suzanne, that you care deeply about others."

"I do! But it only brings me pain." She tilted her head to the side and studied him. He stood only a few centimeters taller; they met almost eye to eye. "How do you know that about me?"

Rubbing his neck, Jean looked away, then back again. "I, um, I've seen how you look at your brother. It seems to me you're struggling to let him go but are doing so out of love. You want the best for him."

He'd read her like a book. She couldn't decide if she liked that or not. Her mouth twisted a bit as she tried to think of something to say.

He looked down the road. "You know, it's getting darker by the minute. We should head back to the house before it's impossible to see. It'll be awhile before the moon's light grows strong."

They turned and started down the path to the hamlet. Along the way, he gathered a few more dried pods and stalks. In front of Rolland's home, he handed her the unlikely bouquet, his face full of questions. By drawing together what appeared to be dried weeds, he'd created something lovely. She accepted the offering, murmured her thanks, and avoided his eyes as they entered the house. Relieved no one was around to see their return, Suzanne said goodnight and went on to her room.

That man continually surprised her, and she wasn't sure what she thought about that or about him. Well, it didn't matter. Early tomorrow morning, she'd depart and probably never see him again. She reached for the candle, blew it out, then settled into a dreamless sleep.

CHAPTER 20
EXECUTION

12 August 1702
Pont-de-Montvert
Northern Cévennes

Abraham adjusted his position, taking care not to jostle the branches of his hiding place. The last thing he needed was to draw attention as he crouched between a stone wall at the end of the Pont-de-Montvert bridge and a massive broom bush, brimming with small yellow flowers. The brilliant blooms presented a jarring contrast to the scene before him.

He wiped the moisture off his forehead with his sleeve. Two weeks earlier, Governor Bâville's soldiers had arrested Esprit Séguier. After searching for hours, they'd finally found the old prophet, who surrendered without a fight. They'd led him away with his hands bound behind his back and roped to an officer's horse.

For the past few days, Abraham had stayed with sympathetic Huguenots who allowed him to hide in their barn. They brought him food and water, as well as news of Séguier's capture. The info had passed from one Huguenot to another throughout the region, all telling of his courage. Séguier had accepted his fate. Maybe that's what the old prophet heard from God in the cave before the Huguenot fighters had dispersed, before Esprit had headed out on his own.

During his trial, Séguier confirmed his participation in killing the Abbé du Chaila, declaring himself proud to have struck the first blow. Holding nothing back, he testified to burning churches and taking part in the execution of the Château de la Devèze family.

Shock waves reverberated through the Cévennes at his sentence. Condemned to die, Esprit Séguier would have his right hand cut off, then be burnt alive at the Pont-de-Montvert. Authorities deemed it appropriate that his execution took place on the bridge where the rebels killed the Abbé du Chaila.

The tribunal also handed death sentences to two other Huguenot prisoners taken in the forest raid. One was to be broken alive on the Wheel and then burned in front of the Château de la Devèze, the other to be hung facing the razed church. Governor Bâville's order of those sentences served as a warning meant to stamp out any further revolt and to put an end to the uprising.

Sweat dripped down Mazel's neck, dampening the collar of his white linen shirt. He'd also taken part in all those incidents. Until the day of Esprit's capture, the prophets had received inspirations in complete unity. Whatever Esprit believed the Almighty said to him in the cave had contradicted what Abraham heard. Had one of them heard wrong? Or were both inspirations part of God's plan?

Abraham felt he owed it to Esprit to bear witness to his execution, despite the risk. None of the remaining fighters, now called Camisards after the local dialect's word for their white shirts, had elected to join him. It didn't matter. Concealment was easier on his own. And if discovered, only he would pay the price.

The atmosphere shifted, the heavy summer air growing still. Cicadas stopped their constant chirping, and even the trees seemed to hold their breath as soldiers led Séguier to the front of the crowd. Abraham parted the long flower-filled branches of his hiding place and strained to watch. Séguier walked with his gray head held high. His rumored courage and serenity were evident as his captors led him onto a small platform.

Several interrogators stood before him. "Your name?"

"Pierre Séguier."

"Why are you called Esprit?"

"Because the Spirit of the Lord is with me."

"Your domicile?"

"In the desert and soon in heaven."

"Do you request pardon from the King?"

"I have no other King than the Lord."

"Do you not repent for your crimes?"

"My soul is like a garden full of shelter and fountains."

Folks in the crowd mumbled and shook their heads. Abraham couldn't tell whether they admired or were astonished at Séguier's unusual answers. For Abraham, almost nothing Esprit said or did was a surprise anymore. Now Esprit stood before a pyre, while Abraham hid and watched.

The executioners grabbed their tools and prepared to carry out the sentence.

"Make him suffer!" cried one.

"He deserves a slow death for all he's done!"

"Burning churches and killing priests does not go unpunished!"

"Extinguish the old man!"

Séguier trembled. His voice rang out clear and strong. "I did only what the Holy Spirit told me to do!"

Soldiers shoved him toward a rough-hewn stake surrounded by dry firewood. The executioner seized Séguier's arm, raised his axe, and chopped Séguier's right hand. Gasping screams erupted from the crowd as the hand remained attached by a piece of skin. Séguier tore it off with his teeth and tossed his head to throw the severed hand into the pyre.

Eyes steady, Séguier presented his left hand to be cut off. "Have your fill. Be satisfied."

The executioner stepped back, stunned. After a moment of confusion and conferring with the members of the tribunal, he proclaimed the sentence did not include that instruction. He refused to comply with Séguier's request.

Abraham's scalp prickled as the old man, bleeding profusely, sang in a loud voice a phrase from Psalm 69.

> *But as for me, afflicted and in pain, may your salvation, God, protect me. I will praise God's name in song and glorify him with thanksgiving.*[5]

Suddenly, Séguier stopped his worship. A profound hush fell over the onlookers. Gazing high above and far beyond the crowd, he prophesied. "This place! Before long, water will cover this place where you execute me. Afterward, the river Tarn will change its flow to a new bed."

---

[5] Psalm 69:29–30 (NIV)

Abraham looked at the river Tarn, flowing below. Even if the waters rose and overflowed the banks, it seemed impossible for them to flow where Esprit stood. The river would need to rise many meters. And then it would flow in a new bed? Was the prophecy accurate? Or was his friend spouting vengeance?

With two chains, soldiers attached Séguier to the wooden stake. His manifestations grew into violent agitations. He cried out, "My brothers, desolate Carmel will grow green, and the roses of Lebanon will flower again."

The old prophet passed out. Frowning, the executioner checked for a pulse. He shook his head and pronounced Séguier dead. A rush of gratitude welled in Mazel. *Thank you, God, for your mercy.* His friend's soul departed before the fire consumed his body. Esprit was now in his eternal home and at rest.

Abraham slipped away along the stone wall, then followed the brush-lined river and disappeared into the forest. Moved by his friend's courageous death, he needed time to pray and to listen. He had much to ponder. With Esprit gone and the fighters dispersed, he needed new guidance. This Camisard war was indeed a holy one. God had ordained it so. But how was it to go forward?

CHAPTER 21

REPERCUSSIONS

20 August 1702
Montpellier
South of France

Governor Bâville watched a scorpion scuttle across the oak parquet floor of his study. Despite deterring sprigs of dried lavender the housekeeper placed in windowsills throughout his home, one of the primitive-looking creatures had made it in, maybe through the chimney.

Bâville glared at the cold hearth. The woman should've seen to that. He'd make sure no such slipup occurred again. He strode across the room and crushed the tiny black pest with his raised-heel shoe, grinding the remains into the floor's herringbone pattern. If only he could achieve the same with the heretical Huguenots.

He regretted last week's letter to the King's court, claiming that the public executions at Pont-de-Montvert would end the nascent uprising. He'd been proven wrong by the insurgents' continued attacks.

Slamming his fist against a windowsill cracked the pane of glass above. A sharp edge cut open his knuckles. He swiped away the blood and squeezed his other hand tight around the abrasion, defying its flow.

A timid knock sounded on the door of his study. He stomped across the room and flung it open. The housekeeper stood on the other side.

"Excuse me, sir. I heard a noise like something breaking." She did not meet his eyes, and her hand-wringing raised Bâville's ire further.

"How kind of you to check unbidden on my welfare," he snarled. "Get out of my sight."

The woman scurried away, reminding him of a scared mouse. He slammed the door and the paintings tilted on his study wall.

He paced the room. How dare the rebels call raiding churches, destroying statues of the saints, and killing priests and leaders a God-given mission! With their vendettas, they were bloodthirsty fiends, burning ecclesiastical buildings with impunity. Surely, that none of the surrounding homes ever caught fire was a sign against the rebellion.

Bâville lowered his tall frame into a polished wood armchair as fury gave way to a mantel of despair. He rubbed the cleft in his chin, then tightened the ribbon around his ponytail of graying hair. No matter how hard he tried, the Huguenots never gave up. Despite punishments, restrictions, torture, and public executions, they carried on, growing ever more bold in their actions. They seemed to thrive spiritually and physically under pressure.

Exhaustion mixed with his frustration. He'd grown to hate this thankless task. After all, he was in his fifties and had served as Governor of the Languedoc for seventeen years, doing his utmost toward stamping out the Protestant pestilence but with no permanent results. With his right-hand man defeated and dead, what was he to do? Who would serve alongside him and replace the Abbé du Chaila to stop this rebellion? Who would help rid France of the Protestants forever?

The Governor stood and crossed the polished floor to his *escritoire*, his steps resounding throughout the room. He wrapped his bleeding knuckles tight in a fresh handkerchief, then snatched the chair from the writing desk. Flicking the long tails of his blue coat out of the way, he sat down and pulled a fresh sheet of paper from a shelf to the desk, then grabbed a quill and sharpened it with fierce strokes from a small flint knife. He dipped the quill in the waiting well of black ink and tapped off the excess.

The first missive he had to compose was a request to the King for a military marshal and fresh, trained soldiers. He gathered his thoughts, considering how to put them into persuasive words while suppressing any evidence of his own failure.

Ideas came, and though his bound hand slowed his writing, he scribbled furiously, emphasizing the stain the Camisards wrought on the honor of the *Roi Soleil*, as Louis XIV styled himself. The Sun King. A bit much if you asked Bâville, but why not appeal to the man's outsized sense of importance?

A pertinent example came to mind, and he applied his pen to it.

> *Recently, Huguenot forces murdered a baron of particular use to me. A former Protestant, the baron was known for his ruthless persecution of the heretics. The "Camisards," as they now style themselves had the audacity to order the baron to say his prayers and prepare to die. The rebels grow in number and a certain recklessness.*

"Like cockroaches," the Governor said aloud, dipping the pen again. Bâville underlined that with the death of the Abbé du Chaila and the Camisard uprising, he needed a skilled commander to carry out his orders. A tight smile pulled the corners of his mouth as he signed his name.

That letter set aside to dry, he pulled out another sheet of paper. The words for this second document flowed freely, full of fire and a particular clarity. Pride surged through his chest as he exercised his power as the "King of the Cévennes."

> *By order of the Governor of the Languedoc, Nicolas de Lamoignan de Bâville,*
> *20 August 1702*
> *The Governor proclaims the following:*
> *Any person, be it man, woman, or child, with the least suspicion of practicing the Pretend Reformed Religion known as the Huguenots, shall be arrested. Proof not required. Due to the treasonous uprising of the same people, the so-called Camisard Revolt, they shall be held without trial. Soldiers may execute any resisting arrest. Anyone aiding the heretics in any manner whatsoever will be subject to the same sentence.*
> *Effective immediately.*

Bâville tossed his quill on the desk and reread his work. Yes, that would do. Even while waiting for a military marshal and additional soldiers, this edict gave his men already on the ground broader authority to wipe out the Protestants, whether Camisard fighters or inhabitants of any Huguenot home that offered aid. Now all his troops would carry the same power he'd extended to the Abbé du Chaila.

Chin held high, he pushed back his chair, walked to the bell sitting on fireplace mantel, and rang for his manservant. The letter and the edict would go out immediately. Soon, the prisons would be full, the scaffolds busier than ever. Bâville returned to the scorpion and pulverized it further, delighting in the sound and sight. He'd exterminate the Huguenots once and for all. He'd do whatever it took and would win. After all, wasn't the God of his King on their side? Success was just around the corner.

CHAPTER 22
HOME

31 August 1702
St Hippolyte du Fort
Southern Cévennes

In the early hour before dawn, Suzanne walked through town, reviewing the events of the night. Despite a few complications along the way, a healthy baby boy was born. The joy of new life welled in her. A miracle every time.

As she stepped up the road to the Planque bridge, her elation evaporated. Just ahead stood the guarded gate. Her home lay beyond it, on the far side of the river.

It wouldn't do to show fear when harassed and questioned by the guards. If only Grand-mère hadn't needed to stay behind and attend to the new mother and baby.

"Your Father in heaven will see you safely home," Grand-mère had proclaimed. "He's seen me through on my own many a time."

Suzanne had held her retort about the difference in their ages and the effect that had on the soldiers. Now she lifted her chin and walked toward the guards, recalling her parents' surprise that the rampart walls encircling the town had left the Château de Planque and the Lacombe manor on the outside. Overall, this was to her family's advantage, but it meant passing through the checkpoint to attend births or any other time they wished to go into town. Her heart sped up as she approached the exit point. The most recently arrived troops were rougher than ever.

A soldier stepped in front of her, his partner close beside him. Both loomed large, each with a hand on the saber strapped to his side.

"What have we here?" asked one.

"Out early, mademoiselle. Busy night?"

Both soldiers leaned close enough for Suzanne to smell their putrid alcohol-laden breath. She forced her voice steady and explained her reason for being out, then opened her basket of midwifery supplies to prove it. The men blanched at the soiled cloths, then waved her through. She stepped onto the bridge, biting the corner of her lip to hold back a nervous giggle, then breathing a prayer of thanks for safe passage and for Grand-mère's proven method of getting by royal soldiers.

The river Vidourle trickled along at its end-of-summer low. The front vineyard stretching from the Château down to the riverbank exuded scents of grapes and earth. Inhaling the fragrance, she quickened her pace at the sight of her home ahead. She was ready to catch up on sleep.

First, though, she'd check if Marc-André and Marie were still tucked into their beds. Suzanne loved participating in births but not that it sometimes meant leaving her younger siblings alone. There hadn't been time to see if Aunt Anne could stay with them, and the housekeeper wasn't available. Marc-André, almost thirteen, had assured he could take care of himself and their little sister.

Suzanne shivered at the usual temperature drop just before sunrise. Coral hues streaked the sky as the sun crept to the top of Le Cengle mountain on her left, filling the atmosphere with a rosy glow. Wasn't that just like God? Bringing beauty out of the darkness.

Since returning home from taking Gabriel-Isaac to Mialet, her soul seemed more wide open, more able to search for the good amid challenges. That made little sense given circumstances. Gabriel-Isaac had joined Rolland and their uncles just in time for what appeared to be an ongoing uprising. She'd left Mialet bereft of her brother and with all sorts of terrible possibilities looming large.

Then the report came of Esprit Séguier's courageous death. His prophecies and faithfulness to the end had shaken something deep within her. Instead of shutting her down, the description of his final moments acted like a light, illuminating and activating her faith. A shift she couldn't explain had occurred in her way of seeing and responding. It felt like a move toward freedom.

As she stepped across the threshold of home, the familiar scents of family and the very existence of the three-story manor house spoke to her of solidity. She set her basket on the terra-cotta floor in the entry and rushed up the stairs, two at a time. Marc-André and Marie slept snug in their beds. All was well.

A debate rose inside her over dropping into bed herself or going back downstairs for a warm cup of tisane made of sun-dried herbs from the garden. Something warm to drink promising to be a balm to her weary body, she headed to the kitchen, pulling her woolen shawl tighter around her shoulders.

She started a fire in the kitchen hearth, grabbed two ceramic water jugs, and walked out back to the well. The sun now shone bright over Le Cengle, releasing a welcome warmth onto her shoulders. The scent of damp grass and the earthy odor of horses and chickens added up to a surrounding sense of life.

With a full load of water, Suzanne returned to the house. She filled a small cast-iron pot and hung it over the fire, then sank into Grand-mère's chair, positioned closest to the warmth. Her body relaxed, and she dozed, her head bobbing as she waited for the water to boil.

Loud raps on the front door resounded through the entryway and into the kitchen. She jolted fully awake and onto her feet. Who could it be so early? Had one of the royal guards watched her return home and come to harass her after all?

She smoothed her apron and strode toward the door before the pounding continued and woke her siblings. Too late. Marc-André and Marie stood at the bottom of the stairs, traces of sleep still on their faces. How long had the knocking persisted?

Suzanne pointed at the kitchen. "Go now!" she mouthed to her siblings. "Hide!"

Long ago, the Lacombes had prepared a *cachette*, a hiding place, dug into the ground under the bottom shelf of the pantry. The area extended beneath the kitchen floor and could hold up to four crouching people. Her siblings knew to lift off the wood plank, slip underneath, then replace the shelf over their heads.

Since her return from Mialet and news of increased arrests after the incident at Pont-de-Montvert, Suzanne had made them practice hiding at least once a day. She prayed they remembered to shut the pantry doors behind them and pull the shelf back into place. Following another prayer for all their safety, she opened the front door, squinting against the bright sunlight.

"Bonjour, Suzanne!" Aunt Anne's voice rang clear and strong.

"Oh! It's you!"

Aunt Anne stepped inside and gave Suzanne three *bisous*. "Who else would it be at this hour?"

Suzanne opened her mouth, then shut it again. How could she explain that despite her growing trust in God, fear still exploded in her at anything out of the ordinary? That she continued to battle slinging arrows of anxiety?

She changed the subject. "Why do you insist on knocking? We've told you to just come in."

"You know I'm not comfortable entering your home without knocking."

Suzanne sighed, then gestured for Aunt Anne to follow her. In the kitchen, Suzanne opened the pantry doors and lifted the bottom shelf. Two relieved faces smudged with dust grinned out at them.

Aunt Anne's eyebrows raised. "Really, you had them hide? Because someone knocked on the door?"

Suzanne helped Marie, then Marc-André hoisted himself out on his own. "It might've been soldiers," said Suzanne with a shrug. "You two step out back and dust yourselves off."

"I don't think royal troops knock and then wait for someone to answer. Anyway, I have something to tell you, but let's prepare some tea."

A strange sensation rippled up Suzanne's arms. What news could Aunt Anne bear?

Cleaned off, Marc-André and Marie returned and took their seats at the table. Suzanne reached for a cloth-wrapped loaf on the top shelf of the pantry, grateful they'd baked yesterday before the birth started. She cut thick slices, then grabbed a pot of *confiture*, Grand-mère's jam made recently from wild berries. Using garden herbs, Aunt Anne prepared tisane for everyone, then passed cups around.

Once settled, Aunt Anne gave thanks to their heavenly Father for the food and drink.

"So?" Suzanne prodded after the prayer.

Aunt Anne set down her tisane. "I have some news of your parents."

Icy shock jagged through Suzanne, undoing the benefits of the warm tisane and crackling kitchen fire. She'd longed to have word of her parents, but now resistance rose within her. Not knowing had kept a door open for hope. She looked at Marc-André and Marie, their eyes wide in pale faces. She needed to be strong for them all.

"Go ahead, please. Tell us whatever you know."

Sorrow etched across Aunt Anne's face. "Your papa is with his heavenly Father. We can trust he is well and at peace. We will meet him there one day."

Little Marie crumpled, lay her head on the table, and wept. Marc-André appeared stunned and absentmindedly patted his little sister's shoulder. Suzanne stared at her aunt, feeling nothing at all. She reached her arm around Marie and stroked her hair. Aunt Anne pulled her chair close to Marc-André and spoke words of comfort.

Sometime later, Aunt Anne added hot water to each cup of tisane, encouraging everyone to drink. Across the table, Suzanne met her aunt's eyes. "And Maman?"

"She's in prison. Here in St. Hippolyte du Fort."

Suzanne shut her eyes, wishing to keep them closed forever. Knowing her parents' fate didn't bring comfort. Quite the opposite.

Suzanne, child, I am with you. The words came from the depths of eternity, rising from within her shaken soul. *Beloved! Fear not. Fix your eyes on me. I am with you always.*

Like a lifeline, the Voice cut through her emotional swirl. Out of long-standing habit, she pushed it away. Then, in a flash, she understood that receiving its truth would save her from the despair lapping at the edges of her heart. She grabbed the truth with both hands.

Beloved! Fear not. Through the mist of pain, she hurled her understanding as close as possible to the reality that her heavenly Father loved her and that his love was meant to chase away fear. Although not yet able to anchor herself fully to that truth, she clung to it. What else could she do?

"Listen, today is the open market," said Aunt Anne. "It would do us all some good to get out of the house."

Suzanne gaped. How could that be a good idea? Everything within her wanted to crawl into bed and fall into a dreamless sleep.

"Let's go now before the heat is fully upon us," Aunt Anne continued. "Breathe some fresh air, see normal things. We cannot change what is, but getting out of here will help a little."

Lacking the energy to resist, Suzanne sent her brother and sister upstairs to get dressed. She and Aunt Anne sat in silence, sipping the rest of their tisane.

A short time later, all four stepped outside and crossed the bridge toward town. Suzanne put one foot in front of the other, keeping her arm linked through Marie's. At least Aunt Anne was there to deal with the guards at the gate, and as it was market day, their family passed through with only minimal harassment.

They retraced Suzanne's steps from earlier and arrived at the stalls set up along the river's edge. Every Friday morning, farmers and artisans brought their wares: seasonal vegetables and fruits, cheeses, olive oils, and wines, plus cloth, baskets, tools, and animals. Townspeople and folks from surrounding villages brought homemade and homegrown items, ready to sell their surplus or trade for what they lacked. Chickens clucked and flapped in their crates, waiting for new homes. At an open field at the far end, cows lowed and sheep nibbled grass.

Marguerite's voice carried across the crowd as she directed her helper in the setting up of their stall. Busy with the surplus bags of flour she sold on market day, Marguerite didn't look up. Suzanne walked the other way. She'd tell her friend the bad news later, in private, most likely when Marguerite visited on Sunday.

On a normal day, Suzanne loved going to the market. Its sights, sounds, and scents mingled into a sensory experience unlike any other. Neighbors stopped to chat, catching up on local gossip. Rectangular limestone blocks set along the way provided resting places. Despite the continual presence of soldiers, community life in St. Hippolyte carried on.

Today, she observed the food stalls, the animals, and the passersby as if from the tiny end of Papa's handheld telescope. Papa! Pain seared through her chest. He was gone from this life.

She sat with Aunt Anne while Marc-André and Marie wandered over to the livestock.

"Tell me more about Papa. How you found out, how it happened."

"My Bedos in-laws learned authorities condemned your father to the galleys of Marseille, as we suspected. For unknown reasons, they didn't send him right away but incarcerated him in the prison-fort in Alès, until news came of the Abbé du Chaila's death. Governor Bâville retaliated by executing several imprisoned Huguenots, including your father."

Suzanne shifted on her hard seat. The incident in Pont-de-Montvert had changed everything. Aunt Anne stood and brushed off her skirt. Gentle and firm, she took Suzanne's hand and pulled up. Suzanne tried to focus on her aunt's face, her words.

"I'm so sorry. I know this is a shock and will take time to sink in. But as I told you, your mother is still alive. And nearby, in St. Hippolyte's main prison-fort."

"She's been right here all this time."

Aunt Anne placed her basket laden with fresh produce on one arm, crooked her other through Suzanne's, and started easing them along.

"Can we visit her?" Suzanne whispered.

"Possibly. Uncle Bedos believes it could happen but could require a bribe of some sort."

They joined Marc-André and Marie, then made their way back through the market, attempting to respond to friendly greetings with a semblance of normalcy. Suzanne steered them away from where Charles stood at the Domaine La Grand'Terre stall, selling wine. She wasn't sure how much more pretending she could take. Would her family ever be able to stop?

They walked home in silence, again passing through the checkpoint. Their basket of produce provided proof they'd gone to the open market. A warm gust of summer breeze swept across the bridge, and the sun shone bright above. Suzanne took in her favorite view of the river below, reflecting the beauty of the blue sky above and the green foliage and brilliant yellow and purple wildflowers on its banks. On the other side, Le Cengle stood majestic as always, calling her to look up and take a higher perspective, like the eagles who soared above its cliffs.

Her gaze lowered onto the St. Jean Tower, down on the left riverbank. Unlike the smaller watchtower high on the corner of the Château de Planque property, this one had been built at the same time as the St. Hippolyte fort. Embedded in the rampart walls encircling the town, the round limestone edifice brought her thoughts crashing back to earth. This watchtower served as another entry gate, with soldiers permanently stationed there. Even worse, the bottom level of the tower functioned as another Huguenot prison. Almost all incarcerated there died due to the damp cold of the river or sickness. Heavy rains caused the waters to rise and snuff out the lives of those trapped inside. At least

Maman wasn't being held there. Nausea roiled in Suzanne's gut at the thought.

She forced herself to look toward home. Hadn't she trusted she was God's beloved? Thinking that his love would enable her to function without fear seemed impossible given her circumstances. But if not now, when? She determined to try for hope, even amid such loss.

A measure of peace wafted through her, like a tiny bird alighting in her soul. A water-scented breeze rose from the river. She drew a breath and moved forward.

CHAPTER 23
PRISON-FORT OF ST. HIPPOLYTE

1 September 1702
St. Hippolyte du Fort
Southern Cévennes

The Lacombe family sat at the oak dinner table, their reddened eyes staring at food they pushed around their plates. No one had an appetite. Grand-mère and Aunt Anne had insisted on serving dinner, saying that routine would be beneficial for them all. And maybe it did help to gather around a meal as usual, even if no one ate a thing.

After the first day of stunned numbness had worn off, each member of the family experienced raw pain in his or her own fashion. Suzanne's grief, now mixed with that of her siblings, bore down on her like a heavy blanket, a shroud. Marc-André's rigid back and face concerned her more than Marie's quiet weeping. Suzanne didn't know what to do. How does one console for the loss of a father? Especially when one carries the same sharp sorrow?

Yesterday, they'd sent a messenger to Gabriel-Isaac with the news. Suzanne wished her brother would come home to grieve with them. It wasn't likely.

He'd find comfort from Madame Laporte and his uncles, although the news would be a blow to them as well. Papa and Uncle Gabriel hadn't always agreed, but they were brothers and had come to an understanding. Uncle Paul would greatly mourn his eldest sister. Maman and he had many adventures before he left.

And Jean Massip? Was he still there? Suzanne didn't know why she was thinking of him.

Marc-André closed the curtains tight while Aunt Anne walked to the sideboard. She lifted the mirror from the wall and turned it over. All watched in silence while she performed the nightly ritual Papa used to do. Before. A strangled noise escaped Marie. Suzanne moved to her little sister and held her tight.

Aunt Anne opened the secret compartment on the back of the mirror and lifted out the hidden Bible, plus the tiny psalter. She returned the mirror to its normal position on the wall, in case soldiers suddenly interrupted their reading. Whether or not there was time to conceal the holy books, it was important not to give away their hiding place, since most Huguenots used the same method.

She set the Bible before Grand-mère, who shook her head. "I'll continue with the readings tomorrow. Tonight there will be comfort in listening and receiving the truth through your voice, Anne."

Sadness ridged Grand-mère's eyes, yet they carried a profound strength. She smiled. Light in the darkness. It was beautiful to behold.

Aunt Anne sat down at the table, opened the psalter, and began reading the familiar words of Psalm 23.

Suzanne looked out the window to the front vineyard, picturing the grassy meadow on the far side, next to the river. Never had she laid down in a pasture. Wouldn't the grasses poke and itch? The bugs bite and annoy? She shook her head. That hadn't been shepherd David's point. He must have rested in fields while watching over his sheep and understood the connection to God's care and provision for himself. He'd written that he feared *no* evil, even in the darkest places.

The truth flowed into Suzanne's innermost being. There was that word again: *fear*. Hadn't God repeated it to her enough, while reminding her she was beloved? It felt as if a warm shaft of light wrapped round and seeped into the cold dark knot in the pit of her stomach.

Grand-mère spoke up. "Dear ones, your papa is with his God and experiencing the joy of heaven at this very moment. I don't know how it all works, but it's possible he's looking down on us, watching over us all. And I'm certain that our Father God will never leave us. Never fail us. Never forsake us. We're not alone."

Marc-André's shoulders loosened a degree. Grief for their papa wouldn't soon be gone, but they'd find a way through the pain, together, with God's presence and help.

Aunt Anne closed the psalter. "I think that's enough for tonight."

Grand-mère stood. "Come Marc-André and Marie. Let's go upstairs and prepare for bed. The blessing of sleep will be good for us all. *Bonne nuit.* Good night."

"*Bonne nuit,*" Suzanne and Aunt Anne responded in unison, giving *bisous* and gentle hugs all around.

Once they were alone, Aunt Anne turned to Suzanne. "We need to talk about visiting your mother in prison. I received word this afternoon that it will be possible."

Suzanne sat down hard, and Aunt Anne pulled up a chair. "They'll move her soon to the prison of Aigues-Mortes and incarcerate her indefinitely in the Tour de Constance, with other Huguenot women. We need to visit her in the next few days, before she's transferred."

A fresh bolt of fear roared through Suzanne, robbing her of a moment's breath. She wanted to see her mother and had longed for this opportunity. But entering St. Hippolyte's prison-fort meant stepping into her worst nightmare. Every time she'd come under the inspiration of the Holy Spirit, she knew the manifestations could one day land her in jail. She'd woken many a night, her pulse racing, from a dream where that very thing occurred.

But hadn't David written she could fear no evil? Even in the darkest valley? Surely, the dungeons of St. Hippolyte's prison-fort qualified on both accounts. At the prospect of going inside, everything in her screamed *Non!* Resistance rose within and fought like a startled, frightened horse, rearing back, beating the air with its hooves.

Suzanne's shoulders heaved as tears burst through the pent-up dam of her emotions. She let the tears flow. Indeed, she couldn't have stopped them.

Finally, the flood subsided, and she dabbed her eyes with her apron. She arranged its soggy fabric out across her skirt and turned to her aunt.

"This scares me more than anything else. The darkness, the confinement, the possibility of never leaving once we enter." Suzanne's voice caught. She gulped some air and let out a loud hiccup that was almost funny, but she didn't have the will to laugh.

"I understand. We'll be together, and we never walk alone. Our heavenly Father is with us always."

Suzanne gave a tiny nod. That was true, but in this situation, his presence didn't seem real enough.

Aunt Anne continued. "I propose we go tomorrow. We don't want to lose this chance to see her."

In the early morning, they crossed town together. Ripples of nervous energy emanated from Suzanne, and she sensed the same from Aunt Anne. Arms linked, backs straight, they approached the guarded front entry of the prison-fort. Along the walk there, they'd prayed for the favor of being admitted. Visits came down to the whim of the guard on duty.

"Bonjour, monsieur. We're here to see the prisoner Jeanne Lacombe." Aunt Anne's voice rang clear and steady.

"Jeanne Lacombe?"

"Yes, sir."

"What's your relationship with the prisoner?"

"Jeanne Lacombe is my sister," said Aunt Anne. Tipping her head at Suzanne, she added, "And her mother."

The man scowled and scanned his list of prisoners. "I see we transfer her to Aigues-Mortes this week."

"Yes. It's for that reason we have come."

Hearing the man speak out Maman's sentence struck Suzanne like a slap. After today, her mother would be out of reach. Visits were not allowed in the infamous Tour de Constance.

Suzanne tried to fix her inner eyes on Jesus. *The Lord is my shepherd*, she recited. *I have everything I need.*

The guard took his time looking them over, head to toe. Aunt Anne remained tranquil, her example reminding Suzanne to do the same.

"What's in there?" he asked, pointing to the basket on Aunt Anne's arm.

"A change of clothes, food, and a few medical supplies."

The man snatched the basket, glowering as he dug through. He swore under his breath. Aunt Anne's posture grew rigid. Why? They had nothing to hide. Finally, he handed the basket back and opened the gate. Another soldier appeared to escort them to the cells.

They crossed the enormous interior courtyard, open to the late summer sky. On an upper terrace of the fort, a child appeared through a door. Suzanne suppressed a gasp. A family lived here? With a child? How awful! A palpable sense of evil flowed from every stone.

The soldier ushered the women through a low door and down a steep, winding staircase. She placed her feet sideways on the narrow stone steps, one at a time, taking care not to misstep and take a tumble.

They descended into darkness, blinking to adjust their eyes as their bodies acclimated to the damp chill from the limestone walls.

At the bottom, the soldier led them down a tight arched hallway. With each step, Suzanne's breathing grew more shallow. They stopped at another guard, sitting on a three-legged stool inside a massive iron gate.

The guide soldier consulted his list again. "Take these two to prisoner Jeanne Lacombe," he ordered. The guard rose and lifted an iron ring off a peg, located a large key, then rattled it in the rusty lock. He threw open the door, crashing it against the vaulted wall on the other side.

Suzanne's throat squeezed tight. What if the guard didn't let them out again? What if this was a trap? The prison authorities knew they were Huguenots.

Beloved! Fear not. I am with you always. Suzanne drew a long breath and let it fill her lungs. She held it for a minute, picturing the glow of the life-giving force of the Holy Spirit dwelling within. She exhaled slowly and stepped through the door.

The guard started down a dark passage lined with iron doors bellowing "Where's Jeanne Lacombe?"

Silence.

"Jeanne Lacombe? Speak now!"

"Here. I'm in here."

The guard motioned for Aunt Anne and Suzanne to follow as he moved farther down the corridor. He stopped at the third door on the right and used a different key to unlock it. Blood pounded and roared through Suzanne's ears.

Then she saw Maman. Unkempt and thinner than ever before. Suzanne hurtled past the guard and straight into her mother's open arms. Maman stroked Suzanne's back and spoke soft words of comfort. Aunt Anne moved to her sister's side and reached an arm around her shoulders. The three women barely registered the guard's announcement that they had ten minutes.

Maman pulled away and looked into each face. "Suzanne! Anne! I can scarcely believe you're here."

"Neither can we," said Aunt Anne.

"How are the rest of my children?"

"Well," said Aunt Anne. "Unfortunately, only those over sixteen can visit." She caught her sister up on the family, leaving out the news of Gabriel-Isaac's move to Mialet.

Maman's eyes glistened. "I'm surprised they allowed anyone to come at all."

"Since you'll move to Aigues-Mortes soon, we're allowed this one visit."

Maman drew Suzanne back into her embrace. After a moment, Maman looked at Aunt Anne and whispered the question Suzanne dreaded. "And Pierre?"

Quietly, Aunt Anne relayed the news of his death. Maman shut her eyes for a moment as tears coursed down her cheeks. "I sensed he'd gone on before me. We'll all be together again."

Suzanne sniffled, then wiped her nose on her sleeve. "Maman, have they hurt you? Have you been ill?"

Maman smiled. "I've always loved how God made you, my eldest child. Since you could walk, you've thought of others' needs and brought whatever help you could. I'm well. Truly."

"I'm glad." Suzanne glanced around the dank cell. It hurts to care so for others, Maman."

"I know. You'll grow in understanding of how to use your gift without letting it wear you down. That's possible only when you abide in God and receive his love, then let it flow out to others."

"He's been telling me I'm his beloved, that I can be free from fear. I'm trying to accept this."

A joyful light on Maman's face expelled the darkness in the room. "Nothing could make me more proud of you."

"It's a struggle to hold on and believe it all the time. I'm so weary and afraid of so much. I thought if I did the right things, everything would be alright. But it doesn't seem to work that way."

"He's with you, through it all. That's what it means to have peace that surpasses understanding. Keep asking for his wisdom and leading. Only do what he shows you. Let him be God. He's good at it. And he'll continue to help others through you in significant ways."

Suzanne drew a ragged breath.

"Have you had a Holy Spirit visitation recently?" Maman whispered.

"No, but the Voice comes often, most of the time quietly, bringing comfort and guidance. If the manifestations do come, I'll try to not suppress them. We need his direction now more than ever."

Maman looked to her sister, who leaned close and spoke in muted tones of the Huguenot uprising of the past few months.

"By now, Gabriel-Isaac must be with his uncles," Maman murmured, "preparing to join the battle."

Aunt Anne and Suzanne exchanged small smiles. How had they thought to keep anything from Maman?

Like a cloud covering the sun, seriousness darkened Aunt Anne's face. She pulled the basket off her arm, set it on the floor, then crouched next to it and shuffled through the items inside. "Here's clothing, food, and some of Isabeau's best herbal remedies. And Marc-André and Marie each wrote you a letter."

Fresh tears welled in Maman's eyes as she accepted the precious missives.

Then, with one swift motion, Aunt Anne ripped the cloth lining out of the basket. Suzanne's mouth dropped open as her aunt extracted a small object wrapped in linen. The Tessier family psalter!

Aunt Anne stood and handed the gift to her sister, taking care to speak softly. "Your eldest son rescued this from our hiding place. You can tuck it in your chignon, your thick hair will conceal it well. Take it with you to Aigues-Mortes, and may it bring you great comfort."

Maman clutched the treasure to her heart. "To have this book is blessing upon blessing. It brings true sustenance. Thank you."

Her face shone from an inner light as she drew her sister into a tight hug, making worthwhile every anxious moment Suzanne experienced while Gabriel-Isaac retrieved the psalter. So this was Aunt Anne's plan all along.

After a moment, Jeanne turned to her daughter. "My beautiful Suzanne, I pray for you daily. Be free, my beloved child, and continue in the fullness of who your Creator made you to be."

The steps of the returning guard echoed down the corridor. Maman slipped the psalter into her bodice, then drew Suzanne into an embrace. Suzanne clung tight, wishing to never let go. Maman kissed Suzanne's cheek, then looked deep into her daughter's eyes. "Now go in peace. All will be well."

CHAPTER 24
HOLY WAR

9 September 1702
Collet-de-Dèze
Eastern Cévennes

Deep in the pine forest, Abraham Mazel and Gédéon Laporte stood before the Huguenot fighters. Mazel glanced at Laporte and thanked the Almighty for supplying not only a fellow leader but one with experience as a soldier, plus an innate strategic sense. Leading together, they complemented each other well.

The Lord had seen to it that the Camisards regrouped quickly after Esprit Séguier's execution. The way the old prophet's courageous death acted as fuel to the dry tinder of long-repressed Huguenot hearts no doubt opposed Governor Bâville's expectations. Throughout the Cévennes, Protestants had found inspiration from Esprit's last words.

"We now carry a formidable reputation," said Laporte. "Only through God's will have we survived and had victory over the King's troops."

Mazel nodded. "It defies logic. It has to be the Almighty. And the addition of your band of sixty men points to more of the same. Those two over there, the ones who've been with your nephew Rolland for years, are forces to be reckoned with. Gabriel carries passion and authority, and Paul seems to ponder matters in depth."

"They're an intense pair, even more so now that they're finally seeing some action."

Keenly aware that he was younger than many of the men he led, such as Gabriel and Paul, Abraham turned his spiritual eyes upward. He

135

lived to please God alone. He'd previously partnered with the "old prophet" Séguier and now led with Gédéon Laporte, a man twice his age. The ways of the Lord were indeed mysterious.

Laporte had taken to calling himself "colonel of the children of God who fought for liberty of conscience." Abraham chuckled under his breath. A bit much, and way too long for a title. But the phrase conveyed their overarching motivation.

Séguier's death had unleashed a flood of action. Maybe that's what the old prophet and God had discussed that day in the cave, before Séguier went out on his own, setting himself up to be arrested. Maybe he'd understood what was ahead of him and had agreed to it willingly. Abraham exhaled long and slow. He grieved for his fallen friend and doubted the scenes of the execution would ever leave his mind. But whatever happened between Séguier and the Almighty had resulted in greater unity and sense of purpose among the Camisards. Was that God's plan all along?

Finally, after several days of the Camisards hiding deep in this forest, resting between skirmishes and waiting for divine direction for their next move, guidance had come yesterday. If their prophesied mission succeeded, it would be the first of its kind.

Mazel understood the men looked to him, following his spiritual leadership. Their obedience to his every prophetic utterance as from the Almighty led him to seek the Lord soberly and with all his might. He'd obeyed fully even when the guidance surprised him, like the time God directed him to let a priest go in the northern Cévennes. But what if he got an instruction wrong? Led them astray? Today's unusual action would be a proof that his interpretation could be trusted, if their ruse worked. They'd soon know.

Yesterday, posing as an informant, Laporte had sent a letter to the leader of a company of soldiers stationed nearby. The missive contained the intelligence of a supposed underground gathering of Huguenots, including location, day, and time. Today was that day.

"Ready?" Laporte asked Mazel.

"We still don't know if they bought it, but there's only one way to find out."

"Lead us in prayer, Abraham, before we go."

They called the men to attention. Mazel lifted his face to heaven and prayed a benediction on the unique mission ahead. Then Laporte organized the fighters and led them out. Abraham brought up the rear—praying, without ceasing, for protection and success.

The Camisards moved with caution through the forest until the foliage grew sparse. Laporte motioned for the company to halt and hide. He pointed at Gabriel and Paul. "You two go ahead. Get the lay of the land, then return with a report."

The pair disappeared down the path in an instant. In less than a quarter of an hour, they returned.

"Good news!" said Gabriel. "The officer and his garrison are absent, not a soldier in sight."

"Apparently, they believed your information to be authentic," said Paul, "and have gone to raid the alleged Huguenot assembly."

As word spread, Camisards emerged from various nooks and shrubs. A few let loose shouts of glee and clapped each other on the back. The ploy worked!

Mazel raised his hands. "Quiet! Certainly, there are villagers around. Some may be all too willing to sell us out for Bâville's generous rewards."

Barely concealing their excitement, the fighters moved through the narrow streets toward their destination, the last remaining Protestant temple in the Cévennes. That it had escaped demolition over the past two decades was a miracle for the Huguenots, though they'd not been able to use it as intended. Until today.

Gédéon bounded up the stone steps to the entrance of the empty temple, flung open the arched wooden door, and entered. The fighters streamed up the stairs, slowing to a reverential pace as they neared the top. The last to cross the threshold, Abraham couldn't contain his welling joy. He hadn't expected to experience anything like this feeling of redemption, of home. He'd been only seven or eight years old the last time he'd attended a service in such a place.

Since the outlawing of their faith seventeen years ago, few of the Camisards present had ever worshipped inside a temple constructed for that purpose. Today, that changed.

The men removed their worn caps, held them against their dingy white linen shirts, and sang psalm after psalm. Attempts to keep voices low to avoid drawing attention from the villagers didn't last long. Hearts soared with previously unexperienced freedom, releasing years of anguish. Gabriel and Paul sang the loudest, both old enough to have worshipped inside a temple when young.

Sunlight streamed through a high round window, across the upper wooden gallery, and down onto the worshipping men. A holy benediction. Abraham basked in the warmth, his soul responding like a plant long deprived of light.

From the depths of his being, he believed that darkness would never ultimately win. God was with the fighters. Here was a tangible sign. Huguenots worshipping in a place of their own. The light that overcomes all darkness pouring over them. Light that darkness can never extinguish.

Laporte stood by his side, and the Lord of heaven's armies directed them. God had given the Camisards a mission, and they'd carry on until he told them to stop.

CHAPTER 25
MISSION

9 September 1702
St. Hippolyte du Fort
Southern Cévennes

Lost in thought, Suzanne took her time crossing the street between her home and the Château de Planque. A few golden leaves drifted across her path, reminding her to look up. The cerulean sky, filled with puffy white clouds morphing into various shapes by unseen currents, lifted her spirit. All around her, the dazzling natural beauty of September communicated life. The great artist Creator of such wonder was with her, always.

She continued on the Rue de Planque, past the Château, her mother's childhood home. Maman. Would Suzanne ever see her again?

Last week's visit to the prison had shifted something in her soul. With Aunt Anne by her side and their heavenly Father with them, Suzanne had faced one of her greatest fears and made it through. She'd entered the prison and made it back out again.

But the biggest miracle came from her time with Maman and the words they'd exchanged. Suzanne had emerged with a fresh perspective and renewed strength.

She reveled in the swallows swooping and swirling in the afternoon sunshine. What would it be like to fly free like the birds, to have their view? Well, maybe she could feel free, even with her feet on the ground.

She'd long admired her mother's faith and courage. But last week, in that dank prison, Maman's joy had glowed brighter than ever. An inner light shining from her had caused darkness to flee. The presence of God in her changed the atmosphere and reached a deep place in Suzanne. She didn't fully understand the experience, but that made it no less real.

At the slight bend in the Rue de Planque, Suzanne turned and arrived at the *moulin*. Approaching the Marolle family home, she quickened her steps. Marguerite loved Suzanne's parents like family, fiercely grieving the loss of Papa and worrying over Maman's imprisonment. Suzanne had already sent word to Marguerite that the prison visit had gone well, but now she could fully share the beauty of the encounter.

The unmistakable sound of the immense circular millstone reverberated through the large limestone building as Suzanne entered. To everyone's relief, the summer drought had finally ended. Recent rains provided ample water rushing from the river, through a canal, and into the *moulin*. She watched the crashing water turn the enormous wheel that powered the millstone.

September sunshine reached through the eight large windows on the opposite side, backlighting the *moulin*'s operation. The scent of crushed wheat filled the air. In a few more months, they would harvest olives, and the same stone would grind them into oil.

Marguerite stood across the room, absorbed in her work. Suzanne admired her friend's intensity, the way she put her entire being into whatever was before her. Skirting the millstone, one eye on the powerful instrument, Suzanne moved toward Marguerite.

"Oh! Bonjour, Suzanne! I didn't see you there!"

"I know how you are, my friend, fully focused."

"Let me finish this batch of wheat, and then we can sit and catch up."

Suzanne helped her complete the process. Together they filled large cloth sacks with freshly ground flour that the farmers would pick up for personal use or to trade for needed items. The job finished, the friends dusted themselves off and stepped outside.

Marguerite pointed to a small trail on the foothill opposite the *moulin*. "Let's go up and sit in our spot, in the sunshine. We can talk freely."

A smile tugged at the corners of Suzanne's mouth as they started up the path. How did her friend know she wanted to talk in private? Perceptivity was yet another thing she loved about Marguerite.

Within minutes, they reached the destination and settled themselves on their usual flat boulders. Marguerite's keen gaze bore down on Suzanne. "So, tell me. What's going on?"

Suzanne shut her eyes, welcoming the sun's warmth on her face. After a moment, she tried to put into words the internal changes visiting Maman in prison had brought about. "Honestly, I expected to be devastated after seeing Maman, but it's the opposite. Of course, I miss her terribly. Papa, too." Suzanne drew a shaky breath, inhaling the surrounding scents of wild plants and sunbaked earth. "But I've turned a corner, Marguerite. Something slotted into place. A part of me that has been dead is now alive. Or at least waking up."

Marguerite nodded.

"So, I'm wondering how I can help. Fight, I mean." She almost laughed at the quaver in her voice. These thoughts and ideas were so new, bringing them out into the light of day left her feeling exposed.

Marguerite studied her with intense eyes.

"Maman and Papa understood who they were, what they were called to do. They fought against repression, for all of my life. Now, I want to do my part."

"Are you considering actual battle, like your brother and uncles?" Marguerite's voice carried a pointed tone, something Suzanne couldn't quite identify.

"*Non!*" You know that wouldn't work. I can barely harm an insect in the house."

The friends laughed.

"All right," said Marguerite. "We agree that wielding a gun is not exactly your destiny. Any ideas of what you can do?"

"Uh, yes actually. When Aunt Anne gave Maman the psalter, an idea came to me. That tiny tome of truth is such a source of comfort to them, both the contents and the book itself. It made me wonder." She stopped, looking down.

"And now I wonder," said Marguerite. "Go on!"

Suzanne rolled her eyes at her demanding friend. "You remember when we were in school, how I loved learning history? Despite our lessons being given by priests and nuns, with their particular perspective, I found it interesting."

Now it was Marguerite's turn to roll her eyes. "I never understood how you could enjoy the most boring subject of all. But you soaked it all up. Why?"

"Well, I think it's about knowing the context and the connection between events and the people involved."

"I didn't mean why you like history! Why are you bringing it up now?"

"Oh! Well, I'm thinking of writing the story of my parents' lives and grandparents' lives and maybe also recording current happenings, the history that's unfolding right now."

Marguerite leaned back on her boulder, supporting herself by both hands from behind, her face lifted to the sun.

"What do you think?" asked Suzanne.

"I think that's exactly what you should do. It's a perfect fit."

"I'm not sure if it counts as fighting like my brother or like the guide Jean Massip. At tremendous risk, he helps those fleeing get to a safe place, to freedom. He almost died in the fire in the Abbé du Chaila's prison and still limps from the ordeal. Anyway, at least writing is something I can do now. Maybe it could bring comfort to whomever might read my words someday."

Marguerite sat up straight and looked her in the eye. "It *is* resistance. Recording the events and the suffering of our people preserves the memory of their courage and faith. It gives *our* side of the story. I believe it will instruct and inspire people in the future."

The encouragement melted into Suzanne, bolstering her resolve.

"What about you, Marguerite? You're a born warrior. Didn't Grandmère say you entered the world with the umbilical cord around your neck?"

"Oh, I've never heard *that* story before," Marguerite said, sardonic grin well in place.

Suzanne ignored the sarcasm. "But you rallied immediately and burst into the world. And you've fought for the people you love ever since. Have you thought about what you will do to help our cause? To resist?"

Marguerite's face grew solemn. "I have more than just thought about it. I'll explain soon. But first, let's talk about this Jean Massip."

Betrayed by her flaming face, Suzanne sucked in her breath. Her hands flew to her cheeks.

Marguerite's chortle reverberated across the mountain.

Mialet
Southeastern Cévennes

Warm in the early autumn sun, Gabriel-Isaac knelt by Madame Laporte, yanking weeds from the kitchen garden. Why couldn't he do drills with the men? Since the news came of his father's death and his mother's imprisonment, they'd treated him like a child. Hot tears pricked, and one dared trickle down his cheek. He gulped air, then wrenched out several weeds at once and threw them on the growing pile. To be sidelined was the last thing he wanted or needed.

In the beginning, they'd let him take part in the preparations for war. Just thinking about the training sped up his pulse, the inner drumbeat of battle he carried with him always. But receiving the information about his parents after the Abbé du Chaila's death and Esprit Séguier's execution had changed everything. Now, his uncles mostly sent him to help in the kitchen or to tend the *potager*, stating Madame and her daughters needed help with the end-of-summer harvest. What a waste! Just as the men finally fought back.

Gabriel-Isaac ripped out the last weeds in his row and deposited them in the burn pile. He stared at the untethered plants, clods of earth clinging to their roots, and identified with their plight. You start to thrive, then suddenly you're tossed aside. Brushing his hands on his woolen pants, he stomped toward the far end of the garden. His foot bobbled on a rock, wrenching his ankle a little. Using the other foot, he kicked it hard and high, aiming at blackbirds perched in a fig tree, feasting on ripe fruit. The little flock rose as one, flapping and fluttering to safety.

"Gabriel-Isaac! That is *not* how we treat God's creatures." Madame Laporte's voice rang stern.

"Even when they eat our food?" He rolled another rock around under his foot. He didn't care if he sounded disrespectful. Was anybody respecting him?

"Gabriel-Isaac!"

He drew his breath in slowly, then let it out in a rush. It wasn't her fault. "*Excusez-moi*, Madame."

The situation wasn't fair. Hadn't he come here to fight? Now, with a revolt heating up, they tell him he's too young? Not ready? He didn't buy the story that keeping everyone nourished was as important as actual fighting. Did they think he was an idiot? Try telling them to stay home and cook.

Gabriel-Isaac walked to the row of onions, picked up his wooden trowel and inspected the only weapon he could use these days. With a glance at Madame, he restrained himself from hurling it across the garden. He dropped to his knees among the onion plants and attacked the dandelions, placing them in the basket Madame set there earlier. Although they grew wild like weeds, they were rather delicious cooked or raw. And Madame insisted they were good for you. Not that he cared about any of that.

Stinging sweat dripped into his eyes. Just what he needed. He blinked hard, not allowing himself to rub away the burn. Reddened eyes would only justify his uncles' decision to hold him back.

Except they weren't here at the moment. Had been gone several days. Now lieutenants, they helped lead the growing band of men following Gédéon Laporte. Gabriel-Isaac stabbed the dirt with his trowel, unearthing more dandelions. Rumor had it the fighters were quite successful too, especially against Capitaine Poul and his troops. Why couldn't Gabriel-Isaac be part of that success?

He looked across to Madame. Head down, she plucked fresh green beans from their vines and added them to the pile in her basket. Gabriel-Isaac's belly rumbled as he imagined tonight's dinner. He had to admit the Laporte family's cuisine was delicious, especially when Madame's eldest daughters, Gabrielle and Esther, cooked. But that didn't mean he enjoyed one minute of helping in the garden or preparing the meals. He could've stayed home and worked the vineyards in his father's place if they wouldn't allow him to fight.

Grand-mère understood his need to engage in action. That's why she'd allowed him to leave St. Hippolyte. Even Suzanne had given her blessing in the end, despite her constant attempts to keep him home and under her wing. More tears stung and spilled over. Gabriel-Isaac turned his head away. No way could he let Madame see this sudden flow.

Maybe he missed his family a little. Maybe even a lot. He wasn't homesick exactly but did *miss* them. Especially Maman. He sucked in a large breath. Should a man of thirteen miss his mother so much? He dragged his rough woolen sleeve across his face. He'd probably never see her again.

She and Papa had always been ready to die for their faith. More than once he'd told Gabriel-Isaac so, wanting him to understand. Papa made it very clear that he loved them all more than anything except God. And if called to die for his faith, he would do so, proclaiming it an honor. Papa's belief anchored him in this life and gave him hope for the one to come. The whole family would reunite in heaven, spending eternity together in complete peace and joy. Gabriel-Isaac pulled out a grubby handkerchief and blew his nose hard.

He finished his task, stood, and plodded back to the house. An honor to die for God. Was *he* ready for that? He wasn't sure but knew he wanted to be brave and useful, like Papa. He'd just have to figure out a way to join the action, permission or not.

In the house's entryway, Rolland's youngest sister, Michèle, directed him to wash his basket of vegetables in the stone sink with the waiting pitcher of water. Once finished, he headed toward the kitchen. His thoughts elsewhere, he tripped over Rolland's iron hayfork propped against the wall. The tool clattered to the ground.

Staring at it, Gabriel-Isaac thought of Rolland's words when he left several days ago to preach and call men to join the Camisard uprising. He'd mentioned the town of Calvisson. Somewhere near Nîmes, it was a walk of only a day and a half from Mialet, in the opposite direction from Uncle Gabriel and Uncle Paul.

Gabriel-Isaac could try to figure out on his own how to get there. But why do that when there was a guide in residence? Just yesterday, Jean Massip announced his healing was progressing and he'd be on his way in the next few weeks. A grin lit Gabriel-Isaac's face.

With buoyant steps, he entered the kitchen and offered to help Rolland's sisters with the meal preparation. Ignoring their surprise, he set about stirring the pot of soup simmering over the fire.

He had an idea. He had a plan. He had hope.

CHAPTER 26
A CALL TO WAR

9–10 October 1702
St. Jean du Pin
Southeastern Cévennes

The first pinpricks of light appeared in the darkening sky. Despite having all senses on high alert, the men following Rolland single file through the scrubby brush had little time to notice the evening stars. A barely suppressed yelp revealed that an inattentive man had neglected to hold back a branch for the next in line. Rolland crouched his large frame low. The others did the same. Such a sound could betray their nighttime mission. Such a sound could get them all killed.

Hadn't he made it perfectly clear that silence was of the utmost importance? For his new recruits, this was their first time out, their first foray into unknown territory. Still, he expected complete cooperation and obedience to his orders.

After several minutes with no shooting soldiers descending upon them, Rolland stood and forged ahead. He'd deal with the noisemakers later.

He led the way up a small incline, then stopped on a narrow plateau to observe the cluster of stone houses and barns nestled in the valley below. The mental image the Holy Spirit had given him matched this place perfectly. He shot up a prayer of thanks for the specific guidance, then started down the hill.

Not knowing what or who they'd find, he only had the divine direction to go there. Within minutes, they reached the edge of the tiny hamlet. Rolland huddled against an outside wall. His fighters concealed themselves in scattered bushes.

One of them crept forward and pointed to a dimly lit window in a house down a narrow road. Rolland held up a hand to wait, then listened for further guidance from God. No specific word came, but he sensed they were free to move ahead.

From behind the stone wall, he motioned for the others to follow, then took the first steps, walking toward the light. He entered a cobbled passageway between houses. Ducking under a low limestone arch, he hoped none of his men's heads made contact and induced more noise, especially dangerous this close to buildings.

A little farther in, he stopped. The sound reaching his ears was definitely not the cry of a man striking his head on a stone arch. This sound flowed soft and golden, like the light beaming through the window.

He listened hard. Was that singing? He leaned in. For the past year, reports came of angelic song throughout the Cévennes, the singing of Psalm hymns familiar to the Huguenots. Was this a sign from God?

Rolland signaled for the others to stay in place. Alone, he moved forward toward the melody. Yes, singing flowed from the window above. He placed his feet on the single stone step and put his ear to the door. Muffled music, but definitely one of their tunes. Slowly, he turned the doorknob. Locked. He straightened and raised a fist to knock.

His hand poised midair, the door cracked open, a sliver of light escaping. From under his white linen shirt, Rolland grabbed the Huguenot cross on the chain around his neck and raised it to eye level. The woman on the other side of the threshold did the same.

The door opened wider. Rolland stepped through, then turned and gestured for his men to follow. Inside, they found a worship gathering.

The leader stepped toward him. "Are you not Rolland Laporte?"

"I am. How do I know you?"

"I heard you preach and prophesy in Grotte de la Roquette before the raid. I'm glad you escaped."

"You as well, my brother."

"You are welcome here," another man said. "Please have your men sit. Would you share something from the scriptures?"

Rolland agreed, and the Camisards wedged in between fellow Huguenots in the small space. To the flicker of candlelight, Rolland walked through the packed crowd. Once in front, he paused, waiting on the Lord. No trembling occurred in him, just a profound clarity that matched the silence of the room.

You already know why you're here, what you are to say.

God had sent them to call others to resist the authorities and to engage in the revolt. He needed no further instruction until they accomplished this mission.

"My brothers and sisters, like you, we're here in obedience to the Almighty. The Holy Spirit led us to this place, at this exact time. We didn't know why. We didn't know what or who we would find." He glanced at his men standing nearby, then scanned the crowd, only able to see those near the front in the candlelit room. "We're here to exhort you to join us. Our time has come. Since the incident at Pont-de-Montvert, we've entered a holy war."

Again, Rolland surveyed the room. "My uncle, Gédéon Laporte, along with Abraham Mazel, leads men to purge our land of those who've long persecuted us for following our consciences. Despite a few defeats, they've had multiple successes against the Governor's troops led by Capitaine Poul."

A murmur rippled through the assembled Huguenots. Were they questioning the validity of these events? He'd heard rumors that some disagreed with the acts of violence against priests and churches, stating God would never condone such a thing. He gave his head a quick shake. *Non!* He would not entertain such thoughts or speculate on their opinions. Only God's orders and complete obedience in carrying them out were of importance. Only God's opinion mattered.

Tremors in his limbs started small and grew. Holy Spirit inspiration surged through his body. After a moment, words flowed. "I urge you to enter the battle. Don't be afraid. We're on God's mission, and our reward is eternal. Be strong! Be courageous! As it says in Psalm 68, 'Let God arise, let His enemies be scattered.'[6] The time is now!"

Rolland peered across the crowded room. "Who will join us?"

A young man strode toward the front, another right behind him. Several more followed.

Rolland narrowed his eyes at the first and then the second. "Gabriel-Isaac! Jean Massip! What are you doing here?"

---

[6] Psalm 68:1 (NKJV)

Gabriel-Isaac met his gaze. "We've been searching for you almost a month. You're hard to keep up with. We'd hear you were in one place, and by the time we'd get there, you'd disappeared."

Rolland gaped at Jean. "You helped Gabriel-Isaac search for me? Where are his uncles? Have they agreed to this?"

Jean turned to Gabriel-Isaac. "I'll let you explain."

"Uncle Gabriel and Uncle Paul now serve your uncle as lieutenants. Along with Mazel, they gather men and fight somewhere in the northern Cévennes. They all left not long after you did."

"You didn't answer my question. Your uncles want you to join me?" The last he'd heard, Gabriel-Isaac's uncles wished to keep him in Mialet.

The boy's chin dropped a bit, then he stood straight. "You need fighters. Isn't that what you're doing here tonight? Calling men to battle?" He gestured at the others who had come forward.

Rolland forced his lips into a firm line, holding back the smile tugging at the corner of his mouth. He appreciated Gabriel-Isaac's audacity but needed to keep him in check. "Your uncles don't know you're here, do they?"

Gabriel-Isaac looked him in the eye. "I belong here. I believe in our cause, and you need men."

"Yes, *men*." Rolland stared him down, his gaze fierce. He must establish his leadership, especially with this one. The boy didn't flinch. Rolland's admiration grew, but he forced his face stern.

"Jean, what's your business in all this?"

"With my leg healed, it's time for me to be back about my mission. There's always a need for a guide in this region. Leading people to freedom is my call and my contribution to our cause."

"And you brought along a thirteen-year-old? Without his uncles' permission?"

"I believe his family would prefer him to be in my company rather than wandering the Cévennes alone while looking for you."

The guide had a point, even if Rolland didn't like it.

"He'd have set out to find you on his own," Jean continued. "I know my way around, and we're here and safe."

"We'll talk more about this later," Rolland said. He needed time to think and pray about what to do with the boy. Send him back to Mialet? Risk him running away again?

Rolland scowled at the pair. "Stand aside for now."

A couple dozen other men had volunteered to join the fight. He must not lose focus; he must obey the Almighty's directives. There was oppression to throw off, and nothing must stand in the way.

CHAPTER 27
UNFINISHED BUSINESS

18–19 October 1702
Near Florac
Northern Cévennes

Rain lashed across the mountains and down the plains, making it almost impossible to see. Abraham Mazel and Gédéon Laporte pushed through the night, their band of soaked-through fighters following their lead.

Abraham glanced toward the back of the group. "Check the men, especially the rear."

Laporte turned and walked along the long line of men pressing on despite the constant downpour. He nodded and murmured encouragement along the way. A quarter hour later, he fell back in step with Mazel. "Everything's in order. Rolland guards the back end, as directed."

"And the boy?"

"He's in the middle, with his uncles."

Abraham's lips pursed. He didn't appreciate having the unseasoned youth along. When Gabriel-Isaac showed up with Rolland last week, sending the boy back to Mialet chaperoned by Jean Massip had been the first thought. Abraham glanced over his shoulder at Massip. The guide's vast knowledge of the land kept the Camisards on the right path and gave them a definite advantage. So they allowed Gabriel-Isaac to stay, for now.

Today, they marched toward the home of a notorious *notaire*. A former Huguenot, this town lawyer renounced his Protestant faith long ago. Likely enticed by the financial and security benefits handed out by Governor Bâville, the *notaire* was proving his loyalty to the King's church by vicious persecution of the Huguenots.

Even worse, he employed the Abbé du Chaila's former secretary who had somehow escaped the Pont-de-Montvert the night this all began. To the Camisards great chagrin, the secretary now roamed the Cévennes collecting the ever-increasing fines imposed by the Governor.

A stately villa came into view just down the road. Abraham held up a hand, and the troop stopped. He turned to Jean. "This is it?"

"Yes."

Mazel and Gédéon gave the signal to charge.

The band of Camisards descended on the *notaire*'s home. After infiltrating its ground floor, they faced a line of armed servants attempting to protect their boss. Gédéon raised his pistol and opened fire. The *notaire* yowled, clutched his face, and crumpled to the ground. Chaos erupted.

As fighters and servants tussled, the injured *notaire* got to his feet, helped by a woman who could be his wife or sister. They shuffled together to an open window.

"STOP THOSE TWO!" Abraham shouted, his words lost in the tumult. The woman assisted the *notaire* out the window, then followed close behind. Mazel pushed his way through the brawl. Too late. The pair escaped. He leaned out the window as they disappeared down the street below.

Mazel grabbed the arm of the closest Camisard. "Go! Take a few other men and pursue the *notaire* and his helper. They're running down the road, to the left."

The man carried out Mazel's orders immediately.

Another shot fired. Mazel swiveled toward the sound as the Abbé's former secretary dropped to the floor, his blood splattered and pooling on the terra-cotta tiles. Abraham crossed the room to where Gédéon stood over the body. The leaders' eyes met, acknowledging the closure this brought them both. This man, who eluded them at Pont-de-Montvert, had since caused the Huguenots much misery. No longer.

With no employers left to protect, the servants fled.

"Let them go!" Abraham cried.

The room emptied of all but the Camisards. Chests heaving, they raised a victory cry.

"We've taken possession of the land!" shouted Gabriel.

"The Lord of heaven's armies is on our side!" proclaimed Paul.

Mazel gave orders. "Search the premises! Seize anything valuable to our cause!"

Fighters scattered through the house. With Gédéon by his side, Abraham stayed in the main room, praying, listening for the next instructions. They came loud and clear. *Burn the buildings!*

Camisards returned whooping and waving their bounty: eighty gold coins and several firearms. Plus food supplies. A veritable treasure! God's favor was with them indeed.

Abraham called them to order. "Once again, the Almighty requires we purge the land, using iron and fire as first instructed in my dream. Burn the buildings!"

Men obeyed at once, setting ablaze the homes of the *notaire* and the parish priest, as well as the church.

Fighters filled a street lit and warmed by flames. Heads held high, the men sang Psalms as they trooped out of town and into the forest. Far into the woods, they sought shelter, soon settling behind a stack of granite boulders. After a quick, cold dinner, most fell into a dreamless sleep despite the wet ground. Abraham slept little, rising well before daylight for time alone with God. How else would he know what to do next?

Not long after sunrise, Mazel and Gédéon led their band north, toward the Almighty's next assignment. Damp clothes dried in the autumn sun, and faces turned upward toward the warmth. Many a heart soared, grateful to be on the journey. No matter how it ended.

Midmorning, Gabriel and Paul fell in beside the leaders.

"Where's the boy?" demanded Abraham. "I don't want him left unattended."

"At the rear," said Gabriel. "No need to worry. My nephew will get away with nothing under Rolland's watch."

Paul leaned in. "Sir, for some time now, someone's followed us. He conceals himself in the foliage along the road."

"We propose that Paul and I go ahead a bit," said Gabriel, "then slip undetected into the forest. We'll circle back around and make the man's acquaintance. If he's an enemy, we'll convince him we're on his side."

"And discover what he's up to," added Paul.

"You've got it all figured out, haven't you?" Gédéon's eyes narrowed at the lieutenants. "Then what?"

Keeping in step with his leaders, Gabriel spoke with force. "Once we know if he's for or against us, we'll take action accordingly."

The men marched on in silence. Finally, Gédéon spoke. "It's not a bad plan. I say go."

Abraham nodded. The pair took off.

A little over an hour later, Mazel, Gédéon, and the fighters arrived at a hamlet. Drawn by thirst, they headed as one toward the central village fountain.

"Hey! What's this?" cried Gédéon.

The fighters picked up speed and surrounded the water basin. On the edge sat a man, bound and gagged. Gabriel stood to his right, Paul to his left.

"Our spy!" said Gabriel.

"Tell us what happened," demanded Abraham.

"We came around behind this man and followed him as he trailed you all," Paul said. His face darkened.

Gabriel took up the story. "We caught up with him and let him believe we were part of Bâville's civilian militia."

"From another region," said Paul.

"He made the mistake of boasting that he followed a band of Camisards, collecting information to pass on to the Governor's soldiers." Gabriel spat at the man's feet.

Fighters jostled and surged, ready to tear the prisoner apart. Informants were among their worst enemies.

Gédéon flung his arms wide and ordered the men to stand down. "Gabriel and Paul are his guards. No one else touch him, for now."

Mazel and Gédéon looked to each other. Without speaking, they knew the next move. God's orders for the day meant reaching their destination, a village farther ahead. They had business to attend to in that place.

After drinking their fill and replenishing their gourds, the Camisards marched on, their prisoner in tow. With Gabriel gripping one arm and Paul the other, they hauled the man down the road.

As the troop entered the village, Gédéon directed the men according to God's predawn instructions. Jean Massip confirmed which was the home of a local noble, yet another ruthless persecutor of the Huguenots.

154

There wasn't a villager or clergy in sight. Had someone warned them, after all?

"Iron and fire!" Gédéon shouted, repeating the line from Abraham's dream. "The land shall be purged of all evil, all injustice. All of you go, carry out the Almighty's will. Burn the buildings!"

The Camisards dispersed and set ablaze the home of the local noble, the church, and the presbytery.

Abraham grabbed Rolland as he ran by. "Where's the boy?"

"Right here," Rolland said, gesturing behind him into empty space.

"We left him under your supervision!" shouted Gabriel, wrenching the prisoner's arm as he stepped forward.

"There he is!" Paul pointed to the side of the church.

Gabriel-Isaac scrambled up a low limestone wall. At the top, he prepared to jump to the other side. Rolland raced forward, grabbed one of his legs, and yanked him to the ground. With a scowl, he jerked Gabriel-Isaac back onto his feet, then dragged him out to the road.

Faced with the two leaders and his uncles, Gabriel-Isaac squared his shoulders.

"You were meant to stay with me," said Rolland, eyes blazing.

"How can I help our cause if you won't let me do anything?"

"Following orders is the first duty of every soldier," growled Rolland.

"This is exactly why we didn't want you out here," said Uncle Gabriel. He took a step toward his nephew, then tightened his grip on the prisoner's arm. "We'll deal with you later."

Sparks filled the air as the church roof collapsed, shooting flames high into the sky.

The rest of the fighters regrouped in the street around the leaders, panting from exertion and exhilaration. Sweat dripped from many brows despite the cool temperature.

Gédéon turned to Mazel. "We've accomplished our mission. But there's one more matter."

Abraham gave a slight nod. What to do with the prisoner?

God spoke swift and clear. Abraham faced Gédéon. "The Lord has declared the spy must serve as an example. We are to execute him."

Gabriel reached for his musket. Gédéon stopped him. "I'll do it."

Gédéon carried out the order, then propped the body against the remains of the charred church door. Grabbing an unburnt plank and a piece of charcoal, he scratched a warning: "So it will be for traitors and persecutors of the children of God." He propped the sign on the dead man's chest, then stood back with the rest of the men. Tomorrow, when people flocked from the countryside to this place for a regional fair, the message would be clear. Anyone who dared betray the Camisards paid a steep price.

Abraham led in giving thanks to the Almighty for protection and victory. With raised voices, the troop sang the Psalm that had become their anthem.

Let God arise, let His enemies be scattered.[7]

Violence was part of war. Abraham no longer questioned the Camisards' actions. They'd followed God's orders to the letter. To have done otherwise would be disobedience. With every fiber of his being, Abraham believed that God had led them down this unexpected path, Abraham merely the recipient and communicator of the Almighty's plans.

Mazel turned to Gédéon, again grateful they created an unstoppable team, a unity of spiritual leadership and military skill. They still needed to figure out what to do with Gabriel-Isaac, but that could wait.

"Onward!" Mazel cried. "To the next assignment. We continue southward."

Gédéon barely contained his glee. "Yes, right through Capitaine Poul's hometown. His troops garrison there, plus his family resides within the fortified walls."

Abraham ran his hand across his face. They had experienced more victory than defeat over Capitaine Poul and his troops. Why, then, did it seem Gédéon still had a score to settle?

---

[7] Psalm 68:1 (NKJV)

CHAPTER 28
RESISTANCE

21 October 1702
St. Hippolyte du Fort
Southern Cévennes

Suzanne lay her writing quill on her oak desk and shook her cramped hand. She shut her eyes for a moment, contemplating her next words. A rush of wind rattled a branch against the window before her, and she opened her eyes in time to witness a spray of autumnal leaves in the early dawn light.

Scarlet, amber, and ochre, they floated, then fluttered toward the ground. She loved this view from the second-story bedroom she shared with Marie, who dozed nearby. Rising before the rest of the family to write was working out well.

Suzanne touched the letter lying to her right on the desk, dated four weeks prior but only delivered yesterday, delayed for unknown reasons. It didn't matter. Gratitude filled her at her brother's familiar scrawl and his assurances that all was well. Gabriel-Isaac didn't write often. This was only the second missive in three months. Both times the messenger delivered the precious words from her brother, something inside her loosened. The assurance of his safety, at least at the time he wrote, soothed some tight part of her soul.

His report split her prayers between Rolland, out recruiting men in the eastern Cévennes, and Uncle Gabriel and Uncle Paul, who had joined Gédéon Laporte and Abraham Mazel in the north. Best of all from her perspective, they'd left Gabriel-Isaac behind, deeming him not yet ready for battle. Her brother's frustration came through loud and clear in the note, but Suzanne thanked God and her uncles for holding him back.

She glanced outside again, the growing light reminding her to focus and write down more thoughts before the day began. Once she finished recording her personal reflections, she slipped the pages into a dossier left from her school days and concealed the folder under layers of fresh parchment in her desk drawer. These words were private and not meant to be read by others, at least not now.

After placing a clean sheet before her, she picked up her quill pen and dipped it into the glass inkwell. She tapped the pen a few times against the well's edge, then began describing current events. The pen's sharpened end scratched along the thick paper, another satisfying part of recording history in the making.

A smile touched her lips. Gabriel-Isaac's letters informed her on events in the region, enabling her to write about happenings well beyond St. Hippolyte. Also, she gained information chatting with their neighbors during their weekly trips to the open market. Truly, God arranged things well.

Across the room, Marie yawned and sat up. Suzanne smiled at her sleepy sister. "Ready to start your day?"

Marie nodded and rubbed her eyes. "Finished with your writing?"

"For now. If there's time between chores later, I'll add to the story of our parents' adventures."

"I can't wait to read the next part." Marie stood and slowly pulled on her maroon wool skirt. "I love reading about Maman and Papa. It helps me feel . . . I don't know. Closer to them."

"Writing it out helps me too, Marie. Maybe someday others, at least in our family, can read it and be inspired by their courage."

The sisters descended to the kitchen where Grand-mère sliced bread fresh from the oven. Her wild berry jam and hand-cranked butter sat ready on the table. Marc-André appeared at the back door with a pail of milk from a neighbor's cow. Suzanne took it off his hands and poured the contents into an iron pot she then placed on the hook over the kitchen fire. Once it warmed, she ladled the milk into drinking bowls, and the family, now reduced to four, held hands and thanked the Lord for the food and the day ahead.

After Marc-André and Marie left for school, Suzanne began working her way through her list of daily chores, washing the breakfast dishes before grabbing her cloak from a peg and stepping out the back door. She fed the chickens, enjoying their skirmish over kitchen scraps, then added their eggs to her basket before joining Grand-mère in the potager. Suzanne knelt between rows of vegetables and medicinal herbs and set about weeding and harvesting. She didn't look up until the arrival of their part-time cook and housekeeper, Flore.

Suzanne rose to greet the adult daughter of the Tessier family's longtime servant Marion, then handed her a basket of fresh vegetables for the day's soup and followed her into the house. Heading back upstairs, Suzanne whispered a prayer of thanks to God for the funds earned through midwifery that allowed them to employ Flore for cooking and laundry. Without Flore washing the family's clothes and linen bedsheets in the freezing water running through an outside basin at the far end of the Château, then toting the heavy items back to the Lacombe house to dry, it would be impossible for Suzanne to find the time and energy to write.

Back at her desk, Suzanne wrote another chapter of her parents' story. Her mother's nocturnal adventures leading pastors to hidden meetings was admirable. But not something Suzanne could do. She laughed out loud. Her sense of direction was notoriously awful. Papa's contribution had been passing messages of meetings and other vital information as he delivered his wines. Had anyone betrayed him for doing so, the authorities would have sent him to the galleys long ago.

Suzanne had always assumed such bravery was only for her parents. Why, then, did she long to do more? A hidden inner well had unlocked within her, revealing a long-buried part of herself. On one level, her acute sense of responsibility plus her God-given nature had kept her focused on caring for others. There was nothing wrong with that. But as those characteristics had combined with her desire to have life under control, to feel secure, fear had entered and taken root. With her slow and steady acceptance of God's love, the old, fearful ways and patterns receded, and in their place came new strength and resolve.

She rose from her desk and stretched, then walked a slow circle around her bedroom, musing, pondering surprising news Marguerite shared recently—of how she transmitted secret messages regarding underground meeting places and other resistance-related activities and had also become a night guide, leading visiting preachers to the gatherings. Marguerite filled the void left by Maman and Papa.

According to Marguerite, the Huguenots taking part in active resistance could use more help. There were arms and supplies to get to the fighting Camisards, plus information on certain people and locations. Despite admiring Marguerite's activities, Suzanne had dismissed the idea of being involved in that way herself. But that strong desire to do more remained.

She stopped to gaze out her window at the enormous gingko marking the edge of their front garden and standing sentry over the front vineyard beyond. Like her mother before her, Suzanne loved that tree and its glittering golden leaves. She opened the window, inhaled fresh air, and listened to the wind rustling through the branches.

It was time, and she felt ready. She would step out into the world and resist actively, but only in a way that matched who she was. And she had an idea of how to do just that.

———————————

"So you want to become a messenger?" Marguerite asked. "While you do midwifery rounds?" Her voice was stern.

Suzanne stood her ground. In the past, she'd given too much place to others' opinions. Especially when it came to Marguerite, whose strong and sure beliefs made it easy to follow her lead. But no longer.

"That's what I said, and that's what I intend to do." Suzanne attempted to hold her friend's gaze.

Marguerite looked toward the tall windows lining the length of the *moulin*. Just beyond, the river Vidourle rushed along, almost overflowing after days of torrential rains. "You understand the risk, right? If you're caught—"

"Of course! I know the danger involved and the consequences. I'm not ignorant."

"I never said you were!"

"Then don't treat me like a child," Suzanne said. "I'm ready to join your resistance work. It's the most natural thing in the world for me to transmit information on my midwifery rounds. Even when the dragoons first came to St. Hippolyte, Grand-mère used such visits as an excuse to be out and about."

Marguerite shrugged. "Alright then. In fact, this is good timing. I've received word that there will be a worship gathering tomorrow night.

The first in our area since the raid, since your parents . . ." She lowered her head. "Are you sure you're ready for this?"

Suzanne huffed. "Marguerite! You don't have to tiptoe around me or the subject of the last assembly. I was at the raid and certainly don't need to be shielded from the results. I believe God wants me to take this step. It's my way of contributing like my parents, but in a way that fits me."

Marguerite's face softened. Suzanne loved how her friend's compassion always leaked through her tough exterior.

"So, give me the information on the assembly and I'll get it out. Grand-mère has agreed that I take over most of her routine visits. She knows and approves of my delivering messages as well as babies." Suzanne grinned.

Marguerite rolled her eyes. "The meeting will be around midnight in the *grotte* about a half hour walk up the eastern mountains from your home. Up the Route de Lasalle, toward Monoblet. We haven't met there in a while, so it should be a secure location."

Suzanne nodded. "I'll start sharing the news this afternoon on the other side of town. Besides checking in on two mothers, I'll visit Aunt Anne. I haven't seen her in a while."

"Perfect! Start with her. Word will spread quickly through her Bedos in-laws." Marguerite glanced at the wheat mill and a stack of empty sacks. "I must get back to work. I have orders to fill. People are so impatient when it comes to their flour. As if they lived by bread alone." Marguerite nudged Suzanne and laughed. "You're not the only one who can make puns about her work."

"Very funny. We're both rather clever today. Or is it silly? Either way, it feels good to laugh. I need to go, too. Marc-André and Marie will return soon for the midday meal."

With three *bisous*, the friends bid each other goodbye. Suzanne stretched the five-minute walk between their homes into ten. Swollen gray-black clouds hovered overhead but dropped no rain for the moment. So far, the day had brought a welcome lull in the ongoing stormy weather.

Suzanne's new assignment filled her with energy, a lightness, along with an undercurrent of anxiety. She breathed a prayer for courage. God had given her this task, and she welcomed it. But that didn't prevent fear from rearing its ugly head.

Under the gingko tree, she opened her arms wide as a few golden leaves sprinkled down. She received her heavenly Father's goodness and assurance, letting the beauty wash over her like a cleansing rain.

At the midday meal, Suzanne listened to Marc-André and Marie recount their morning at school. Normally, she made mental notes of the theological errors in what they'd learned, to address them with reteaching in the evening. Not today. Her attention drifted across town, where she'd soon start spreading news of tomorrow night's assembly.

They finished their chestnut soup and sausages, and she jumped up to stack the dishes. The sooner the cleanup was behind her, the sooner she'd be out the door.

"I'll tend to that." Grand-mère's eyes carried a spark. "And I'll make sure Marc-André and Marie get back to school on time. Go ahead and prepare for your rounds."

"Aren't you going, Grand-mère?" asked Marie, her little face filled with concern. "Are you sick?"

"I'm perfectly well, child. But your sister is ready to take on more responsibility."

Suzanne met her grandmother's gaze, unspoken thoughts understood. Today, she entered into the role of midwife more fully *and* into active resistance work. Her shoulders tightened a bit at the sense of a mantle settling on them.

"*Merci*, Grand-mère."

"Be sure you supply your basket correctly. If you need anything, you can take it from mine."

"*Oui*, Grand-mère." Suzanne hid her smile. Her grandmother was passing the torch while keeping a firm eye on the new bearer.

Under a sprinkling of autumn rain, Suzanne crossed the bridge over the river. Bursts of crimson foliage dotted the bank of the swollen Vidourle. Scents of greenery and minerals from the river rocks filled the moist air. She adjusted her bonnet and wrapped her woolen cloak tighter, attempting to keep dry out on the open bridge. Gusts of wind blew, swaying branches and releasing colorful leaves onto the damp ground. She passed the guards without trouble then ducked around the corner. The tall row houses lining the narrow streets provided some protection from the weather. Just in time. Within minutes, the light drizzle became driving sheets of water.

Caught in a Cévenol episode, including dazzling flashes of lightning and earsplitting cracks of thunder, she picked up her pace. Within minutes, the streets filled with water streaming toward the river. Cold moisture pierced her leather shoes, reaching through woolen stockings to her skin.

Head down, skirts raised to midcalf, she waded along as briskly as possible. She didn't see him. Without warning, a hand reached out of the driving rain and pulled her into an alcove.

CHAPTER 29

SAVING LIGHT

21–22 October 1702
La Vallée Française
Northwestern Cévennes

Sheets of unending rain, borne on ferocious winds, slashed across the plains. Mazel and Laporte led their troop onward, intent on following God's orders to head south. The sunset hour had taken with it the meager fragments of light piercing the storm. Putting one foot in front of the other, the bedraggled Camisards no longer had any sense of time. Maybe it was past midnight.

Abraham wiped his drenched face with a soggy handkerchief and turned to Gédéon. "Do you know where we are?"

"No. I was hoping you did."

Glancing to the back of the line, where Rolland brought up the rear, Abraham wished Jean Massip would somehow appear. "We could really use Massip's guiding skills right now."

"Yes. Too bad it was necessary he escort Gabriel-Isaac home to St. Hippolyte. The boy couldn't be trusted to obey orders."

Abraham nodded. The troop trudged along in silence, weary from traveling for days under nearly continuous torrential rain.

Another hour down the road, Abraham prayed out loud. "Lord, we're lost and can't see the way forward. Literally. Please show us where to go."

"Amen," said Gédéon. "Should we stop and wait? Maybe the rain will cease."

"That could take hours, and we're all exhausted and famished. We must keep moving until we find shelter and food, trusting the Almighty to guide our steps."

Not five minutes later, Mazel came to a sudden halt. "Wait!" He held up a hand.

Gédéon collided into Abraham, men down the line into each other. They waited, listening. The only sounds were splashing rain and the rustle of the fighters gathering around.

Suddenly, a brilliant light surrounded the men, illuminating their faces. It then moved to the right.

"What is that?" Gédéon cried.

"You see it too?" Abraham's voice cracked.

"It doesn't make sense!"

"Rays of light? How could that be?"

"Is it angels?"

"It twinkles!"

"Like the crystals of a chandelier reflecting candlelight!"

"Or diamonds!"

Abraham put a finger on his lips. "Quiet!" All gazed at the miraculous light for another minute, then it faded away.

"It's a sign from God," said Mazel, "showing us the direction we need to go." His voice was thick with awe. Doubt had crept into his soul as they'd forged through hours of darkness under driving rain. Every time he questioned the veracity of their mission, his heavenly Father reminded him of his presence, protection, and power.

"Let's get going, then!" said Gédéon. "We move to our right."

Without another word, the men marched on through the rain, the troop fortified by God's intervention. Within a half hour, they arrived at an auberge. Murmurs of gratitude rippled through the ranks. The Almighty had led them to shelter and sustenance.

Seated around the inn's dining room, the Camisards guzzled tankards of ale and consumed quantities of cured sausages. That the sympathetic innkeeper allowed them entry in the middle of the night was yet another miracle. The men crowded by the roaring fire, taking turns rotating themselves back to front like roasting chickens, attempting to thaw their bodies and dry their clothes.

Abraham observed his men, grateful for each one, especially Rolland and the lieutenants Gabriel and Paul. But why did Gédéon look like a caged animal pacing in the corner? Mazel crossed the room and joined his fellow leader.

"You aren't resting and enjoying the repast with the others. Why?"

Gédéon's eyes darted from one side of the room to the other, then he leaned close. "There were three servants here when we arrived. Now there are only two. Our men continue to eat and drink at such a rate, you'd think all three servants would be required."

Abraham scanned the room, then shrugged his shoulders. "I can't say I took any notice."

"You, my brother, focus constantly on the spiritual, the unseen. It's my job to keep an eye on practical matters."

"True, my friend. What is significant about a servant's absence?"

Gédéon's eyes flashed. "I can't explain it, but I think he's gone to report our presence here to the local authorities. As you know, Capitaine Poul has men stationed throughout this region."

Abraham studied his colleague. Was this about Gédéon's fixation with the capitaine? Gédéon still seemed to carry a grudge against the man.

Mazel shut his eyes and listened to the Almighty. Receiving clarity only took a moment. "I believe God prompted you to notice the servant's absence and is again providing protection. We must leave."

Gédéon strode to the front of the room. "Men, we're moving out. Now."

Several grumbled.

"God has spoken," Abraham said, his voice firm. "We go."

In short order, the Camisards were on the road again, wishing they could have tarried longer in the dry warmth, with food and drink at hand. But safety and God's word propelled them on.

Three hours later, they stumbled into a village. Again soaked to the skin, they found shelter in an empty *bergerie* on the outskirts. Huddled together for warmth like the sheep usually inhabiting the place, they immediately fell into deep slumber, many no doubt dreaming of flocks.

Sunrise came only a few hours later. Abraham rose early as usual but allowed the bone-weary men to sleep. After prayer, he awakened Gabriel and Paul and sent them to scout ahead.

Midmorning, the lieutenants returned with the report that the next town was well guarded by Capitaine Poul's soldiers. Abraham paced, seeking the Lord for guidance. Clear direction came. They were not to enter that place but to head east.

Mazel gave the orders, and the weary band headed out. God smiled on them, this time in the form of a bright autumn sun, which did much to lift the fighters' spirits and dry their clothes. As they walked, Abraham prayed for their strength and morale.

Three hours later, they arrived at their God-given destination in the valley called Française. The town *lavoir* provided a somewhat sheltered spot for rest as the sun moved into the western half of the sky. Mazel paced and prayed and received more guidance. They were to hold a nocturnal worship assembly. He wasn't sure where, but God would show them.

Rolland, Gabriel, and Paul volunteered to spread the information through the nearby hamlets and towns. Abraham and Gédéon sent the three off, grateful they had men willing to give up needed rest while submitting to further risk.

In the early evening, Rolland and his lieutenants returned with the news of a cave that sat below a perched village and would work for the worship service. Again, Abraham stood in awe of God's continual provision.

Toward midnight, Mazel and Gédéon led their men through the forest. At the mouth of a cave, the two leaders glanced at each other, then bent over and entered together. If there was any danger, they'd face it first.

Torchlight and the flickering of candles held by a hundred Huguenot brothers and sisters filled the cave with warmth and light. Abraham drank in the sight.

His eyes landed on a familiar figure waiting at the bottom, someone he hadn't seen since the incident with the Abbé du Chaila at Pont-de-Montvert. Abraham made his way down, careful to avoid slipping on the slick rocks and boulders lining the way.

Although he didn't know any of the gathered Huguenots, he murmured bonsoir as he passed through the crowd. More than once, he overheard his name, along with mentions of "the dream," "black cows," and even the Abbé du Chaila. Someone greeted him as Chef des Camisards, acknowledging him as the leader of the fighters. He fulfilled that role with his men but hadn't realized others saw him as such.

He ducked his head, absorbing this revelation as he continued to the bottom of the cave. Water seeping down the walls and escaping through hidden nooks and crannies in the dark recesses beyond left the floor mucky. Abraham barely registered all that and instead focused on his fellow prophet and friend Salomon Couderc, greeting him with three *bisous*.

"Salomon! Brother! You are a welcome sight."

"Abraham! It's good to see you, too. Hard to believe it's been three months since our confrontation with the Abbé. However, your exploits throughout the Cévennes have reached our ears."

"We follow God's instructions only. Nothing more, nothing less. I heard you were farther in the north with Jouany, leading up to eighty men."

"*Oui.* Also following the directions of the Almighty."

Mazel locked eyes with Couderc. "We live in a remarkable moment in history. May we be faithful to the entirety of God's purposes." Abraham scanned the packed cave, filled with expectant Huguenots. "Salomon, will you preach to us all tonight? It would be an honor to hear what God has to say through you."

Couderc bowed his head, then lifted it to meet Abraham's gaze. "It would be my privilege."

Gédéon joined them in prayer, then he and Mazel sat near the front, Gédéon dozing off almost immediately. Abraham chuckled to himself. He couldn't blame his companion. They'd been on the road in terrible conditions for days.

Absorbed in Couderc's impassioned preaching, Abraham hadn't noticed a man making his way through the crowd, until a Camisard stepped in to intercept the rough-looking intruder and brought him to the front. Salomon ceased speaking, and a hush fell over the assembly.

Mazel stood. "What's your errand?"

"Sir, local resisters sent me to invite you to our village of Canourgue tomorrow. It's the one you see perched on the hill above this place."

Despite the man speaking in low tones, Gédéon startled awake and onto his feet.

"Why, may I ask?" Abraham studied the villager.

"Many of us support the cause of resistance. You fight for us all."

"That's good to hear. But why should we come to Canourgue?"

"Our mayor is also the chief magistrate of the region."

"Get to the point," Gédéon muttered.

The peasant turned his attention to Gédéon. "This man has denounced your troop, sir. To Capitaine Poul."

Gédéon jolted. Abraham had never seen his coleader's spine as rigid or his eyes as fierce.

"How can you know this information?" Gédéon demanded.

"My sister works as the mayor's housekeeper. She hears things, including the *maire*'s boast of bearing information of your troop's movements to Capitaine Poul."

Gédéon reared as if shot. "Let's stop him. Now."

Abraham placed a firm hand on his arm and pulled him back. "We'll pray on it and wait for the Almighty's guidance."

The peasant bowed his head and melted back through the crowd.

"What if this *is* from God?" Gédéon asked. "This man just handed us valuable information. We should strike now under cover of night, deal with this mayor and any others who inform on us."

"Prayer first, Gédéon. In the morning, I'll let you know how God directs us."

Abraham motioned for Salomon to resume preaching. Gédéon struggled for self-control, finally taking his seat with a curt nod. Mazel sat too, his thoughts drifting elsewhere. Was this news to be trusted? Or was it a trap? God would show them.

Mazel's greater concern was for Gédéon. Something in his colleague's reactions still didn't sit right. Once again, an edge had surfaced, an odd intensity that revolved around mention of Capitaine Poul.

Couderc preached well and long. All present had great respect for the prophet and were hungry for the teaching, but the relative warmth from so many bodies crammed into the space made the pull of sleep hard to resist. More than one Camisard dozed off until nudged awake by another.

A few hours before dawn, the gathering ended. The local Huguenots streamed out and toward their homes. The Camisards would stay put for what remained of the night. Within minutes, most were sound asleep, though not Abraham. Like Jesus, he met with his Father during the quiet night hours. He needed that time to pray and hear what God would have the Camisards do. Were they to go to the village clinging to the mountain above and deal with the mayor?

169

Abraham paced until the Voice came through strong and clear. They were to avoid Canourgue and the renegade mayor. He tiptoed through the sprawled fighters until he found Gédéon and Salomon leaning against tall boulders, still awake. Abraham delivered the message, then moved back to his spot near the bottom and settled into sleep.

As the first rays of dawn crept into the mouth of the cave, he stirred and sat up. Movement near the opening drew his attention. Blinking off the remnants of sleep, he watched two figures creep out. He rose and moved toward the men, stepping over sleeping Camisards.

The two men disappeared into the early morning mist, but not before Abraham saw who they were. He sucked in his breath. Gédéon and Couderc had left despite God's instructions. A chill ran through his body, and he fell to his knees.

CHAPTER 30

THUNDERSTRUCK

21 October 1702
St. Hippolyte du Fort
Southern Cévennes

Terror spiked through Suzanne's every nerve. A boom of thunder shook the ground, and lightning cracked so close she thought her heart might stop. At least the flash illuminated the alcove and revealed the person who'd pulled her into the tiny space.

Charles Fesquet grinned down at her. "You must not have heard my greeting!"

Rivulets of rain ran off his face and onto hers. Stunned, she couldn't respond for several seconds. Finding herself crammed next to Charles was not part of her plan. She tried hard to ignore their touching shoulders and his eyes, soft as brown velvet.

"Bonjour, Charles! I didn't hear or see you. You scared me half to death."

"I'm so sorry. What are you doing out in this weather?"

"I could ask you the same."

"I'm on my way to the Château de Planque, to see Lord Valmalle."

"Lord Valmalle? But aren't you in a partnership with my uncle Philippe?"

"Yes! And I'm grateful that your Grand-mère suggested it. Your uncle's *vendange* this year were even better than expected, and his grapes complement ours from Domaine la Grand'Terre well. The vintages that result from the combined harvest should be interesting."

"I'm glad it worked out. Your trip to Tornac was worth it then. Even with Gabriel-Isaac and me along for the ride."

Charles met her gaze directly. "That was the best part."

Suzanne's pulse raced while everything else inside her seemed to melt. This wouldn't do. Charles was off-limits. She looked away, at the cords of rainwater filling the street.

What if Charles discovered she was on her way to deliver information about an illegal Huguenot gathering? As long as the Fesquets weren't aware of when or where the services took place, they could look the other way. He could never know the details or her new role in transmitting messages.

She looked back to Charles. "You haven't answered my question. Why were you on the way to the Château de Planque?" She tried to appear firm and not waver at the shadow of disappointment crossing his face.

"Well, that's a funny thing. Lord Valmalle is desperate to partner with us. Especially since your father is . . ." Charles's face drained of color. "Suzanne, I'm so sorry."

She stared at the rain splashing hard in the street. "You've heard, then?"

"Our family greatly regrets your loss. Pierre Lacombe was an excellent man."

"Thank you, Charles."

"That's why I'm on my way to the Château. Without your father overseeing the vineyards, Valmalle needs us."

"Will you help him?"

"I don't know. Today, I'll find out what he proposes. My father and I will decide from there. Anyway, he only needs help until your brother is ready. Lord Valmalle awaits the completion of the apprenticeship with impatience. How's Gabriel-Isaac doing? I've been back to Tornac twice, but he wasn't around."

Here was yet another subject that must remain hidden between them. What would Charles think once he discovered that Gabriel-Isaac wasn't returning to work the Château de Planque vineyards? That their trip to Tornac was a cover for his true destination?

A bolt of lightning filled the street with its blinding light. Almost immediately, a clap of thunder shook everything around them. A welcome distraction.

"Suzanne, look! The water's rising over the first steps of the houses. The street's flooding." Charles leaned out of the alcove, then pulled back in, drenched anew. "I can't see very far. I think we best get on our way."

"Yes, of course. We should go before it gets worse." She patted the basket hooked over her arm. "I'm on my rounds to check on expecting mothers, then I'll visit my aunt Anne." Grateful the storm spared her from lying outright, she spoke the truth, just omitting the most significant reason for her outing. She needed to toughen up and get used to eluding detection.

"Au revoir, Charles. It was nice to see you."

"Hold on! Can't you visit them later? You should return home, while it's still safe. You know how quickly these streets turn into rivers. We can go together, since I'm going that way."

Suzanne shook her head. She couldn't ignore the spark of hope in his voice alongside his genuine concern. As much as she wanted to spend more time with him, she had to put a stop to this.

"*Merci*, Charles. But I really must visit these women. It cannot wait." Childbirth and all that surrounded it provided her with the best cover. Though the mothers could wait another day for her visit, communicating the information about tonight's meeting could not.

"Suzanne! It isn't safe!"

She wanted to laugh. If he only knew.

"Charles, I'm going. It's what I must do." Today, she was stepping more fully into her calling in more ways than one. She could let nothing and no one stop her. Even him. Especially him.

Charles's brow ridged. "Then I'm going with you. The rain doesn't show any sign of stopping. We can deal with flooding and blockages together."

Elation flashed through Suzanne at thinking of him by her side. But how was she supposed to pass on the information of the underground service with him there?

A half hour later, the pair sat by the fire in Aunt Anne's salon, sipping hot tea. Warmed by the hearth and proximity to Charles, Suzanne fought the temptation to stay and prolong the moment. She cleared her throat.

"Aunt Anne, didn't you tell me earlier in the kitchen that there's something wrong with your father-in-law's wine barrels? A leak or something?"

"Ah, yes." Aunt Anne met her eyes. Suzanne had explained her true errand while they prepared the tea. "Charles, I wonder if you could take a look. Two casks seem to have significant leaks. They're down in our cellar."

"Of course. I'll take a look, see what I can do."

"*Merci*, Charles." Aunt Anne stood. "Follow me."

"And I'll be on my way." Suzanne rose to her feet and smoothed her still-damp skirt. "Those expecting mothers are, uh, expecting me."

Charles stood and glanced out the window, brows knit together. "Suzanne, although the rain has slowed down, the streets remain full of water. Can't you visit them tomorrow? I'd like to accompany you home once I check your aunt's wine casks."

"I'll be fine, Charles. I grew up here, just like you. Rain doesn't scare me, and I do know how to swim if needed."

Her attempt at humor didn't erase the worry from his face.

"She'll be fine," Aunt Anne said. "But my casks threaten to swim in puddles of wine if they're not fixed. Come, follow me." Without waiting for an answer, she turned and headed out of the room.

Charles searched Suzanne's face and then, with a sigh, followed her aunt to the cellar.

---

22 October 1702
Between St. Hippolyte du Fort
and Lasalle

Past secret journeys to gatherings had caused Suzanne a great deal of anxiety. With Marguerite leading the way, tonight hadn't been as difficult. Stars twinkled overhead, and the autumn evening was unseasonably warm. But entering the cave in the dead of night raised a flood of horrific memories, the stuff of nightmares.

What Suzanne experienced her last time in a cave was no dream. Images of her parents' arrests passed through her mind. Each step farther into this cave brought sharper stabs of grief.

Seeming to sense her turmoil, Marguerite grabbed Suzanne's hand and led her to a seat near the front of the assembly. They settled on the least-damp boulders.

Though Marguerite gave the appearance of being fearless, Suzanne knew her friend carried terrible sorrows, witnessed daily in her father's broken hands and her maman's facial scars suffered at the hands of the dragoons. Marguerite had vowed to let no such thing happen again, to herself or anyone else she loved. Suzanne appreciated Marguerite's strength and presence.

Being accepted by Marguerite into the network and spreading the word of tonight's meeting had filled Suzanne with a sense of purpose, almost as satisfying as helping a mother bring a child into the world. With this new way to contribute, Suzanne was finding her place in the resistance.

Light and warmth filled the cave as torch-bearing Huguenots streamed in. They arrived in small groups of two or three at a time to avoid detection.

Most of the local believers hadn't attended a meeting since the July raid. They'd needed to lie low as Governor Bâville increased pressure to wipe them out. Every week, more royal soldiers arrived to guard St. Hippolyte's fort, each new batch rougher than the last.

With armed Huguenot sentinels posted at the cave opening, the service began. As those gathered sang several Psalms, Suzanne let their truth comfort her soul. How she'd missed being with other believers and worshipping God together. She shut her eyes and soaked in the fellowship.

A stirring inside her started small and grew. She didn't recognize the inspiration at first, such a long time had passed since a major one had fallen on her. The stirring moved outward into her body, and her eyes opened wide. She almost pushed the trembling away.

Beloved! Fear not.

Choosing not to give in to fear, she stood. A hush spread through the crowd.

An elder approached. "The Holy Spirit is upon you. Speak! We will hear the impartation."

Suzanne let the words flow. Her voice spoke them out, but their origin came from above.

"Beloved children of God. I have seen your suffering. Be assured that I am with you always. I will never fail you. I will never abandon you. Who shall separate you from my love?"

The tremblings increased. Marguerite rose and reached her arm around Suzanne's waist as the message continued. "Nothing can separate us from the love of Christ! Not any type of trouble, hardship, persecution. Not even danger or the sword."

Suzanne paused, listening.

"Who shall separate us from the love of Christ? Shall trouble or hardship or persecution or famine or nakedness or danger or sword? Yes, we face death constantly, like sheep waiting for slaughter. But, in everything, we are more than conquerors because of His love for us."

A holy hush followed Suzanne's prophecy, until a cry pierced the silence. Marguerite's grip tightened.

"They're here!" shouted a watchman. "Royal troops!"

Shots rang out. Screams erupted from trapped Huguenots as they huddled and covered their young or stood and took aim with ancient muskets. Suzanne froze. It couldn't be happening again.

Beloved! Fear not. You are more than a conqueror through me, through my love.

Marguerite pulled Suzanne to the side. Crouched behind a large boulder, Suzanne waited for guidance. The Voice had led her to safety before, along with Gabriel-Isaac. Surely, God would do that again.

She peered around the edge of the boulder. The scene played out before her as an eerie déjà vu. Royal troops swept through the smoke and confusion, rounding up Suzanne's friends and neighbors. Children screamed when separated from their parents, the volume of the screams increasing to high-pitched wails as soldiers dragged Huguenots up and out of the cave.

A question wove through Suzanne's numbness. *Where are you, God?*

Beloved! Nothing shall separate you from my love. Even this. Two soldiers appeared before Marguerite and Suzanne and grabbed each of them by the arm, hauling them to their feet. One yelled to his captain. "This *fanatique* was 'prophesying' when we arrived."

"Good! One less self-proclaimed prophet to stir up the people. Keep going, men! Arrest them all!"

Marguerite wrestled hard and stomped the soldier's boot. He slapped her face, then dragged her toward the cave opening, Marguerite clawing at him and yelling the entire way.

Suzanne's captor looked around, muttering. "Any more rats hiding in dark corners?" He wrenched her along, then reached behind a large boulder and snatched a young man to his feet. Was she dreaming?

Jean Massip!

The soldier yanked Suzanne and Jean up through the cave. Behind the man's back, Jean spoke. "Fear not, Suzanne! More than conquerors through God's love."

Everything in Suzanne stilled even as the soldier continued dragging them toward the exit. She nodded at Jean, unable to find words.

Jean tilted as near Suzanne as possible. "Suzanne! I love—" The soldier shoved him through the cave opening, but not before Suzanne saw the love illuminating Jean's face. Light in the darkness.

CHAPTER 31
DISORDER

22–25 October 1702
La Vallée Française
Western Cévennes

Into midmorning, Abraham watched for the return of Gédéon and Salomon. Trouble was coming, possibly disaster. The only other time a fellow prophet disobeyed divine orders had led to his death. Perhaps, in Séguier's case, the Holy Spirit had led him on a unique path. Certainly, his martyrdom had inspired and inflamed the Huguenots of the Cévennes. But this situation was different.

Abraham watched as his fighters, now wide awake, stretched out stiff limbs and dug through rucksacks for scraps of food. Water pooling in low spots on the granite boulders would have to serve for quenching the men's thirst.

Since Gédéon and Salomon's desertion at dawn, Mazel had sought the Almighty's wisdom. To his surprise, God instructed him to go up the mountain, to the perched village of Canourgue, certainly the destination of the missing pair. God's original guidance to avoid the place had now been modified because of their disobedience. Abraham trusted his heavenly Father but couldn't shake the sense that difficulty lay ahead.

"Men!" he called out. "Time to pack up and go."

Rolland approached him, speaking low. "Where are Gédéon and Salomon? I don't see them anywhere."

Abraham shook his head. "Not now. I'll explain later, as the Almighty leads."

Rolland raised one eyebrow, studied Abraham a moment, then took up the position of rear guard.

Confusion and disorder would likely break out once the men knew that Gédéon and Couderc disobeyed God's earlier directions. Abraham could hardly believe it himself.

With Gabriel and Paul in the middle of the ranks, the Camisards moved out and up toward Canourgue, trudging along under an icy mixture of driving rain and sleet. They arrived at the outer wall around midday and gathered in a cluster of green oaks to rest a moment under the dripping branches. Eighty men huddled for warmth despite having walked for an hour and a half. Would they ever again experience the comfort of dry clothes or enough food to fill their bellies?

Clapping his hands for their attention, Abraham stood on a small boulder and waited until they quieted. "Men! I need to inform you—"

"Mazel, look!" Rolland shouted from the back of the troop.

The crowd parted as Gédéon and Salomon pushed through, hauling along a bound man. Mazel hopped down and strode toward them.

Gédéon spoke first. "Abraham, we apologize for our unsanctioned departure. But voilà!" He pointed at his prisoner. "This is the mayor of Canourgue, the very one who informed Capitaine Poul of our movements and led to us losing certain battles and many of our men."

Mazel didn't like the vengeful gleam in Gédéon's eyes. It was one thing if God led them to take such steps. But the Almighty's original direction was to avoid Canourgue, and here they stood with the village's mayor as their prisoner. Abraham could only deal with the issue at hand and address the disobedience later.

"What do you plan to do with the man?" he asked.

"You didn't mention I had a visitor when you abducted me," the mayor interrupted. A smirk plastered on his face, he focused on Gédéon. "While confronting me with all sorts of false accusations, you let him escape."

"We are concerned only with you," said Gédéon.

The mayor laughed out loud. "I'd be concerned about my friend if I were you. He has undoubtedly already informed my son, who will spread the news of your presence and of my capture at your hands. Surely the troops of the surrounding towns mobilize at this very moment."

Abraham's every nerve sprung to high alert. Because of the mayor's direct link to Capitaine Poul, who commanded many hundreds of troops plus the militias made up of local bourgeois, the Camisards would soon be under attack.

Gédéon blanched. His fingers dug into the prisoner's arm. Salomon bowed his head, probably praying. It was their only solution.

As the information traveled through the gathered Camisards, the sound of horses' hooves thundering through the valley below.

"That'll be Capitaine Poul now," said Gédéon through gritted teeth. "With his dragoons and the bourgeois militia he forces to march with him whether or not they want to—as he did my cousins from St. Hippolyte du Fort, both killed in a skirmish with Huguenots in a neighboring village."

Rolland climbed a nearby boulder. "Abraham! I also see a disturbance in the brush in the valley below us and to the west."

"And I see the movement of trees from the east," yelled another fighter, his frightened voice followed by others.

"They'll surround us soon!"

"We're trapped between this mountain and Poul's troops, coming from below and both sides."

"We're only eighty against their hundreds."

"We've only thirty guns. Most will malfunction in this rain. And the gunpowder is soaked."

Abraham listened for God's voice. It came swiftly. "We must leave immediately. The Lord of heaven's armies is with us and can overcome any number. But this time, his instructions are to flee. Now."

Gédéon planted his feet. "I disagree." With that, he lifted his musket and pulled the trigger. The mayor crumpled to the ground, dead. Salomon leaped away, his face hard as stone.

Before Abraham could decide the next step, the roar of advancing dragoons drew closer.

Again, Gédéon raised his musket. "We'll do the same to Capitaine Poul."

A sudden blast of wind drove sheets of rain and sleet through the trees. Disoriented, the Camisards swiveled right and left, trying to keep track of the troops approaching from all sides.

Capitaine Poul and his dragoons pierced the gray mist. Musket fire rained down on Mazel, Gédéon, and their men. Shots erupted from the Camisard fighters. Abraham kept his gun poised and ready for action. If only he could see clearly.

The crack of a musket shot exploded to his right. Mazel whirled toward the sound. At his feet lay Gédéon Laporte, dead, blood pooling under him.

"Go!" ordered Abraham. "Everyone flee!"

With royal soldiers on their heels, he didn't need to urge his men to make haste. He led the way down and across the river then up toward another high village. Under the barrage of constant fire by Poul's troops, the Camisards flew up the mountain.

Abraham and his men pushed through the scrubby brush and dripping trees to the village of Pompidou, where Poul's soldiers normally garrisoned. The location high on a mountain above the southern Cévennes made it an ideal location for Poul's troops and meant they were familiar with the surrounding area. Yet Mazel led true Cévenol men, born and bred on such terrain. Still, they needed a miracle to escape Capitaine Poul's troops bearing down on them on almost every side.

Despite the urgency, Mazel directed the Camisards to the royal troops' barracks, empty of the same soldiers pursuing them now. Certain Gédéon would find a measure of vengeance in the act, Mazel commanded his men to gather as many arms and supplies as possible. In minutes, they returned with a significant amount of gunpowder and bullets. Rolland waved a capitaine's uniform overhead. Gabriel held up two drums, Paul a musket.

Abraham led them out of the village just as Poul's soldiers entered it from another side. Shouts from the royal troops echoed through their raided barracks. The Camisards scrambled up steep, wet slopes toward the peak of the mountain. Too far ahead to stop a man from throwing a drum down at Poul's soldiers, Mazel grimaced. He didn't appreciate wasting supplies they'd procured at significant risk. Neither did Rolland. He grabbed the man's arm and hauled him on up the mountain.

At the top, Abraham motioned for the fighters to hurry on. Night would fall soon, and they needed refuge from the soldiers and the incessant rain. Mazel prayed for the fighters as they crossed the ridge, putting distance between themselves and Poul's troops. Even his lieutenants, Gabriel and Paul, were lagging.

Silence descended with the growing dark of night. Had the royal soldiers abandoned their pursuit until morning? Abraham directed the men to the wooded foothills of the towering Mount Aigoual. Soaked and exhausted, the fighters dropped immediately into whatever shelter they could find, under trees and behind or between boulders. Despite the surrounding wetness and complaints of ravenous hunger, sleep came to the men quickly. Except for Abraham.

Propped against a rock, he sat with his head in his hands. He thanked God for the Camisards' escape against all odds. Yet a dozen of his men had lost their lives in that day's conflict. Remembering his fellow leader shot dead at his feet, Mazel wept. If only Gédéon hadn't gone his own way and ignored God's direction.

Throughout the night, Abraham prayed, drifting in and out of sleep. Just before dawn, the Holy Spirit jolted him awake. *Leave now!* Abraham roused the bedraggled men with the warning. They hoisted rucksacks on weary shoulders and moved on, not a moment too soon. The sound of soldiers pursued them through the woods. Rolland brought up the rear, shouting orders like a sheep dog yapping at his flock to protect them from predators, while Gabriel and Paul served as side guards.

The Camisards followed paths known only to locals, moving swiftly and with stealth. Along the way, Abraham received more guidance. The men needed to return home. Drained after days of marching through cold, rain, and hunger, in and out of high mountain elevations, they needed time to recuperate their strength. And grieve their losses.

Once they outdistanced the royal soldiers and arrived in a safe location, Mazel called the remaining fighters together. They clustered behind a large granite outcropping, huddling close for warmth. Pale and dirty faces turned to him, waiting for his anointed words.

"Men, you have fought well, and the Almighty has seen fit to bring most of us to safety. Despite their great numbers, we eluded the royal troops." Abraham paused, his hand on his chest. "We mourn the loss of Gédéon Laporte and twelve brothers. They've given their lives for a just and holy cause."

As one, the men fell on their knees, heads bowed, pouring out their hearts to God. Afterward, they rose to their feet and, in low voices, sang Psalm 68, their battle hymn.

Abraham gave orders for the men to return home, then rendezvous in six days. With the words barely out of his mouth, the men breathed a collective sigh of relief and took off in different directions. Rolland, Gabriel, and Paul headed to Mialet, the rest to their respective villages. The prospect of a warm hearth and reconnection with family already lifted their spirits.

Once his men disappeared into back routes and out-of-the-way paths, a burden he hadn't known he carried fell from Abraham's shoulders. Not only was he relieved of the responsibility of leading alone, but he now had a few days to think and pray and rest.

But where to go? He couldn't return to his parents' home in St. Jean du Gard, as much as he'd like to see them. His notoriety had grown since the incident at Pont-de-Montvert and the subsequent fiery raids. A trusted friend who lived in a secluded valley came to mind. The man lived alone and would welcome Abraham despite the danger and potential consequences.

For Abraham, the simplicity of traveling alone after months of guiding others with peril all around was freeing, and the journey passed swiftly. As expected, his friend received him with open arms, and after a simple but warm meal of chestnut soup and fresh bread, Abraham slept the better part of two days.

On the third morning, his friend shook him awake with horrendous news. Capitaine Poul had ordered the decapitation of Gédéon Laporte and the twelve Camisards killed in the battle. Poul then organized his troops to march into Abraham's hometown of St. Jean du Gard in rows of two. Each of the first thirteen dragoons carried the head of one of Abraham's fallen men, displaying the gruesome trophies on bayonets held high in the air.

Word came that the grotesque parade would continue on to Anduze, where the dragoons would exhibit their bounty on the bridge. Next, the soldiers would move to St. Hippolyte du Fort, then on to Governor Bâville in Montpellier. Capitaine Poul's march served as a severe warning of the fate awaiting those who dared defy the authorities.

Despite risk of discovery, Abraham ran into the woods behind his friend's house. As he rocked on his hands and knees, his empty belly retched only bile. How much more could he endure? What effect would this grisly display have on his fighting men and on the Huguenot community?

Beloved! Fear not. I am with you always. The Voice came soft and gentle, without trembling other than that of Abraham's battered body still responding to the sickening news. He crumpled and added hot tears to the soaked earth.

CHAPTER 32
LIGHT IN THE DARKNESS

27 October 1702
St. Hippolyte du Fort
Southern Cévennes

Suzanne wrapped her woolen cloak tighter around her shoulders. She tucked the edges around her legs, trying to stave off incessant shivering, but to no avail. No matter what she did, it wouldn't stop. And no vision or prophetic inspiration accompanied this trembling.

She looked around the dank cell, drawing only quick breaths of the refuse-soaked atmosphere, then buried her face in her cloak, wishing for the release of tears. Hers had dried up for a while, hardening into a permanent lump in her throat.

Marguerite scooted closer, and the two huddled for warmth, knees tucked under their chins. A dozen other women—many she knew—filled the small cell, with only the icy stone floor for sitting and sleeping. Constant cold and hunger pierced them. One bowl of weak broth and a stale crust per day didn't help.

Suzanne lay her head on Marguerite's shoulder. The guards refused to give them any indication of what would happen. Would she and Marguerite be put on trial? Or executed with no process, a frequent occurrence since the Abbé's death?

What about Grand-mère, Marc-André, and Marie? They must know of Suzanne's capture but not her location. It had taken two months for Aunt Anne to get information on Maman's imprisonment. How long would it take this time?

Maman's face rose in Suzanne's mind, as it was the day they'd said goodbye in this very place. Her mother's strength and peace had marked Suzanne indelibly. The brilliant light of love, God's and Maman's, overcame the darkness of the circumstances. Maman had reflected the possibility of God's presence in any situation.

Suzanne sat straighter and looked at Marguerite. At least they were in this together. Marguerite had first argued daily with the guards, demanding more food and blankets. The only results were two beatings, leaving her subdued. *Lord, don't let the fire go out of my friend. Please give her wisdom in choosing her battles.*

Doors clanged down the corridor, announcing guards approaching with their fifth midday meal. Five days had passed, then, since the raid. How much longer would the Huguenot women arrested in the cave be kept here? And where was Jean Massip? How had he come to be at the worship gathering, not in Mialet with Gabriel-Isaac?

Suzanne hadn't seen Jean since the dragoons brought them to St. Hippolyte's prison-fort. The soldiers had separated the female prisoners from the males, then hauled them off in different directions. She didn't know where they'd taken Jean and the other men.

Despite her chilled bones, warmth spread through her chest as she remembered the moments with Jean as the soldier dragged them out of the cave and shoved them onto horses. Jean, perched behind the soldier assigned to take him away, had looked at her with such intensity. She would've expected to see fear or anger in him, but he only had a look of love. The crumbling chaotic world receded for the merest breath, and a bond formed between them that held an element of eternity.

She leaned back against the cell wall and ducked her head. Was it the love of Jesus shining through? She breathed deep. Yes, it was God's love beaming through Jean, straight to her heart. And if she wasn't mistaken, there was more. Did Jean love her as well? The experience of God's love and quite possibly Jean's stirred something in her that brought comfort, even in this place.

Perfect love drives out fear. The Voice's whisper broke the dam of Suzanne's tears. She cried on Marguerite's shoulder, releasing hard bits of anxiety that still clung to her soul.

Marguerite leaned her head on Suzanne's and joined her in the cathartic release. Shortly, a moment of peace descended over them, giving Suzanne hope like a light in the darkness. Then the iron door to their cell crashed open.

Pintarde entered, the guard who inspired the most terror. Not that any of the guards who worked the dungeons were kind. But the burly, unpredictable Pintarde appeared slightly unhinged. The women scooted together in a corner of the cell and cowered, watching the man's every gesture. A few days ago, he'd taken two of their cellmates away, where they did not know.

Pintarde dropped a tray at his feet, thin soup sloshing over the sides of tiny bowls. He reached into his pocket, pulled out half a baguette, and threw it on the filthy floor. No one moved. They'd not give him the pleasure of seeing them dive for food like starved animals. Nor did any woman wish to draw individual attention. Marguerite's earlier actions had proven that engaging their captors only brought more punishment.

Crossing his broad chest with his arms, Pintarde widened his stance. Usually, he left immediately after depositing the food. He eyed the huddling women, a leering sort of smile pasted on his cragged face.

"Ladies! I have good news! Well, not good for you." He sniggered. Suzanne's skin crawled from more than the fleas that were the prisoners' constant companions.

"Today, your Huguenot rebellion ends." He spat on the floor, close to the tray of soup. "Several days ago, your Camisards suffered a great defeat at the hands of our troops, led by Capitaine Poul." He paused and let the information sink in.

"Get on with it," Marguerite muttered.

Pintarde took a few steps toward her, his boot knocking into the tray and spilling the rest of the soup. "You have something to say?"

No one moved. Suzanne prayed her friend would keep her mouth shut and eyes averted. Marguerite did both. The guard glared at her a moment. Suzanne wasn't sure her hammering heart would ever return to a normal pace.

Pintarde spun toward other women in the cell. "Capitaine Poul and his men surrounded and killed a great number of your fighters, including the so-called military leader Gédéon Laporte. Ha! As if untrained peasants could compete with royal troops. What folly led them to believe they could ever hold out against our forces?"

The women remained silent, eyes cast downward.

"Now, Laporte and twelve of his fallen comrades are here in St. Hippolyte du Fort! They've been taking a brief tour of the region."

Suzanne glanced sideways at Marguerite. How could Laporte travel if he was dead?

"Capitaine Poul removed their heads to display his conquest in various villages. Right now, they're hanging on the bridge in the center of town. Every person in St. Hippolyte will see them at today's open market."

Suzanne's emotions swirled, looping like bats at dusk. She wanted to stomp around the cell, hit things, scream. It was sorrow enough that Gédéon Laporte was dead. He'd saved Jean from a fiery end in the Abbé du Chaila's dungeon, then brought him to Mialet. Now Gédéon's decapitated head hung in the middle of town? Had her uncles been involved in the battle? Were their heads among the others on display?

Pintarde belched, then continued. "Tomorrow, these trophies travel to Governor Bâville in Montpellier. Your little uprising is as dead as those heads outside." The guard cackled, then narrowed his eyes.

"Which one of you is Suzanne Lacombe?"

Marguerite grew rigid.

"I am," Suzanne blurted, before her warrior friend could defend her and create more trouble.

"Stand up!"

Suzanne rose to her feet and stood with her arms wrapped around her middle.

"And which is Marguerite Marolle?"

Gripping Marguerite's arm tight, Suzanne dug fingers in as a warning for her friend not to speak while scrambling to her feet.

"You're to come with me." Pintarde strode across the cell and grabbed each of their wrists. He hauled them out into the hallway, then dropped their hands to turn and lock the dungeon's door.

For a wild second, Suzanne considered fleeing. But there would be no escape from the depths of St. Hippolyte's prison-fort. No one had ever managed it in the fifteen years of its existence.

"Where are you taking us?" demanded Marguerite.

Suzanne ground her toe on her friend's foot and shot her a warning look. The last thing they needed right now was to annoy the guard. Marguerite's lips pursed tight. She gave her friend a slight nod.

Pintarde took them each by the arm and led them down the narrow, dark corridor. Beyond the guarded gate, he shoved them up the tightly curved staircase. With each step, Suzanne's stomach clenched tighter. Was he taking them to their deaths or to another prison? Why them?

On the ground floor, he led them out to the open courtyard. With her free hand, Suzanne shielded her eyes against the bright light, a shock after days in dim captivity.

Pintarde dragged them toward an imposing man standing in the yard's center, wearing an elegant waistcoat of blue and gold brocade. Completing his finery were wide crimson cuffs, silk stockings, and a plumed tricorn hat.

"Stand straight, ladies," Pintarde whispered. "The prison director awaits you."

The guard's mocking tone transformed to one of deference in front of the director, who stood like a statue next to a carved limestone well. "Monsieur de la Haye, I present you the requested prisoners."

Soldiers stood on the director's right and left. Their long curled wigs and wide mustaches and the gold embroidery on their blue coats struck Suzanne as ludicrous in the setting of the prison.

De la Haye looked down his aquiline nose at her, then Marguerite. "Are these the two requested?"

"Yes, sir."

"Which one is Marguerite Marolle?"

Pintarde pushed Marguerite forward. She tripped and fell to her knees.

"This clumsy one's Marolle," said Pintarde, yanking her up.

Marguerite shot him a fiery glance but said nothing.

De la Haye studied her, taking his time. Suzanne held her breath. *Please God, please God, please God. Don't let Marguerite make this worse.*

Finally, the director spoke. "It's your lucky day."

Marguerite lifted her chin.

De la Haye stepped closer. Marguerite didn't budge a centimeter.

"Mademoiselle Marolle, you're to return home. Now."

Suzanne stifled a cry of relief. What was happening? Had she heard correctly?

The director leveled a fierce glare at Marguerite. "We need the services of the Planque mill to keep us supplied with flour and olive oil. Your parents clearly aren't up to the task."

Marguerite's body stiffened at the mention of her parents.

Suzanne tensed. Don't give in now, Marguerite. Hold your tongue. No sign of weakness or belligerence would do.

De la Haye waved his hand, and the soldiers flanking him snapped to attention. "Lieutenant, escort Mademoiselle Marolle to the Planque mill. Take an additional man with you and leave him as a guard. We wouldn't want any messages to pass from Mademoiselle Marolle to the customers."

Were they aware Marguerite took part in the resistance in that way? Suzanne swallowed hard. Did they suspect her as well?

De la Haye addressed Marguerite. "Do not escape or run away, unless you want your family to pay a steep price." He fixed his eyes on her and let the threat sink in. Marguerite held his gaze, her face white.

"*Bon.* I see you understand." De la Haye turned to the lieutenant now holding Marguerite's arm. "Go now."

Marguerite looked at Suzanne. "What about—?"

"You want to know about your friend?" De la Haye smirked. "Of course, she remains under arrest. We can't let a so-called *inspirée* walk away."

Marguerite opened her mouth but clamped it shut. Suzanne couldn't see through a wave of dizziness.

"Mademoiselle Lacombe will be detained elsewhere. We have more prisoners arriving today and are in need of space."

De la Haye turned to the other soldier. "Lieutenant, take Mademoiselle Lacombe to the Château de Planque. Deliver her to Lord Valmalle, who is extremely happy to oversee her house arrest. We thought incarcerating her next door to her family would be a suitable punishment. So close, yet so far." A frigid smile stretched across his face, his eyes hard as glass. "Make sure you take both prisoners by the central bridge. See to it they take in the full view. These two need to see what happens to those who rebel against Governor Bâville, representative of our glorious King."

Suzanne's head spun, and her world turned black.

CHAPTER 33
HOMECOMING

27 October 1702
St. Hippolyte du Fort
Southern Cévennes

The crack of gunfire rang through the woods. Gabriel-Isaac ducked behind a large granite outcropping. The racket came from the direction of St. Hippolyte du Fort, beyond the forest of green oaks.

Another flurry of shots filled the air. His heart hammered. A battle in his hometown? Maybe he could join in. Could Jean Massip be there?

It wasn't likely Jean had decided Gabriel-Isaac could finish the journey home on his own. The guide took seriously Mazel's orders to escort Gabriel-Isaac back to his family in St. Hippolyte. No harm had seemed to come from Gabriel-Isaac's one act of disobedience except to him, unless Jean had been arrested or worse on this journey.

Guilt squeezed through Gabriel-Isaac's chest. He should've gone to the worship service too, shouldn't have hid with his painful memories while soldiers marched through the forest. At least he'd kept his promise to wait as long as reasonable for Jean's return.

Gabriel-Isaac had been tempted to strike out on his own. He could go anywhere, perhaps return to the home in Calvisson where he landed when he first ran away from Mialet. The two older sisters who sheltered and fed him there were active in the resistance. They had informed him where to find Mazel and would know of another band of Camisard fighters to join. But a surprising compulsion to go home and see his family kept rising in Gabriel-Isaac's mind.

The gunfire ahead stopped, and birds overhead resumed their chirping songs. He rose and continued pushing through prickly vines, holding the stems to avoid puncturing his fingers. At the next small crest, he hid on rocky ledge, leaning out to scan St. Hippolyte below.

As the scene came into focus, he gasped and stepped forward, releasing a spray of rocks. He jerked back and sat down hard, wrapping both arms around his middle. Nausea spasmed through his gut. It was just as well he'd eaten little in days, only what he'd foraged in the woods. He leaned against a boulder and covered his face with both hands. If only he could block out what he'd seen.

Royal soldiers below guarded a grisly display. At least a dozen decapitated heads lined the stone wall along the central bridge. Judging by the swagger of the troops, the heads belonged to defeated Camisards. The earlier gunshots must have been intended to draw attention to the grotesque spectacle.

Did he know any of the men whose heads hung on the bridge? He clamped his hand over his mouth. What if his uncles were among them? Or one of the Camisard leaders?

Gabriel-Isaac stood and waited a moment for his head to clear. He moved closer to the ledge, avoiding stones that could roll down and alert the soldiers below. Dropping to all fours, he crawled the last bit to the edge, then lay flat to peer over it. Besides a better view, his shaky body welcomed the solidity of the earth beneath it.

There were thirteen heads, bloodied but, as far as he could tell, not newly dead. After resting his own sweaty head on his hands for a minute, he resumed the inspection. None of them resembled his uncles, though it was hard to tell. He studied them one more time, and his certainty grew that neither Uncle Gabriel nor Uncle Paul were among the display.

But there was something familiar about the head in the center. The soldiers spat at it and hurled epithets, as if insults made a difference at this point. Gabriel-Isaac shimmied closer, blinking hard. Gédéon Laporte!

Gabriel-Isaac retreated from his perch and nestled back behind the boulders, where he sat for a long time. Did the uprising continue without Laporte? Mazel was a forceful leader and constantly received guidance from God. But he'd relied heavily on Laporte's strategic skills.

A light breeze wafted through nearby trees. Under a canopy of dappled sunlight, Gabriel-Isaac's shoulders relaxed a little, and he inhaled the fragrance of green oaks, wild thyme, and earth. His family might need him now, and maybe he needed to go home to rest and regroup. Wasn't Suzanne always saying they should remain together, safe? He'd scoffed, but right now, safe sounded like heaven. Tears welled, and even though he was way too old for such things, he let them flow.

After a while, he stood and started moving back through the forest. Within the hour, he arrived at the top of the Château de Planque's property. Standing in the watchtower's doorway, he remembered the last time he was there, with Suzanne right after their parents' arrests. He swiped away more tears with his sleeve, then straightened his shoulders. He needed to get hold of himself before seeing his family. Wasn't he supposed to be a fighter by now? Or at least on his way to becoming one?

He began working his way down the side of the mountain to his home, not sure how long he'd stay. At the street, he paused and observed the guard tower on the Planque bridge for activity. As best he could tell, none of the soldiers on duty looked his way.

He ran across the road, slipped into the Lacombes' back garden, then hurried across to the back door. The familiar sound of the wood door scraping over terra-cotta tile welcomed him as he stepped into the back corridor and shut the door behind him.

"Bonjour?" he called. "Anyone here?" No response. Where was everyone?

He stood still a moment, thinking, then noticed that the baskets used for market day were missing. The family must be out shopping for needed supplies.

In the kitchen, he helped himself to room-temperature soup from the large iron pot ready for the midday meal. A freshly baked loaf of bread lay on the hearth, waiting for the family's return. After a few minutes of attempting restraint, Gabriel-Isaac grabbed it and tore out a huge chunk. Nothing had ever tasted so good.

He ate his fill, then drank several cupfuls of water from the kitchen jug. He wandered to the salon, curled up in a wide chair, and fell into a sound sleep. Some time later, he woke with Grand-mère, Marc-André, and Marie standing over him.

"You're home, Gabriel-Isaac!" said Grand-mère. "What a wonderful surprise!"

His siblings' wide-eyed stares gave way to smiles. Were their faces paler than usual? He stood and embraced each one. Marie clung to him.

"So, you missed me!" he said. "Sorry, Grand-mère, but I couldn't wait for the soup. It's delicious, chestnut, my favorite. And the bread too."

Grand-mère shook her head. "I don't mind. Come, join us *à table*. You must have much to tell us."

Gabriel-Isaac's lips pressed tight. He should have prepared a story explaining why he was home. One that left out why Mazel and Laporte had sent him away. Best change the subject. "Where's Suzanne?"

The air sucked out of the room. Marie hid her face in her hands, and Marc-André grew paler still.

Grand-mère pulled out a chair. "Sit down, Gabriel-Isaac. There's much to tell."

What was going on?

Only once they had all settled did Grand-mère explain. "Five days ago, there was a service in a cave north of St. Hippolyte. I stayed home since one of my mothers was close to giving birth. Marc-André and Marie were here with me, but Suzanne attended with Marguerite."

Grand-mère straightened her spine. "There was a raid by soldiers. They arrested your sister and Marguerite. Many others as well."

Time stood still as Gabriel-Isaac struggled to fully take in the words. "Suzanne? Arrested? Marguerite too?"

"Yes. We have reports from those who escaped."

Gabriel-Isaac shook his head, resisting the news. This was Suzanne's worst nightmare. Had they caught her in the middle of a prophecy?

Grand-mère reached across the table and placed her hand over his. "We don't know for sure, but it's possible they're in the prison-fort here. One of our community saw a group of prisoners, male and female, ushered inside in the early morning hours after the raid."

Gabriel-Isaac pushed away from the table and crossed to the kitchen window. His jaw clenched. The soldiers must have arrested Jean as well.

What would happen to them all? He placed his palms on the cool stone sink and gazed out the window. He'd been worried about what to tell Grand-mère and Suzanne about why he was home. None of that mattered now.

His world crumbled around him as one reference point after another fell and left him unmoored. First, the Camisards' defeat and the sickening display of heads. Now, the news of his sister's arrest and most likely Massip's.

The stomp of boots from across the street drew his attention. A group of royal soldiers emerged from the Planque bridge, marching toward the Château. Two of them held tight to someone's arms. A woman, a prisoner. She stared at the Lacombe house as they dragged her toward the Château. Suzanne!

CHAPTER 34

ESCAPE

28 October 1702
St. Hippolyte du Fort
Southern Cévennes

The prisoner tossed a crumb of his bread into the corner, grinning as his pals scurried and fought for the morsel.

"Don't give up, Jeremiah! You let Ezekiel win far too often."

Jean Massip chuckled as Daniel stole the bread while the other two rats fought over it. A wily one, that Daniel. For Jean, it was worth giving up a precious bit of his meal to watch his furry cellmates tussle for the scrap. In his six days of detainment in the St. Hippolyte prison-fort, he'd only bothered to name three of the rats, although several others shared his space.

He stood and stretched his limbs. Not for the first time, he gazed up at the open window, a rectangle with a vertical iron bar in the middle. Already slight of build, the meager rations since his incarceration had further reduced his already slight build. With the bar removed, he'd slip through without a problem. But could he manage to get it out?

Only three months ago, almost to the day if he remembered correctly, he'd been the prisoner of the Abbé du Chaila. Thanks to Gédéon Laporte and several other brawny Camisards bashing in the wall of his cell as the Abbé's house burned around them, Jean had escaped. Barely. The injuries to his leg and lungs had taken months to heal. He rubbed the center of his chest. He was ready for more adventures, starting with getting out of here.

Yesterday, he overheard the guards talking about the recent release of two women. The prison director sent one home to run the town's water mill and the other to the Château de Planque under house arrest. Gabriel-Isaac and Suzanne lived in the Planque domaine. Certainly the guards spoke of Suzanne and of her friend Marguerite, the girl he'd seen scratching, and screaming at the soldiers dragging her out of the cave during the raid. She fit Suzanne's description perfectly.

Suzanne. The guards had mentioned that Lord Valmalle would prove to be a more vicious jailer than those in the prison-fort. Already determined to escape this place before they sent him to the Marseille galleys, Jean now felt a greater urgency. He needed to get her out of the Château de Planque and Lord Valmalle's grip. Maybe Marguerite would help him. Jean was pretty sure she'd fight hard to set her friend free.

He leaned through the bars and peered into the corridor. The guard's grunting snores reverberated off the stone walls. Jean tipped over his cot with care. One of the wooden legs was already loose. A second one gave him a bit more trouble, but he finally pulled it off.

Glad he didn't have a cellmate, he moved the extra bed under the window. With the two wooden pieces in hand, he climbed up on it, then stopped and listened. The snorting racket continued down the hall. *Thank you, Lord.* The noise would cover his activity.

Using one of the bed legs as a wedge and the other as a hammer, Jean tapped as quietly as possible at the mortar around the vertical iron bar in the window. To his surprise, it chipped out somewhat easily, baked by the summer sun.

Pausing every few minutes to check on the level of snoring from the guard's station, he worked for close to an hour. He pushed the bar out at the bottom, and the top slid out and into his hand.

Brushing limestone dust out through the slit and replacing the iron bar cleaned up the mess. Satisfied the window looked much as it had before, he reattached the legs to his bed and stretched out on it, hands behind his head. A smile played on his lips. Hopefully, he'd finish the process tonight. And then go.

He drifted into sleep and dreamed of walking with Suzanne through a forest, others following behind them. He woke up happy, imagining her joining him in guiding Huguenots to safety. But it wasn't likely she'd enjoy traipsing through woods and being in constant danger. She'd shared her desire to be safe at home, with loved ones gathered around.

He swung his legs over the side of the cot, sat up, and rubbed his neck. It was just a dream.

After dinner, he waited until the prisoners and guards settled for the night, then resumed his task. A brilliant moon shone outside, so bright he almost had to shield his eyes. Grateful God provided such illumination, he worked through the night, carefully chipping away at the outer window slit. Just before daylight, he extricated a large stone from the narrow opening.

He replaced everything and cleaned up after himself. Checking the window one more time to make sure the guard bringing meals would see no difference, Jean lay down to sleep.

Time in a cell had a strange shape to it. He drifted in and out of sleep well into the next day, then woke to a loud conversation between two guards just beyond his cell.

"Did you hear? Antoine Lagarde brought Monsieur de la Haye more information."

"He's certainly been a reliable source of Huguenot activity." A sneering laugh followed, grating Jean's every nerve wide awake. Antoine Lagarde was a traitor!

"Those fools still think he's one of them. Loyal to the cause and all."

"What did Lagarde bring this time?"

Jean sat up, then tread softly across the cell. More than once, he'd stayed at Lagarde's home in Lasalle, considering him a friend.

"Those idiots plan to gather for their illicit worship yet again. Some cave near Le Cengle mountain."

"They never give up!"

"Lagarde says it's planned for night after next. In two days."

"Ha! Surely this will be the last one. We'll arrest them all!"

Jean tiptoed back to his cot and stared up at his cell's window. He'd trusted Antoine, believed him to follow the faith and its principles of loving one another. It was hard to fathom Antoine betraying neighbors who'd never caused him any harm.

With a moat just below the window, Jean would wear very little for the swim to freedom and had planned to visit Lagarde for clothes. Jean breathed a prayer of thanks to God for the warning. Returning to Lagarde's home now or ever was out of the question. Jean would have to find clothes elsewhere. His heavenly Father watched over him and would provide.

The next hours dragged. After the disturbing news, Jean could no longer doze. Finally, the cell block quieted for the night. He slipped off his shirt and undershirt and used his suspenders to tie them to his hat. Heart pounding, he stepped on the cot and pulled out the iron bar and then the large stone. He put them under the blanket on his bed. It didn't exactly look like a human lying there, but it would have to do.

He pulled himself up and leaned out the window, scouting for night sentries patrolling on top of the high wall across the dry moat. All was quiet. He shimmied up and through the window, then hung on to the outer ledge for a moment. Aiming for a silent entry into the water below, he pushed away from the outer wall, holding himself straight as he let go.

After waiting underwater for a moment, he surfaced. No commotion. Good. With a huge gulp of air, he swam underwater to the rock wall lining the far side of the moat. He searched along its length. No way out.

Show me the way, Lord. He swam back toward the prison, then along the length of the inner rampart wall. Under the entry bridge into the fort, he paused to catch his breath. Thanks to the bright moon, he noticed an emergency door covered by an iron gate at the far end. He dove underwater and swam to the portal. Grabbing hold of the iron bars, he climbed up the gate and over onto the bridge.

He lay low, aware he was in full view of guards at the sentry point inside the fort, directly across from him. Breathing a prayer, he stood and ran across the parapet.

"Who goes there? Who goes there?"

Cold prickles spread through Jean's drenched body. *Just keep going. Don't look back.*

"Who goes there?" A shot pierced the night.

Keep going. I am with you. There was no time to analyze, but it seemed God was directing Jean's way. He ran. Arriving at a defensive perimeter, he searched along the wood stakes comprising the fence and found two wide enough apart for him to squeeze through.

Rifle shots continued but grew distant as Jean progressed away from the fort. He arrived at a large vineyard and slipped into its rows of barren vines. Too bad the *vendange* was months past. The empty vines didn't provide much cover.

Bent over, he ran through the vines until the forest outside town appeared. Sprinting far into the woods, he stopped at a thicket of brambly bushes beside a pile of granite boulders. Had God put so many huge rocks throughout the Cévennes so his people could hide?

Jean slipped behind the prickly bushes, ignoring scrapes, and slipped into a space between two tall rocks wide enough for his body. Grateful, he sank to the ground. He'd catch his breath, then continue on.

He had to get to Suzanne. But where was the Château de Planque? He was unfamiliar with St. Hippolyte du Fort and had counted on Gabriel-Isaac showing the way. Jean never should have left the boy alone. Where was Gabriel-Isaac now? Had he run away, attempting to join another band of Camisards? Or had he done the sensible thing and returned to his family? Either way, Jean decided he'd head first to the Lacombe home, if only he knew where it was.

A slight breeze ruffled through the trees and chilled his wet body, growing colder with each passing minute. Maybe he should keep moving, even if his bare feet screamed the opposite. Maybe resting a little longer would help. His eyelids slid shut.

Some time later, Jean awoke with a start. Early rays of daylight seeped through the forest. Despite the chill, he'd fallen into a deep sleep and now had the challenge of traveling during daylight. He stood, stepped out of the crevice, and stretched his creaky limbs. Only natural forest sounds reached his ears—birds chirping at the rising sun, brittle autumn leaves crunching under his sore feet, and the rustle of small animals searching through the underbrush for breakfast. A growl from his belly reminded him to eat. He foraged for some edible greens and came up with a handful. Not the best on an empty stomach, but what choice did he have? At one time, he'd hidden for eight days in the shelter of a thick fig tree. How he wished for such a treat right now.

Early morning dew on the plants he ate quenched his thirst a little, but he needed to find clean water soon. As a guide, he'd gone many times with little food and drink, but never after escaping a prison-fort. Lightheaded, he resumed his journey.

With the help of the sun in the eastern end of the sky, he oriented himself and set out north, praying he remembered correctly. During the night, he'd dreamed of Gabriel-Isaac telling him that the Lacombe manor was on the Route de Lasalle, just down the road from the underground gathering where he'd been arrested. He chuckled. Gabriel-

Isaac hadn't mentioned how close they were to his home the night Jean left for the worship service.

He shook his head a little as he walked through the trees. God had given him directions in a dream. How biblical! Was it his imagination or wishful thinking? But what else did he have to go on?

North. He'd head north and find a way to liberate Suzanne.

CHAPTER 35
CHÂTEAU DE PLANQUE

28 October 1702
St. Hippolyte du Fort
Southern Cévennes

Suzanne woke and looked around. Where was she? She stared at a crack running in a jagged line between the ceiling's massive oak beams. Gentle whiffling from the woman sleeping in the adjacent bed brought back the situation, house arrest and bunking with a housemaid on the third floor of the Château de Planque.

Soaking in the relative quiet, Suzanne lay wondering what the day would bring, distressed by the dark moments from yesterday afternoon. The royal soldiers escorting her past the display of Camisard heads, the oppressive darkness swirling in that place causing her knees to buckle. The price for the luxury of passing the checkpoint at the Planque bridge without question, soldiers gripping her arms and joking with the guards waving them through. Seeing but being unable to enter her own home, hoping her family there might see she was alive but not see her as a prisoner.

At least Lord Valmalle's receipt of her had involved only a brief speech ordering her to the servants' quarters with the housemaid, Marthe. Though locked in the room, Suzanne had received dinner, and this room had a window looking over the back garden to the terraced hill beyond, vast improvements over a prison cell.

She gazed through the window, taking in the splash of autumnal colors dotting the landscape. Her favorite season was on full display.

Despite being confined, the room brought some comfort. If only a fire blazed in the limestone hearth.

Marthe's breathing changed. There'd been no words exchanged between them. Was the maid frightened or upset at sharing her room with a Huguenot prisoner? Did the inhabitants of the Château know Suzanne was an *inspirée*? Time would tell.

Time. Now, on the first morning of her house arrest, fear-wrapped thoughts circulated through her mind. Would her incarceration go on indefinitely? Unthinkable. Would Lord Valmalle confine her to this room? Would he put her to work outside it? She wasn't sure which she'd prefer. Not that it mattered; she had no choice.

Beloved, I am with you. Suzanne shut her eyes. *Fear not, little one.* Her hands clutched the rough wool blanket under her chin. *Non!* How could her heavenly Father let this happen to her? Hadn't she suffered enough? How could this be love? Tears slid down her cheeks, wetting her hair. She'd never felt more alone.

Her emotions tangled into a tight knot in her chest. The days inside St. Hippolyte's prison had seemed unreal, disconnected from regular life. Finding herself in her own neighborhood but inside the unfamiliar interior of the Château was disorienting. Loved ones were so close yet so far. Hope rose at the thought she might catch a glimpse of them, might connect with them somehow. Just as quickly, the spark extinguished at the improbability. She gulped back a sob.

Marthe stirred, then sat up. Out of the corner of her eye, Suzanne watched the maid dress, then leave the room in a rush. In the prison-fort, Suzanne had been with Marguerite and other Huguenot women. Was she now to remain isolated, cut off from all normal human contact?

Suzanne pushed off the bedcovers, rose, and pulled her filthy dress on over her grubby shift. She used and covered the chamber pot and slid it back under the bed. After a moment's hesitation, she splashed her face with icy water from a wide porcelain bowl sitting in a stone sink nestled into the wall. Dabbing her face and neck with the linen on the ledge of the sink, she longed for a hot bath and a fresh set of clothes. Probably not an option for her here.

She looked at the bowl of used water, sludge color. Should she pour it into the sink to let it run through the pipe in the wall to the outside? Better not. Someone in the garden might notice. The less she did to draw attention, the better. She wrangled her curls into a chignon, using a small, cloudy mirror hanging on a nail. At least she'd landed in a room with a few amenities.

Marthe returned with a breakfast tray of warm milk and bread and butter, setting it on a small table in the corner. The maid gestured for Suzanne to come sit and eat, then pulled out another wooden slat-back chair for herself.

"Drink while it's still a little warm." Marthe's voice was soft. Suzanne detected a note of kindness behind her reticence.

"*Merci.*" Suzanne lifted the small bowl of milk and drank, watching the maid over the rim. It tasted delicious. Her hunger awakened full force, and she restrained herself from guzzling it down. Finished, she set the bowl back on the wooden tray and ate the bread, studying the maid, wondering why she stayed. Had Valmalle ordered her to do so?

Suzanne smiled. "Do you know what I'll be doing here? Am I to be confined always to this room?"

Marthe fidgeted, then stood and walked to the stone sink. She turned and looked at Suzanne, but said nothing.

Suzanne broke the silence. "I hope you don't mind that I used the water and your linen for my face this morning. I'm still quite dirty from the prison."

Marthe shook her head. "No, I don't mind. I'm glad you did. You must be very uncomfortable in those . . ." Her cheeks blossomed pink.

"Yes, these filthy clothes are unpleasant to wear and even more so for you to look at and smell."

The maid glanced toward the narrow armoire in the corner, then back at Suzanne. "I have a second dress. I think we're similar in size. You could borrow it while I get yours washed and dried. Valmalle said nothing about your clothes, and I doubt he'd even notice." Her color heightened, clearly this was quite bold for her.

"That would be incredibly kind. Thank you."

Marthe nodded, turned, and dumped the dirty water from the porcelain bowl out through the drainpipe. She poured fresh water, then grabbed a small block of olive oil soap from a wooden shelf and set it on the granite sink. "Get out of those clothes and wash yourself. Quickly. We mustn't keep Lord Valmalle waiting too long." From the armoire, she pulled out the spare dress, a clean linen shift, and stockings, laying them across Suzanne's bed. "I'll step out for a few minutes."

Once Marthe shut the door behind her, tears sprang to Suzanne's eyes. Her body sang with relief as she liberated it from prison filth. Dressed in the clean clothes, she vowed to never again take for granted such blessings.

Marthe returned, a shy smile on her face at Suzanne's fresh appearance. The two women hastened down the servants' stairs to the second-floor landing.

As the maid knocked on double doors, Suzanne took in the elegant staircase behind them, leading down to an inner courtyard on the ground floor. An oval-shaped limestone well stood in the center, decorative ironwork arching over the opening. A wooden bucket with a rope attached sat on the ledge, waiting to pull up fresh water as needed.

So this was the inside of the Château de Planque. At least the part of it she could see from here. Yesterday she'd been too overwhelmed to notice much.

The door flew open, and a butler ushered Marthe and Suzanne into the grand salon, lit by five high windows that spread across the front of the building. Growing up in the Château's shadow, Suzanne had seen those windows from the outside every day. Now she stood inside, a prisoner.

Valmalle dismissed Marthe. If Suzanne wasn't mistaken, the maid shot her a tiny glance of sympathy on her way out as the master of the house stepped closer. Would he also send the butler away, leaving them alone together?

"Mademoiselle Lacombe," Lord Valmalle began, sneer firmly in place. He looked her over, head to toe, walking around as if assessing the purchase of an animal. She'd heard reports of his cruel nature but had never expected to experience it firsthand. "Too bad the prison had no more room for you. All the better to have you here, my dear. Don't even consider running away. It will not go well with you if you attempt escape. One of my servants will stand guard at the front door, day and night from now on. The rest of the Château and the grounds are surrounded by an impenetrable wall."

Suzanne's skin crawled at the look on Lord Valmalle's face as he circled close. She felt his hot breath on her neck and regretted cleaning herself up. Probably wouldn't have made a difference to this vile man. He ran his fingers lightly up her arm. She felt ill.

Beloved! Fear not. I am with you. The words barely registered. *Beloved, you're not alone. Look up, child.* The last sentence penetrated through the fog of fear like the light streaming through the salon's windows. *Look up, child.* Her heavenly Father had not and would not abandon her.

You are more than a conqueror through me, through my love. She felt nothing like a conqueror at the moment. Suddenly, the biblical words that had flowed from her mouth at the assembly replayed in her mind. Nothing at all, in any form, could separate her from the love of Jesus. Even abuse, even death. His love made her unconquerable in the truest sense.

Lord Valmalle pulled back and stood stock-still. A warmth rose into Suzanne's body as if through the floor, calming her frantic heart and clearing her head. Peace, steady and strong like the river Vidourle after a healthy rain, flowed through her. Truth seeped into her soul. She was never alone. And God said she could get through this ordeal. The strength of his love filled her to overflowing like liquid light as brilliant as the recent full moon.

"Stop that!" Lord Valmalle screeched, his marble-gray eyes fierce under thin eyebrows. He whirled and strode to the far end of the room.

What was happening? She'd been standing still and silent. Unless he sensed or somehow saw the strengthening from the Lord she was experiencing.

Valmalle bellowed orders to the butler. "Take her down to help the cook. Keep her out of my sight."

"Yes, sir." The butler crossed the room.

Suzanne hid her relief behind an expressionless face. God had spoken truth and enabled her to receive it. Lord Valmalle hadn't been able to tolerate the resulting spiritual shift and had sent her away. She offered up a prayer of thanks.

With a tight grip on Suzanne's arm, the butler ushered her out of the grand salon. He escorted her down the wide staircase and into the kitchen. A rush of cool air met them as they crossed the threshold and stopped.

"Justine!" He called. "Where are you?" Suzanne couldn't discern whether his unwillingness to venture farther into the kitchen himself was out of disdain or disgust. Maybe a mixture of both. The man hadn't made eye contact with her and dropped her arm as the kitchen door shut behind them.

"Justine! I haven't got all day."

A middle-aged woman bustled out from somewhere within the kitchen compound, sweat beading on her paunchy face. "Sorry, Monsieur Bernard. I was—"

"I don't care what you were doing. Here's the Huguenot prisoner. Your new help, at Lord Valmalle's behest."

The cook frowned as she waved the long iron spoon in her hand near Suzanne's face. "Can she even cook?"

"How would I know? You'll follow orders and put her to work." With a frosty glare over his beaklike nose, he stalked from the kitchen.

Justine swiveled in the other direction, shouting at Suzanne over her shoulder. "Keep up. I've got the midday meal over the fire. You want to be responsible if it burns?"

She followed the woman into a medium-sized room. Smoked meats and sausages hung from the rafters. Chestnuts lay drying on racks. Light shone through a window over a stone sink on the far side. The window Gabriel-Isaac had jumped through to retrieve the psalter!

As the cook hustled on to yet another room, Suzanne slowed and looked out the window. Directly across the street, in the Lacombe kitchen window, stood her brother. Gabriel-Isaac! Her breath caught. Why wasn't he in Mialet with their uncles? Why was he home?

CHAPTER 36
PLANS

28 October 1702
St. Hippolyte du Fort
Southern Cévennes

Gabriel-Isaac offered to wash the breakfast dishes, letting Grand-mère sit with his siblings and finish drinking her warm milk. At the stone sink, he stacked the bowls, then glanced out the window at the Château. What was happening with Suzanne inside? Lord Valmalle hated Huguenots.

Across the street, the form of a young woman appeared in the Château's kitchen window. Was that Suzanne? He couldn't be sure. Had he imagined her there, conjured out of a desire to know how she fared? Or had Lord Valmalle put her to work in the kitchen?

He turned to tell Grand-mère but stopped as the sound of the back door scraping open reverberated down the hallway. Grand-mère sprang to her feet.

Gabriel-Isaac stepped forward. "I'll go. Hide Marc-André and Marie in the *cachette.*"

Grand-mère shepherded the children into the hiding place as he exited the kitchen. He walked at a deliberate pace, giving them time to get into the *cachette* and put everything in order. The hair on the back of his neck stood on end. Who could it be? Why come in the back, unannounced?

A slight movement in the space between the door and the adjacent armoire that stored extra foodstuffs sent his pulse racing. "Who's there?"

he called, forcing his voice deep and strong. At least he hoped it sounded that way.

A shadow emerged into the corridor. "Gabriel-Isaac? Is that really you?"

"Jean?" Gabriel-Isaac moved closer to confirm. "What are you doing here?"

Massip stepped into the light, grinning wide, and drew Gabriel-Isaac into a tight embrace. Pesky tears threatened to spill from Gabriel-Isaac's eyes, fueled by relief that the intruder was actually a friend and that this friend was safe.

After a moment, Gabriel-Isaac pulled back, questions redirecting his emotions. "What happened at the worship gathering? Were you arrested?" He paused to draw a breath. "Wait. Come with me to the kitchen so Grand-mère can hear."

Jean followed him to the kitchen, where Grand-mère washed and put away dishes, hiding evidence of how many had eaten the midday meal.

"Grand-mère, this is my friend Jean Massip. He's a guide, helping Huguenots on their escape routes to Switzerland or wherever they need to go."

Grand-mère dried her hands on her apron, came forward, and greeted Jean with three *bisous*. Her smile faded as she took in his damp and dirty appearance. Gabriel-Isaac noticed his friend's disheveled state for the first time.

"Jean, come sit at the table," Grand-mère said. "I imagine you'd like some vegetable soup and bread? Then we'll see about a change of clothes."

Jean glanced down, then nodded with a crooked smile. "Yes, please. That would be wonderful."

"Take a seat. Gabriel-Isaac, please let the children out of the *cachette*."

"Oh, of course." He pulled out a chair for Jean, then walked to the cupboard built into the wall and threw open the double doors. He removed a ceramic jug, lifted out the wood plank, and helped his siblings out. Both gaped at the stranger seated at the kitchen table.

"Marie and Marc-André, this is Jean Massip."

Marc-André stepped forward, reaching out his hand. Jean rose and shook it. Marie kept her gaze down but offered her hand. Jean kissed it gently, despite its coating of limestone dust. Her cheeks pinked, but she didn't pull away.

Grand-mère set a warmed bowl of soup and a plate of bread slices on the table. "Sit. Eat while it's hot."

Marie, eyes wide as saucers, looked from the disheveled guide to Grand-mère, who sat beside him.

"When he's finished, we'll hear why he's here," Grand-mère stated, her voice firm.

After a second serving of soup, Jean drank a small tankard of cider. "*Merci*, Madame Lacombe. That was delicious."

"You're most welcome. Now, tell us your story."

Three sharp raps of the knocker on the front door echoed through the house. The blood drained from Jean's face. "I might have put you in danger. I escaped from the prison-fort of St. Hippolyte during the night. Surely, they're searching for me."

Grand-mère stood. "Get into the *cachette*, Jean. Marc-André and Marie, too. Gabriel-Isaac, you stay and replace the shelf. I'll go to the door."

"*Non*," Gabriel-Isaac said. "You stay, Grand-mère. I'll go."

More banging came from the front door. He left the kitchen and, for the second time within the hour, went to see if friend or foe would enter the Lacombe home.

After squaring his shoulders, he opened the door with as much decorum as he could muster. There stood Aunt Anne with a basket over her arm.

"Come in, Aunt Anne! Be quick." He reached out and pulled her inside, then shut the door.

"Gabriel-Isaac! I didn't know you were home."

"It's a long story. I'll explain later, but come to the kitchen. We have a guest."

"A guest?"

"Come see."

Aunt Anne followed him to the kitchen and embraced Grand-mère while Gabriel-Isaac opened the pantry doors and liberated his siblings and Jean from the *cachette*. Marc-André and Marie emerged covered with yet more limestone dust and slightly less enthusiastic about the adventure of it all. Grand-mère introduced their guest to Aunt Anne, then gestured for them all to sit at the table.

"Anne, is there are reason for your visit? We didn't expect to see you for a while. Aren't your in-laws more unwell than usual?"

"It's true they're ill. A neighbor is with them so I could come see you. And yes, there's a reason for my visit. Two, actually." She stopped and glanced at Jean, then back to Grand-mère. "But I can wait and fill you in later."

"That's fine. We were just about to hear Jean's story and why he's here. Go ahead, young man."

"*Oui*, madame."

Grand-mère touched the back of Jean's hand. "Please, call me Isabeau. Carry on."

"As you wish. I escaped from the St. Hippolyte prison-fort last night."

Aunt Anne sat back hard against the wood slats of her chair, her eyes ridged with tension.

"I'm aware I've put you in danger, and I won't stay long. I can tell you the story of my escape another time. The hand of God protected me."

Gabriel-Isaac's entire being thrummed with admiration. "You swam across the moat?"

Grand-mère held up a hand. "We'll hear details later, *if* there's time. Jean, why are you here? For food, clothes, help?"

"I could use all of those, but that's not why I came. First, I wanted to see if Gabriel-Isaac made it home safely. Abraham Mazel and Rolland Laporte asked me to do so. I shouldn't have left him to go to the underground service. It'd been so long since I worshipped and heard the word of God taught."

He rubbed his neck. "The soldier who held Suzanne found and arrested me at the gathering as well, then took us to the prison in St. Hippolyte. Once there, they separated us into men's and women's dungeons."

A heavy silence filled the room. Marie wept softly, comforted by Grand-mère.

"How do you know Suzanne?" asked Aunt Anne.

Gabriel-Isaac jumped in. "Suzanne and I first met him in the forest on the way home from the raid in the Grotte de la Roquette. Then, when Suzanne and I arrived at Rolland's home, Jean was there. Recovering from his injuries at the Pont-de-Montvert."

"You fought the Abbé du Chaila?" Awe filled Marc-André's voice.

"No," said Gabriel-Isaac. "Jean was a prisoner in the Abbé's dungeons, along with several others he'd been leading to Switzerland."

Grand-mère's eyes widened. "You're *that* guide?"

"Yes. And by the grace of God, Gédéon Laporte and others got me out."

A strangled sound escaped Gabriel-Isaac. "I saw him. Laporte. At least I think I did. I mean his, uh . . ." He shot a look at his siblings. "On the central bridge two days ago." He buried his face in his hands.

Grand-mère reached her arm across his shoulders. "I'm so sorry you witnessed that grotesque demonstration. We heard about it and that Gédéon Laporte was among them. I managed to direct us away from the bridge end of the market."

"Oh, *non, non, non, non,*" said Jean, his face pale.

Aunt Anne sat up. "That's one reason I came here. To see if you'd seen or heard of Capitaine Poul's barbarous act." She turned to Grand-mère. "And to let you know that I've confirmed that none of the others . . ." She glanced at Marc-André and Marie. "That none of the others were your Gabriel or my brother Paul."

"That's what I thought!" Gabriel-Isaac blurted.

After a moment, Jean stood and looked from Grand-mère to Aunt Anne. "I don't want to put your family in danger. But the main reason I'm here is to free Suzanne from the Château de Planque. I don't know if you're aware, but I believe she's being held there under house arrest."

"So she *is* there!" cried Aunt Anne. "That's the second reason I came today. To find out if that rumor might be true. Are you certain, Jean?"

Gabriel-Isaac interrupted. "I saw her escorted into the Château by soldiers yesterday and saw her again this morning through the Château's kitchen window, just before Jean showed up. At least, I think the woman in the kitchen was her. A woman about Suzanne's size walked by the window and seemed to look our way and pause before moving on."

"You *saw* Suzanne?" Marie's quavering voice ended on a high pitch.

"I think so. And if I did, then it's a good thing Lord Valmalle has her working in the kitchen. We can catch glimpses of her."

Jean stroked his chin. "You can see the Château kitchen from here?"

"Yes, come see."

They stood side by side at the Lacombes' window, studying the scene across the street.

"I made it in and out of that window recently, retrieving a family treasure hidden in the Château pantry. Maybe you could go in that way and get Suzanne out."

Grand-mère paced the kitchen, stopping at the iron pot to stir the rest of the chestnut soup. "Suzanne's a prisoner. I doubt they'll leave her alone for long. Plus, you never know who'll come along the road, like Charles did that day. Now that he manages the vines for Lord Valmalle, he'll be in and out of there frequently."

"Charles works with Valmalle?"

"Yes, with the help of his father's workers. The Fesquets are taking your papa's place in the Planque domaine and collaborating with Uncle Philippe, plus carrying on with their own vines. It's grown into quite the enterprise."

Gabriel-Isaac sat down. So much change!

Grand-mère turned to Jean. "We need a plan to get Suzanne out of the Château. Quickly. Surely, the authorities are looking for you."

Aunt Anne cleared her throat. "I have an idea. Did I ever tell you about the tunnel that runs from the Château's cellar to the *moulin* down the street?"

"A tunnel?" Gabriel-Isaac gaped. "To the *moulin* run by Marguerite?"

Grand-mère nodded. "During the first rounds of the wars of religion, the Château's Protestant inhabitants used it to flee King Louis XIII's troops."

"I can't believe neither of you told us this before," said Gabriel-Isaac.

"We didn't want any of you children getting ideas about exploring the tunnel and creating adventures. It's too dangerous."

He tried not to squirm under his grandmother's intense stare. It seemed he was the child she most had in mind.

A soft smile crossed Anne's face. "We've held back this information for a time such as this. We can use the tunnel to get Suzanne out of the Château de Planque."

CHAPTER 37
WINDS OF CHANGE

29 October 1702
Between Montpellier and Carnon Plage
South of France

Governor Bâville jostled along in his gilded, black-lacquered carriage, content to be on his way to the coast. With the Huguenot revolt effectively over after Capitaine Poul's victory and the parade of Camisard heads, Bâville finally had time to visit his mistress. A satisfied smile spread across his face.

Without warning, the driver reigned in the four bay mares drawing the vehicle. Bâville's body jerked forward and then back hard against his seat as the carriage stopped. A red-coated footman appeared at the passenger door as Bâville burst from the cab, almost knocking the man over.

Before him, a royal soldier slipped off his roan gelding, reached into his saddlebag, and withdrew a letter.

"What's the meaning of this?" Bâville growled. "I left instructions for no interruptions."

"Bonjour, Governor Bâville. I arrived with this missive after you left this morning. Sent by one of our officers in the central Cévennes, it's marked urgent and needs your immediate attention."

The Governor grabbed the letter and strode into a thicket of trees lining the road. He broke the wax seal and unfolded the parchment, dated the previous day.

28 October 1702
To the honorable Governor Bâville,
We pray this finds you in good health.
My fellow officers and I deem it important to inform you of disquieting developments throughout the Cévennes. Despite Capitaine Poul's victories, the Camisard revolt continues. The Huguenots grow ever bolder, marching in broad daylight and singing psalms. In some locations, they dare to gather openly for worship services. The heretics seem to have lost all fear of confrontation.

With reluctance, I add that great discontent has grown among Catholics frustrated at the inability of the royal soldiers to stop the revolt. In Catholic opinion, the parade of heads signaled too much consideration for the defeated Camisards.

In addition, the so-called Camisard leaders, Rolland Laporte and Abraham Mazel, have joined forces and burn a great swath through the region.

Bâville stomped farther into the woods. He kicked a stone out of the way, then another and another. The heel of his dress boots caught on a fallen branch, tumbling him to the ground. Grabbing the limb with both hands, he stood and thrashed it wildly against a wide tree trunk. The branch shattered, leaving several splinters embedded in the Governor's raw palms.

The green oak stood unperturbed by his abuse and glower. Every part of Bâville prickled at the tree's audacity. Just like the Huguenots. No matter how much suffering he heaped on them, they stood strong, as if their roots grew deeper still, drawing up some kind of nourishment despite their troubles.

Feeling suddenly hot, the Governor ripped the black three-cornered hat off his head and threw it across the forest floor. He kicked another stone, yelping at a sharp pain piercing his foot. Since his edict had removed the need for trials before executions or prolonged imprisonments of Huguenots, many had been duly exterminated. Yet he couldn't get rid of their kind. No matter what he tried, they wouldn't go away. Like a persisting infestation of cockroaches, more came out into the open.

He continued reading the letter.

The Cévenol Catholics complain that the latest royal infantry regiments are barely out of childhood, untrained, and wear no uniforms. Indeed, their attire is little above the state of rags. It appears either that the King is out of seasoned troops due to wars elsewhere or that he believes the Camisard revolt is all but over. Either way, these "soldiers" fear direct confrontation and make sure they arrive after the departure of Camisards. Then the regiment pillages the locals of whatever the Camisards have left behind.

Finally, with great reluctance, I am obliged to report that the guide Jean Massip, the very one who survived the Abbé du Chaila's imprisonment, has now escaped St. Hippolyte's prison-fort.

Bâville reread the last paragraph, unable to believe it possible. Never had anyone accomplished such a feat. These Huguenots made him look like a fool.

He spied his fur-trimmed tricorne under a berry bush. Reaching through the prickly vines, he wrenched the hat out, leaving long scratches across the back of his hand. Resisting the urge to toss the hat back down and stomp it flat, he brushed it free of stickers and prickly weeds and placed it on his head. At least he was well dressed and remained dignified.

Grinding his teeth, he paced in a circle, dry leaves crunching underfoot. The King believed the Camisard uprising to be nearly over, because that's what Bâville had reported after Capitaine Poul's defeat of Gédéon Laporte. Before the King knew otherwise, something must be done—and quickly—about the unsuppressed revolt.

"Sir!" The footman approached, flushed. "We've been looking and calling out for you!"

The Governor scowled. No one could know about his hearing. He'd concealed his growing deafness from everyone, including his wife. He raised his chin and looked down his nose. "What do you want?"

"Sir, the driver says we must be on our way if we're to arrive before dark."

Bâville strode back to the carriage. Once settled inside the cab, two ideas came.

First, he'd neutralize Rolland Laporte. Today, when Bâville arrived at the seaside home of his mistress, he'd send soldiers to arrest Laporte's family—a mother and several sisters, if the local priest had informed correctly. That ought to weaken and distract the man. A method for stopping Abraham Mazel would require more thought.

Second, he'd write a new letter to the King. Without mentioning the failure in suppressing the rebellion, the letter would request a military marshal to secure peace. A grin spread across Bâville's face. He had in mind just the man.

Château de Fressac
Eastern Cévennes

Abraham Mazel paced the interior perimeter of the crumbling medieval Château perched high above the village of Fressac. Spread throughout the former dining hall, the exhausted Camisards regrouped from their recent raids.

Outrage at Poul's egregious display of Camisard heads had flared through the Huguenot community, and much of the countryside had erupted into literal flames. Abraham had never dreamed of being in the middle of such a conflagration, much less leading the Camisard revolt. Then again, maybe he had. That dream of his from almost a year ago, with the black cows and the order to bring iron and fire to rectify wrongs, provided the spark that now blazed as a full-blown revolt. In his wildest imaginings, he'd never expected the life he now lived.

He blew out a noisy breath. The stench of smoke from Camisards setting fire to Catholic enclaves and from royal soldiers burning Huguenot villages lingered in his nostrils and gathered in the pit of his stomach like a heavy stone.

At least he'd now found someone to lead by his side. Rolland, a natural leader like his uncle, had stepped into Gédéon's shoes and shared the weight of responsibility for hearing God and directing the fighters. Rolland's skill at recruiting and leading forays, proven even before joining Mazel, brought strategic experience to their band. Daily, the daring young man from Mialet grew more cunning.

But the success of the Camisards came down to hearing the voice of God and obeying it fully. Hadn't they prayed on their knees before battle, sometimes even as royal troops rushed toward them? Only the hand of God could've brought about their victories.

As Abraham continued his circuit through the Château, he found Gabriel and Paul sitting with a group of fighters, sharing battle stories. The other men now accorded great respect to the two lieutenants who discovered and apprehended the spy following their band on the road to Florac. Again, Abraham was grateful to not be in this battle alone. As long as unity reigned among them, all would be well.

He stopped to listen to the men's banter.

"That spectacle of Camisard heads has backfired," said Gabriel.

"It's outraged Protestants and Catholics alike," Paul added.

"And they thought displaying them on market days would shrivel up our revolt!"

"Au contraire! It's only fanned our conviction into greater flames."

"And not just for us fighters! My entire village now works to gather provisions, food, and weapons."

"Mine as well."

Moving on through the Château, Abraham imagined hearing the Governor's furious roars all the way from Montpellier.

In the kitchen, Abraham found another group of his men huddled close around the unlit hearth, as if the memory of heat could warm them now. Mazel had forbidden lighting fires in the Château, since chimney smoke would alert enemy troops to their location. The men distracted themselves with tales of God's intervention for their cause.

"Seems even the natural world is on our side," said one as he pulled a ragged blanket tighter around his shoulders. "Did you hear the story of the flock of sheep unexpectedly passing by a hidden prayer meeting?"

"*Oui!* The clanging of the animals' brass bells alerted the Huguenots to approaching soldiers!"

"And they fled in time! A miracle!"

The men paused and marveled a moment.

Another Camisard tugged on his beard. "Have you heard about the hive of bees swarming royal soldiers as they ransacked a farm?"

"Yes! The bees drove 'em away. Ha!"

"Serves 'em right!"

"And I heard a most intriguing story of a blackbird."

"I heard that one too! The bird sings a portion of Psalm 68!"

"Our fighting anthem!"

"*Oui!* When the King's soldiers heard 'May God arise, may his enemies be scattered,' they assumed Camisards hid nearby."

"Then the clever bird flitted to another location and the soldiers followed, thinking the 'rebels' moved."

"Ha! The bird had the soldiers running in circles."

"And our men got away!"

Abraham chuckled softly at the image of royal troops outmaneuvered by a bird. He knew that phenomenon was not wholly supernatural, as wily Huguenots had trained the bird. His smile faded. The ruse would be more amusing if the stakes weren't life and death.

Abraham grabbed a chair and joined the circle. "The ways of God are beyond our imagining."

The men nodded, faces solemn.

Abraham continued. "An hour ago, I received ammunition sent by a local militiaman. He'd collected it in secret, even emptied the militia's own guns. He and many others, former Protestants, don't have the heart to fight us."

"They know we're here?"

"Apparently, some locals are aware. So far, none have alerted the royal authorities."

A younger Camisard spoke up. "Some of the coerced militiamen abandon their assigned posts in the wee hours and return home to sleep!"

The men began nearly talking over each other again.

"And I heard that some troops in the north sing psalms through the night, communicating to concealed Camisards the freedom to pass without consequence."

"It's also said that some former Protestants sent to infiltrate one of our hidden worship gatherings have converted back to our faith!"

Abraham lingered a bit longer with the men, then rose and continued his rounds through the Château. In an inner courtyard, he found Rolland. Alone. Mazel walked toward him, observing. Besides their partnership leading the fighters, they'd become friends. And today, his friend appeared troubled.

"What's on your mind, Rolland?"

Laporte stared at Mazel, as if looking right through him.

"Rolland, is everything all right?"

Laporte started a little, as if returning from a distant dream. "I've had a vision." His brow furrowed, his eyes darkened.

Abraham studied his friend. Was it happening again? Would he lose another fellow leader through disunity?

Laporte focused in on Mazel. "Arrests. My mother and sisters. Soon." Rolland turned and walked away, his head bent low and his broad shoulders stooped under the burden of the revelation.

CHAPTER 38

DREAMS

Suzanne stood at the wooden table under the kitchen window, chopping vegetables for the midday potage. Late harvests from the Château's prolific garden yielded a satisfying soup daily. There were pumpkins, leeks, and something called a cauliflower, which she'd never seen or tasted before. Not bad.

Lord Valmalle, ever trying to prove his unearned nobility, demanded that an extensive array of produce be grown on his land in imitation of the King's *potager* in Versailles. He behaved as if he'd been born a noble. Suzanne chopped out her disgust at his aristocratic aspirations on the vegetables under her knife.

At least the repellant man had avoided her since that meeting four days ago. Instead, he'd ordered that while his servants rested after the midday meal, she spend an extra two hours outdoors in the cold *potager*, guarded by one of his men. Since she was only allowed her shawl, it took hours to thaw afterward. And no one offered sympathy.

As Cook Justine had informed Suzanne with a sneer, they all knew she was an *inspirée*. Maybe the soldiers who heard her prophesy at the raided gathering had shared that information with the prison director, who informed Valmalle. No matter how they knew, the reputation of her prophetic gift and accompanying manifestations worked for her good here. She pressed her lips together, hiding a tiny smile. Master and servants alike kept their distance, as if she might erupt in flames at any moment. All except Marthe.

Suzanne understood their discomfort. Hadn't she resisted the outpouring of the Holy Spirit as strange and potentially dangerous? But she'd survived one of her worst fears, imprisonment in St. Hippolyte's dungeon. Through it all, she'd been carried, filled, surrounded, and sustained. The love of God shone bright and warmed the darkness of the prison-fort. She'd experienced God there in a tangible way, and that made all the difference.

The image of her brave mother rose in her mind, how she'd appeared during their last visit. Maman's inner strength had radiated all around her, changing the atmosphere. Now, Suzanne had experienced the same strength.

She placed the chopped vegetables into a ceramic bowl and carried it to the next room. A fire blazed in the wide stone hearth. Justine stood in the middle of the largest of the warren-like kitchen rooms, punching down bread dough at a long table.

"Add those vegetables to the water," she ordered, motioning to the iron pot suspended over the fire.

Suzanne added the vegetables slowly. Despite taking care, boiling water splashed on her hand. She yelped, then grabbed the pitcher of cold water sitting on the stone sink and poured it over the rising blister. If she wasn't mistaken, there was a glint in the eye of the cook, who said nothing and likely thought Suzanne deserved the pain.

Thankfully, Marthe differed from the rest of the servants. The shy housemaid continued to show little kindnesses. Besides washing and drying Suzanne's clothes, she brought extra bits of food up to the bedroom serving as a cell.

At least working in the kitchen provided a change of scenery and gave Suzanne the opportunity to try and catch a glimpse of her family. Since seeing Gabriel-Isaac on her first day in the Château, there'd been no other sightings, but that didn't prevent her from hoping for more.

While house arrest here provided more comfort and food than the prison-fort, she couldn't imagine living out the rest of her days in this manner. She longed to know how her family was doing and why Gabriel-Isaac was home. Was he just visiting, or was something wrong?

"Don't just stand there doing nothing," growled Justine. "Go fetch more water."

"*Oui*, Justine."

Relieved to step outside, Suzanne picked up the wooden bucket beside the fireplace and exited the kitchen. At the well in the center courtyard, she secured the iron hook on the rope wound round the pulley to the handle of the bucket, then lowered the bucket into the well. When she cranked the bucket back up, it brimmed with cool water. She plunged her hand in it for a moment, savoring the icy numbness on her burned skin.

Her thoughts wandered for the hundredth time to Marguerite. How was she faring at home, running the mill under guard? Would she continue her resistance activities? Knowing Marguerite, she'd manage just fine. Suzanne missed her friend and family so much it physically hurt, a constant dull ache.

She hefted the bucket and started back to the kitchen. A gust of wind slammed shut a low door behind her, at the back of the courtyard. She thought it led to the storage area. Curious, she waited a moment. No one emerged, and there were no other servants around. Why not peek inside? Justine wouldn't miss her for a few more minutes, hopefully.

Sloshing the bucket beside her, Suzanne ducked into the dim, cool cellar. She set the pail on the packed-dirt floor and paused until her eyes adjusted. The unmistakable scent of grapes fermenting released a flood of memories of Papa. He'd worked in this very room, as well as his cellar at home, transforming Lord Valmalle's harvests into outstanding wines.

At the far right end of the long rectangular room, a man emerged through an arched doorway. With the dirt floor muffling his footsteps, his entrance caught her by surprise. Her eyes scanned the room for a hiding place.

He took a few more steps in, then stopped.

"Suzanne? Is that you?"

That voice! Could it be? "Charles?"

He crossed the distance between them. "It *is* you! I'd heard you were, uh, here."

She stared at him, unable to speak.

"Suzanne, I'm so glad to see you. Are you all right? Are they . . . ? Are you being treated well?"

Her chin dropped. Warring factions whirled through her. Should she throw herself in his arms and beg him to get her out of here? Or should she pick up the bucket, exit, and pretend this encounter never happened?

Charles reached out and took hold of each of her hands. "Suzanne, I'm so sorry you're in these circumstances. But I'm glad you're relatively safe and not in . . ." He swallowed. "I'm glad you're not in the prison-fort."

Relieved at his honesty, she met his gaze. Oh, those dark brown eyes and that mouth! She slammed the mental door shut on that line of thinking. No matter what they both might desire, they could only be friends. And right now, having a friend standing in front of her was a miracle.

"Charles, it's so good to see you." Her voice cracked, and she buried her face in her hands. He drew her into his arms, and the warmth of his embrace released a flow of tears, wetting his shirt.

After a moment, she drew back and dried her eyes with the corner of her apron. "I need to get back to the kitchen. Is my family all right? Gabriel-Isaac?"

"As far as I know, they're all well."

"And Marguerite?" she asked.

"I haven't seen her either."

"Could you get word to them that it's not too bad here? I'm mostly in the kitchen or in the room I share with the housemaid, who's very kind."

"Of course, anything. I'll visit your family, then the *moulin*, as soon as possible."

She nodded, a myriad of emotions constricting her throat.

Charles glanced toward the back of the cellar. "You know, your papa built those wine casks. I think of him often as I work in here. His mastery of experimental vintages is far beyond me, but I'm trying to figure out how he did it."

His eyebrows scrunched. "I hope you don't mind me talking about him and working in his place."

She shook her head. "Not at all. It's a relief to talk about him, and although I've never been in this place, I feel connected to him here."

"SUZANNE!" Justine's roar ricocheted off the inner courtyard walls.

"Follow my lead, Suzanne," said Charles. He picked up her bucket, then stepped through the door into the courtyard. "Justine! She's here with me. I had a question for her about the wines. I thought her father might have imparted some of his knowledge."

Charles handed her the water pail. "Thank you, Suzanne. That was very informative. I'll think about what you told me."

Justine's scowl deepened. She swept her arm out, indicating Suzanne's path back to work. Suzanne shot Charles a grateful look, then hurried away. Justine followed close behind and shoved Suzanne hard toward the kitchen door.

Back in the kitchen, Justine barked orders. Suzanne tried to keep up, sweat trickling down her back. She stirred the potage, taking care not to splash herself again, then took a large ham down from an overhead hook. After slicing and arranging the meat on a platter, she cleaned up.

"Anything else, Justine?"

The cook's eyes narrowed, then flitted around the room seeking further tasks.

"Should I go to the oven room and check the bread?"

"You think I'm letting you out of my sight again?"

Suzanne opened her mouth to repeat Charles's story but snapped it shut. The less she said, the better.

Marthe stepped into the kitchen. "Justine, is the midday meal ready to be carried up?"

"Almost. Take the prisoner back up to your room. I'm done with her for now. Then come back for Lord Valmalle's meal."

"*Oui*, Justine." Marthe turned and walked out of the kitchen. Suzanne followed up the wide stone staircase to the second floor. Her heart raced when they walked by the grand salon's double doors, like passing a bear's lair. Would Lord Valmalle emerge hungry?

Up in their room, Marthe turned to her. "It seems Justine's on the warpath more than usual."

"Yes, she is."

Marthe waited a moment, studying Suzanne. "Well, I'll be back with your meal when I can get away."

"*Merci*, Marthe." She met the maid's eyes. Did she read a question there?

Before she could figure it out or ask, Marthe left the room.

Suzanne removed the wooden clogs given her to wear inside, then stretched out on her bed, grateful for the unexpected break. After a moment, she curled on her side and thought about her meeting with Charles. Had it been mere coincidence? She didn't think so. *Thank you, heavenly Father, for letting me see Charles.*

Her eyes flew open, remembering how he'd held her in his arms. How she'd longed for that. Yet, while enormously comforting, his embrace felt more like a hug from a brother than anything else. The feeling surprised her, but it was just as well. The blessing of his friendship would be enough. He'd reassure her family and Marguerite that she was all right. And if Justine ever let her out of sight again, he'd bring news of Suzanne's loved ones. Her eyelids grew heavy.

Suzanne! You can't stay here! You must leave. Maman's hazel eyes filled with love and concern.

Maman, I can't leave. I'm a prisoner.

Suzanne! Papa stepped toward her. *You are more than a conqueror, through the love of Jesus.*

Papa! Maman! How are you here?

Maman held up her hand. *Suzanne, we came to warn you. Escape, as soon as possible.*

Escape?

Papa looked her in the eye. *One of the wine casks I built, the largest one, has a removable cover. Unlike the others, there are two iron hinges holding it in place. It should be on its side in the cellar's far right corner, on the shelves next to the wall. Do you understand?*

Uh, yes. Where was this going?

I knew the day would come when a way of escape would be necessary. I wedged the fat cork on the barrel's lid tight in place. Use it as a handle to lift off the lid. You'll have to remove the straw I placed inside the cask, then climb in. Don't forget to replace the straw and shut the lid behind you.

Suzanne squirmed. *I hide there?* She hated confined spaces.

Papa leaned closer. *The barrel has a false bottom. It should come off easily using the two finger indents on the upper right side. Behind it is a hole of the same size in the stone wall. Beyond the wall is a narrow, arched passageway. Enter it, then go to the right. At the end, there's a small trapdoor in the ground. Lift it out. I put a handle on it that lies flat until you pull it up. You'll see.*

Really? She didn't see now.

Once you pull the trapdoor up, there's a small stairway leading down. Descend it, remembering to replace the cover over your head once you're through.

It leads to a tunnel that runs under the Château and to the moulin. Maman's eyes fixed on her. *Do you see?*

Suzanne woke to the fragrance of a bowl of soup on the table beside her, indication she'd slept through Marthe's return. After splashing cold water on her face, Suzanne sat and swallowed a spoonful of lukewarm soup.

What she had dreamed returned with a rush. Maman and Papa! Suzanne looked around the room, as if they might be standing in a corner. She shut her eyes and replayed the dream.

Escape! A way out. But could she actually take it?

CHAPTER 39
MESSAGES

31 October 1702
St. Hippolyte du Fort
Southern Cévennes

"You really think we can trust him?" Gabriel-Isaac looked up at Marguerite, his face pinched tight. Why was she so much taller than him? And so pretty, with her hair so dark and shiny? Confused, he drew back and suppressed that line of thinking. He narrowed his eyes. "I know Charles is friendly with our family, especially Suzanne, but he's a Fesquet. He's Catholic."

Marguerite crossed her arms and peered down at him. "I know he'd never hurt Suzanne. We need her to know about the tunnel and the escape plan. How else can we do that if not through Charles? His daily work at the Château gives him access without suspicion."

Yes, Charles and the Fesquets were family friends, but were they beyond the temptation of betrayal? Gabriel-Isaac didn't like the plan, but he had to admit it could work.

Earlier discussions with Grand-mère, Aunt Anne, and Massip had suggested multiple ways of getting information to Suzanne but hadn't found a solution. Jean had offered to sneak into the Château, find Suzanne, and then escape with her through the tunnel. But all agreed that would put them both in great danger. If caught, the authorities would execute them without delay. That's why Gabriel-Isaac stood here, discussing possibilities with Marguerite. Also, as the tunnel ran from the Château's cellar to the *moulin*, she needed to be in on the plan.

"Good thing I have connections," Marguerite said. "I only recently learned of this tunnel myself. Decades ago, someone blocked off its exit near the waterwheel. I thought the tunnel might be useful someday and had a colleague reopen the access and install a door."

"Did you explore the tunnel? What did you find? Do you know where it opens in the Château?"

"Patience, young man! We went as far as possible before the tunnel dead-ended at a stone wall with a narrow staircase against it."

"Where did it lead?"

Marguerite frowned. "To a trapdoor in the ceiling above. Water trickling from the door made the stairs slick. We couldn't open the trapdoor, no matter how hard we tried. I suspect we were under the Château, but I don't know where exactly. Anyway, we needed to return to the *moulin* before my guard grew suspicious."

"So, we still have the problem of where Suzanne can access the tunnel. Aunt Anne only knew it started in the cellar somewhere." Gabriel-Isaac's shoulders tightened. How was this going to work?

Marguerite glanced out the window at the soldier posted outside. "Speaking of my guard, you need to leave soon. Do you agree we ask Charles to convey the message to Suzanne? Maybe he knows or can determine where to access the tunnel on the Château end."

"Yes," he sighed. "Will you or I talk to him? We need to act fast. Authorities continue searching for Jean. If he's discovered hiding in our cellar or *cachette*, they'll imprison us all—or worse. And he won't leave until Suzanne is safely out of the Château."

Marguerite thought for a moment. "Leave it to me. I'll send a trusted messenger to the Fesquets' home with word that their flour is ready. We've already delivered it, but I can pretend I've forgotten."

"Do you ever make that kind of mistake?"

"There's a first time for everything."

"What will you tell the messenger?"

"To ask Charles to come see me today as I have an important question about his family's flour deliveries. Then I'll inform Charles of the tunnel and ask him to relay to Suzanne that she must find it and then escape through it at midnight tomorrow. We'll wait for her here."

"Who's 'we'?"

"Me, of course. And Jean."

"Massip?"

"As you said, he needs to disappear and soon. So does Suzanne. With his skills, we can trust she's in safe hands." Marguerite offered her signature sardonic smile.

Until now, Gabriel-Isaac's primary concern had been getting the information to his sister and praying she'd escape safely. He'd not thought about afterward, not considered the implications. Like Jean, Suzanne would never be at liberty in St. Hippolyte, even in their home.

"You agree?"

Gabriel-Isaac nodded, unable to speak.

Marguerite picked up a medium-sized bag of flour. "Go, now. Take this, your 'order.' I'll send word to you when I have Charles's response."

Gabriel-Isaac hefted the sack on his shoulder, relieved it shielded his face from Marguerite, lest she see the tears pooling in his eyes.

Marguerite placed a hand on his shoulder. "Tell Jean to be here tomorrow before midnight. He can make his way through the front Planque vineyard and then hide in the stone storage hut near the *moulin*. I'll make sure the door's unlocked and meet him there. He'll need help finding where the tunnel exits the *moulin*."

Gabriel-Isaac murmured goodbye, then left, avoiding eye contact with the guard stationed outside. He walked home at a slow pace, his heart as heavy as the bag on his shoulder. As he approached the Château, he shifted the scratchy sack to the other side, revealing his face, in case Suzanne looked out a window. Even if this risky plot worked, would he ever see her again?

---

1 November 1702
St. Hippolyte du Fort
Southern Cévennes

Once again preparing vegetables in the kitchen, Suzanne kept watch on her home across the street, still hoping for a glimpse of her family. The chopping knife grazed her finger. She gave her head a little shake and focused on the task before her, lest she add a cut to her slowly healing burn.

The warning dream from her parents stayed with her. Should she take it seriously, or was it born out of a longing for freedom? It conveyed so many details. A hinged cask. A hole in the wall. A passageway leading to a tunnel. Even her overwrought imagination couldn't invent all that. But how could she know for sure?

There was only one way—going to the cellar and looking for the cask. Justine would never give permission to go there, since finding Suzanne with Charles yesterday. Suzanne set the knife down for a moment. Should she risk stealing away from the kitchen to search the cellar?

She didn't want to live in the Château for the rest of her life, a prisoner of Lord Valmalle. Rumor had it he'd soon marry, and children would likely follow. Was she consigned to live at the margins of someone else's family while longing for her own? *Heavenly Father, please show me what to do. Was that dream from you? Can I really escape? Show me the way.*

A loud knock on the kitchen's entry door interrupted her prayer. She wiped her hands on her apron and waited to see if Justine would get it. Who could it be? Servants entered without knocking.

Rap, rap, rap. Justine didn't appear, so Suzanne started toward the entry. The cook emerged from the depths of the kitchen, cut Suzanne off, and thrust open the door.

"Bonjour, Justine." Charles stood there, a warm smile on his face. He looked only at the cook, yet Suzanne sensed he was aware of her presence.

"What is it, young man? I'm busy and need to tend to the meal." With the back of her pudgy hand, Justine wiped sweat off her forehead, leaving a smudge of wheat flour.

"I'm sorry for the interruption, but there's a problem with one of the wine casks. Since Suzanne's father built it, I wonder if she could help solve the issue. I've discussed it with Lord Valmalle, and he's given permission for her to investigate the matter, under my supervision. When it's convenient for you, of course."

Justine's lips pressed into a straight line. She threw Suzanne a look that could burn down a forest, then glared at Charles. Suzanne studied his face. What was he up to? And how strange that he mentioned her father and a cask. Could this be connected to the dream?

"All right, if the master says so. Only if she's done with the vegetables."

Suzanne kept her voice calm. "I've finished the task. Should I add them to the potage?"

"No, I'll do it. Go, but come back quickly and clean the floor."

"Yes, of course."

Justine held open the door and shooed Suzanne through, letting it slam shut behind.

"Hurry!" Charles spoke low as he headed toward the cellar.

She followed him into the cool interior, then waited while he shut the door.

"Charles, what's this all about?"

"Marguerite sent a messenger with word from your family."

Suzanne stepped forward. "Are they well?"

"Yes, but there's more. Apparently, there's a tunnel running underground from somewhere in here to the *moulin*." His dark eyes bore into hers.

Could it be? Was this a dream as well? "Wait, Charles. You're telling me there's a tunnel from here to Marguerite's *moulin*?"

"Exactly. Problem is, your aunt Anne knows of its existence but not where to access it in the cellar."

"But I do."

"What?" Charles gaped. "You know where to find it? How?" He shook his head. "Never mind, we have little time. Where is it?"

"I thought you knew! You told Justine there's a problem with a cask. Papa said he made a special one that conceals a hole in the stone wall leading to a passageway and then to an underground tunnel."

He shook his head. "I just made up the problem with the barrel to get you in here. Your Papa told you all this?"

"No time now for that story. He said it's the biggest one, on the far right end of the shelf."

Charles pointed to a cask. "That one differs from the others. Besides being the largest, there are hinges on the top piece. A servant told me your father said it leaked and couldn't be used until repaired."

"Hinges! That's what Papa said."

They rushed across the room and began examining the barrel. He tapped it in several places, confirming it wasn't full of wine.

"Papa said the cork is like a handle."

Charles tugged at the cork and the top swung up and open despite its rusty hinges. Winey scents from the past flowed into the room.

She stood on tiptoe, peering inside. "Just as Papa said! He put straw in here to help conceal the false bottom at the back end. Hard to see in the dark, but I can just make it out."

"Suzanne, most of your family just learned of the tunnel, but not its exact location. When did your Papa tell you all this?"

"It came to me in a dream."

"A dream? What? Well, I'm glad you knew." He leaned closer. "Suzanne, there's more to the message."

She met his eyes.

"You're to escape through the tunnel tonight, around midnight. Marguerite will wait for you at the *moulin* end."

Suzanne sucked in her breath. Tonight? Everything was happening so quickly, there was no time to think the plan through. Yet, between the dream leading her to this point, Charles's help, and Marguerite waiting for her on the other end, it all seemed to be falling into place.

"I'll do it," she whispered.

Charles held her gaze, his own full of questions. "You're sure?"

"Yes."

His head dipped, then he turned to the barrel. "All right then. I'll let your family know we found the passage to the tunnel and that you'll follow the plan. The top will be back in place and the hinges oiled to ensure they open easily. I'll place a large rock or something on the ground below to help you climb up into the cask. Once you're inside, remember to close the cover."

A tiny smile played on her lips. "Papa said the same thing about the trapdoor in the passageway floor, leading to the bigger tunnel."

Charles looked through the barrel, studying the false bottom. "I wish we had time to practice, to make sure you can get through. Hopefully, the passageway isn't much lower on the other side. And it'll be very dark. You'll need a candle or a torch."

He paced, walking in a small circle. Finally, he stopped and put his hand on her shoulder. "Suzanne, you're *sure* you want to do this? You could be caught by one of Valmalle's servants. And if you make it to the *moulin*, then what will you do? Hide for the rest of your life?"

Suzanne looked at the cask, then back at Charles. Despite her throbbing pulse—not from proximity to him for once, but for all that lay ahead—she'd take this path to freedom. At least she'd try. Her heavenly Father had given her a way out. Literally. Hope bubbled up, like a life-giving ground spring, filling her soul with a well of peace. Charles's legitimate concerns should've had the opposite effect. But this was God's plan. He'd be with her every step of the way.

"Charles, this is for the best. God is with me and will provide all I need." Her knees weakened a bit as she spoke the thought out loud. Not that she didn't believe it to be true. She did. But there was a lot of ground to cover between now and standing in Marguerite's *moulin*. And then what would she do?

"Suzanne!" Justine's voice screeched through the courtyard. "I need help. Now!"

"I have to go. Please tell Marguerite and my family all we found and that, Lord willing, I'll go through the tunnel tonight at midnight."

Charles shut the cask lid. "I'll leave you something you can use for light. A lantern, a torch, whatever I can find. But you'll have to bring a lit candle to make use of it."

"Thank you for everything, Charles."

He drew her into his arms for a last quick embrace, then gave her cheeks three *bisous*. She returned them, blessing him in the name of the Father, the Son, and the Spirit.

"SUZANNE!" The little patience Justine possessed had disappeared.

Suzanne glanced at the cellar door. "Charles, there's one more favor. I've been writing for the past few months. Could you get word to Grandmère about the parchments inside my desk? I'd like her to hide them somewhere safe. Maybe I'll return some day and collect them."

"Of course, Suzanne." His eyes shone with unshed tears.

"Adieu, Charles."

"Go with God, Suzanne. Adieu."

CHAPTER 40

MEASLES

1 November 1702
Mialet
Eastern Cévennes

From the valley below Mialet, Rolland and a handful of his men snaked their way through brambles and bushes in the dark before dawn. One by one, they slipped into the narrow streets of the hamlet, hopefully unnoticed. Were Governor Bâville's soldiers waiting, assuming Rolland would come home?

Rolland heaved a sigh. Maybe he didn't care anymore. Yesterday's word confirming the arrests of his mother and sisters had ignited a blazing fury beyond anything he'd ever known. He'd thought himself prepared for repercussions on his family, but the boiling rage flowing through his veins testified otherwise.

His last visit to Mialet was only a week ago, on Mazel's orders for all the men to return home and regroup after the debacle with Capitaine Poul. As always, Rolland had known it could be the last time he'd see his family. Still, the news of their arrests came as a punch to the gut, knocking the wind out of him. Was their suffering all his fault?

Hadn't he only acted as the Holy Spirit led? Putting an end to enemies under God's orders like the Old Testament heroes? No other recourse for justice existed, no other manner for the Huguenots to regain their freedoms.

He signaled Gabriel to hold the men back and conceal themselves well. For now, Mazel's band had divided into two smaller ones for greater stealth. Rolland had taken charge of one, Abraham another.

Fewer men increased mobility and the element of surprise. No one knew where they'd next appear.

Rolland would enter the house first, alone. If they walked into a trap, only he'd be caught in the snare. Also, he needed a moment by himself. The weight of sorrow in his chest increased with each step.

He crept up the winding back staircase to his home, less open to view than the front entrance. At the top, he paused for a moment, then opened the wooden door. Finding it unlocked was normal. Mialet was, after all, a Huguenot hamlet. But with royal soldiers roaming the countryside and possibly surveying his family home, he wasn't sure what to expect at any turn.

The first of the kitchen rooms was empty. Standing on the uneven terra-cotta tiles, he peered into the room beyond, with its wide fireplace. No one. Tears filled his eyes, and he felt his last measure of hope leave him. The reports were true. His entire family had been taken.

He strode through to the inner room and out to the covered terrace, where his mother and sisters cooked in the heat of summer. Normally, they filled the space with joy, chatter, and the delicious smells of hearty food. Today, not even the mice stirred.

In a daze, he wandered to the inside kitchen and stood at the cold hearth. Usually, this time of year, a fire blazed there from dawn until bedtime. He toed the ashes with his leather boot. Were his mother and sisters alive? If so, where were they? Could he rescue them?

A snuffled noise behind him drew his attention. He pivoted fast and crossed to the window, scanning for enemy troops. All appeared still, inside and out.

If royal soldiers appeared, he could hide in the *cachette* beneath the cupboard next to him. The *cachette*! Why hadn't he thought of checking it first thing? His capacity for hope had grown so small. Dared he hope now that the sound he'd heard came from there?

He opened the carved oak doors, knelt, reached for the bottom shelf, and lifted the wood plank, using the barely visible fingerholds made by his father years earlier. Rolland had helped Papa carve into the limestone on this side of the house nestled against a hill, creating a hiding space that could fit up to six people.

Holding the shelf, Rolland looked into the hole below, then leaned over to get a good look at the dugout area extending back under the floor. The plank clattered to the ground. Two pairs of wide eyes stared at him, and his heart surged with joy.

"Joséphine! Michèle!"

The girls shuffled forward, blinking at the light. "Rolland!"

Emotion clogged his throat. His youngest sisters were safe! He reached in and pulled out one, then the other. The girls fell into his arms, clinging tight. He savored the moment, whispering thanks to God.

"Are you hurt?" Rolland asked, his voice husky.

Sixteen-year-old Joséphine, the older of the pair, spoke up. "We're not harmed."

"Just freezing," Michèle said. Two years younger than Joséphine, her slight build meant she was often cold.

"How long have you been in there?"

"What day is it?" asked Joséphine.

"Wednesday, the first of November."

"The soldiers arrived on Monday. Maman sensed they were coming—or God told her. As the troops came up the stairs, she insisted we hide in the *cachette*."

"Have you been hiding this whole time?"

Joséphine shook her head. "After what seemed like a day, we came out and ate. We hid again when we heard someone coming up the stairs. I'm so glad it was you!"

"There wasn't time for Gabrielle or Esther to join us," Michèle said, her eyes glistening.

Rolland paced in a rapid circle, tamping down his anger. "I'm grateful that at least you two were spared. We'll pray for the safety of our mother and sisters. May God deliver them from the hands of the enemy."

All three wiped away tears. Rolland led the girls to the kitchen table, settled them on a wooden bench, then went to fetch blankets from the bedroom. He returned and draped them over their shoulders. Lifting a ceramic pitcher left full on the stone counter, he poured each of them a cup of water.

"I need to let my men know they can join us, then let's find something to eat. We don't dare light a fire; the smoke would alert anyone watching." He opened the kitchen window and whistled the prearranged signal, the distinct sound of the hoopoe bird. Within minutes, several Camisards appeared, minus Gabriel and Paul, who stood watch below.

"Men, these are my younger sisters, Joséphine and Michèle. Safe, by God's grace!"

The fighters removed their caps and greeted the girls.

"They could use your help to prepare food for us all. Without fire, for obvious reasons."

No one needed to be asked twice. The men and girls searched the cupboards and served up cured sausages, an aged cheese, and dried figs. Rolland offered a prayer of gratitude for his family's constant endeavors in the garden and in preserving what they grew. They always had enough to eat and even enough to share. He sent plates of food and pewter tankards of ale to his lieutenants on watch.

The rest of the day passed without incident. All needed rest. At twilight, Rolland ordered a rotation of guards throughout the night. Propped in a chair, he watched over his sisters, not ready to let them out of his sight. Sleep came to him only intermittently.

While enormously relieved to find his younger sisters, he needed to figure out what to do with them. Leaving them here alone would leave them vulnerable in multiple ways. Taking them to nearby family members would be dangerous for all concerned, and he could not trust them to anyone in the hamlet with certainty.

He dropped his head in his hands and prayed his mother and other two sisters lived and were safe. If only he knew where they were. Should he now concentrate on finding and rescuing them?

A gentle hand landed on his shoulder. He jerked to attention, trying to focus on the figure standing beside him.

"Michèle, is anything wrong? Couldn't you sleep? I'm here watching over you." He wished to tuck her back into bed and protect her like a young child.

"I know," she said, smiling. She pulled a chair close and sat down. "I just want to tell you something that Joséphine and I discussed. We know you can't leave us here. So, we want to come with you and help. All these years you've prepared for such a time as this, we've been watching and waiting for our turn. We can play our part, too."

Rolland stared at his sister, a hundred reasons against the idea swarming through his mind. When had she become this articulate, strong young woman?

"I know you'll think it's not appropriate or safe," she continued. "But where are we truly safe? Only as we follow God's leading. The outcome is in his hands."

He couldn't find his voice. How did his sister have such wisdom and trust?

She held out a folded parchment. "Maman handed me this letter for you before we hid in the *cachette*."

Rolland reached for the letter. Michèle leaned over, kissed him on the cheek, and returned to her bed.

His eyes blurred at his mother's familiar script.

> *Cher Rolland,*
>
> *If you're reading this, then you'll already know of my arrest. I've long planned to hide your sisters in the cachette with this letter should such an event occur, knowing you'd come when you heard the news.*
>
> *Be assured that I'm at peace. God has prepared me. I do not go into the unknown alone or afraid. He'll never fail or forsake me. I trust him entirely for all the days of my life, and I will dwell in his house forever.*
>
> *Please don't attempt to rescue me. Instead, attend to your divine calling and continue to lead the Camisards entrusted to your care.*
>
> *As for your sisters, all four wish to join you in the fight for freedom. They have my blessing to do so, and I know your father would agree. Your sisters and I have discussed and prayed over the matter, and I believe they can be of great service. God will show you the way.*
>
> *You are always in my prayers.*
> *All my love,*
> *Maman*

Rolland read the words again, then folded and slid the letter into his pants pocket. How like his mother to prepare them all for a time such as this. Through her wisdom, clarity came, at least for the next few steps. Though resistance ran high in him at the idea of not attempting a rescue, his mother was right, as usual.

Would it actually work to bring his sisters along? Everything in him longed to protect them, to find them safe shelter. Yet he had to admit they could be helpful, and he knew they wouldn't give in to fear. How would it all work?

He drifted into a light slumber until early light. At dawn, he rose and checked his sisters' beds. Empty and neatly made. The sounds of breakfast preparations emanated from the kitchen. His belly rumbled in response. He rose to his feet, massaged a knot in his neck, then walked to the window. Turning the iron handle, he threw it open, letting a rush of fresh air fill the room.

Movement below caught his eye. A lone figure approached through the narrow street leading to his home. Rolland leaned farther out just as Gabriel stepped into the man's path, stopping him, then clapping him on the back. Gabriel gestured toward the house, and others stepped out from hiding places.

The leader's face came into view. Abraham Mazel! What was he doing here?

Rolland hurried down the stairs to greet his friend.

"Mazel! This is a surprise! Is all well?"

"We were nearby and needed provisions. And your family?"

"I've good news in that regard. My two youngest sisters hid in the *cachette* and went undetected."

"Praise be to God! And your mother and other sisters?"

A layer of peace beyond comprehension encouraged Rolland, weaving through the familiar sorrow of loss. "Arrested. I don't know where they are, but my mother left a letter urging me to carry on with God's mission."

Abraham placed his hand on Rolland's shoulder. "I'm very sorry. Your mother is a woman of great faith, who trusts in the plans and the goodness of God."

"That is so, and there's more. She advocates for my sisters to join us in our fight."

Mazel looked away, then back at his friend. "God's been speaking to me about that very thing. We need the wisdom and inner strength women bring."

Abraham's response surprised Rolland, yet it provided one more confirmation, like a puzzle piece slotting into place. Still, he struggled to picture his sisters or any women on the road or near a battle.

"Abraham, bring in your men. My sisters have prepared breakfast and we're happy to share."

Fighters flew up the stairs, overrunning the dining table and kitchen to enjoy a decent meal, a rare experience. Without the use of fire, the sisters served up cold smoked ham, cured sausages, and sun-dried figs. Talk was sparse as hungry Camisards tucked in. Rolland ate little, his mind preoccupied with the next steps.

After stomachs were satisfied, Abraham turned to Rolland. "My band will move on. No need to draw attention with too much activity here."

Rolland nodded. One never knew who would report them to the authorities. Abraham half rose from the table, then fell back in his chair and slumped forward. Joséphine set down a platter of ham she held and touched his forehead.

"He's burning up with fever."

Gabriel and Paul came to Mazel's side, then helped him to the nearest bed.

"I'm not feeling too good either," said one man. "Hot, cold, then hot again."

"Me too," said another.

"And I've got these red spots on my chest and stomach."

"And your neck."

"Oh! So do I."

Rolland lifted the closest man's shirt. Small red dots covered his torso. "Measles." Rolland looked at his sisters. "A few men were sick when we were last together with Mazel's troop in Fressac. We left them in sympathetic Huguenot homes."

"The sickness has recently passed through the area," said Joséphine.

"Some recover," Michèle added. "Some don't. But we'll do our best to ensure all survive."

The young women sprang into action. Once the home's beds were full of men fallen ill, the women created resting places on the floor. Throughout the afternoon and night, they bustled about, serving water and light food and placing cool cloths on burning brows.

Following the sisters' instructions, Rolland and other men helped best they could. By midnight, he collapsed into a chair, no longer able to fight the dizziness and growing weakness that had stalked him for the past hour. Michèle appeared at his side, and her cool hand on his forehead confirmed what they suspected. Joséphine checked others and announced that most had high temperatures and the telltale red spots.

Rolland's strength ebbed. Barely able to pray, he managed a quick plea for healing, as Michèle helped him to a nest of blankets prepared on the floor.

CHAPTER 41

DISAPPEARANCE

1–2 November 1702
St. Hippolyte du Fort
Southern Cévennes

Lying in bed, listening to Marthe's rhythmic breathing, Suzanne guessed it must be close to midnight. No timepiece existed in the room, but considering the kitchen cleanup after the evening meal, plus the hour since Marthe blew out the candle, it must be close.

Suzanne needn't have worried about falling asleep and missing her escape. Little chance of that. Her pounding heart roared through her ears, noisy in the nighttime silence. She lifted her woolen blanket. It was time.

Bare feet on the floor, she reached for the clothes she'd placed at the end of the bed. She slipped the blouse over her head, stepped into her skirt, and fastened the buttons on the only things that were her own. After pulling her hair into a tight chignon, she set her bonnet in place. Marthe slept on. Thanking God for her many kindnesses, Suzanne prayed what she was about to do wouldn't bring repercussions on the housemaid.

Suzanne pulled on her stockings, picked up her leather shoes, and tiptoed to Marthe's nightstand. Charles's plan to leave a lantern of some sort required bringing something to set it alight. Suzanne reached for the extinguished candle so very close to Marthe's head and slowly pulled it out of the iron candle holder. One obstacle cleared, many more to go.

With care, she moved to the fireplace, relieved to find a few red embers glowing in the dark. Kneeling on the terra-cotta tiles, she extended the candle into the ashes, pushing the wick against a live coal, praying it would ignite. A tiny flame, then a larger flare. She drew the candle out, stood, and walked to the door. With her hand on the iron knob, she turned to bid Marthe a silent farewell.

Suzanne jumped, fumbling the candle. Her roommate sat up in bed, watching. The two women held each other's gaze. Suzanne swallowed hard, trying to think of an excuse, chiding herself for not coming up with one in advance.

"Fear not, Suzanne," Marthe said, her voice low.

Suzanne blinked at the echo of her heavenly Father's oft-repeated words.

"I . . . uh . . . Marthe, I must go. Now. It's my chance for freedom."

Marthe held out a key. "You'll need this."

"Oh! I didn't realize you locked us in at night."

"Valmalle's orders. I waited till you were asleep each night, which doesn't take long."

"Except tonight. I only pretended to sleep but still didn't hear you lock the door."

Suzanne crossed the room and took the key. Marthe tapped two fingers on her own forehead, then left and right across her chest, signing the cross of Christ. She kissed those fingers and raised her hand toward Suzanne. "Go with God."

"*Merci!*" Suzanne leaned toward her friend. "I pray they don't blame you."

"I'll say I accidentally left the key in the lock and slept through your departure. Don't worry. My prayers are with you."

"And mine with you. Thank you for everything."

Suzanne blew Marthe a kiss, unlocked the door but left the key in place, then slipped out. Glancing both ways, she began her journey down the dim hallway, tiptoeing past servants' bedrooms. At the hall's far end, she descended the service staircase to the ground floor, into the back of the kitchen.

Clack! Was that a door shutting? She flattened herself against the wall, holding her candle low. Maybe a wooden shutter had come open in the wind. Hard to tell. When no one appeared, she moved on through the labyrinth of rooms, pausing at the window above the sink to convey a silent goodbye to her family across the street. Would she ever see them again?

Careful to shield her candle from the blast of air, she opened the main kitchen door and peered into the central courtyard. Heart racing, she glanced at the front door across the entryway to her right. The guard's chair sat empty. Presumably, the man Valmalle ordered to guard the door since her arrival was either patrolling on the outside or off relieving himself. *Thank you, Lord.*

Everything in her wanted to run the short distance to the cellar, but keeping the candle flame alive required slower movement. Several windows lined the upper floors surrounding the open space. Was that someone looking out one of them?

Head bent forward, Suzanne crossed the courtyard, pushed open the wooden door to the cellar, and stepped inside. She closed the door, then scanned the area with her meager light. The cask, with its doorway to freedom, lay in its usual position on the shelf. A small wrought-iron lantern sat beside it, tucked back a little against the wall. Charles had kept his word; of course he had, but at significant risk. If Lord Valmalle or any authorities found out Charles had known of her plans and helped her carry them out, the repercussions would be severe. *Lord, protect him.*

Suzanne hurried to the cask, pulled forward the lantern, and lit the larger candle inside. Relieved, she held up the lantern by the top iron ring, then pulled the wide cork on the front of the cask. No movement. She tried again. Nothing budged. Was the lid stuck? Maybe Charles had wedged it firmly into place.

After a few more tugs, the lid popped open and up on the hinge, newly oiled thanks to Charles. Suzanne stepped up on the crate he'd left to aid her climb into the barrel. With care, she pulled out the straw stored inside and set it on the shelf, then slid the lantern into the cask. She kneed herself up onto the shelf and crawled inside, headfirst. Inching along on her stomach, she pushed the lantern farther until it illuminated the false bottom's fingerholds. She reached up and tugged hard, releasing the wooden round.

Cold, musty air flowed from beyond. Setting the false bottom inside the cask, she nudged the lantern to the edge, then shimmied forward. She grasped the lantern and gently swung it out through the hole in the back wall, then she poked her head out. She moved the light up and down the passageway. Something on the right caught her eye. A small stone ledge protruded just within reach, the perfect width to hold a lantern. As if someone had prepared for this exact need. Papa? The ledge seemed like something he'd create. She set the light on the little shelf.

Hanging on tight to the edge of the cask, she assessed the depth of the passage. Thankfully, the drop looked manageable. She could jump, but how then to reach the lantern?

Look down, child.

Suzanne blinked, then saw it. Slats of wood attached to the wall right below her, spaced at intervals. A ladder! Papa had planned a way down and back up.

She left the lantern and wriggled back out into the Château cellar. Standing in the dark, she drew a deep breath and reentered the barrel feetfirst. Pushing her skirts down, she rolled onto her stomach and reached back outside, tapping around with her hand to find the straw. She grabbed as much as possible, pulled it into the cask, and shoved it under her body. Pulling the lid closed, she prayed Charles would arrive early in the morning and cover her tracks.

Using her forearms, Suzanne wiggled through the barrel until her feet stuck out into the cold passage, then she inched farther back and down until her feet made contact with the top of the ladder. Standing on the ladder's slats, she pulled the false bottom back into place. Then she picked up the lantern and made her way down into the passageway.

She landed with a splash, glad to have both feet on solid, if wet, ground. Rivulets of water ran across the dirt floor below, probably overflow from the cistern on the other side. She held the lantern high but couldn't see the end of the passageway. She'd made it through several obstacles but there was still a long way to go. Without warning, discouragement seeped in, like the water penetrating her shoes.

Rocking back on her heels, she shut her eyes for a moment. Before her rose an image of Papa, smiling. Beside him stood Maman, courageous to the end. *Beloved! Fear not.* So much love, from her heavenly Father and her earthly parents, infused Suzanne with new resolve.

She started her journey through the illuminated passageway, which turned to the right as Papa instructed in the dream.

After several minutes, she arrived at the wall marking the end of the passageway. Using one foot, she searched for the trapdoor, unsure exactly what it would feel like. So far, she'd walked through a silty mixture of dirt and water. Nothing here felt different. She scraped harder, but only dug into mud. Isn't this where Papa said it would be?

Panic swirled like the water around her ankles. Fear beat its wings once again, whispering doubt into her soul. *You're stuck, there's no way out. This'll never work. Go back.*

Non! She'd not give in to the lies. *Lord, help me.*

She knelt, ignored the cold water soaking her skirt, and used her free hand to search through the sludge. Working from left to right, she scraped methodically until her shoulder muscle spasmed. Shifting the lantern to the other hand, she carried on. She had to find the way out.

After what felt like at least a quarter hour of moving mud, rocks, and other substances she tried not to think about, she made contact with metal. Pushing aside the muck, her hand bumped against a large iron ring. The handle!

She grasped it hard and tugged with all her strength. Thunk! As the trapdoor popped off, Suzanne staggered back. Murky water trickled down the already wet stairs below.

With the water evacuated, she placed one foot on the slick top stair, testing the stability. No guard rail, so she took one step at a time, her left hand on the stone wall, her right holding the lantern. Only ten steps down, but it seemed to take an eternity to reach the bottom.

On the ground below, she raised the lantern, illuminating a portion of the tunnel. Beyond that, utter darkness. Fear crept again around the edges of her heart. *Non!* Jesus is with me, even here in the depths and the darkness. Strength steeled her soul, and she stepped out.

Light flickered off the flat stone ceiling. She imagined this portion of the passage ran under the Château's outer courtyard, the one she'd only seen briefly from an upstairs window. Quite some distance remained if the tunnel opened somewhere at Marguerite's *moulin*. Only one way to find out.

Suzanne placed one soggy foot in front of another, moving down the long, straight path. Water trickled through the wall on her left, again most likely from the Château's immense underground cistern. After several minutes, the tunnel curved to the right and continued on. Guessing she was now under the street, heading ever closer to the *moulin* and safety, she picked up the pace, then tripped over an unseen object and crashed hard to the ground. The glass in the lantern shattered and its light extinguished.

Complete darkness descended. Disoriented, she could barely breathe. Shaky, she stood and brushed off her muddy hands, letting out a yelp at a stab of pain in her right palm. She pulled out a shard of glass, then used her forearms to brush the hair off her face. Had she come this far to fail? She couldn't see a thing.

Beloved! Fear not. I am with you. Was that truly God's voice or just her own mind repeating the words? Did it matter? Either way, the assurance was true.

Walk with me. I am the light that overcomes the darkness. This was new. The Voice had never spoken that biblical truth to her directly. But she'd never been stuck in an underground tunnel in utter darkness. Was God saying he'd guide her, be her light when she had no other?

Shuffling left, she found the wall. Still unable to see a hand in front of her face, she took a step forward, then another. As she moved, something like light surrounded her. Not a physical light, but a presence, strong and full of love, infusing her with the courage to carry on.

She made slow progress. Her neck ached, the cut in her hand stung, and her clothes were soaked through to the skin. How much farther? Would Marguerite be there? What if something detained her or she'd fallen asleep? Then what would happen? Suzanne shivered, then banished the thoughts and turned her focus to the path ahead.

Stepping through inky blackness for several minutes, she beat back fiery darts of fear. *I am more than a conqueror through Christ's love. I am Beloved and never alone.* Repeating these truths imparted strength.

The limestone wall under her hand veered right. A point of light appeared, tiny in the distance. Was it just her imagination? Was she seeing what she wanted so desperately? Several steps farther assured her it was real.

She accelerated her pace until she passed through an unlocked door in a stone wall. She emerged next to the huge stone basin at the bottom of Marguerite's *moulin*. The gentle splash of river water turning the giant waterwheel was music to the ears. Moonlight streamed through a nearby window, casting shadows across the limestone walls. Where was Marguerite?

Suzanne followed a small passageway that descended on her left, plunging her back into total darkness as it wound under the main floor of the mill. Where did this tunnel end?

Around a corner, a small light shone, illuminating a portion of night sky before it extinguished. Suzanne stopped, despite longing for fresh air, for freedom. What if someone had betrayed them, exposing their plan?

With caution, she approached the end of the tunnel, then leaned out into the night.

"Suzanne!"

"Marguerite!"

The friends fell into an embrace, relief and joy enveloping them both.

"Bonsoir, Suzanne!"

Suzanne jolted and drew away from Marguerite. Jean Massip!

CHAPTER 42

GROTTE DE LA ROQUETTE

2 November 1702
St. Hippolyte du Fort
Southern Cévennes

Gabriel-Isaac threw the knapsack over his shoulder and lifted the candle from the table beside his bed. He looked at his sleeping siblings, silently bidding them goodbye. Slipping out the bedroom door, he tiptoed downstairs and placed the note to Grand-mère on the kitchen table. She'd understand, but he wanted her to know his reasons.

As the grandfather clock in the salon chimed midnight, he stepped through the back door into the dark. A nearly full moon shone overhead, casting dancing tree shadows across the garden to the sound of a night owl's plaintive cry. He blew out the candle and stuck it in his sack as a rush of energy pumped through his veins.

Hunched over, he made his way across the garden to the gate opening into the road. He looked up at the Château de Planque. Was Suzanne on her way to Marguerite's *moulin*? What if she didn't make it? He gave his head a shake. He needed to concentrate.

Leaning out, he scanned up and down the road. All clear. A few tentative steps into the street, then he ran toward the wide field in front of the Château. Bypassing the tall wrought-iron entry gate, always locked, he leaped over the short limestone wall, landing on hands and knees on the lower side. He straightened up, brushed off his palms, then dashed to the stone storage shed in the middle of the front vineyard, following Marguerite's instructions for Jean.

Inside, he paused to catch his breath. Had anyone seen him? Ducking his head through the low door, he peered through the vineyard. No one. He darted through rows of harvested vines, the nubs on their bare branches forming strange nighttime shapes.

Arriving at the river side of the *moulin*, he skirted the edge of the building, running beneath the eight tall windows of the workspace where he'd met with Marguerite yesterday. Her idea had worked. Charles had not only communicated the plan to Suzanne but returned with the report that she'd known of the tunnel and how to access it. God definitely seemed involved in all this.

Gabriel-Isaac rounded the back corner of the moulin and crept along the side. At the opposite corner, movement in a grate-covered drainage hole beside his feet drew his attention. He knelt and looked inside, now seeing nothing.

"Marguerite, is that you?" he whispered.

Nothing.

"It's Gabriel-Isaac. Are you down there?"

Marguerite's face emerged from the dark, her pale skin reflecting the light of the moon. "Gabriel-Isaac! What are you doing here?"

"I'll explain later. Why are you in there? Is this the tunnel?"

"Get down here," Marguerite hissed, pushing open the grate.

He jumped into the space, and she replaced the covering.

Jean stepped out of the dark, Suzanne behind him.

Gabriel-Isaac smiled wide. "Suzanne! You made it!"

"What are *you* doing here?" Jean whispered through clenched teeth.

"I'm going with you."

Suzanne gaped at her brother.

"I suppose you just can't stay away from adventure," said Marguerite, smirk well in place.

Gabriel-Isaac's eyes flashed. "It's not just for that. I must find a way to fight."

Jean stepped closer. "You sent me off tonight letting me think we'd said goodbye forever."

"Would you have let me come if I'd asked?"

Jean didn't answer.

Suzanne placed her hands on her hips. "I don't know if I should throttle or kiss you."

"I'll take the kiss, please."

She reached out and pulled him into a warm embrace. "So, I *did* see you from the Château kitchen window. Why are you home?"

"I thought I saw you too! Why I'm home is a long story for later." Maybe never, if he had his way.

Suzanne studied him, then turned her attention to Jean. "How on earth are *you* here? Last I saw you, soldiers were dragging you to another part of the prison-fort."

"Also a long story for later," Gabriel-Isaac said. "He escaped through the window of his cell and came to rescue you!"

Suzanne stared at Jean, her eyes shining bright with something Gabriel-Isaac didn't understand. Why were her cheeks so pink?

Marguerite cleared her throat. "You all need to get going. At some point, they'll discover Suzanne's absence and alert the authorities."

"You're right," said Jean. "Best to travel under cover of night as well." He rubbed the back of his neck. "Gabriel-Isaac, I should send you home, but I don't think you'd go. Or stay. I guess we're stuck with you."

Holding back a grin, Gabriel-Isaac nodded with all the solemnity he could muster.

"Where are we going?" Suzanne asked Jean.

"First thing is to disappear far into the *garrigue*, through the densest trees, bushes, and rock outcroppings. Somewhere no soldiers will find us. The rest will make itself clear as we go. God will be our guide."

"So go!" ordered Marguerite. She embraced Suzanne again, squeezing her best friend close.

"Thank you, Marguerite, for everything. May God continue to bless you and your work."

"We'll see each other again, if I have anything to do with it!" The cheer in Marguerite's voice sounded forced. "Now GO!"

"Au revoir, Suzanne."

"Au revoir, Marguerite."

Both women avoided the finality of the word *adieu*.

Jean led the way out, down to the river's edge at the end of the property, where their troop disappeared into a copse of trees. Brittle leaves crunched underfoot as they made their way downriver.

Under the central bridge, they huddled against one of the supporting arches and caught their breath. Gabriel-Isaac swallowed down revulsion at the memory of Camisard heads hanging up above only a week ago.

"Jean, I have an idea." Gabriel-Isaac spoke low. "Less than an hour from here is a cave. We've used it in the past for worship services."

"Grotte de la Roquette," whispered Suzanne, shutting her eyes.

"What is it Suzanne?" Jean's forehead ridged.

"It's where they arrested our parents."

Jean put his hand on her arm. "We'll go somewhere else."

She shook her head. "*Non.* It's a good idea."

"The soldiers don't know of all the hidden caverns and hiding places like we do." Gabriel-Isaac's voice rose with excitement.

"Shhh!"

"Sorry!"

Jean looked at Suzanne. "You're sure?"

"Yes." She rose to her feet and brushed off her wet skirt. "Let's go."

Jean turned to Gabriel-Isaac. "You lead the way. Remember the things I taught you about leaving no trace of our passage. We're right behind you."

Gabriel-Isaac's mouth fell open at being given the scout position, then shut quickly at the amusement on Jean's face. He squared his shoulders. "Let's go!"

Weaving their way through scratchy bushes and bending low under trees, they walked in single file, Suzanne behind her brother, with Jean bringing up the rear. She held back an overgrown branch and glanced back at him, meeting his eyes. Her pulse sped up, not just from the nighttime hike.

He'd escaped the prison and come to rescue her? That sounded like a fairy tale, like the ones Maman used read to Suzanne at night when she was little. Except Suzanne had escaped on her own, with help from Charles and, above all, her heavenly Father. It touched her deeply, though, that Jean had risked so much for her. And, at least for now, she wasn't alone.

They trudged along in silence as Gabriel-Isaac led them away from the river and up the side of the foothills. Moonlight beamed over the land, illuminating the way but also requiring that they take a longer, more surreptitious route.

Memories flooded Suzanne of the last time she and Gabriel-Isaac had followed the same path, the night of their parents' arrest. Fatigue wove through her body and she shivered, her soaked clothes adding to the chill.

A cloak descended on her shoulders. Warm and dry. She turned to Jean, his face lit with compassion and more. Heat spread into her chest, reaching her heart. She smiled and his lopsided grin stretched wide.

Gabriel-Isaac forged the way, turning to check on them from time to time. The spring in his step and his concentration on the task gave one more proof that he thrived in such circumstances. How many times would she have to let go of her desire that he stay under her wing, nearby, safe?

"Halfway there," announced Gabriel-Isaac.

"Let's take a quick break," said Jean.

"It's only been half an hour!"

"I know Gabriel-Isaac, but it's good to be aware of the needs of your group." Jean nodded in Suzanne's direction.

"I'm fine," she said. "We can rest at the cave."

Gabriel-Isaac looked at Jean, who studied Suzanne.

"Jean, I'm all right." She pulled the cloak tighter around her body, beaming her thanks.

"All right, then."

The path widened as they continued along the edge of a foothill. Suzanne slowed and fell in beside Jean. "You needn't baby me. I can walk a lot longer than this and have done so many times."

"I'm sure you have, but never after escaping through a dark, wet tunnel. Your clothes are soaked, and it's already been quite an evening."

"I'd say so!"

"Later, I'd love to hear how you found out about the tunnel and all the rest."

"It was quite unusual. And I want to hear how you escaped from St. Hippolyte's prison-fort. No one gets out of there."

"God led me each step of the way."

"Same for me. He provided every need. Even when my lantern broke, his presence lit the dark from inside me. It's hard to explain."

"I know exactly what you mean."

Jean reached for her hand, enveloping it in warmth and strength. She returned his gentle squeeze. Something in her heart slotted into place, like coming home. But this was different, something she'd never experienced outside her family, and she liked it. A lot. In the distance, a solitary owl hooted, the soft sound adding a magical note in the moonlit forest.

Gabriel-Isaac started down the side of the mountain as they approached the cave. Feet wobbled and slid on loose rocks until they arrived at the bottom of the hill. Farther on, they located the opening. One at a time, they bent under the overhang and stepped into the large interior.

"Jean, do you have those flint rocks with you?" asked Gabriel-Isaac. "We need light. "There are lots of slippery boulders on the way down."

"I've been wondering if you'd ask for them."

"I just thought of it."

"A good guide anticipates needs."

Gabriel-Isaac's shoulders sagged. Then he straightened up and reached into his knapsack.

"I have a candle!" he said, pulling it out.

"Good. I do too, but let's start with yours."

Jean passed him the pair of rocks and watched as Gabriel-Isaac rubbed them without success. After several minutes, he huffed and handed them over to Jean.

"It takes practice," assured Jean, achieving a spark within seconds. He lit Gabriel-Isaac's candle, then pulled two more from his own knapsack and set them alight, handing one to Suzanne.

Each candle beamed only scanty light, but together they sufficed. More than once, Jean held Suzanne's arm as she climbed over rocks coated in slimy clay. More than once, he didn't let go when on level ground. She drew close to him as they navigated their way.

At the bottom, they stopped to rest. Suzanne found a semidry boulder, sat, and pulled Jean's cloak tight around her. She tried to relax despite the cold and the onslaught of sounds and images from the past. *Lord, help me deal with this, please. It's hard to be here, right where Maman and Papa were taken and where other Huguenots died.*

Beloved, I was with you then, am now, will be always.

She shut her eyes for a moment and reveled in the peaceful presence of God.

Jean and Gabriel-Isaac found torches, probably discarded by fleeing Huguenots. Using their candles, they lit the ends, then held them high, scanning the back of the cave.

Gabriel-Isaac pointed. "There's a pathway through there. It starts narrow but widens farther back."

"What do you propose we do next?" asked Jean.

"Well, I say we need to go farther in. Find a nook and rest a while. Secure and dry, if possible."

"Good plan. Dawn will break in a few hours. We could continue outside and take advantage of what's left of the night. But with the full moon and the shelter this cave provides, this is a good time to rest."

Suzanne watched the interaction, appreciating how Jean trained her brother.

"Then what?" Gabriel-Isaac asked. "How long do we stay here? We should go find the fighters and serve with them."

"I don't need to remind you the stakes are high," Jean said. "The authorities may or may not have given up on me. But once Lord Valmalle realizes Suzanne is missing, soldiers will scour the countryside."

Gabriel-Isaac's torch wavered. He shut his eyes for a moment, then opened them and focused on Suzanne. "Why don't we ask Suzanne to hear directions from God?"

Fear raced through her veins. Not only were they at the scene of her parents' arrests, but the last time she'd prophesied in a cave, she'd ended up in prison. Right now, she only wanted warmth, rest, and more time next to Jean. Plus, she'd never asked for the Holy Spirit to overflow her. It had always happened unbidden. Would it even work like that?

"Could you do it?" Gabriel-Isaac asked her. "Get guidance from God, like Abraham Mazel and the other prophets?"

The excitement in her brother's eyes and the care written across Jean's face imparted courage. "I'll try."

"Let's ask together," Jean said. He bowed his head and prayed. "Lord, thank you for leading us safely this far and for this shelter. Would you please show us our next steps?"

In silence, Suzanne agreed. Almost immediately, the still, quiet Voice spoke to her, giving clear directions. She waited a moment, asking for confirmation. The message came again.

She looked at Jean and her brother. "At next nightfall, we're to go to Sauve. We'll be needed there."

"Why? What's in Sauve?" asked Gabriel-Isaac.

"I only know that we're to go. God will show us when we're there."

CHAPTER 43

SAUVE

Abraham, Rolland, and the remainder of their men huddled around the fire burning in the center of the cave. Thin from illness and hunger, their bodies shivered in the moisture-laden air. Abraham glanced across to Rolland's sisters, grateful for their nursing care through the measles outbreak. But they'd lost a dozen men as the contagion spread. These fifty were the survivors.

They'd moved back out on the road as soon as possible. Tarrying any longer in Mialet increased the chance of discovery by Bâville's soldiers. The travel, the constant lack of provisions, and the damp conditions while hiding in yet another cave had slowed the restoration of their strength.

Despite the hardships, Rolland stood by Abraham's side, the two of them continuing to function in unity. Still, there were issues to solve. Mainly lack of food and arms. They'd joined their depleted forces with those of Jean Cavalier, a rising Camisard leader who'd had much success in the southern plains of the Cévennes. With Cavalier's men added in, they now numbered around two hundred fighters. But could they work together?

Abraham spoke low to Rolland. "What do you think of Cavalier?" They observed the impressive young leader walking among the men. "He's only nineteen."

"I'm only three years older. You're the old man around here at twenty-five!" Rolland elbowed his friend, grinning. "Anyway, I've appreciated Cavalier's leadership since I fought alongside him before joining you. His men work as one and live up to their reputation of being extremely mobile and determined."

"His strategy of attacking a different area each night gives the authorities the impression of a considerable Camisard army." Mazel paused. "We made the right decision, asking him to join us."

"Despite his youth, he's an excellent strategist and has also earned respect as a preacher and an *inspiré*. What's the concern, Abraham?"

Mazel lifted a small smile. "You know me well, my friend. We still sorely lack guns and ammunition. I expected Cavalier's men to bring more. Now, we've increased in number *and* in needs."

"Joining forces was the right move. Winter's full upon us, and we need reinforcements for both offensive and defensive actions. We prayed about it. We can't go wrong following God's leading, both in joining with Cavalier and coming to Sauve."

"You're right, of course. I fear the sickness weakened me. My faith's a bit shaky. Like my body, it will recover. Your sisters' cooking helps restore both."

Rolland nodded, glancing across the cave to where Joséphine and Michèle worked on the next meal. "We're sorely lacking provisions."

"We need a fresh strategy. Maybe Cavalier will have an idea." Abraham placed a hand on his friend's strong shoulder. "I need time alone. I'm going for a walk outside. I'll be careful."

"Keep your wits about you. We're only a kilometer from Sauve. You could easily run into villagers. They're all Catholic, you know."

"Yes, since the former Protestants here converted. Cowards."

Rolland's dark eyebrows rose at the uncharacteristic tone. Abraham didn't care. He meant it. True, all Huguenots who hadn't fled the country pretended conversion to the King's religion, but most remained secretly loyal to their beliefs. He had no respect for those who hadn't.

Outside the cave opening, he stepped onto what locals called the Sea of Rocks, granite slabs that rose and fell like waves across the top of a mountain ridge. Taking care to remain concealed, he wandered through clusters of trees growing between the boulders. The frosty fresh air breathed life into his soul and lifted his spirits.

He crawled to the edge of a swath of limestone and looked down. The village of Sauve clung to the mountainside between his position and the river Vidourle below. Surely, those homes had stocks of food, possibly even arms and ammunition. Just as surely, none of the population would share with the hungry Camisards.

Help us, Lord. You sent us here. You know our needs.

Quiet inspiration washed over him. Not the usual quaking. This time, a vision played out before his open eyes. *Was that really you, God?* The scene played again.

Mazel scooted down the boulders and sought shelter in a crevice. He slipped in, grateful for a place to process what he'd just received. A waft of freezing air reached him from farther inside. He squeezed through a tight passage, then stepped down into the mouth of a cave. Perfect!

Inside, he found a comfortable spot and sat. Leaning his head back against the wall, he waited and prayed.

"Achoo!"

He scrambled to his feet and pulled his pistol from his belt. "Who's there?"

No answer. He extended his gun. "Show yourself. This instant!"

One, then another, then a third form emerged from the shadows. Two men and a woman. They stepped into the light, hands up and open. "We're unarmed."

Abraham lowered the pistol. "Jean Massip!" He stepped forward. "And Gabriel-Isaac? Last I saw you, we'd sent you home for insubordination."

"I'm very glad to find *you* here, Abraham!" said Jean. "And not an enemy."

The woman narrowed her eyes at Gabriel-Isaac, then looked to Mazel. "You're Abraham Mazel? I'm Suzanne Lacombe, Gabriel-Isaac's older sister, and this is the first I'm hearing of insubordin—."

Gabriel-Isaac stepped forward. "We've been here a month, waiting. God told us to come to Sauve. That we're needed here. We just don't know why yet. Maybe it was to connect with you!"

Abraham studied them. "The Almighty directed you here? To help?"

"Yes," said Gabriel-Isaac. "We all prayed. But, as usual, God spoke clearly to Suzanne. She's an *inspirée*."

"That's enough about me." Suzanne crossed her arms.

"The Almighty led us here a few days ago. We didn't know why either. Until today." Abraham fixed his gaze on Suzanne. "A moment ago, God gave me a vision, a strategy for our next move."

"Can you share it?" asked Jean.

"We're to attack Sauve, but by deception."

"How?"

"I'll explain the rest back with Rolland and the others."

"Rolland's here as well?"

"And Jean Cavalier. We've joined forces."

"How can we help?" asked Gabriel-Isaac.

"The Lord will show us. Until I'm certain you can follow orders, I'm not sure you'll have any role at all."

Gabriel-Isaac dipped his head.

Abraham addressed all three. "It seems God has you here for a reason. Come with me and we'll see how it unfolds."

Jean looked at Suzanne. She nodded. "Let's go!"

Mazel led the way across the rocky ridges and into the Camisards' hiding place. All activity stopped at the sight of three additional people.

Gabriel and Paul stepped out of the crowd, speaking over one another. "Suzanne! Gabriel-Isaac! What are you doing here?" The uncles embraced their niece and nephew.

"I'll explain," said Abraham. He moved to the center, then introduced the newcomers. "I found them in a nearby cave. I believe meeting them today was a divine appointment."

Questions rippled among the fighters.

"I'll share more later. Suzanne, my sisters Joséphine and Michèle are with us. Maybe you'd like to meet them?"

Among so many men, Suzanne's face lit up at the sight of the women. She crossed the space to join them.

Rolland approached Abraham, and the two stepped aside to talk. "So you found our famous guide, Jean Massip, and the uncooperative Gabriel-Isaac?"

"Quite by accident. The sister is an *inspirée*. Like us, they received the Almighty's direction to come to Sauve. Just prior to finding them, God gave me a vision, with a tactic for meeting our needs."

"Go on."

"Walk with me at the cave's far end and I'll explain," said Abraham. "Ask Cavalier to join us."

259

Out of earshot of the rest, Mazel relayed the contents of the vision to his two fellow leaders. All agreed it was indeed an inspired plan.

Abraham returned to the center of the cave and stood on a boulder. He called the fighters to attention.

"God has revealed a strategy to meet our needs. Gabriel and Paul!" The lieutenants stepped forward. "You'll dress as royal officers, using the uniforms we obtained in the raid on Capitaine Poul's barracks. Take forty men of your choice to the entrance of Sauve. Pose as a bourgeois militia from the Vivarais region. Ask permission to enter and search for Camisard rebels rumored to hide in the area."

"Good one!" called one man. "The lieutenants will pretend to search for *us*!"

Abraham nodded. "Yes. Gabriel and Paul, take the two drums we procured. If the locals buy your ruse, pound them as you enter the village. Explain this is your custom, to honor those who welcome you."

"Understood," said Gabriel.

"Rolland, Cavalier, and I will hide close by with twenty of our fighters. Ask the mayor if they have food, arms, and ammunition you can buy. If they agree and show you the location of the provisions, beat the drums a second time. This will be our signal to join you and ambush the town. Now go!"

Everyone moved into action, bringing out the royal soldiers' uniforms and helping Gabriel and Paul transform into officers of the King's army. The lieutenants chose forty men to accompany them, designating two as drummers. Abraham called the troop to prayer. As one, they fell to their knees.

"Lord, you've given us a strategy. Now go with us and lead our men to success. We trust you for all we need, and we go in your mighty name. Amen."

Gabriel and Paul stood and led their men out. Mazel, Rolland, and Cavalier gathered twenty fighters, then followed. The three leaders hid close to the village entrance, crouching behind an outlying building. Their men hid farther back, concealed by wide trees and clumps of prickly bushes.

Boom, boom, boom! Drumbeats filled the air. The leader's eyes met. Gabriel, Paul, and their troop had gained entrance to the village. How long would it take before the second signal came?

Gabriel-Isaac watched from his position behind Mazel, Rolland, and Cavalier's men. So far, so good. He'd gone undetected by the leaders and their men as he followed them down to Sauve. Thankfully, Suzanne, helping Joséphine and Michèle, hadn't noticed her brother's departure. And Jean Massip seemed preoccupied. By what, Gabriel-Isaac didn't know. It all worked in his favor, and he'd slipped out of the cave unnoticed.

He pressed himself flat against a large tree trunk as a drumbeat sounded from the village gate. His uncles' troop had gained access! Finally, Gabriel-Isaac would see some action.

None of the leaders would give him permission to fight. His only choice was to seize this opportunity. Once he proved his worth in battle, surely they'd accept him as a full-fledged Camisard. He'd need a white linen shirt, a slightly dirty one to fit in with the others.

More time passed. He looked at the eagles soaring overhead. Should gaining access to the town's provisions be taking this long? He shivered, more from anticipation than cold.

The village church bell clanged loud. Voices cried out. There was no second set of drumbeats as planned. What did that mean?

He peered around the boulder. Ahead, the Camisards emerged from their hiding places and poured toward the village gate.

Gabriel-Isaac sprinted to catch up, then hovered at the back of the fighters.

"They must've been discovered," said one.

"We'll get 'em out and then take all we need," said another.

No one noticed Gabriel-Isaac as they entered the village. Mazel led the way up through the narrow, winding road. In the town center, Uncle Gabriel, Uncle Paul, and their fighters stood, arms drawn.

Uncle Gabriel called out. "They figured out we weren't royal soldiers. We made it into the mayor's home while the rest of our men waited outside. They say their good manners betrayed them to townspeople, who sounded the alarm."

"Apparently, the King's men are rude and swear a great deal," added Uncle Paul.

"The people store food and arms throughout the village. The mayor agreed to sell us what we need. We were negotiating the price when the cries 'To arms! To arms!' reached our ears. We exited the mayor's house immediately. The mayor and his wife barricaded themselves inside."

"Lead us back there," said Cavalier. "My men will get in. The rest of you spread through the streets and fight any villagers who take you on."

"Strange they haven't done so yet," said Rolland, glancing around. "No one's here. It appears they're not so eager to fight us off."

"Then why did they sound the alarm?" asked Mazel.

Rolland shrugged. "Take half the remaining men and go up to the left. I'll take the rest and circle right."

Abraham nodded. The leaders divided the troops and took off in opposite directions.

Gabriel-Isaac followed Cavalier, his uncles, and their fighters to the mayor's house. "Set the house ablaze!" ordered Cavalier. "We must force them out." Avoiding his uncles, Gabriel-Isaac blended in with the men as they used their flints and sparked a fire. Snatching a small burning branch, Gabriel-Isaac helped spread the flames. But all fizzled out. After several minutes' work, the fire would not catch hold and spread.

"Perhaps it's not the will of God?" asked Uncle Paul.

Cavalier's face hardened. Gabriel-Isaac found his intensity unnerving. Rolland could be tough, even harsh, but his gruff exterior covered a tender heart. Abraham appeared otherworldly, always serious, but not unkind. Something about Cavalier made Gabriel-Isaac want to keep his distance.

A messenger from Mazel's men approached. "The villagers welcome us! Most with joy, despite their firm conversion to the King's faith. Others display great fear but pose no threat. Several nobles have even invited us in and are *giving* us food and arms. Their local militia look the other way. The few that sounded the alarm seemed to have disappeared."

"Good," said Cavalier. "We inspire fear."

He looked at his men. "You four stay here and guard the mayor's house. Two in front, two in back. Arrest them if they try to escape."

Cavalier and the rest of his fighters returned to the town center. Mazel and Rolland arrived with their troops, arms full of supplies and other plunder.

"Victory is ours!" cried Rolland.

"A colonel, retired from the King's army, welcomed us into his home and offered clean clothes," said Abraham. "His own, quite fancy."

"Why have you not changed?" asked Cavalier.

"How could I fight in anything but the shirt by which we are known?"

"Yours is filthy, full of lice."

"Luxury and fighting God's war are irreconcilable."

Gabriel-Isaac listened to this exchange from behind a hefty Camisard. His admiration for Mazel grew. Here was a true warrior of God!

Abraham led them in prayer, thanking the Almighty and listening for the next steps. They came without delay.

"We go on to the next village, Quissac, and do the same. Quickly, before word of our subterfuge spreads."

The Camisards cheered and exited Sauve. Swords, pistols, and other valuable objects filled their arms as they marched down the road, reveling in their triumph.

Within minutes, the pounding of hoofbeats shook the earth beneath them. They spun around, eyes widening at the sight of hundreds of mounted dragoons. Riding hard toward them.

CHAPTER 44

WOUNDED

1 December 1702
Outside Sauve
Southwestern Cévennes

Gabriel-Isaac froze. The joy of victory vanished. Camisards dropped the bounty collected from Sauve and drew their arms.

"Some villagers must've warned the garrison in St. Hippolyte," Rolland yelled.

"Don't back down!" cried Cavalier as royal soldiers dismounted and raised their rifles. Other dragoons remained in the saddle, charging forward, sabers in hand.

Shooting broke out on both sides. Unarmed, Gabriel-Isaac dove behind a cluster of brambly bushes lining the road. Blood seeped from his calf through his pant leg. He stared at the spreading stain as if watching from afar. Did it hurt? He couldn't tell.

What now? His first battle and already wounded. He tried to stand. Not possible. Several dead Camisards lay nearby, their blood flowing into the earth. He shuddered and leaned against a tree trunk, no longer caring to hide himself.

"Gabriel-Isaac! What are you doing here?"

He looked up through blurry eyes. Uncle Gabriel towered over him.

"Paul!" Uncle Gabriel yelled as the fighting moved down the road. "Over here. Gabriel-Isaac's wounded!"

Uncle Paul stepped out of the fray as the royals continued to push the Camisards back. "Gabriel-Isaac? What's he doing out here?"

"I've no idea, but we've got to get him to safety."

Uncle Gabriel grabbed his nephew under the arms. When Uncle Paul lifted Gabriel-Isaac's feet, searing pain shot up the wounded leg. Gabriel-Isaac's vision darkened, filled with tiny sparks of light. His uncles carried him farther into the *garrigue* and lay him behind a cluster of bushes.

"We've got to get him back to the cave," said Uncle Paul. "Suzanne can tend to him."

"We'll have to carry him."

"Means we have to leave the fighting."

"Our men are already retreating. At least we took out about a dozen of the dragoons, judging by the bodies on the ground."

Gabriel-Isaac listened to his uncles through the fog filling his brain. Was he floating somewhere above them? Disconnected from his body?

"Put him on my back, then you cover us from behind," said Uncle Paul. "I'm younger and my back's stronger."

"No, I got him. You're the better shot. We can trade off if needed."

"All right. Let's go."

Uncle Gabriel knelt and helped Gabriel-Isaac sit up. Pain flashed through him like a bolt of lightning, followed by a wave of nausea.

"Take a deep breath," said Uncle Gabriel.

Uncle Paul draped Gabriel-Isaac over Uncle Gabriel's back. "Reach your arms around your uncle Gabriel's neck and clasp your hands tight."

Gabriel-Isaac tried to follow orders but couldn't hold his grasp. His vision dimmed until darkness engulfed him.

———————

Suzanne stood over the fire in the middle of the cave, adding shelled chestnuts to a boiling pot of water. Uneasiness swirled inside her as she stirred the mixture. Something was wrong.

Her gaze swept across the clusters of fighters who'd stayed back. Jean looked up from a conversation and met her eyes. Without smiling, he crossed the space to her.

"Suzanne, I have something to tell you."

"What is it?"

"Gabriel-Isaac's missing."

"Missing? You're sure?" Cold prickles spread up her arms. She scanned the space, looking for her brother. No sign of him. "How have I not noticed?"

"You've been busy preparing food with Joséphine and Michèle. Getting those spiny shells off the foraged chestnuts was no small feat."

Suzanne studied her battered hands. "He's followed the fighters, hasn't he?"

"Most likely."

She sank down on a low boulder. Jean joined her, sitting close. A bustle of movement at the mouth of the cave drew them right back to their feet. Through the crowd of Camisards, Uncle Gabriel emerged, walking toward the fire with someone on his back. Uncle Paul followed.

Uncle Gabriel dropped to one knee. Suzanne's hand flew to her mouth as Uncle Paul gently pulled her brother to the ground, wounded and unconscious, his pant leg soaked with blood.

Her midwifery training sprang to the forefront. She knelt beside him and touched his forehead. No fever. Good.

"We can help, Suzanne," said Joséphine. "What do you need?"

Suzanne looked up. "Thank you. Please find strips of cloth for bandages. Michèle, bring me water. Someone's drinking gourd, a bowl, anything. As much as possible."

The girls rushed off.

"Jean, I need a small knife."

He pulled one from his pocket and handed it to her. "Anything else?"

"Sit beside him and make sure he doesn't move his arms. Pain could jar him awake, and he needs to stay still."

Joséphine returned with the bandages plus a folded shirt to use as a makeshift pillow. Jean slid it under Gabriel-Isaac's head. Fighters who'd gathered around stood back, watching.

Suzanne drew a deep breath. She'd dealt with many urgent situations related to birth, but never a gunshot wound. *Lord, give me wisdom and direct my hands. Please save Gabriel-Isaac's life.*

Using the tip of the knife, she slit his pant leg. Bit by bit, she ripped the thick woolen fabric until the wound lay exposed. She opened the drinking gourd Michèle placed next to her and poured water on his leg. Using a cloth, she wiped away dried blood, revealing a fresh flow. He flinched but remained unconscious. Jean patted his arm.

A bullet had entered Gabriel-Isaac's right calf. A second wound on the back of his leg showed it had gone right through. With her fingers, Suzanne probed the area between the entrance and exit and found nothing amiss other than two holes seeping blood. She wrapped a cloth tight around his calf, covering both wounds, and tied it off. Then she sat back, pushing an errant curl off her forehead.

"What do you think?" asked Jean.

"The bullet shot straight through, which is good news."

"God be praised."

"He's already lost a fair amount of blood, judging from his pant leg. We must stop the bleeding. Elevating his foot on a rock or something will slow it down. And we need to keep him warm."

Several men immediately took off their shirts and handed them to Suzanne. She covered Gabriel-Isaac with two, then folded the others and put them under his foot. Jean stood and talked with her uncles, then returned with bowls of steaming chestnuts and broth.

"Here, Suzanne. Eat." He sat beside her, both of them watching over Gabriel-Isaac.

She took the bowl. "I'm not hungry. Shouldn't we wait for the rest of the fighters to return?"

"Your uncles told me they were already losing ground to the dragoons from St. Hippolyte when Gabriel-Isaac was shot. They won't be coming back here, wouldn't want to lead the enemy to the rest of us."

She nodded absently.

"Suzanne, eat a little. You'll feel better."

She swallowed a few mouthfuls. "That experience was extraordinary!"

"Yes. Your skills were much needed. You've done everything possible to ensure Gabriel-Isaac's recovery."

"Thanks, but what I meant was that no great fear overwhelmed me. Of course, I'm very concerned for my brother, but I felt so . . . alive. A clarity came. And a strength. Like God was so close and working through me. Sometimes I've experienced that at a birth, but never as much as today."

Jean met her gaze. "I think I understand. The same happens to me when I guide people to safety. Despite the danger. Like I'm made for exactly that."

"Yes! After what feels like a lifetime of being anxious and longing for security through external circumstances, everything shifted. Came into focus. Does that make sense?"

He reached for her hand, enveloping her in warmth. "It does."

"One of my biggest fears was just this—my brother being shot or worse. Now that it happened, God's presence was and *is* so tangible."

"His light shines brightest in the darkest moments."

"Just as he did for me in the tunnel when my lantern fell."

"Just as he does every time I'm leading people. Or escaping prison." Jean's crooked grin spread wide, his emerald eyes danced.

She chuckled. "I love that story. I can listen to it again and again."

"Hopefully, we'll have plenty of time, in fact all—"

"Jean! He's waking!" She scooted closer to her brother's head.

Gabriel-Isaac's eyelids fluttered. He blinked slowly, trying to focus. "Suzanne?" His voice rasped.

"Drink some water first." She lifted his head and raised the drinking gourd to his lips. He swallowed a few sips, then drew larger gulps. He looked at his bandaged leg, then lay back down. Jean moved to his other side.

Gabriel-Isaac looked from one to the other. "How bad is it?"

"God's hand was upon you," Suzanne said. "The bullet missed the bone, went straight through."

"So I'll walk normally?"

"It's possible. We don't know how much damage there is to the muscle. Right now, my primary concern is stopping the bleeding completely and preventing infection."

Gabriel-Isaac's face scrunched.

"Are you in much pain?" she asked.

"It hurts. I'm so tired."

"Rest. Sleep if you can."

Gabriel-Isaac shut his eyes.

Suzanne turned to Jean. "If only I had my herbs, ointments, and other supplies."

"Maybe Joséphine and Michèle brought some. I'll check with them."

By the time Jean returned with a handful of herbs, Gabriel-Isaac was sleeping soundly. "They apologized for not thinking of these sooner and for having little on hand after nursing the men through the measles."

"I'm grateful for anything at all," Suzanne said. "But Gabriel-Isaac can't stay here. The healing time could be weeks or even months."

From somewhere behind her, Uncle Gabriel stepped forward. "I've been thinking." He paused.

She looked up at him. "Weren't you wounded when the dragoons first came to St. Hippolyte?"

Uncle Gabriel nodded. "And here's my namesake also shot by dragoons. Capitaine Noguier brought me to Mialet to heal, at significant risk."

"Are you thinking we should do the same for Gabriel-Isaac?" asked Jean.

"Yes, but not in Mialet. We need to take him home."

Suzanne rose and brushed off her skirt. "I've been thinking the same. We have plenty of healing supplies there, and Grand-mère has more experience than I do. She's dealt with gunshot injuries in the past. But how will we move him?"

"I've had a similar problem," Jean said. "When I led a small group to the border of Switzerland, one of our party twisted his ankle and couldn't walk. We found a horse-drawn vegetable cart going to a local fair and hitched a ride."

"Didn't that draw attention to your fugitives?" asked Suzanne. "Did you disguise yourselves?"

"We hid under the vegetables. Onions actually. Smelled like them for weeks. Couldn't get the scent out of my clothes. Worth it though. We made it to safety."

"We'd need a horse, a driver, and a cart full of something that would conceal Gabriel-Isaac and me."

"And me. It's dangerous for you to return to St. Hippolyte." Jean's face conveyed protection and more.

"It's not safe for you either!" She met his eyes, grateful he'd be by her side. She needed to see her brother safely home.

Beloved, you're never alone. I walk with you always. The Voice came gentle and soft. *And often I provide companions to help along the way.*

"We'll take Gabriel-Isaac home together," she said.

"Paul and I will take a few men and locate a horse and cart," said Uncle Gabriel. "A hamlet or village nearby is bound to have left one unattended. We'll, uh, borrow it for a short while. Once we have what we need, I'll send Paul back with word of our rendezvous point. We'll bring it as close as possible to the cave."

Suzanne frowned. "As we're up on rocky crags, won't we need to bring Gabriel-Isaac down somehow?"

"I got him up here, didn't I?"

"Yes, of course, Uncle Gabriel!"

"A few of us here can carry him down," said Jean. He turned to Uncle Gabriel. "Why don't I go with you? I can bring the message back to Suzanne once we've got the cart. You two can guard it at our rendezvous point."

"Good plan. I'll gather the others. The sooner we get Gabriel-Isaac home, the better."

Suzanne sat beside her sleeping brother. "We're taking you home, Gabriel-Isaac. We're going home."

CHAPTER 45
JOURNEY HOME

1 December 1702
Outside St. Hippolyte du Fort
Southern Cévennes

Suzanne covered her nose and mouth, pressing tight. The sneeze slipped out anyway. There was no way to stop it. Then another and another. Buried under a hefty pile of hay, bouncing along the rutted road in the back of the "borrowed" cart, she could do little but attempt to muffle the string of sneezes.

Her uncles and Jean had found the wagon, hay and horse included, at a small farm outside Sauve. The owner didn't appear, most likely hiding in his house, fearful of the events of the day.

Now, Gabriel-Isaac lay between her and Jean, all three concealed for their return to St. Hippolyte. Two fugitives and a youth wounded in battle couldn't openly walk into town. Uncle Gabriel insisted on driving them home, which they should reach soon, before nightfall.

How would they get through the entry guards? If caught, they'd never be free again and would probably be executed. Suzanne's breathing grew shallow. *Beloved! I am with you always.* How many times did she need to hear it? Several times a day for the rest of her life, be it long or short. At least now she believed it, embracing the truth that God loved her and would never abandon her. Especially during the hardest moments.

Gabriel-Isaac groaned as the cart jostled over a pothole. She murmured soothing words, not sure if he was passed out or awake. Jean did the same, filling her with peace. She loved how he cared for her brother, for her.

The wagon slowed to a stop. They must have arrived at the bridge. Almost home. *Please conceal us, Lord. Don't let the soldiers search beneath the hay.*

A guard's rough voice boomed. "What's your business in St. Hippolyte?"

"I'm making a delivery to the Château de Planque at the request of Lord Valmalle." Uncle Gabriel spoke slower than normal, accentuating a peasant accent.

"Hay? Didn't he recently receive a delivery for his horses?"

"I don't know about that. I'm just doing as Lord Valmalle's servant asked."

Gabriel-Isaac moaned low. Uncle Gabriel coughed loud. Suzanne placed her hand gently over her brother's mouth.

"Seems unusual they'd need more hay so soon."

Suzanne pictured her uncle's shrug and lifted eyebrows. "Some also goes to the *moulin*."

Another pause. "Go on, then."

She let out a long breath as the cart moved forward and onto the bridge. She imagined the view. Despite the presence of soldiers, she loved the walk across the bridge, loved savoring the wind blowing across the river, rustling through the surrounding trees. If she were on foot, her eyes would rise to Le Cengle mountain behind the river. Were eagles flying near the cliff tops?

By now, they must be passing the gingko tree at the end of the bridge. Almost there. Instead of turning left to home, the cart turned right in front of the Château. They went farther down the road, then stopped at Marguerite's *moulin*. Before leaving Sauve, Suzanne had suggested delivering some of the hay there to carry out their ruse.

Uncle Gabriel stepped down from the driver's seat and lifted off armfuls of hay. "Don't move," he whispered.

Through the layer left to conceal them, Suzanne saw bits of the dusky sky. Night came early in winter.

"What's the meaning of this?" Marguerite's voice rang out. Suzanne pressed her lips together, holding back laughter at the indignation in her friend's voice.

"Shhh! Please! I'm Suzanne's uncle Gabriel. You must be Marguerite Marolle. I knew your parents when I was young."

"I've heard of you. Aren't you supposed to be fighting somewhere with Rolland? And why are you dumping hay in front of my *moulin?*"

"I'll explain everything later. I have precious cargo in the back."

"Precious cargo?"

Suzanne sneezed.

Silence from Marguerite.

"Do you understand?" asked Uncle Gabriel.

"Yes, I think so."

"Wait a quarter hour, then come to my mother's house. It'll all make sense."

Suzanne imagined Marguerite's expression, somewhere between intrigue and irritation.

Within minutes, Uncle Gabriel pulled behind the Lacombe house. The wagon jostled as he jumped down from his seat.

"You can come out now."

Suzanne sat up and brushed hay off her face, bonnet, and shoulders.

"You go in first, Suzanne, and let your grand-mère know we're here. She'll have seen the cart pull in and be concerned. Jean and I will bring your brother."

"Let me check on him first." She wiped the hay off Gabriel-Isaac's face. Awake, he gave her a weak smile.

She scooted down the bed of the cart and slid off the back. After straightening her skirt and picking off the last pieces of straw, she entered the back door. The familiar scents of home enveloped her.

"Grand-mère? Marc-André, Marie? It's me, Suzanne."

Grand-mère stuck her head out from the kitchen door. "Suzanne? How can it be? Praise God!"

Suzanne ran and fell into her grandmother's arms. "There's much to tell you, but first—"

The back door opened again, followed by a gust of cold air. Uncle Gabriel and Jean stepped through, carrying Gabriel-Isaac between them.

Grand-mère's mouth fell open. "Gabriel, my son! Jean! And, oh *non*, Gabriel-Isaac. What happened?"

"Dragoons shot him in the calf," Suzanne said. "I tended him the best I could, but with limited supplies, so we brought him to you."

"Carry him to the salon. Then, Jean, please let the children out of the *cachette*. You know it well. I hid them when your cart pulled in behind the house."

"I'll get blankets," said Suzanne.

Minutes later, everyone gathered in the salon around Gabriel-Isaac, lying awake on a wide chair. Grand-mère checked the wounds, then nodded at Suzanne.

"As you surmised, the bullet shot straight through, which increases his chances of healing well."

"Should we clean it with wine? Then apply honey? I didn't have either with me."

"Yes, Suzanne. Exactly right. Also, salt before the honey. Marie, go fetch these from the kitchen."

Marie remained tight by Suzanne's side, where she'd been since emerging from the *cachette*.

"Go on, Marie." Suzanne gently nudged her little sister. "You can help us when you return." Marie brightened a bit and left to get the supplies.

Marc-André stared at his brother's wounds. "Will he be all right?"

"I certainly plan to be," said Gabriel-Isaac.

Uncle Gabriel stepped to his youngest nephew's side. "The Lord's brought him this far. He's home now, with your grandmother and Suzanne to care for him."

Grand-mère straightened and looked each of them in the eye. "Suzanne and Jean cannot stay here long. Since her escape from the Château, the soldiers have been here several times. If they find Jean, that would be the end. For both of them."

The back door scraped open. Everyone froze.

"I'll go," said Uncle Gabriel. "It should be Marguerite. I asked her to join us."

Suzanne filled Grand-mère in on the fake hay delivery to the *moulin* as Marguerite strode into the room, Uncle Gabriel right behind. Marie followed, holding a basket containing a jug of wine, a clay pot of salt, and a jar of honey.

"So what's the meaning of—?" Marguerite caught sight of Suzanne, Jean, and the wounded Gabriel-Isaac and stammered.

Smiling at Marguerite's uncharacteristic loss of words, Suzanne embraced her friend. "I didn't expect to see you again. Not so soon, maybe not ever."

"Me neither." Marguerite held her tight, then pulled back and pointed at Gabriel-Isaac. "What happened to *him*?"

"St. Hippolyte dragoons shot him yesterday in a battle on the road outside Sauve."

"I won't even ask why you were in Sauve. Is he going to be all right?"

"We brought him home to Grand-mère, where he has the best chance of healing."

"But it's dangerous for you to be here!" Marguerite's face tightened.

"Suzanne and Jean cannot stay," stated Grand-mère.

Jean stepped forward. "I've given this some thought. Suzanne and I could go to my aunt and uncle in St. Paul Trois Châteaux, north of here, in the Drôme region. Their home is at the foot of a mountain that has forests spread wide across it. Perfect for escape if need be."

He looked at Suzanne, a question on his face. She nodded, her eyes conveying her complete agreement.

"How far is it?" asked Uncle Gabriel.

"I estimate a two-day walk. Or a full day's ride if we borrow the horse and cart a little longer."

"I'll accompany you. We don't want to raise any concerns with your family or others about the propriety of you two traveling alone together."

"I was hoping you'd say that. Thank you."

"We'll take the horse and cart with you both hidden in the back under the hay Marguerite doesn't actually need."

Grand-mère stood up. "Stay here tonight. Should the soldiers come knocking, the *cachette* can hold Suzanne, Jean, and the children. Gabriel, you have the excuse of visiting me."

She knelt beside her grandson. "Marie, you help me clean him up here. After, Gabriel and Jean can move him upstairs. If authorities arrive and insist on searching, we'll say he has the measles."

Suzanne looked around the room at the people she loved. She'd known she couldn't stay. If she were seen by Lord Valmalle or any of his servants except Marthe, the authorities would arrest her again, with more severe consequences. One more night in her childhood home, then she'd be gone. Probably for a very long time.

She swallowed hard past the growing tightness in her throat. "Grand-mère, why don't I see to some food while Marie helps you? It's been a while since we've eaten."

"Good idea. You'll find vegetable soup in the pot, some dried sausages on the shelf. There's also half a loaf of bread."

"I know my way around the . . ." She stopped. She'd been gone for over a month and would leave before sunup. Her stomach hollowed from more than hunger.

Suzanne led the way to the kitchen and served up the food. Uncle Gabriel and Marc-André ate in silence. Jean sat across from her and caught her gaze. Yes, they had things to discuss. It would have to wait.

Marguerite joined them at the table. "You should know that the authorities questioned Charles Fesquet about your escape. The cook—Justine, is it?—mentioned him visiting you in the kitchen."

Suzanne's cheeks flushed. She avoided looking at Jean but sensed his alertness. She focused on Marguerite. "What happened?"

"Seems they suspected him of helping you. Which he did, of course. But, with his usual charm, he convinced Lord Valmalle that he didn't know your plans."

"I'm sorry he had to lie, but I'm thankful Lord Valmalle believed him. Any news about the maid, Marthe? She helped me a great deal, from the beginning right through to giving me her candle the last night."

"Word has it, Valmalle beat her, at first not believing you managed to get out of the locked room on your own. Then he questioned all his servants and the night guard vigorously. But in the end, he believes you acted alone. Or with outside help." Marguerite's signature smirk appeared. "I've overheard more than one customer mention your 'uncanny' escape, that you simply disappeared."

Suzanne smiled, reached across the table, and squeezed her friend's hand. "Thank you for everything."

"Just doing my job." Marguerite's eyes glistened. "So, you're going on an adventure. Actually, a whole new life." She winked at Suzanne and tipped her head toward Jean.

Suzanne threw a pointed look at her friend. "Ironic, isn't it? All I've ever wanted was to stay home. Now, I'm ready to go wherever the Lord leads me. Honestly, his presence and love are my security."

Jean took her other hand. "And she'll have my company. Long as she'll have it." He looked from Suzanne to Uncle Gabriel, who gave him one sure nod.

Joy bubbled up through Suzanne like sparkles of light. She held back a giggle at the red spreading across Jean's face.

"Suzanne, can we talk somewhere?" he asked. "Privately?"

Marguerite cackled. "Go on, you two lovebirds. I'll clean up here."

"Lovebirds?" Marc-André looked confused.

"I'll explain everything," said Marguerite.

Suzanne rolled her eyes at her friend, then led Jean down the back hall to the cold storage room. "Sorry it's freezing in here, but this is the best I can do for now."

"Suzanne, being with you is all I care about. I love you with my whole heart." He took both of her hands, looked deep into her eyes. "I know it may seem a bit rushed, but I've known since Mialet that I wanted to spend my life with you. Will you marry me?"

"Since Mialet? I wasn't so sure about you then. I never expected to see you again, much less all we've experienced together."

"So . . .?

Suzanne grinned wide. "Of course! Yes, I'll marry you."

He drew her into his arms. "May I kiss you?"

She leaned in and gave her answer without words, hopefully leaving no doubt in his mind.

They pulled apart, his crooked smile wide, his green eyes bright. How she loved him.

"Let's go talk with your grandmother," he suggested.

Back in the salon, they found everyone gathered. Pillows propped Gabriel-Isaac up on the wide chair. Jean took Suzanne's hand.

"We have an announcement," he said. "With your permission, Madame Lacombe—uh, Isabeau—we'd like to be married. My family's pastor can perform the ceremony."

Grand-mère stood before the couple. "I would've preferred Suzanne to be a little older before marrying. Given the circumstances, though, this is for the best. You have my every blessing. And I have to say, I'm not the least bit surprised!"

Laughter rippled across the room. Marie hugged Suzanne tight, tears streaming. "I'll miss you so! But I like Jean." She grew shy. "I'm glad he'll be my brother."

Suzanne and Jean reached their arms around Marie. Happiness filled the room, despite the imminent departure.

"Congratulations," said Marc-André. "I'll miss you, Suzanne. And Jean."

"I'll miss you too, little brother." She kissed his cheek and pretended not to see the tears shining in his eyes.

Suzanne crossed the room and sat next to Gabriel-Isaac. Their eyes met and held for a moment. So much had passed between them. So much had changed.

"It seems God sent us to Sauve to participate in this battle," she said. "I think he's used the experience as part of our training, for our next steps." She glanced across to Jean.

"God said we were there to help," said Gabriel-Isaac. "I'm glad you were there when I was shot. And that we could come home together, so you could say goodbye."

"It's funny, isn't it? You were determined to leave, and I resisted it so. Now, I'm the one going."

"And I'm staying. Truly, Suzanne, I'm glad to be home. Besides the need for healing, I'd like to remain here for a while. And, when I'm able, work the vines, if Charles and Lord Valmalle permit it. I wasn't much use in a physical battle after all. And will that really make a difference? How many need to die before we gain our rights? I'd like to try to fight in another way. Maybe help Marguerite with her activities."

Marguerite's left eyebrow raised. "I can see you being quite useful."

"You want to work in the *moulin*?" asked Marie.

"No. Something else, still helping our cause." Gabriel-Isaac leaned back, tired.

Grand-mère held up her hands. "Let's all get some rest. Everyone to bed. We'll rise before dawn to see off the travelers. Suzanne, you stay here a minute."

Uncle Gabriel and Jean carried Gabriel-Isaac up the stairs. Suzanne winced at every yelp of pain.

Grand-mère walked to the mirror on the wall and lifted it off. Opening the back, she lifted out the family Bible, then handed Suzanne a stack of parchments. "Charles passed on your message to hide your writings. These are your personal thoughts, which I only glanced at. I hid the rest, your documentation of current events, in the wall behind my armoire. I chiseled out a stone months ago in case such a need arose. Would you like me to get those as well?"

"Oh, Grand-mère! Thank you." Suzanne clutched the parchments to her chest. "I'll take these but leave the rest here. In case we're apprehended on the way."

"As you wish, my dear girl. I will miss you so. But this is your path, your destiny. The Lord will use you and Jean greatly, in ways beyond your imagining. May he bless and keep you both."

"*Merci*, Grand-mère. For everything." Suzanne embraced her grandmother. After a moment, they pulled apart, both wiping away tears. "I'll send a message when we arrive in St. Paul Trois Châteaux."

Grand-mère placed her hand on the Bible. "Also, let me know when you're married. I'll record it here. Right under your parents' names. Pierre Lacombe and Jeanne Tessier. Suzanne Lacombe and Jean Massip. The lineage continues. Now, get some sleep. You have a whole new life ahead of you."

CHAPTER 46
NEW LIFE

November 1703
St. Paul Trois Châteaux
Drôme

Suzanne followed the narrow trail up the mountain behind the Massip family home. She breathed in the piney scents released as fallen needles crushed under her feet. Walking through the forest always restored her soul.

Only a day's ride to the north of the Cévennes, the sights and smells were different. Fewer rocks, more trees, a bit greener. Looking up through the lacy canopy created by the tall pines, she glimpsed patches of bright blue sky.

"Beautiful, isn't it?"

She smiled over her shoulder at Jean. Her husband. They enjoyed climbing this hill together, spending time alone away from the small house they shared with his aunt and uncle. Maybe someday they'd build their own home, but not now.

Tomorrow, Jean would lead a group of Huguenots to the Swiss border. The increased repression in the Cévennes brought continual waves of *réfugiés* fleeing to safety. For the first time, Suzanne would be by his side, her basket of supplies filled and ready to tend people as needed. She laughed.

"What's so funny, my wife? I love calling you that."

The path widened, and they walked side by side.

"Oh really? I hadn't noticed." She nudged him with her elbow, then took his hand. I find the idea of me on the road humorous. It's something I've fought against most of my life. Now, I'm looking forward to it. To helping people, danger and all."

"You mean being with me isn't the main thing you're excited about?" His crooked grin appeared.

"Well, that too." She stopped, leaned in, and kissed him well.

"I'm convinced." He tucked a curl back under her bonnet, his emerald eyes lit with love. "I'm grateful we're called into this adventure together. Come what may."

"Me too."

At the top of the mountain, they found their favorite flat stone and sat, taking in the breathtaking view of the valley below.

Suzanne pulled an envelope from her pocket. "A messenger delivered this letter from Grand-mère earlier today while you were outside doing chores. I thought we could read it together."

"Thanks for waiting. It's been a month since her last letter, hasn't it?"

Suzanne nodded and opened the letter.

November 1703

Chers Suzanne and Jean,

I trust this missive finds you both well. I realize it's been a while since my last letter. We are all well.

Gabriel-Isaac walks more each week with the use of a cane. He spends time in the vineyards daily, along with Marc-André, both under the tutelage of Charles Fesquet. Marguerite continues to visit on Sundays, and I believe Gabriel-Isaac and she have grown in their friendship. They're both quite convinced that fighting through their form of resistance is more effective than actual battles. As much as his leg will allow, Gabriel-Isaac delivers messages like his papa and is building strength in using the skills Jean taught him in guiding Huguenots to underground worship services, like your maman.

Marie and I have been busy here with several births in the village plus planting the spring potager. Your sister helps me tremendously with both, and we find joy working side by side, although we miss you very much.

Suzanne sighed. "I miss them, too."

"Of course you do." Jean reached an arm around her.

"I'm grateful that Gabriel-Isaac is healing well enough to work in the vineyards and help with Marguerite's resistance network. Who would've guessed he'd change his need for action in this direction? I think his wounding in Sauve led him to reconsider the best way for him to fight."

Jean leaned his head against hers. "Not all Huguenots agree with the violence and physical fighting. It's hard to sort out as the Camisard leaders believe they follow God's instructions. The Almighty's ways are not the same as ours."

She turned to look deep into his eyes, kissed his cheek, then lay her head against his shoulder. "Well, I'm glad they're safe at home in St. Hippolyte and that I have a new home here."

After a moment, Suzanne continued reading.

> *Governor Bâville's new military leader, Marshal Montreval, burns hundreds of villages and hamlets throughout the Cévennes. Smoke fills the air, and once again it seems as if the entire world is aflame. Many Huguenots are homeless, and royal soldiers have increased arrests. In Mialet alone, over five hundred villagers were arrested before the soldiers destroyed the village. Thank God, Rolland's family and your uncles were not there at the time.*

Suzanne dropped the letter to her lap. "It breaks my heart. So much suffering. Will it ever stop? Is it all worth it?"

"The Camisards follow the will of God above all else, no matter the consequences. The timing and the outcome is in his hands."

Suzanne drew a deep breath and picked up the letter.

> *At a recent worship gathering, I learned that Mazel and Rolland carry on despite Bâville and Montreval's severity. They, along with Cavalier, have divided their fighters into smaller bands again. These fearsome Camisard leaders and their men give the impression of a much larger army, striking often and in different places with force. Apparently, they keep the royal troops guessing and on the defensive.*
>
> *Yet we are all praying against the apprehension of Mazel, Rolland, and your uncle. Governor Bâville recently recruited*

mountain men from the Pyrénées who understand how to fight in our terrain better than the royal troops from the north. Many now think the capture of the Camisard leaders just a matter of time.

In an important skirmish, one of Cavalier's men knocked Capitaine Poul off his horse with a stone thrown at his head. The Camisard fighter then finished off that Goliath by sword.

Suzanne and Jean stared at each other for a moment, eyebrows raised.

"So biblical!" Jean turned his gaze back to the view. "What a spectacle that must've been!"

"Truly incredible. It's a wonder the Camisards persevere and have such victories."

In other news, remember Esprit Séguier's prophesy just before his execution? He proclaimed the river Tarn in the Pont-de-Montvert would overflow, then change to an adjacent riverbed. And now it has done exactly that.

I must finish this missive and return to my chores. Please know you both are in my prayers daily. Give my greetings to Jean's aunt and uncle and to your community in St. Paul Trois Châteaux.

With love,
Grand-mère

Suzanne snuggled closer to Jean, loving the sensation of his warm arm holding her tight. "Despite how awful and out of control everything seems, God remains in charge. We are his beloved. He'll never fail or forsake us."

"The safest place is in the center of his will. No matter the outcome."

"So very true."

They sat in silence, enjoying each other's company. Like a fragrant breeze, the strong and gentle presence of their heavenly Father filled and surrounded them.

Jean stroked her back. "Why haven't you prophesied in a while? Is it because you're here with me and my family?"

"Oh, but I have! Just not with wild physical manifestations. God speaks to me all the time. Sometimes it's just for me. Other times, I'm to share the message, and I will."

"So, prophecy includes just hearing from God? Shouldn't we all be doing that?"

"Yes, exactly. It's a relationship. I think how the communication happens is different for everyone."

"Well, I'm glad he made you exactly the way you are. And if you hear in a wild way, that's fine. Of course, it's also fine if your communications are more personal, between you and him. But I'd love to hear whatever you can share."

Suzanne nodded, her heart full.

The sun moved closer to the horizon, a cool breeze swirled around them. Without words, they stood and made their way back down the mountain. To all God had in store. No matter the outcome.

CHAPTER 47
TOUR DE CONSTANCE

January–July 1705
Montpellier
Southern France

Abraham Mazel stood tall, his hands cuffed and attached to the chain around his waist. The swift tribunal had concluded. Abraham met Bâville's fierce gaze as the Governor rose to pronounce his sentence.

"I, Governor Bâville, of the Languedoc, do hereby condemn Abraham Mazel, instigator of the troubles in the Cévennes, to death by public execution."

Abraham's heart accelerated slightly, but the calm he'd experienced since his arrest in the southern Cévennes two days ago remained. The death sentence didn't come as a surprise.

So this is the end. I've lived and now will die for you Lord. It is a privilege. The soldiers on either side of Abraham grabbed his arms and began moving toward the door.

A priest in a traditional brown robe broke from the crowd observing the trial and made his way to the front. "Excuse me, Governor Bâville. May I speak?"

Abraham studied the middle-aged priest, who looked vaguely familiar. Bâville didn't respond. An aide moved closer to him and repeated the priest's question.

The Governor glared at the aide, then addressed the priest. "Yes, but speak up! No more mumbling."

Mazel noticed glances between the members of the tribunal. The priest had spoken clearly. Had the Governor grown deaf?

"*Merci*, Governor Bâville. I am Father Martin, the priest at the church of Saint-Martin-de-Corconac in the eastern Cévennes. My parish is a half-day journey south of the Pont-de-Montvert." The priest paused and turned his gaze to Abraham. "In the month after the incident with the Abbé du Chaila, Abraham Mazel led his men on fiery raids, burning churches, and often killing the priests."

"Get to the point!" snapped Governor Bâville. "And speak up. No one can hear you."

The priest spoke in a loud strong voice, gesturing at Abraham. "This man spared my life, claiming God told him to do so. Today, I ask you for clemency. I believe the blessing of God will be in it for you."

Bâville appeared confused, then glowered as the priest bowed his head slightly. Silence reigned for several minutes. Finally, without looking at Mazel, the Governor barked orders.

"Get the prisoner out of my sight. Take him to Aigues-Mortes, to the Tour de Constance. I sentence him to life imprisonment, which is guaranteed to be short in that place."

No one moved. "Go now!" Bâville bellowed.

Shock rippled through the crowd as soldiers escorted Abraham out of the room. Within a quarter hour, a detachment of dragoons appeared outside the courthouse, one leading an extra horse. Several soldiers shoved Mazel up onto the mount, then fastened his ankles in irons connected by a chain beneath the animal's stomach.

Resting his bound hands on the horn of the saddle, Abraham held his head high and ignored the blur of red-coated royal dragoons surrounding him as they began leading his horse down the road. *Lord, you never cease to amaze me. Life with you is certainly an adventure. I'm truly in your hands, as always.*

The contingent trotted along in silence except for occasional taunts by the dragoons. Abraham focused on soaking in the sights. The two-hour journey would soon be over, as would his life as a free man, no way of escape open to him now.

As they traveled through the salty marshlands leading to Aigues-Mortes, the air grew increasingly putrid. Mazel mused that the town lived up to its name—Dead Waters.

Soon the infamous Tour de Constance came into view, rising high into the pale gray sky. The limestone cylinder rose to what appeared to be more than thirty meters above the Mediterranean coast and communicated power and intimidation by land and sea. Abraham's heart pounded as they drew close. To be imprisoned in the tower was to be buried alive.

One of Abraham's dragoon guards leaned his way. "Your new home! How do you like it?"

"You'll never want to leave!" said the soldier to his left, laughing at his own joke.

"The prison director has surely prepared a special place for you." The dragoons guffawed and continued their jests.

Abraham kept his mouth shut as they passed through the guarded gate in the rampart walls and rode into the city. The dragoons steered their mounts to the right, toward the tower, where royal soldiers stood outside the entry door. The man who appeared to be in charge stepped forward.

"Stop here!" He scrutinized the prisoner. "So, this is the instigator of all the troubles in the Cévennes, the infamous Abraham Mazel?"

"*Oui*, monsieur," responded the lead dragoon.

"Detach him now and bring him inside."

The dragoons dismounted. Two set to unlocking and removing Mazel's fetters, then yanked him off his horse. Unable to feel his legs beneath him, Abraham crumpled to the ground. Yet an incomprehensible peace remained, strengthening him even as the soldiers jerked him up and pushed him through a small door into the tower.

A narrow passageway through the six-meter-wide walls opened into an enormous round room. Abraham blinked as his eyes adjusted to the dimly lit space. The prison director paced in front of his most famous prisoner to date.

"I have questions for you, Mazel. But we'll wait until you've experienced our warm hospitality for a while."

The man leered, one eyebrow raised in his paunchy face. A ripple of laughter passed through the prison soldiers. Mazel shivered, it was freezing in this ground-floor room, even with a fire lit in a huge hearth on the far side.

"Take him to the other male prisoners on the third floor," ordered the director.

Soldiers strong-armed Abraham across the room, then marched him up a small spiral staircase to the top floor. They shoved him into a round room he guessed to be over twenty meters wide, lit only by feeble light from slits archers would use to defend the citadel. He could barely see. Smoke from a small fire in the center of the room stung his eyes, and the stench of open latrine buckets and unwashed men assailed his nostrils.

"Meet your heretic comrade!" announced the lead dragoon. "I present you Abraham Mazel." With a final shove, the soldiers exited, clanging the creaking iron door shut behind them.

Once the sound of the skeleton key turning in the lock ceased, over thirty Huguenots rose from various positions and surrounded Mazel. All had heard of him. Many knew him. Abraham barely recognized those of his acquaintance. In their gaunt features, all the ragged men resembled one another.

"They finally caught you!" said one, who stood a head taller than the others. "We'd begun to think they never would."

"Unlike your friend Rolland," added the shorter man next to him.

"The Almighty provided means of escape more times than I can count," replied Abraham. "For me and Rolland."

"But he's dead and you're not. We heard he was betrayed by a relative."

Weariness washed through Abraham. "That's true. Surrounded and shot a year ago while hiding in a château in the eastern Cévennes. The lieutenants with him at the time, Gabriel Lacombe and Paul Tessier, were arrested and executed on the Wheel in Montpellier. They died courageously, faithful to the end."

"We heard Cavalier tried to negotiate with Bâville. Tried to get Rolland to do the same."

"That's correct."

"And that Rolland wouldn't comply unless the Governor assured freedom of worship and unless the King restored the Edict of Nantes, returning our legal rights."

"Yes, Rolland held his ground and remained loyal to the cause. Cavalier acted on his own. Disunity never leads to God's best."

"Was that how they captured you? Did someone betray you?"

"I'm not sure. Possibly. Bâville's mountain men from the Pyrénées caught up with me as I traveled alone through the southern Cévennes." Abraham scanned the room. "Men, I need rest. I'll answer more questions later."

The prisoners scrounged a blanket and made a place for him to lie close to the fire. He pulled the thin cover over his body and, despite the freezing stone floor beneath him, fell into a deep sleep.

Abraham, my son. Listen! Be of good courage. You will escape this place before too long.

Lord? Escape this place? How?

You'll discover a way, and you will succeed in overcoming the obstacles.

Abraham woke with a start and lay staring at the high ceiling. *Escape? Before too long?*

Questions flooded his brain as he glanced around the unaired room. Men slept—some quietly, some snoring, some moaning softly. *There are over thirty prisoners in here. I don't know them all. Who can I trust?*

Abraham rose from his meager bed and began pacing the perimeter of the room. The three arrow slits were set deep into small alcoves in the massive walls. He leaned into one alcove. Only his fist fit through the slit. Apart from the locked iron door, no other openings existed.

Mazel returned to his place by the fire. Maybe he'd only imagined the dream. No one had ever escaped this place in the four hundred years of its existence. Overwhelmed by the many obstacles to such an achievement, Abraham fell back asleep.

Through the next months, the dream returned multiple times, but without directions on how to carry out the escape. Night and day, through the damp cold, Abraham paced and prayed. Over time, he figured out which men to trust with sharing what God had told him. Eventually everyone knew, as keeping secrets in such close quarters was not possible.

Several men agreed to actively aid and escape with him. Together, they sharpened a dinner knife over the cooking fire and transformed it into a makeshift saw. Abraham marveled that two cannon balls from some ancient battle had been providentially abandoned in a nook in their room, long forgotten by their captors. These now served as hammer and anvil.

Prisoners with years of experience in the tower informed Mazel that the guards on the roof above them abandoned their posts at night. Still, the imprisoned men worked quietly through the night hours, until they managed to detach the horizontal iron piece that held the stones of one arrow slit in place.

"Hurrah!" whispered one.

"Shhhh!"

"We have a way to go," Abraham said quietly, pushing his dirty hair off his face. "But this is a good start."

One man held up the iron piece. "Tomorrow, we'll start forging this into a chisel."

"I'm grateful for your experience as an ironmonger, brother. For now, we'll put the bar back in place and get some sleep." Abraham began sweeping away traces of limestone dust with his hands and dumping it through the slit. *Lord, thank you for these men beside me, in unity. I feel your presence strong with us each time we work.*

Over the next nights, the men chiseled at the cement around a large limestone block next to the arrow slit, then worked at chipping out the stone. To limit noise, Mazel covered the chisel with a cloth and often reminded them to use tiny strokes.

After four nights work and without suspicion from the guards, Abraham and his men extracted the large stone from the edge of the arrow slit. The narrow window was now wide enough to permit one man at a time to pass through.

"We did it!" one prisoner whispered with intensity.

Another pumped his fist in the air.

Mazel marveled at what they'd accomplished. "By God's grace, we have our way out. Put the stone back for now."

Over the next days, the prisoners braided a long and sturdy cord. Every man contributed a blanket, a sheet, or a shirt. Finally, all was ready.

"Tonight's the night, men," announced Abraham as they huddled close to the fire. "This is the moment of decision. Who's with me? Who will attempt escape?"

The tall man who often served as spokesperson glanced at his fellow prisoners. "We've all agreed to go." Several nodded.

Abraham's stomach sank. Would the cord hold up for thirty men to descend? What choice did he have? *Lord, you said this would work. Guide me—guide us—to safety.* "All right, we'll begin in a few hours when the guards have quit their post. Get some rest."

Shortly before midnight, the men assembled around the arrow slit and removed the loose stone. They attached one end of the cord to a wood plank that would serve as a seat and tied the other end to the iron bar braced against the window from the inside.

"The Almighty told me to go first," said Mazel. "If anyone is to be caught initially, it will be myself. You can deny any involvement. Once I'm on the ground outside and determine safe passage for the next man, I'll tug the cord as a signal to pull the plank back up."

Abraham slipped through the opening, stood on the narrow ledge outside, and placed his thighs on the plank. The men inside checked that the iron bar on their end held firm, then gave him the signal to go.

Praying as he descended, Abraham could barely believe it when his feet hit the ground. He'd made it! No guards sounded the alarm. *Thank you, Lord.*

He tugged the cord several times and watched as it rose back up to the third floor. Without problem, sixteen prisoners made it down one after another.

The freed men flattened themselves against the outside tower wall to avoid drawing attention, waiting for the next escapee. More than twice the usual time between descents passed. Mazel prayed. *Lord? What's happening?*

Go! Abraham, go now!

"Men, God says go. Follow me."

"What about the others?"

"We obey the Almighty." Abraham ran toward the waterless moat.

"Prisoners escaping! Prisoners escaping!"

The cries emerged from the third floor. Mazel could barely register that the remaining men had sounded the alarm. Without looking back, he fled into and across the dry moat and up over the small outer wall, hoping the other escapees followed. He waited. One after another, all sixteen leaped over the wall.

Behind them in the tower, no guns fired. Shouts that sounded like orders emanated from the citadel, but no immediate threat presented itself for the moment. In the dark, Abraham scanned the men but couldn't find the one he needed.

"Devic, are you here?" Abraham whispered loud.

"Yes."

"Where to now?"

"This way. Follow me."

Mazel motioned for the others to follow the former cowherd. *Thank you, Lord, for the gift of a local.*

Devic led them across a bridge spanning a wide canal that flowed into the surrounding swamplands. On the other side, the band descended into the marshes and continued their flight. All night, they pressed on through swamps, ignoring the leeches attached to their legs.

When the sun rose, the men hid among tall reeds, taking turns watching for soldiers. Once night fell, they continued their flight, hungry and cold. As they headed northwest, shots rang out.

"By order of Governor Bâville, halt!"

More shots.

Without a word, the escapees fled in different directions.

CHAPTER 48

BREAKTHROUGH

21 September 1705
St. Paul Trois Châteaux
Southern France

Suzanne paced back and forth in her upstairs bedroom. She stopped to look through the window for what felt like the hundredth time. Where was Jean? Even though he couldn't completely control the timing of his missions guiding people into Switzerland, he should be home by now. He'd promised.

She stroked her swollen belly and sank into a cushion-filled armchair. Her lower back ached, and she could see through the window from here. Settling in for a little nap, she glanced out once more.

Her heart leaped. Jean! Even from a distance, she recognized the figure of her husband rounding the corner and walking up the long path toward their home, his gait unmistakable. She pushed herself back up out of the chair and waddled out of the bedroom.

At the bottom of the stairs, Grand-mère met her.

"Jean's here!" Suzanne said, continuing toward the front door.

"Praise be to God! I told you he'd be back in time."

"Did you say Jean's back?" Marie popped her head out of the kitchen.

"*Oui!* Yes!" Suzanne and Grand-mère answered in unison.

Grand-mère stopped in the entryway and put her arm around Marie, who matched her height. "Give them a moment."

Suzanne threw open the door and moved down the path as swiftly as her condition allowed. Jean waved and quickened his pace.

"Suzanne! Not too fast!" Jean broke into a run, until he gathered the bulk of her in his arms.

"I'm fine," she said, leaning her head past her belly to kiss him. "Especially now that you're home! You don't need to worry about me or the baby. The little one can come anytime now. Grand-mère confirmed it."

"Grand-mère Isabeau's arrived?"

"And Marie. See?" Suzanne gestured at the open front door, where they stood.

Jean's lopsided grin widened, and he raised a hand in greeting before returning his emerald gaze to Suzanne. "I'm glad you've had the company. I'm sorry not to return until so close to your time."

"You're here now." Suzanne grasped Jean's hand as they walked slowly toward home. "An eventful trip?"

"Incredible."

"Tell about it when we're all together."

Jean squeezed her hand and planted a kiss on her cheek.

A short time later, all four gathered around the kitchen hearth, holding warm tisanes.

"Let's hear all about it, my love," said Suzanne.

"The first day out, I connected in Montélimar with the refugees I'd agreed to guide to Geneva. As we camped that night in the forest, a man emerged, moving toward us." Jean paused for effect, as he often did.

"Go on." Suzanne stroked her belly, drew a long deep breath, and slowly let it out.

"I drew my pistol, of course, and asked his identity." Jean shook his head. "You'll never guess who it was."

"Tell us!" said Marie, bouncing on the edge of her seat.

"Abraham Mazel!" Jean grinned, his green eyes bright.

"Abraham Mazel?" repeated Grand-mère.

"The rumors are true, then?" asked Suzanne. "He escaped the Tour de Constance?"

"Yes! Two months ago, on the twenty-fourth of July, with sixteen others. He's been hiding in the Cévennes and staying with friends as he made his way toward Geneva."

"The twenty-fourth of July?" Grand-mère sat up. "Isn't that the date of the Pont-de-Montvert incident?"

Jean nodded. "Three years to the day since the death of the Abbé du Chaila and the beginning of the Camisard revolt. Abraham said they had no idea of the exact date when they escaped."

"That timing is incredible and I think not a coincidence," said Suzanne. "Where were the other sixteen?"

"The second night of their evasion, royal troops caught up with them. When the soldiers fired, the escapees fled in different directions, as they'd agreed to do. Abraham has not heard of their whereabouts since."

"That could mean anything," mused Grand-mère. "The men would need to hide indefinitely or flee the country."

"Exactly. Mazel was on his way to Switzerland. By God's providence, he discovered us in the forest that night. We traveled to Geneva together."

"Amazing!" said Suzanne. "Again, not a coincidence."

"Tell us about Mazel's escape!" said Marie, scooting her chair closer.

Jean laughed and smiled at his sister-in-law. "Gladly! It was quite a miracle."

Marie's eyes grew wider with each detail Jean shared, starting with Mazel's prison dream.

The spell of silence that followed Jean's story fell to a heavy sigh from Grand-mère. "With Cavalier's earlier flight to Switzerland and with the major leaders out of the way, I expect Governor Bâville believes the Camisard uprising over. And we've heard that many Huguenots are weary of violence and are finding more underground ways of resisting."

"Like Gabriel-Isaac and Marguerite," added Marie.

"Yet there are those who will continue to use arms and battle royal soldiers," Jean said. "One way or another, we cannot give up until our rights are restored."

Suzanne sat up straight and groaned softly. She stared in the distance for a minute, then fell back against her chair.

Grand-mère reached out practiced hands and felt Suzanne's belly. "How long have you been having contractions?"

"Contractions?" Jean jumped to his feet. "Is it time? Let's get her to bed!"

"They started this morning but weren't too bad. Since Jean returned and while we've been sitting here, they've increased in strength and frequency."

"Marie, set more water to boil," ordered Grand-mère. "And check the supplies while Jean helps me get Suzanne up to bed. We've most likely plenty of time, but she needs to be comfortable."

"I'm fine in between contractions," said Suzanne. "Let me walk around."

"Only upstairs," said Grand-mère. "I shouldn't need to remind you that you need a little extra attention. Let's go."

Suzanne let Jean and Grand-mère escort her upstairs. After two miscarriages and a stillbirth, no one was taking any chances. She changed into the shift she wore at night and lay on her side in bed. *Just for a while, then I'll get up and walk.*

The next contraction came on strong and held its grip. Sprouts of fear rose in Suzanne, and her breathing grew shallow. *Lord, please don't let us lose this one. I don't think I could bear it.*

Beloved! Fear not.

Of course! Suzanne smiled and inhaled deeply. She was beloved and never alone. Even if what she dreaded the most came to pass, her heavenly Father would carry her through. Profound peace filled her soul and calmed her body.

Within two hours, a healthy baby girl lay in Suzanne's arms. While Grand-mère and Marie tidied up, Jean sat next to Suzanne on the bed, one arm around her, the other stroking the baby's soft cheek.

"I can't believe she's here already."

"She came so quickly! I guess she knew her papa was home." Suzanne smiled, her gaze never leaving the tiny, beautiful face.

The baby opened her eyes and seemed to study her parents, one little fist sticking up through her bundled blanket. Grand-mère leaned in to observe her great-grandchild. "Unless I'm mistaken, little Jeanne has hints of green in those beautiful eyes. Time will tell. But the shape reminds me of yours, Suzanne."

"I agree," said Jean. "And the way she's looking at us —calm, curious—reminds me of her maman."

"I wish *my* maman were here to meet her," said Suzanne. "Papa and your parents too."

Jean pulled her closer and lay his cheek on the top of her head. "We look forward to the future great reunion. Eternity with no sadness or lack. What joy to be all together there."

"And together here, for now." Suzanne snuggled baby Jeanne closer as the warmth of love washed through her. Never alone. No fear. Beloved.

STRANGER THAN FICTION

Truth is stranger than fiction,
but it is because Fiction is obliged to stick to possibilities;
Truth isn't.
Mark Twain

The most unusual events in this story are based on documented occurrences. Some are shocking. Many are astonishing. I would not have dared invent them, thinking they would not be believable. However, as Mark Twain noted, fiction is limited to possibilities, while truth is not. Nowhere is this truer than when speaking of God's involvement with his creation.

Prophetic Outpouring

An outbreak labeled "prophetic," with the Holy Spirit filling and speaking through children and youths, started in 1688 in a region north of the Cévennes. The first *inspirée* was a young shepherdess, Isabeau Vincent, who spoke long biblical passages in formal French, sometimes while awake, sometimes in her sleep, despite being illiterate and normally speaking only in her local dialect.

Isabeau and the hundreds of other youths involved in the outbreak did not usually speak of future events. Their proclamations exhorted believers to endurance, repentance, and a transformation of life. Hearers responded with a greater awe of God, deep repentance, and increased hope.

Firsthand accounts of proclamations exist, written by both Protestants and Catholics. No one could find a natural explanation for this phenomenon.

In 1701–02, the same outpouring occurred in the Cévennes region. Authorities jailed hundreds of children and brought in doctors to examine them. No one could find a rational explanation for their abilities. Labeling them "fanatics," Governor Bâville sent the children to convents for reeducation or returned them to their parents with strict warnings against future prophesying, including the threat of razing their homes.

These young people were courageous, suffering the abuse of the authorities and sometimes their terrified parents. Overall, they remained remarkably steadfast and exhorted the adults to do the same.

Camisard War

Almost every event related to the Huguenot revolt that began in the Cévennes in 1702 happened as described in this story, including Abraham Mazel's dream, the Abbé du Chaila's death, and Esprit Séguier's execution. Much of the dialogue in these events is lifted from historical accounts, one written by Abraham Mazel during his eventual exile in England.

Also true were the events leading up to the incident at Pont-de-Montvert: multiple unplanned connections with other Huguenots ready to fight, going out in pairs to recruit more men before the rendezvous on Bougès mountain, the subsequent organization of the fighters, and the march to Pont-de-Montvert.

Françoise Brès's prediction that the Abbé du Chaila would die within the year on the same spot as her execution did come to pass. As did Esprit Séguier's prophecy of the river Tarn changing its location. The river flooded and permanently changed its path at the end of 1702.

Jean Massip's escape from the prison-fort of St. Hippolyte du Fort occurred, but not by him. Antoine Gavadon accomplished the amazing feat in 1692, a date too early for this story. I borrowed his escapade and loaned it to Massip. History does not record what happened to Massip after he gained his freedom at Pont-de-Montvert.

Also true is this story's account of a Camisard ruse "betraying" a clandestine Huguenot service to Capitaine Poul's men, sending them on a fool's errand. Subsequently, the Camisards worshipped in the one remaining Protestant temple.

The supernatural light that appeared before the Camisards on a rainy march through the Vallée Française happened as described. Many firsthand accounts tell of animals and birds deceiving royal soldiers and aiding the Camisards. From the beginning of the prophetic outpouring, both Protestants and Catholics heard angelic singing, often of the Huguenots' songs. Again, there are eyewitness accounts, even by those intending to disprove it.

Gédéon Laporte's death and the subsequent display of heads occurred as written here. Capitaine Poul's death also.

Historically, authorities arrested Rolland's father and brothers. I changed that to mother and sisters.

Rolland, Mazel, and their men fell sick with measles in November 1702. Many Camisards died, and Mazel struggled with recurring illness in the following year.

The Camisards deception at Sauve occurred as told here, except for Gabriel-Isaac's wounding afterward.

Under Governor Bâville's order, Marshall Montreval and his troops burned a swath through the Cévennes, starting in 1703. Once again, this persecution only increased the Huguenots' determination to fight for their rights.

Salomon Couderc helped lead Camisard troops until 1705, when he was captured and burned at the stake.

Rolland's death by betrayal happened in 1704 while Cavalier attempted negotiations with authorities. Abraham Mazel continued fighting and was arrested in January 1705 as Jean Cavalier worked on peace negotiations with a new military marshal. Mazel's incredible escape from the Tour de Constance occurred as written here. After his flight to Switzerland, he joined fellow Huguenots in England, then returned to France in 1709 to lead an English-backed insurrection. Tricked by a formerly sympathetic supporter of the Camisard cause, Mazel was killed in a skirmish with royal soldiers in 1710.

Nicholas Jouany continued to lead troops of up to four hundred Camisards until his capture and execution in 1711.

Château de Planque
St. Hippolyte du Fort

By the 1690s, the Valmalle family purchased the Château and added the noble designation "de la Planque" to their name.

During this time, the Château's lands included two water mills and vineyards requiring the work of fifty men.

Prison-Fort of St. Hippolyte du Fort

After rendering Protestantism illegal in 1685, King Louis XIV ordered the construction of several prison-forts in the Cévennes. Only those in Alès and in St. Hippolyte du Fort were finished. Included were rampart walls surrounding the towns, with guarded entry ports. While only remnants of the walls remain today, both forts survive.

Religious Freedom

Fighting between the government and the Camisards largely ceased after 1704, only to resume in 1710 and continue sporadically for the next five years. Suppression of the Huguenots continued until the death of Louis XIV in 1715.

At that time, the heir to the throne, Louis XV, was only five years old. France came under the rule of a regent who had little interest in continuing the persecution of Protestants. While the kingdom's religious laws did not change, their application diminished. The Huguenots began to celebrate their religion a little more freely. However, there remained men in power who advocated severity in the treatment of the Protestants.

Persecution finally ended with what is commonly called the Edict of Tolerance, signed by Louis XVI in 1787. After the French Revolution two years later, the Declaration of the Rights of Man afforded Protestants equal rights as citizens and the freedom to worship.

PRIMARY AND HISTORICAL CHARACTERS BY LOCATION

*historical person

Southern and Southwestern Cévennes

St. Hippolyte du Fort

Suzanne and Family

Suzanne Lacombe – eldest daughter in Lacombe family; *inspirée*

Gabriel-Isaac Lacombe – Suzanne's younger brother; eldest son in Lacombe family

Marc-André Lacombe – Suzanne's youngest brother

Marie Lacombe – the youngest child in the Lacombe family

Jeanne Tessier Lacombe – Suzanne's mother

Pierre Lacombe – Suzanne's father

Grand-mère Isabeau Lacombe – Suzanne's paternal grandmother; midwife

Aunt Anne – Suzanne's maternal aunt

Other Huguenots

Marguerite Marolle – Suzanne's school friend and neighbor; mill manager

*Antoine Lagarde – Jean Massip's acquaintance

Catholics

Charles Fesquet – Suzanne's school friend; vigneron
Pintard – prison guard in St. Hippolyte prison-fort

*Monsieur de la Haye – governor of St. Hippolyte prison-fort

*Lord Valmalle – owner of Château de Planque

Justine – cook in Château de Planque

Marthe – housemaid in Château de Planque

Tornac

Philippe Delapierre – Suzanne's great-uncle, Grand-mère Isabeau's brother; vigneron

Florence Delapierre – Suzanne's great-aunt, Philippe's wife

Sauve

*Jean Cavalier – Camisard leader

Northern Cévennes

St. Jean du Gard

*Abraham Mazel – prophet and Camisard leader

Génolhac/Bougès Mountain

*Nicolas Jouany – Camisard leader

Pont-de-Montvert

*Abbé du Chaila – priest and Governor Bâville's superintendent in the Cévennes

*"La Violette" – Abbé du Chaila's manservant
*Father Roux – priest in Pont-de-Montvert

Eastern Cévennes

Mialet

*Rolland Laporte – prophet and Camisard leader

Madame Laporte – Rolland's mother

Joséphine and Michèle Laporte – Rolland's youngest sisters

*Esprit Séguier – oldest prophet in the resistance

*Jean Rampon – Séguier's guide

*Salomon Couderc – prophet and Camisard leader

*Jacques Couderc – Camisard fighter; Salomon Couderc's cousin

*Gédéon Laporte – Camisard leader; Rolland's uncle

Gabriel Lacombe – Suzanne's paternal uncle, serves as lieutenant to Gédéon Laporte

Paul Tessier – Suzanne's maternal uncle; serves as lieutenant to Gédéon Laporte

South of Cévennes

Montpellier

*Governor Bâville – King Louis XIV's governor of the Languedoc region

Displaced and Itinerant Characters

Huguenots

*Jean Massip – guide from St. Paul Trois Château

*Celestin sisters – *inspirées*

*Françoise Brès – *inspirée*; executed at Pont-de-Montvert

*David Devic – Camisard prisoner from Aigues-Mortes

King's Officials

*Capitaine Poul – royal captain

*Marshall Montrevel – military marshal under Governor Bâville

GLOSSARY

abbé – father; used as a title designating any priest

à table! – come eat!

bergerie – sheep pen

bien sûr – of course

bisous – kisses

bon – good

bonne nuit – good night

cachette – hiding place

Cévenol – a person from the Cévennes region

ça va? – how are you?

chef – leader

cher(s) – dear(s)

chérie – sweetheart

confiture – jam

dames – women; shortened version of *mesdames*

déjeuner – lunch

escritoire – writing desk

excusez-moi – excuse me

fanatique – fanatic

garrigue – scrubland, hinterland

grotte – cave

inspiré (male), *inspirée* (female) – an "inspired" one; mostly young people enabled by the Holy Spirit to preach and prophesy

lavoir – outdoor stone basin used for communal laundry

maire – mayor

merci – thank you

moulin – mill

moulin à huile – olive oil mill

non – no

notaire – civic lawyer; notary

oui – yes

potager – vegetable garden

réfugiés – refugees

Roi Soleil – Sun King (Louis XIV)

vendange – grape harvest

ACKNOWLEDGMENTS

I'm always impressed at how many people it takes to create a single book. While writing is a solitary process, a community is truly required to bring it forth into the world.

A heartfelt thank you to Kelsea Tripod, Liz Cowley, Donough O'Brien, Sarah Soon, Cynthia Godwin for their close reading and wise advice. I'm amazed at the time and care you each invested, resulting in excellent input.

My wonderful Writers Group, the Lady Lits–Linda, Mari, Susan, Sarah, Cindy, Jill–contributed enormously as well. I've learned so much from you all, directly and indirectly, through our many discussions and brainstorming sessions. This book bears your fingerprints and is the better for it.

Another gift in my life is author Ginny Yttrup, whose life-giving approach to writing spurred me on while offering valuable instruction. Ginny's Fiction Crafters Cohort has brought innumerable blessings, including relationships with other authors.

What an incredible privilege it was to have the talented Jill Wilson as editor. I cannot overestimate the clarity and increased depth she brought to the story. Any remaining errors are one hundred percent mine.

The support and prayers of friends around the world have made an enormous difference. I'd especially like to thank Brett and Lyn Johnson for their encouragement, hospitality, and for connecting me with the Good Lit retreat where I wrote the first chapter of this book.

Cynthia Alliman's cheerful service, and deep love for God and others, are a fountain of life. Thank you, dear friend, for who you are and all you do.

As always, my husband Dudley's listening ear helped this verbal processor sort out story issues. Thank you for helping me through the technical aspects of wine casks and prison escapes.

Above all, I'm grateful for the privilege of writing with the Father, Son, and Holy Spirit.

Cover photo by Simon Wilkes on unsplash

J anet Joanou Weiner grew up in southern California and studied French against her 6th grade teacher's advice that she'd never use it. Janet has now lived in France for over twenty years. First in the Alps, followed by several years in the center of Paris.

Janet has also lived in Amsterdam, the San Francisco Bay Area, and Kona, Hawaii. In addition, she's traveled for her work in Christian ministry to over forty countries.

Currently, Janet and her husband reside in southern France, in St. Hippolyte du Fort, nestled in the heart of the Cévennes region. History abounds, centered on the Huguenots and the persecution they suffered. Dramatic, true stories of courage and faith inspired *The Huguenot Resistance Series*.

Despite missing her children and grandchildren, who all live in the US, Janet loves her life. She delights in the endless opportunities to discover inspiring stories of the past while soaking up the beauty, culture, and history.

Based on actual events, *The Huguenot Resistance Series* takes place in her region, village, and home, the over 500-year-old Château de Planque.

www.janetjoanouweiner.com
Blog: Fig & Vine

If you've enjoyed *The Light Shines Through* and would like to leave an honest review on Amazon, Janet would be very grateful.